THE PINK BUS
CHRISTOPHER KELLY

LETHE PRESS
MAPLE SHADE, NEW JERSEY

Published by Lethe Press
118 Heritage Ave, Maple Shade, NJ 08052
lethepressbooks.com

Copyright © 2016 Christopher Kelly

ISBN 978-1-59021-613-2

No part of this work may be reproduced or utilized in any form or by any means, electronic or mechanical, including photocopying, microfilm, and recording, or by any information storage and retrieval system, without permission in writing from the Author or Publisher.

This is a work of fiction. Names, characters, businesses, places, events and incidents are either the products of the author's imagination or used in a fictitious manner. Any resemblance to actual persons, living or dead, or actual events is purely coincidental.

Cover and Interior Design:
Inkspiral Design

PART ONE
THE PINK BUS

1979

On that hot late morning in October 2014, three weeks and six days before the election, in the moments after the bullet pierced the flesh of his abdomen, as the awareness that he would not be long for this world rapidly settled upon him, Patrick Francis Monaghan was seized by a memory that he had never before considered in his adult life; a memory he never would have guessed was still stored within the gray matter of his cerebrum.

This is what I'm thinking about?

This was not an entire life flashing before his eyes. This was a silly little episode of childhood, scary enough at the time, but then quickly forgotten—and yet now looming so large in his mind that it occluded all other competing thoughts in his final seconds on Earth. Indeed, the cosmic cruelty that here he was *dying*—at age forty, just when he had found what had eluded him for so long, a place in the world, widespread embrace for his ideas, *a platform from which to make his voice heard*—seemed to him far less perverse than the notion that *these* would be his last thoughts; that he was doomed to relive, one final time, the fifth day of kindergarten at P.S. 42 in Staten Island, New York.

He was only five years old, tall and sometimes clumsy, prone to a nervousness whose cause he didn't yet have the vocabulary to articulate. He was sitting at one of the long white tables in the lunchroom, waiting to be loaded onto the bus that would take him home. There were six different bus routes, each coded by a different color. Early that morning, owing to the fact that there were more students assigned to ride the "green" bus than there were seats, it was announced the routes had been changed: Patrick and one other student from his kindergarten class—a snub-nosed, chunky girl named Anne Wade—had been moved from the "green" bus to the "pink" bus.

Except Mrs. Wolfe must have forgotten, or not been paying attention, because as she guided the students into the lunchroom, she directed Patrick and Anne to sit at the table for kids riding the green bus—the same table at which they had been placed each of the four previous afternoons, where they were to wait for one of the three school aides overseeing dismissal to collect them and lead them outside. Patrick was scared of Mrs. Wolfe—she had skin that was white like chalk and eyes that bugged out of her head behind thick, black-framed glasses—but he nonetheless summoned the courage to protest.

"No, Mrs. Wolfe, this is wrong," he said. His voice, even as a little boy, could sometimes be strident and righteous—but only because he *knew* he was right, and because he couldn't understand why the grownups in his life could be capable of such silly, careless mistakes.

"Sit down and be quiet," Mrs. Wolfe snapped at him, and then turned on her heels and disappeared from the lunchroom.

He was five years old. Certainly he had known fear before: Monsters that had convinced himself were hiding under his bed; leering clowns with blood red mouths that drew too close to him at the Big Apple Circus. Yet none of the fears that Patrick had previously suffered seemed to compare to this. After four days of being warned of the above-all-else importance of making sure you got onto the correct bus, on this fifth day he was going to be placed on the wrong bus, which would strand him far from his usual stop, where his mother would *not* be waiting to meet him.

The greatest terror for Patrick Francis Monaghan, at age five, and, come to think of it, all throughout his life, was the terror of being lost.

"We're going to miss our bus," he whispered, leaning into Anne.

Anne Wade looked back at him in a manner that made Patrick think of the elephants at the Bronx Zoo, their faces gray and confused and heavy with sadness.

He looked at the clock. 2:55 p.m. One of the aides was now standing in front of the pink bus table—the table where Patrick and Anne should have been sitting. He watched as she gestured to the children sitting there, who rose and formed side-by-side lines, boys in the one, girls in the other, and then began their march out of the lunchroom.

"I don't know what to do," he murmured.

He said it to himself, but Anne must have thought he said it to her, and she must have thought he was angry that *she* wasn't doing anything either, because just then her pudgy, freckled arm starting shaking beside him, and when Patrick turned to look at her, he could see that there were tears forming in her eyes.

He had to get the attention of one of the other aides. He was sandwiched between Anne on the left and a boy from the second grade on his right, and it took longer than he would have expected to climb out of his seat. He readied himself to take off in a run, so that he could catch up with the aide at the edge of the lunchroom—the one now leading the orange bus kids out the doors—and explain to her that a terrible mistake had been made.

But just then he heard a voice from the other side of the room, high-pitched and squawking—a sound that made Patrick think of the digital alarm clock his parents had recently bought him so could learn to wake himself up each morning for school.

"Stay in your seat until it's your turn," the third aide shouted.

And though he understood the consequences of doing so, that now they were *definitely* going to miss the pink bus, Patrick did as he was told.

"What's the matter, Peppermint Patty?" a boy sitting across from him called out.

Patrick was much too anxious and distracted to pay attention to the laughter that erupted all around him. In the coming years, this epithet would stick to him like gum in a girl's long hair, its assault worsening the more he tried to disentangle himself from it—but he wouldn't actually remember that *this* was the moment when it was first used against him. He was only five years old: how could he possibly know that this how it would always be; that when something bad is happening, you must keep vigilance—or otherwise you will miss entirely the even worse thing that takes form out of the detritus of your misery?

The clock now read 3:02 p.m. He looked over to the doors, and he saw the second aide who had led the pink bus kids out of the building re-entering the lunchroom.

What happened next couldn't have taken more than thirty or forty seconds, but for Patrick it seemed to stretch out longer than the entire first week of kindergarten. He began shouting at the second aide, a string of nonsense and babble about pink buses and green buses. The aide yelled at him, the instant she figured out what was wrong, as if all of this was Patrick's fault: "For Christ's sake, why didn't you tell someone?"

"Get up," she told Patrick and Anne, pulling them away from the table. "You have to run. Go find Mrs. Carter and tell her you're supposed to be on the pink bus. *Run.*"

Patrick's knapsack felt heavy on his shoulders, as if it were stuffed with building bricks. He grabbed for his metal Muppets lunchbox, wrapping his hand so tightly around the plastic handle that his fingernails made tiny impressions in the flesh of his palm. With his other hand, he clasped Anne's wrist, and the two of them took off toward the lunchroom doors. He heard another boy call out, "Peppermint Patty takes the *pink* bus," and then the laughter of his classmates chasing after them.

They made it through the heavy double doors. A cinderblock wall stood directly in front of them, and Patrick couldn't remember which way they were supposed to turn. He decided to go left, and he pulled Anne along with him.

They journeyed about thirty feet before Patrick realized his mistake. "It's the other direction," he said, breathless and furious with himself. He turned without quite breaking stride, dragging Anne with him. She stumbled after him but did not fall. They raced back to the double doors where they had started, faster now, and then past them. Soon he could see the blurry pink light of the exit sign at the far end of the corridor.

Rudimentary physics. He wouldn't take a class in the subject for another ten years, but he got his first lesson right here. When you are running, your body uses your arms to generate momentum; and so when one of your arms is constricted—as Anne's was now, because Patrick was gripping her by the wrist—you are apt to flail the other arm out in the opposing direction. So as to maintain *balance*. So that you don't end up spilling forward and falling flat on your face.

But this corridor was a narrow one. And sometimes there's only so far one's arm can stretch.

Patrick knew right away what had happened, the instant he heard the sound, tin against rough cement, Anne's Strawberry Shortcake lunchbox scraping the wall and then slipping out of her hand and falling to the floor. The contents spilled everywhere, the plastic thermos and unopened can of Mott's apple juice and a half-eaten, peanut-butter-and-jelly sandwich. Anne pulled away from Patrick, and Patrick let go of her wrist. She dropped to the floor, onto her hands and knees. But then she paused and looked up, as if waiting for Patrick's permission to continue.

"Hurry up," he pleaded with her.

She did nothing. She stared at the pieces of her lunchbox all around her. The tears she had been holding back the last few minutes now started to pour out of her.

Patrick faced a decision, which he knew he had only a second to make. He knew that the right thing to do would be to drop to the floor and gather Anne's things for her and get them both moving once again. Patrick was aware, too, of the trouble he might get into if he left Anne behind. All during the first week of school, Mrs. Wolfe and the aides had emphasized that wherever they went—whether to the bathroom or the gymnasium or onto the bus that would take them home—they were required to stick close to their designated partner.

Yet even as Patrick understood this, he also bristled against all this *responsibility*. Why did he have to take care of this little girl who was so *dumb*; who couldn't even manage to hold onto her lunchbox and run at the same time?

Besides, did it really make sense that both of them should miss the pink bus, when there was still the possibility that one of them might still get home safely?

He looked to the end of the corridor. Light sabers of purple-yellow afternoon sunlight shot through the glass of the doors, as if challenging him to some kind of fight. He looked back at Anne, her whole body shaking now with sobs. He mumbled words to her that didn't even sound like words, he wasn't even sure what he was trying to say, maybe it came out as *I've gotta go*, or perhaps simply *I'm sorry*.

Then he ran. He ran faster than he had ever run in his young life, in the hopes that he might still make it onto the pink bus.

THIS IS WHERE PATRICK'S MEMORY stops. Or at least jumps ahead. The next thing he can picture is sitting on the pink bus, alone on a double-wide seat near the back. The engine turns over, an enveloping *whirr* that—as the adrenaline of the previous few minutes finally begins to crest—tempts him to sleep. But he stays awake. The bus cruises through the familiar streets of his neighborhood, along Ridgewood Avenue, stopping at Katan and Lamoka and finally Wilson, *his stop*, where his mother is waiting for him.

What happened?

As the adult Patrick lay slumped on the front porch of the Fort Worth Stockyards Museum, aware but only distantly of a tumescent stinging centered in his belly, he found himself outraged. *Indignant.* First that his final thoughts should be hijacked by the long-forgotten Anne Wade, and now that he wasn't even able to remember what had happened to her.

What kind of sadistic final joke was God playing on him? He was going to die without knowing how it ended.

Once he made it onto the bus, did he have the wisdom and courage to tell the driver to wait, because there was still one last student they couldn't leave behind?

Did Anne somehow make it onto the bus?

Did she ever forgive him his abandonment?

In those final seconds of consciousness, Patrick tried to recall other memories of his life, the triumphs that might have counterweighted this sadness, his friendship with Nora, his romance with Oscar, that gloriously silly run on television, this strange and exhilarating campaign for the United States Senate that—who knows, given a little more time and a lot more funding—might yet have turned into a victory. But of course by then it was too late, and the very final thought that occurred to him was a version of one that this restless, ambitious, generous, angry, hopelessly self-critical, endearingly earnest man had considered many times before in his life, in many other, decidedly less *terminal* circumstances.

He thought to himself: *Did I really just screw this up?*

Did I not even manage my own dying right?

PART TWO
THE STORY OF A MAN

1 9 8 5

IT ONLY TAKES ONE BULLET. A gun and good aim. Depending on your regard for self-preservation, a halfway-decent escape plan.

This is American history's prescription if your wish is to irrevocably silence a man.

On November twenty-two, 1963, at 12:30 p.m., three or four shots—depending on whose version of the story you prefer—were fired at President John Kennedy, as he traveled by motorcade through Dealey Plaza in downtown Dallas. The gunman, Lee Harvey Oswald, employed an Italian Carcano bolt action rifle loaded with 6.5x52 millimeter bullets. If you subscribe to the "single bullet theory," and thus the conclusions of the Warren Commission that Oswald acted alone, one of those bullets would miss and another would strike Kennedy in the upper back, travel through his neck and exit his throat, then strike Texas Governor John Connally, and travel through *his* chest and wrist before coming to rest in the Governor's thigh. Not entirely plausible, but, at least as far as Kennedy's fate was concerned, ultimately beside the point—the wounds from that bullet were not the fatal ones. The next bullet that struck the President created a fist-sized hole in the rear of his head, spraying pink chunks of brain matter across his open-roof limousine. Whether in the moments between injurious bullet and deadly one the President maintained consciousness or spoke a few last words remains open to debate; a Secret Service agent sitting in the front seat claimed to have heard him exclaim,

"My God, I've been hit," but in the chaos and bloodsplatter, the First Lady and Governor and Mrs. Connally would be able to recall almost nothing. John Fitzgerald Kennedy was rushed to Parkland Memorial Hospital, where he arrived at 12:38 p.m., already too late. He was the fourth sitting President of the United States to be assassinated.

Flash forward fifty years, ten months, and sixteen days, journey approximately thirty-five miles due west: The gun used in the shooting of Patrick Francis Monaghan was an American Tactical .45 ACP with black polymer grip and chrome finish. The full metal jacket bullets used in the American Tactical are small and fat and hard-shelled, like a tick bloated after feeding. They generate a relatively low velocity, which makes them ineffective in combat against body armor. But when fired into the tender white belly of a six-foot, two-inch, two hundred-pound politician, those bullets work awful wonders. They tear open a hole and create a permanent wound channel. They produce a ghastly amount of blood, which mixes with hydrochloric acid in the stomach and usually results in fatal toxemia.

Patrick's eyes fluttered open. His face was pressed against the smooth limestone surface of the porch of the Stockyards Museum—from his vantage point he could see nothing. In the distance he heard shouting, and then the plaintive wail of an ambulance siren drawing nearer. He was aware of a heat and stickiness coming from somewhere in his middle—as if hot candle wax were being poured not onto him but *out of him*—and he knew that it must be blood, his own blood, vast and irreplaceable quantities of it.

"Patrick, just hold on. The ambulance is almost here."

He heard the words clearly, but they sounded impossibly far away. He was pretty sure it was Oscar talking, though maybe it was Nora. He wanted to answer, *Yes, I'm holding on*; and he wanted to ask, *Am I going to die?* For a moment he even heard himself speaking these responses—but then he realized he couldn't be understood; that as with Kafka's cockroach, his coherent thoughts were rendered to human ears as the terrifying and tragic noises of a now-condemned man.

His eyes closed once again. Seconds might have passed, or minutes, or even hours. He next heard the sounds of footfalls racing toward him. He felt hands on his body; fingers prying open his closed eyes; a cuff tightening around his bicep. He saw a light that could have been a dilating pen or perhaps the iridescent gates of heaven.

Had Patrick been able to make sense of his present circumstance, he might have realized then that the EMTs had arrived, and this realization might have given him hope and renewed vigor—throughout his forty years, and especially during the last eighteen months of the campaign, with Nora steering everything so brilliantly, he tended to put up his best fight when he knew himself to be surrounded by professionals, and when he understood the game plan for his victory. But by now Patrick's mind was once again drifting, remembering, his past sliding into his tenuous present, his present folding back into his past, like a shuffled and re-shuffled deck of cards. He was thinking about blood, his own and others; thinking about how, for a few years, the blood was all anyone could talk about.

"They're taking you to the trauma center," said Oscar, on the floor beside him, cradling his head in his arms. "Just hold on, Patrick. Please just hold on."

But this he didn't hear at all. Now he was out of Oscar's reach, and out of Nora's; out of reach of the EMTs, who kept shining the pen light into his eyes hoping for some kind of neural response.

Now he was just eleven years old.

PATRICK ASSUMED THAT THE FIGHT had been carrying on for days or even weeks, night after night leading up to right now, and that this was simply the first time it was being argued within his earshot—though, thinking back on it years later, he wondered if maybe his mother, too, was scared of Ant visiting, unsure of whether she even wanted him here, and so she waited until eighteen hours before his arrival to spring the news upon her husband. It was just before midnight, two hours past Patrick's technical bedtime, though these days he usually stayed up reading thick Stephen King and Dean Koontz paperbacks by the faint light of his bedside lamp. Patrick would always remember that he was on page 361 of *'Salem's Lot*, in the middle of a sentence with the words, "They spill each other's blood with great vigor," when he heard his father's raised voice through the wall.

"I don't want some fairy in this house."

Patrick had recently entered the sixth grade, having escaped from P.S. 42 to I.S. 24—a new school and, due to the vagaries of zoning regulations, a mostly new set of classmates. The taunts of Peppermint Patty that once greeted him daily on the playground had been left behind; if he still had few friends, at least the bullies of this junior high school focused their humiliations on other boys, smaller and more girlish in manner than Patrick. But of course by then he knew. He had long been drawn to his male classmates—not the things they liked, the football games or shiny sports cars or *The A-Team* on television, all of which he found boring, but their very beings, their bodies and smells and sounds, the way they skittered around the school playground, tossing out their elbows, heedlessly crashing into one another. He wanted to be physically near these boys, even if their brashness so often intimidated him. He couldn't deny, either, that sometimes he would start thinking of certain ones of them—the carrot-headed Seth Kearns, I.S. 24's most gifted athlete; the wide-smiling Danny Califiore, with those thin wisps of a mustache growing above his upper lip—and there would follow a stiffening of his penis that he couldn't make go away.

Which perhaps explains why Patrick responded the way he did to his father's pronouncement. He sat up in bed, wide-eyed, breath in abeyance. He was convinced that his father was talking about *him*.

"Keep your voice down."

"You wanna go meet him at the diner, you go. But not here."

Patrick could picture his father, in his threadbare white T-shirt and Fruit of the Loom underwear stained brown at the seat, what he always wore to bed and then pottered around the house wearing each morning. He could picture his father's face—ruddy to begin with—darkening to the reddish-purple shade of raw meat.

"He's family," Patrick's mother said.

"I don't want him around the kids."

"This is how you treat family?"

"Go meet him at the diner."

ALMOST IMMEDIATELY AFTER HE STEPPED into the house that next afternoon, taking note but not thinking much of the boxy brown car parked outside, Patrick sensed a strange, nervous energy all around him; a kind of real-life static cling in the air. His mother called out, high and stuttering, "Jim, is that you?"—which made no sense at all, because Patrick's father wasn't due home for another two hours, whereas he—Patrick—arrived home at exactly 3:37 p.m. every single day. He called up the stairs to say hello, to which his mother breathlessly answered, "Oh, honey, come on up," which also made no sense, because where else could he have gone? The ground floor of their house consisted only of a foyer, a coat closet and a utility room.

As he stepped onto the landing, he saw his mother coming towards him, wiping at her eyes with the nub of her palm. She was obstructing his sight line, so he had to twist his neck to see that, behind her, two men were presently rising from the couch.

"Honey," she said, taking hold of his wrist and leading him forward. "Come meet your cousin Anthony and his friend Cal. Ant is your Uncle Tony and Aunt Patty's son. He's visiting us from California."

"I didn't… " Patrick started to say, and then stopped himself. He sensed that it might be rude to point out that, until this instant, he didn't know he had a cousin in California.

"Ant moved out there right after you were born—when would it have been, Ant—1975? 1976?—my God, I can't believe I haven't seen you in ten years," his mother said; and Patrick couldn't understand why she was talking like this, all in a rush, not even pausing to let the man answer her questions.

Patrick started to move towards them, but then stopped. In that next instant the entire living room was plunged into shadow. The man who his mother called Cal was on his feet now, and his body was blocking all of the light that moments earlier had been streaming through the front window. Patrick opened his mouth, but of course no words came out. Cal was at least six-and-a-half feet tall, with a shaved head and a bushy black beard, a big, broad chest and outsized Popeye biceps. He reminded Patrick of the characters on the World Wrestling Federation telecasts he and Tim sometimes watched with their father, unsmiling giants with names like the Iron Sheik and Ravishing Rick Rude.

"Ant's told me a lot about you," this man said, and to Patrick it sounded almost like a threat.

And that's when Patrick remembered there was another person standing there, a reed set beside this tree trunk, a man with the slim shapeless body of a boy. He wore clothes not unlike what Patrick's sixth-grade classmates might wear: a black zippered sweatshirt with the words "San Francisco" printed across the front; white Converse high-tops; faded blue jeans that hung loose around his waist.

Except when you looked at his face, you saw he wasn't a boy. Nor was he Cal's age, which Patrick took to be about thirty. His light brown hair had fallen out in a donut shape, leaving a tuft in the front surrounded by ring of shiny, pockmarked skin. There were brownish-grey pouches beneath his eyes. He had a smear of acne on his right cheek, dark red and scabby, that made it look as if that side of his face was sinking into his skull.

And though he wasn't sure how he knew it with such certainty—because it wasn't like either one of them wore silk scarves around their necks or made exaggerated, limp-wristed gestures, the way the gay people you saw on television always seemed to do—and though it didn't entirely compute—because wasn't it weird for a young man like Cal to be interested in a man who was twenty or twenty-five years older?—Patrick in an instant understood.

Anthony was the man his parents had been arguing about the night before.

This was the "fairy" his father didn't want in the house, and Cal was this fairy's "lover."

All Patrick could think was that his father was going to be furious if he came home and found them here.

"It's good to finally meet you," Anthony said, and he stepped forward and held out his hand to Patrick to shake.

There was a long moment of awkwardness, as Patrick tried to figure out what to do. He didn't want to have to shake Anthony's hand; didn't even want to have to speak to him. He was convinced in that moment that Anthony would sense a softness in the bones of his fingers, or something timid and girly in his voice—and because Anthony had once been a boy just like him, a boy who didn't want anyone to know he liked other boys, he would at once know Patrick's secret. At the same time, though, he feared even more that his mother was going to insist that Patrick greet Anthony the way all family members were greeted, with an embrace and a kiss on the cheek. His guts churned with the thought that if he were to come into such close contact with a gay man—even one as old and deformed-looking as Anthony—it might cause him to have an erection.

He was trying to discreetly rub his palm on his pants, to dry the moisture that had gathered there—he had decided it would be best to just *quickly* shake Anthony's hand—when the front door opened, and miraculously he was rescued. Patrick turned his body in the direction of the stairwell, toward the competing voices and laughter rising up from the ground floor. A moment later, they were in the living room, his brother Tim, four years older than Patrick, and his sister Laura, a year older than Tim.

Another round of introductions followed. Tim and Laura shook Anthony and Cal's hands both, without any noticeable displays of self-consciousness. Laura claimed she remembered when Anthony said he used to play with her when she was a little girl—though Patrick couldn't tell if this was true, or if she was just saying it to make their cousin feel more welcome. Tim launched into a monologue when Anthony said he'd heard he liked to play baseball—the middle Monaghan sibling had always been the friendliest of the three of them around strangers. Patrick watched all of this in silence, taking small, half-unconscious steps away from them. He longed to slip into the kitchen, and then into the dining room and his bedroom at the back of the house, but feared that his mother would catch him and call him back—and draw all of Anthony and Cal's attention towards him.

"Why don't you kids go watch TV and give us a half-hour to talk," Patrick's mother said, a few minutes later. "Then you can set the dining room table for seven."

"No, Marilyn..." Cal began.

"I won't take no," she said. And then, to Laura, Tim and Patrick, she added: "I made spiedini and stuffed artichokes and rice balls"—which Anthony and Cal wouldn't have known but Patrick recognized at once as his and Laura and Tim's favorites.

"I don't think it's a good idea to put James out," Anthony said.

"Who's putting anyone out? He's going to be thrilled to see you."

And from the way she said it—with exaggerated stress on the word *thrilled*, with a good cheer she rarely displayed when talking about Patrick's father—Patrick and everyone else could tell that she was lying.

Laura and Tim went ahead first, out of the living room and through the kitchen and dining room, and then down the long hallway that led to the bedrooms. Only fourteen months separated Patrick's sister and brother, and from the effortless way they had always gotten along, and the frequency with which they shared confidences, many people initially mistook them for twins. They excluded Patrick from their conversations and activities less out of ill-will than unthinking habit—no matter how old he got, they would always see him as their baby brother, emphasis on the *baby*.

So at present Patrick had to hurry to stay close behind them, and he had to strain to hear them, because they were keeping their voices low. He missed the first few things they said to each other. But what he did hear he heard clearly.

Tim said to Laura, "He's our cousin?"

And Laura answered: "I've never heard them talk about a cousin in California."

And then Tim, sensing Patrick drawer closer behind, dropped his voice to a whisper and said: "Anthony's hand is really *cold* when you shake it. It's weird."

And Patrick was just barely able to make out Laura's response: "I think they might be fairies."

"So you didn't grow up in San Francisco?" Patrick's mother asked, after Cal made them all laugh, explaining that for nearly fifteen years now he'd been putting up with "Cal-from-California" jokes. The dining room table was set for seven, and they were presently gathered again in the living room. Cal and Anthony and Laura sat on the couch, with Patrick and Tim across from them on the two fraying yellow armchairs that had been handed down from their grandparents. Patrick's mother kept popping her head in every few minutes from the kitchen. Patrick's father still wasn't home from his job delivering pallets of Coke and Sprite to supermarkets and bars in Brooklyn—traffic on the Verrazano almost always delayed him on Friday afternoons—but Patrick could feel his heart racing in anticipation, knowing he would be here any second.

"Lawrence, Kansas," Cal said to Patrick's mother. "I got out as fast as I could."

"I've never been to that part of the country," Marilyn Monaghan offered.

Cal frowned and said, "You're not missing much."

Patrick couldn't really comprehend this statement—or, if he could, he didn't want to think about what it might mean. Most of the people he knew came from close-knit Italian or Irish families and grew up on leafy streets in Queens or Brooklyn or Staten

Island, next door to or no more than a few blocks away from aunts and uncles and cousins and grandparents. He had never heard anyone speak about where he was from with such disgust; with such obvious determination to flee.

"Does your family ever visit you in California?" Patrick's asked.

"My family doesn't want anything to do with me," Cal said, matter-of-fact, like a teacher correcting his pupil.

"Oh… I didn't…"

"A lot of people in San Francisco lie," Cal went on. "They pretend that their lovers are their roommates, just so that they can carry on that illusion with their families. But I couldn't do that with them. So I told them, and they stopped talking to me."

Cal turned to face Anthony and added: "I don't think people can keep lying to their families and friends and co-workers and expect any real progress to be made."

Patrick watched as his mother stuttered through a response, "No, no… of course not… you shouldn't lie… " Then he watched Anthony place his hand on Cal's furry forearm—Anthony's pale fingers seemed to Patrick to get lost inside the thick nest of black hair that grew there—and then Anthony whispered something in Cal's ear, and then Cal responded by rolling his eyes and softly shaking his head.

Patrick wondered once again how much longer they had until his father came home.

Patrick's mother hurried to change the topic. "Kids," she said, "Anthony was a year behind me at Bay Ridge High School. We walked to school together every day down Avenue U. Remember Ant?"

"Your patient and saintly mother," Anthony said, "protected me from all the bullies in Brooklyn."

Patrick's mother said something in response to this, and then Anthony answered back, and then Cal must have interjected with a joke, because suddenly everyone was laughing. Everyone except for Patrick, who heard nothing of what they were saying; who instead stared goggle-eyed at Anthony and Cal. It hit him with the force of an avalanche. It *flattened* him. His mother had celebrated her thirty-ninth birthday the previous July. Which meant that, if Anthony had been one year *behind* her when they were both students at Bay Ridge High School, this man who Patrick guessed to be fifty or even fifty-five years old was in fact just thirty-eight.

Patrick narrowed his gaze and studied his mother's cousin. He considered once again Anthony's thinning hair, and he imagined large clumps of it having recently fallen out. He looked at Anthony's face, his skin the whitish-yellow color of carpenter's glue—so unlike the other, dark-complexioned members of that Italian side of the family. He noted that Anthony's zippered SAN FRANCISCO sweatshirt was much too heavy to be wearing inside the house—and wondered if Anthony kept it on because otherwise the scabs and sores that the newscasters talked about when describing the disease would be visible on his exposed arms.

Patrick saw the word flashing in his brain, hot pink and all-capital letters, as if in neon on a Broadway marquee. The word that he refused to say, for fear that speaking it aloud would serve as a kind of invitation to it; for fear that others would hear him talking and know at once that he, too, was one of its potential victims.

This was what it looked like up close.

Patrick leaned forward on his chair and tried to get Laura's attention, but she was still laughing at Cal's joke and didn't notice her younger brother glaring at her. He then turned to face Tim and tried to communicate a set of questions with his expression. *Can you tell, too? Do we need to say something to Ma?* Tim gazed back at him and made a face like, *What the hell is wrong with you?* When Patrick next looked across to Anthony and Cal, he saw Cal staring right back at him. With his dark, bristly beard and square, jutting jaw, Patrick thought he looked like a German shepherd readying for attack.

And just when Patrick thought he might explode with all of this worry—worry that he needed to tell someone what he alone seemed to know; worry that somehow he might catch this sickness that was so obviously killing his mother's cousin; worry that by now both Anthony and Cal had surely figured him out and were going to expose him to the rest of the family—they all heard the accordion creek of the front door opening, and Patrick was rescued once again.

"That's Jim, finally," Patrick's mother said. "He's going to be so excited to see you Ant."

Anthony gave her a grim little smile and said nothing.

In the wedding photo album that his parents kept in a cardboard box beneath their bed, James Monaghan was slim and shining, with a messy mop of blondish-brown hair that curled into a flip at the back. When he was a little boy and couldn't sleep, Patrick would often ask his mother to haul out the album and narrate to him the circumstances of each of the pictures—to him it was a storybook far more enchanting than the ones by A.A. Milne or H.A. Rey that lined the bookshelf in his bedroom—and he would doze off listening to stories about the bridesmaids and groomsmen and about how everyone who lived alongside them on West Sixth Street in Brooklyn came to St. Simon and Jude that day to see them get married. In those pictures frozen in place beneath a thick dusty layer of protective plastic, Patrick recognized the bride as a younger version of his mother, a beautiful, round-figured woman who people always said reminded them of Elizabeth Taylor. But the groom in his parents' wedding album seemed another man entirely from the one who these days arrived home from work each late afternoon, scowling and beerthirsty, his hand raised as if to swat a fly in response to anyone who might want to talk to him. Eighteen years after his wedding day, Patrick's father was mostly bald, and what little hair remained on the sides of his head had turned dishwater gray. When Patrick's mother recounted to Patrick tales of their wedding day, she spoke of James as a boisterous joke-teller, the man who made sure everyone was having a good time. These days, Patrick couldn't remember the last time he had seen his father even smiling.

They were all silent as they listened to his footfalls on the stairs. Patrick's mother took a few steps closer to the landing. Patrick snuck a quick look at Cal, who was looking at Anthony, who had turned his head away and was gazing out the window behind him.

And then Patrick's father was right there beside them, he had walked past Patrick's mother, brushing her hand away when she tried to reach out for him. Next Patrick felt the pressure of his father's hand gripping his right shoulder a little too tightly. He turned and saw that his father's other hand was gripping Tim's left shoulder—though whether James Monaghan was using his sons' shoulders to keep his hands occupied, so that he wouldn't do something he might come to regret later, Patrick couldn't tell.

"Jim, you remember Ant, and this is his friend—"

"Kids," he cut her off, "go get your jackets, and we'll go to the video store and rent a movie. Let's leave your mother so she can finish up with her cousin."

"No, Jim," Anthony said. "Cal and I were just headed out."

Anthony rose from the couch and dug into his sweatshirt pocket to pull out a set of car keys. But then he turned to face Cal, and Cal wasn't moving.

"I thought we were staying for dinner," he said evenly

"You are," Marilyn declared from the other side of the room. "I made a big dinner for everyone."

Patrick's father kept his voice low and said to Marilyn, "I don't want them here."

"James, *please*, don't be like this."

"I'm not having this conversation."

And then Cal let out a snort and said, "Jesus, Jim, you're a real class act."

Patrick was shocked by the speed with which his father spun around and said to this man whose name he hadn't even yet bothered to learn: "You don't have a say here."

Cal rose from the couch, his shoulders pitched forward, his nostrils flared—less than a German shepherd, he now looked to Patrick like a bull locking in on a matador. In his mind, Patrick imagined a fight between the two men, a bloody and mostly one-sided contest. Cal would rush towards Jim, knocking over the coffee table that now separated them, and he would swing at him with his right fist, his knuckles would smash into Jim's jaw, and Jim would be dazed, but at first he wouldn't fall—he was a big man himself, overweight but solid from unloading countless cases of Coke and Sprite off his truck five days a week. Jim would take a swing back at Cal, though this swing would be wobbly, and of course he would miss, and then Cal would punch him once more and this time knock him to the ground. Patrick knew it was terrible to think this way—so terrible that he would almost certainly have to confess it to one of the priests at Holy Child—but he was nonetheless excited by the thought of Cal hurting his father.

He wanted his father to be taught this lesson, that not all men like Cal and Anthony could be so easily pushed around.

Except Cal didn't make to throw any punches. He stood in place beside Anthony, his fists balled up by his sides, and he inhaled through his nose and then looked to the ceiling and let out a soft, tired sigh. Then he muttered under his breath, so low that Patrick wasn't entirely sure of what he heard—only that it sounded like he was saying that he knew it would be a mistake to come here.

"James, can you please just calm down?" Marilyn said next.

"I told you I didn't want them here."

Anthony interjected and said, "It's okay, Jim, we're leaving. I didn't mean to cause any arguments."

"I haven't seen Ant in ten years," Patrick's mother added, her voice cracking. "Can't we just have a nice dinner together as a family?"

For a moment, Patrick thought that maybe this would be enough to restore order. *Family*. It had been drilled into Patrick's head since birth: *Nothing* is more important than family. After-school sporting events would be skipped, friends' birthday party invitations might be turned down, even schoolwork could be set aside—if any of it conflicted with the obligations of seeing and spending time with the family. All four of Patrick's grandparents were still alive, he had seven aunts and uncles on his mother's side, another three on his father's, nineteen first cousins and counting. Almost all of them lived within a thirty-minute drive of each other, in Staten Island or Brooklyn or central New Jersey. Barely a week passed when there wasn't a birthday or anniversary or baptism or graduation—and that's not even counting the alternating Sunday dinners at their grandparents' houses—*always* they found cause to gather and eat and talk.

Patrick thought that by reminding everyone they were *family*, his mother might have succeeded in settling things down.

James Monaghan turned to his wife and calmly pronounced: "I'm going to take the kids to the video store, and when we get back, I'd like them to be gone."

It came out of Patrick's mouth before he had a chance to second-guess himself. He didn't want to be seen as Anthony and Cal's defender—and definitely didn't want his father wondering why he was so interested in these two men—but he also couldn't bear to stay silent. Not when he was witnessing something so obviously *wrong*.

"Dad, they're nice people," he said. "You should talk to them and you'll see."

"Go get your jacket, Patrick. We're going to the video store."

"Why are you being so mean?" Patrick protested.

His father responded with a violence in his voice that Patrick had never heard before. "Shut your mouth, Patrick. This has nothing to do with you."

"James, please, *stop this*," Patrick's mother interjected. "This might be the last time I get to see Ant. I don't want it to be like this." Patrick—reeling from his father's shouting at him, on the verge of tears himself—looked across the living room and saw that his mother was crying.

"Kids get your jackets," Patrick's father again repeated, but then stopped himself. He paused and blinked and then knotted his forehead in confusion. "What are you talking about?" he asked.

"He's *sick*, Jim. He's very sick."

"*What?*" Jim asked—though Patrick could tell that, by then, his father too understood everything.

"He's dying," Cal pronounced, in that matter-of-fact way of his, the schoolteacher once again setting his misunderstanding student straight. "We both are."

And what struck Patrick wasn't the stark finality of that statement—or even the strangeness of it coming out of the mouth of someone so young and strong and handsome—but that Cal wouldn't say the word, either.

Even infected and dying from it, he wouldn't say he and Anthony had AIDS.

For as long as Patrick could remember, he had understood his father in terms of fearlessness. The son of Harold and Agnes Monaghan, raised in Bay Ridge and educated at Our Lady of Perpetual Help and St. Michael's Boys High School, James Harold Monaghan was the type of guy who friends and other family members sometimes called "a real sonofabitch"—saying it like they were teasing, though Patrick could tell that they really meant it. He almost never hugged or kissed his children. He expected Patrick's mother to clean the house and not bother him for the first forty-five minutes after he came home from work each night, while he drank a beer and watched the news through to the end of Warner Wolf. During the most recent junior varsity baseball season, in just the handful of games that Patrick had attended, he used the words "sissy" three times and "faggot" twice to refer to the boys he regarded as the weakest members of Tim's team—without entirely realizing he was doing it, Patrick had kept a running count.

But now, as his father's eyes widened and he twisted his upper body and head backwards, almost as if trying to avoid some sort of blunt object hurtled across the room,

Patrick realized that all this time he had been wrong. His father wasn't fearless at all. When he sat through their nightly family dinners saying nothing, the only sounds from him the sounds of his fork and knife scraping against the plate; when he barked at his three children to stop making so much noise, even if the loudest thing any of them were doing was Laura practicing her clarinet; when he insisted Patrick's mother return a pocketbook she had bought at Macy's, because she hadn't first asked his permission to spend those thirty dollars, James Monaghan wasn't being fearless, and he certainly wasn't being the kind of father Patrick sometimes read about in books, like Atticus Finch in *To Kill a Mockingbird* or Mr. Tiflin in *The Red Pony*, strict yet fundamentally kind.

James Monaghan was in fact the opposite of fearless. He was, now that Patrick thought about it, quite possibly the most scared man alive.

"You knew about this," he said to his wife, "and you still let them come here?"

"He needs to be around his family," was all Marilyn Monaghan said in response.

"Unbelievable," Jim said.

"It's not contagious," Cal broke in. "You don't get it by breathing the same air as someone who is infected."

"You both need to get out now," Jim said; and from the way he *didn't* raise his voice, it was clear to everyone that no further arguments would be heard.

The rest was mostly silence, and of course Patrick wishing desperately that he could be brave enough to speak up in their defense. Cal and Anthony—their heads held high; their eyes cast straight ahead—made their way side-by-side past James, who said something to them that Patrick couldn't hear. For an instant, the muscles in Cal's back tightened, and Patrick thought that there really would be a fight.

But then Anthony reached for Cal's hand and Cal took it in his, and they carried on walking through the living room.

Patrick's mother followed them down the stairs and then out the front door. Five minutes passed with none of them moving or saying anything, and then through the silence they heard Anthony and Cal's car turn over and pull out of the driveway. When Patrick's mother finally returned to the living room, Patrick could see the streaks of rubbed-away tears in the makeup on her face. She said to them, "Let's sit down to dinner, we don't want everything to get cold," and as they ate Patrick thought of things he could and should say, he wanted to ask his mother: *when you said goodbye, did you at least let them know that not all of us are like him?*, and as he watched his father poke at a second serving of chicken cutlet and take another angry slug of Michelob Lite, he wanted to say: *there's too much food here, and two empty place settings, all because of you—because we were supposed to be having dinner as a family, the seven of us, but you chased Anthony and Cal away.*

Except he couldn't do it. He just kept hearing those words—*Shut your mouth, Patrick*—repeating like a scratched record in his head.

So for the twenty minutes it took for them to eat dinner, Patrick said nothing, and neither did anyone else.

The next day there was a purging. Patrick's father wore yellow rubber gloves that reached to his elbows as he placed the drinking glasses from which Cal and Anthony sipped iced tea, and the plate and bowl from which they snacked on Fig Newtons and potato chips, into a large cardboard box and then carted the box to the front curb for sanitation pickup.

The next week there was a cleaning. Each day Patrick came home from school, five days in a row, to find his mother clutching a squeeze bottle of bleach; mopping the floors in the kitchen; scrubbing and disinfecting the toilet.

Funny thing was, Patrick couldn't remember Anthony or Cal ever using the bathroom.

For the next two or three months, Patrick rehearsed a speech that he intended to deliver to his father. Better late than never, he told himself. *Finally* he would speak up against the injustice that he had watched unfold in their living room. Even if Anthony and Cal never found out about it, Patrick would at least be able to say to himself that he had defended them. He would talk to his father about fairness and equality, about Susan B. Anthony and Martin Luther King, Jr., whom he had learned about recently in school, and their fights on behalf of women and black people in America. He would talk about grace and selflessness and the New Testament story that he knew from his weekly religion class at Holy Child. He would even quote the relevant passage in Mark, which he had diligently looked up in the Bible that his parents kept in the bottom drawer in the kitchen:

> *A man with leprosy came to him and begged him on his knees, "If you are willing, you can make me clean."*
>
> *Jesus was filled with compassion. He reached out his hand and touched the man. "I am willing," he said. "Be clean!"*

And even though he sensed that his father didn't *deserve* the compliment that he would be paying him by engaging him in a civil debate—because as one of Patrick's teachers, Mrs. Bark, liked to say to their class, usually in the aftermath of some stupid playground fight, *when you enter into civil debate, you are saying to the other person, I respect you and think you are intelligent and want to have a conversation and work out our differences*—he thought he could win the man over with one simple piece of logic.

Why would anyone choose *to be gay if they knew it would come at the cost of their family, their friends, all of the world's respect?*

He would think—but would still be afraid to say out loud to his father—*Why would I choose to be gay?*

Yet the moment never felt right. Patrick didn't know how to start the conversation. His father always seemed so impossible to engage.

To his enduring, thirty years' regret, Patrick said nothing.

Indeed, he raised the subject of Anthony and Cal only once more, three years later, when he was walking home from the movies with his mother. It was the thing they always did together, well beyond the age when most boys would be embarrassed to be caught in public with their mothers. That day they had seen *Big*, and twice Patrick had gotten an erection—on the list of actors Patrick liked to watch, Tom Hanks was fourth after Tom Cruise, Rob Lowe and Patrick Swayze.

"Whatever happened to cousin Anthony?" The question just popped into his head. He didn't really pause to worry that he might be making his mother uncomfortable by asking it.

"You remember Ant?"

"He came to our house that time with his friend Cal."

"Oh, that's right," his mother said. "I'm always amazed at the things you kids remember from when you were little."

For a moment Patrick didn't understand: Had she somehow forgotten that only three years had passed since that day? He was about to explain this to her, but then he realized. This was just one of those strange things grownups sometimes did, perhaps in order to contend with their own regret. They pretended something happened a long time ago, until enough time passed that they could pretend it had never happened at all.

"Why did he move away to San Francisco?"

Marilyn Monaghan answered so quickly and confidently, like an actress on stage delivering a well-rehearsed line. "He followed his girlfriend out there."

"He was sick, right?" Patrick asked.

"He passed away two years ago."

"What was wrong with him?"

Again Patrick's mother didn't hesitate as she erased her cousin Anthony's history entirely. "He was diagnosed with cancer. It doesn't run in our family, but he got it, and there was nothing the doctors could do to save him."

1 9 8 9

The ambulance pulled away from the curb at 12:13 p.m., turning onto North Main Street, then NE 28th Street, and then journeying south on Interstate 35, making the eight-mile trip to the John Peter Smith Urgent Care Center in just under ten minutes. An emergency surgical team had been hastily gathered, and hands and forearms were already being scrubbed as Patrick was raced through the hospital's front doors, strapped at his ankles, thighs and shoulders to a steel-back collapsible gurney. At 12:26 p.m., the patient was attached to a series of vital sign-monitoring machines. At 12:32 p.m., the surgeons ordered an intraoperative CT scan and began their assessment of the trauma.

Back at the Fort Worth Stockyards Museum, there was chaos; barely-contained panic; a kind of *no-fucking-way-this-can't-possibly-be-real* sense of wonder. The gunman, first tackled by a bystander and two members of Patrick's security detail, was handcuffed and shoved into the backseat of a police car and sped away to an undisclosed location. The three hundred or so people who had gathered at the Stockyards Museum to hear Patrick's speech, however, would not be permitted to leave the area until authorities could interview everyone. At this early juncture, no one could say whether the alleged gunman had acted alone or what might have been his motive.

The scene looked like a party that had carried on too long and too loud until finally the cops had to be called to break it up. Rented aluminum folding chairs were tipped over like cows on their sides. The speakers mounted on either side of the museum's front porch elicited a whistle of feedback that no one seemed to know how to silence. Bendable plastic signs and placards were abandoned in scattered piles—shiny pools of bright red and white against the green of the lawn.

MONAGHAN 2014
Turning Rejection into Acceptance

They had stumbled upon this slogan unexpectedly, one night in summer 2013. At the time, they hadn't even been talking about work. Instead it was a rare night off, and Patrick had just finishing showing Oscar one of his favorite movies, a tale of unrequited romance called *Gods and Monsters*. He was only musing out loud when he said that he felt as if rejection had been an inescapable part of his existence; that in fact he believed it defined *all* gay men's lives.

"We become so accustomed to rejection that we fool ourselves into thinking that we *need* to be rejected in order to function," he told Oscar that night; and Oscar's brown eyes started to sparkle, and he reached for his laptop and nodded at Patrick to keep talking.

"The expectation of rejection has become our default pose," Patrick declared in August 2013, on the terra-cotta steps of the county courthouse in downtown Fort Worth, during the speech in which he stated his intention to become the next United States Senator from Texas. "We go through our lives now demanding so little—and not even getting that much."

These were words that Oscar had written and Nora had carefully edited, but Patrick was the one who had lived them, and he spoke that day with such naked conviction that many in the crowd began to tear up. He emphasized that this message didn't just apply to the gay men and women of Texas, the most populous state in the union where same-sex couples still couldn't marry, but also to the schoolchildren marginalized by a financially inequitable public school system; the longterm unemployed workers who couldn't find jobs; and to untold numbers of industrious immigrants who were being discriminated against by a state and a country that had turned tragically xenophobic.

He proclaimed, "We need to turn that rejection into acceptance."

In the weeks and months that followed, the journalists assigned to cover the campaign tried to get Patrick to say more—they didn't seem to believe that a handsome, well-respected, confident-seeming man could have faced all that much rejection in his lifetime. And, full disclosure, Patrick *wasn't* being entirely honest: there was a story from his past that he had never shared with anyone. Perhaps he kept it a secret because he still felt such a piercing sense of shame, or perhaps he kept it a secret out of some preposterous, lingering hope that one day he and Baffi might cross paths again and there would be an alternate outcome—a way for them both to take it back and start over. Whatever his motivation, though, Patrick often brooded: Until he spoke of this story openly, did his entire public persona amount to a kind of fraud?

Ironically, he thought he saw Baffi on that very morning, when he announced that he was running for the Senate. Patrick was walking along Weatherford Street, surrounded by an already-too-large phalanx of advisers and assistants. This man-who-would-be-Baffi was waiting at the corner for the traffic light to turn, about fifteen feet away, wearing red track shorts and a grey T-shirt. Patrick first noticed his ass—*always* what you noticed first about Baffi was the ass—and then he raised his eyes to the man's torso, as limber and lean as Baffi's had once been, and then to the back of his head, and his wavy mop of walnut brown hair. Patrick very nearly gasped, as much at the beauty of this sight as with the realization that he might very well be looking at his erstwhile high school rival.

But in an instant the spell was broken—another sort of rejection. The traffic light clicked over from red to green, and the man started to cross, and suddenly Patrick saw that it wasn't Baffi at all, that in fact this man was just a boy, sixteen or seventeen, some sort of teenage reincarnation of Baffi, a Baffi frozen in his mind's eye. And at the very same moment, Nora—who was always two steps ahead of him, literally and figuratively—stopped and waited for him to catch up and then whispered in his ear: "I hate to break this to you, Patrick, but if the good people of Texas catch you checking out high school boys, they are *not* going to give you their vote."

HIS NAME WAS MARCO BAFFI, recently relocated from Wethersfield, Connecticut, the only new member of the sophomore class at Staten Island Technical High School that year. Patrick thought he was cute the first time he saw him, with his hazel eyes and his floppy hair he wore parted to the side. But Patrick was fifteen and gay and horny every single second of the day—cute was a low bar in those days. In which case, the first time Patrick *really* took notice of Baffi was about three weeks into the school year. He was walking past the field where the boy's soccer team was practicing, and he looked across the field, and there was Baffi—*holy shit*, there was Baffi—chasing down a soccer ball, for some reason the only boy on the team presently shirtless, his arms outstretched, his stomach muscles taut, and he had on a pair of white Umbro shorts, and Patrick could make out of the impression of his underwear briefs beneath them, which were black, creating the perfect outline—and perfect, in that moment, meant all that Patrick had ever wanted and all he ever would want from this world—of Baffi's perfect ass.

Patrick stopped in place and stared for who knows how long. Later the same afternoon, and for weeks thereafter, he recalled these images as he masturbated; and of course he soon became obsessed with the idea of recapturing the moment. It didn't happen. The weather was turning colder—throughout October, the boys on Baffi's team all wore sweatpants and long-sleeved shirts—and soon soccer season was over altogether. Beyond the practice field, Patrick had little opportunity for contact with Baffi, who tended to congregate with the jockiest, noisiest boys in the class—the ones Patrick had long since learned to avoid, out of fear that those grade school taunts of "Peppermint Patty" would suddenly flare up again.

Except now here was Baffi standing in front of him in the hallway, looking all sheepish and sweet (and hot! God, he was so unbelievably *hot*!), and normally this would have been intriguing, even exciting, only Baffi was breaking to him this extremely shitty news, saying he hoped there would be no hard feelings, it was just that he thought it would be a good idea, being the new kid in school, to run for sophomore class president.

"I mean, I'm probably going to lose, but I figure it will force me to talk to everyone and meet new people."

"But I was freshman class president," Patrick said, immediately defiant—despite the fact that just standing across from Baffi was inducing the stirrings of a hard-on.

"Yeah, I know. And a lot of people told me they are going to vote for you again." Baffi paused and then added: "But... I was also thinking... elections with just one candidate aren't really democratic, you know?"

"You've been asking people about me?" Patrick said, knowing right away that it sounded *off*; at once lovesick and weirdly paranoid.

Baffi made a face that Patrick would become familiar with over the coming weeks and that would melt him every time, turning his head sideways, squinting one eye shut and arching the eyebrow of the other—Baffi never looked so adorable as when he was perplexed—but then, just as quickly, he regained his assurance, and told Patrick: "You know, it's not like we have to be enemies. I mean, it can be a *friendly* competition."

IT WAS ANNOUNCED THAT THERE would be a campaign, the very first in the history of their only four-year-old magnet school—though almost immediately Patrick wondered if it would be better for him to bow out entirely. He had only volunteered for the job last year because no one else wanted it, and because his English teacher and debate team coach, Mrs. Ansen, insisted that it would help him sharpen his public speaking and leadership skills. Besides, no one else had *wanted* the job—he never would have volunteered if he had actually had to campaign for it. Was he now expected to write speeches and go around school shaking the other kids' hands—all for the questionable privilege of getting to be one of four student representatives at a monthly "community-building" meeting with the principal? Was he who was so studious and who mostly kept to himself—Patrick Monaghan, with his many acquaintances, but almost no one at school he would call a good friend—really supposed to compete against someone like Baffi, who was so quick to smile and crack a joke, so handsome and likable and unthreatening to *everyone*?

"Absolutely not," said Mrs. Ansen, when he relayed to her his doubts.

"But it's just going to be some dumb popularity contest," he protested.

"Give up now," Mrs. Ansen told him, "and you'll never get want you want"—and Patrick never did figure out if what she was talking about was the grown-up life of fame and accomplishment that he sometimes fantasized for himself, or if Mrs. Ansen understood that what Patrick wanted more than anything right now was Baffi.

Even still, he had a hard time throwing himself into this. He already had a already-packed extracurricular schedule: debate team; academic Olympics; founder and editor of

Technical Writing, the school's literary magazine—he couldn't see stretching himself all that much thinner. And, honestly, as much as Patrick thought of himself as competitive and determined and *definitely not a quitter*, a part of him thought he would be okay with Baffi winning. He really was very friendly, once you got to know him (early on in the month-long campaign, Mrs. Ansen insisted they meet for an hour to discuss the needs of the student body and to pledge to each other not to "go negative" in their posters and speeches). There seemed to Patrick many worse kids at Tech to whom he could lose the title of class president.

Or at least that *was* how Patrick was viewing things, until the first Friday in November, when he was perched on a chair in the hallway, taping his hand-drawn, oak tag campaign posters onto the wall. He heard a throat-clearing behind him. He turned to see one of his classmates, Valerie Seelman, staring quizzically at his handiwork.

"I thought you were going to be *vice* president," she said.

"What are you talking about?"

"That's what Baffi's been telling everyone—that you guys worked out a deal so that you would drop out of the race, and then he would choose you as his vice president."

Patrick marched straight to the lunchroom, where Baffi was sitting at his regular table of all boys, soccer and football players mostly. He didn't care that his voice probably sounded a little hysterical and that the other boys were suddenly looking at him like he was an escapee from the Willowbrook mental asylum. Frankly, he believed the situation *demanded* a little hysteria.

"What have you been telling people about me agreeing to be your vice president?"

"Oh... that... " Baffi said, climbing out of the lunch table and gesturing to the doors that led out to the schoolyard, inviting Patrick to go for a walk. "I think people might have misunderstood what I was saying."

Patrick didn't want to follow Baffi outside—he wanted this resolved in front of everyone, where it wouldn't be so easy for Baffi to make up lies without getting caught. But Baffi was already moving, and Patrick had to scurry just to keep up.

"Well, did you say it or not?" Patrick demanded.

"No... no... I just... " and here Baffi paused, because they had arrived at the exit doors, and if you were going out to the schoolyard at lunchtime, you were first supposed to obtain permission, but Baffi only needed to look across to Mrs. Mallette, twenty feet away, and raise his chin toward her and smile, and she smiled back warmly and nodded her consent, and the next thing Patrick knew they were outside in the bright light and brisk November air, and Baffi was waving at three freshmen girls huddled on the opposite side of the schoolyard—who were so besotted by his attention that they immediately closed ranks into a circle and started giggling—and then Baffi inhaled and exhaled in rapid succession, puffing out bursts of vaporous air—he had left his jacket inside and was only wearing a T-shirt—and he wrapped his arms at crooked angles around his body, and Patrick got so caught up in watching all of this—even the way Baffi kept himself warm was cute, like a gangly giraffe giving himself a hug!—that he could no longer entirely remember why he was mad in the first place.

"What were you saying?" Baffi asked.

"I was… the um… the vice president thing… "

"Oh, yeah, that," Baffi answered. "Well, listen, I'm sorry for the misunderstanding. I really want this to be a friendly competition."

"No… I know that… but I never agreed—"

Baffi didn't let him finish. "You know, from what I'm hearing from voters," Baffi said, "this could go either way."

Patrick squinted at Baffi in confusion, but said nothing. What the hell? Was it possible that Baffi had actually been conducting his own polling?

"I think the two of us are going to be a really great example for the school," Baffi continued. "We'll show them that the democratic process works, every vote counts, all that stuff."

"Yeah, I understand that… but you can't lie to people and—"

"Not that I think I'm going to win," Baffi said, cutting Patrick off again. And then Baffi shrugged and at the same time opened his eyes wide—another of this gorgeous boy's gorgeous gestures that seemed to contain within it all the possibilities of the world.

For a few more seconds, Patrick tried to cling to the thread of his rapidly unraveling argument. But as he stared back at Baffi, noticing for the first time that his hazel eyes were flecked at the edges with blue, seeing up close the faintest trace of a dimple in his chin, no words came, only countless confusing thoughts: How was it that he could want so much to run away from this boy, and yet at the same time want to spend every second in his presence?

How come when it came to this sophomore class presidential election, one part of him wanted to crush Baffi, and a larger part of him wanted to be humiliated by him?

"You know, I'm really glad we decided to make this a friendly competition," Baffi told him, when it became clear that Patrick had nothing left to say.

Patrick began to feel a familiar, unmistakable stirring in his pants.

THE MESSAGE CAME TO THEM both in math class, the Friday before the election, that Mrs. Ansen wanted to see them during lunch. Patrick of course feared the worst. These past two weeks he had held tight to his distrust of Baffi as he went about refocusing and strengthening his campaign. For the most part, everything he had been doing was perfectly legitimate: a new set of brighter, more sophisticated posters to replace his original ones; a letter outlining his campaign platform that he wrote and mimeographed and distributed to the entire class. But there were those dubious promises he had made to three different boys, that he would choose them for his vice president in exchange for their votes; and of course he had whispered that fake rumor, that Baffi's family might be moving again mid-year and thus if elected Baffi wouldn't be able to finish out his term.

Had Mrs. Ansen somehow found out about these less noble tactics?

Nope. The news was much worse.

"Gentleman, on Monday we're going to have a special assembly, and you're both going to deliver your final speeches to the sophomores. What I'd like you to do this weekend, though, is work on your speeches *together*. Exchange ideas. Challenge one another. I know that's not how elections usually work, but I think it will be an excellent learning experience for you both. A chance to see how the other side thinks."

Mrs. Ansen—who in her freshman English class had won Patrick over with her very first reading assignment, *The Turn of the Screw*—was far and away his favorite teacher, and generally he regarded her word as a kind of gospel. But, come on, was she *really* asking them to do this? A mental image of Baffi showing him one speech in private—and then delivering an entirely different one at the assembly—quickly flashed in Patrick's head.

"That's a fantastic idea," Baffi piped up, before Patrick could even attempt to protest. "I've been saying all along that this should be a friendly competition."

And then, turning to Patrick, he asked: "You want to come over to my house this afternoon? My parents will be at work, so we'll have the place to ourselves."

"Can't we just do it at the library?" Patrick answered, a little too quickly, way too churlishly. But, *come on*, it was already difficult enough protecting himself against his rival's fast talk and adorable facial expressions. Just the thought now of entering into his house—seeing where he ate and slept and showered; possibly even seeing a stray pair of Baffi's dirty underwear on his bedroom floor—was once again making him hard. How would this be anything other than torture?

"No big deal," Baffi said, his voice now very soft, like his feelings had been hurt. "I just thought… you know… we have Cokes there… and pizza left over from last night… it would be fun."

"That's very gracious of you to offer, Marco," Mrs. Ansen said.

"Patrick probably has other stuff to do… "

And then they were both looking at him, Mrs. Ansen's ovoid black eyes behind bifocals attached to a chain, Baffi's beautiful hazel eyes bright with the promise of *fun* and *friendly competition*, and what else could Patrick say, other than no, he didn't have anything else going on this afternoon, and yeah, come to think of it, Cokes and leftover pizza would be nice.

They met at the bus stop on Hylan Boulevard, twenty minutes after school let out. Patrick found a seat near the front of the bus, while Baffi opted to stand at the back. They departed at the intersection of Richmond Avenue and King Street, a half-dozen stops before Patrick usually got off. They walked alongside each other in silence for about six blocks, until Baffi turned into the driveway of a two-story saltbox, beige brick with faded brown shutters on the windows. Patrick at first felt a rush of relief—nothing particularly fancy about this place; no reason to be *intimidated* to go inside—followed by a sharp, strange stab of disappointment: Previously when he daydreamed about Baffi's private life, he always imagined him living somewhere much grander.

"So this might sound a little weird," Baffi said to him, as he unlocked the front door and stepped inside.

"Uh-huh," Patrick said, thinking that pretty much all of his interactions with Baffi had been weird so far, so whatever Baffi was about to say couldn't possibly be anything special.

"Well, I was thinking maybe we should each vote for the other person."

"What do you mean?" Patrick asked.

"You know… just to prove that this really has been a friendly competition."

"You want to me vote against *myself*?"

"Yeah… I mean… I'd be voting against myself, too."

Oh my God. What was this kid's mental malfunction? Did he *really* think Patrick was so naïve as to fall for this idiotic proposal—because *of course* Baffi would just pledge one thing to Patrick and then go ahead and vote for himself regardless. Patrick felt his eyes burning; his head beginning to pound. Enough of this craziness. *Enough*. He *never* should have agreed to this campaign in the first place—he should have fought tooth-and-nail and claimed his right as the incumbent to run *unopposed*—and he never should have backed down over the vice president thing, and he certainly shouldn't have gotten sucked into coming over here today. He had to stop doing this, what he had been doing all his life. He had to stop being afraid and start demanding justice. He had to learn to make the words coming out of his mouth match the ones in his head.

But yet again, just as Patrick was about to lash out at him, Baffi stopped in the hallway of his house and turned back to face Patrick, though now his eyes were cast down and his lower lip was pushed out awkwardly, an expression that Patrick understood to mean he was embarrassed.

"I'm sorry… it's a stupid idea… forget I even said it…"

And then Baffi was talking way too fast, the way Patrick himself sometimes did when he was nervous, and touring them through the house, stopping in the kitchen to collect Cokes and cold pizza from the fridge, and he was being so *nice*, so *gracious*—did Patrick want some lemon with his Coke? how about his pizza heated up?—and Patrick had no idea what he was supposed to do now, if he should stay here or leave, be nice in return to Baffi or throw his apology right back in his face.

Jesus Christ, were all boys this *difficult?*

Baffi left Patrick in the living room, saying that he wanted to change out of his school clothes. Patrick took the opportunity to examine the two framed photos on the mantle over the fireplace. One was of a much younger Baffi alone, only five or six years old, posed in a red-and-blue-striped shirt against a beige studio background. (Even at six years old, he was the cutest boy Patrick had even seen!) The other photo was a more recent shot, presumably taken over the summer during a family vacation, a brightly smiling Baffi flanked by his parents, with a lake and green, wooded hills in the background. What struck Patrick first was that Baffi's mother and father were both frowning—what kind of parents put out such a sorrowful-looking picture for visitors to see? What struck him next was that Baffi appeared to have no siblings—and because Patrick so often felt like an only child, too, because Laura and Tim were older but so close in age themselves, this was the detail that resonated with him. He started thinking about how, even though he was fifteen now, Laura still sometimes talked to him in a voice you would use with a little kid; about how Tim had always treated him like an attention-starved pet who perpetually needed to be shunted aside. He thought about how—maybe because he was always afraid of other boys suspecting he might be gay—he had also never really tried to find the sort of best friend that lonely young boys in books always seemed to seek out, the Tom to his Huck, say, or the Johnny Cade to his Ponyboy.

Staring at those photographs of Baffi, he even went so far as to formulate a question in his head; something that might clear the air with his rival and offer them both a fresh start. He could ask him, as a *friend* might, what it was like to be an *actual* only child, as opposed to just one inside your own head.

But just then Patrick heard Baffi padding down the stairs and entering into the living room, and he looked up, and nothing was ever the same again.

"I got us pens and pads," Baffi said, holding them out to Patrick.

Patrick let out a gasp like he had just been punched in the gut. He knew it sounded ridiculous—*how stupid! how gay!*—and yet he couldn't stop himself. Months of pent-up desire came rushing out of him in a single hot breath. Baffi was standing in front of him, no shirt, no shoes, no socks, wearing only a pair of cotton shorts, navy blue but for a thin strip of white fabric sewn down the sides and around the hem of the legs.

Patrick looked away, worried that if held his gaze on Baffi for even a fraction of a second longer he wouldn't be able to disguise the desire—the sheer *ferity*, to borrow a word from his most recent vocabulary test—he felt inside. But already he had seen enough, so that he would never be able to forget: the broad, solid torso; the flat stomach with its tiny, protuberant belly button; the convex, inverted V-shape of his quadriceps; the toenails, yellow-white and long and perhaps in need of clipping. When Baffi walked past him, deeper into the living room, Patrick sneaked a look at his ass in those unbelievably *skimpy* shorts, and it was just like the first time he saw Baffi on the soccer field, except now in extreme close-up, *one hundred times more intense.*

It was the most beautiful thing he had ever seen.

"I was thinking that we could both just free-write for awhile, and then show each other what we come up with."

"Uh… OK," Patrick managed to get out.

"Do you want to change? I have shorts you can borrow."

"No… I'm fine… " Patrick answered; and then he quickly made his way to the living room couch, because sitting down was the only way he was going to be able to hide his latest hard-on.

These were the two most agonizing hours of Patrick Francis Monaghan's life thus far, when time seemed to slow and stretch and then stop altogether; when time seemed to be mocking and name-calling him, just as his grade school tormentors once did. Baffi handed Patrick a pen and pad and collapsed into the sunken easy chair positioned catty-corner to the couch. Patrick looked expectantly to him, awaiting further instruction, but Baffi immediately started writing. He tried to take a deep breath and calm down. The cause was a lost one. All of his senses were attuned to Baffi: he could hear his soft, open-mouthed exhalations; could smell his faintly sour afterschool sweat. Thirty minutes along, having written all of four sentences, Patrick cast a furtive glance in his classmate's direction. His heart went pounding anew. Baffi's entire body was now curled up into the chair, the legal pad resting on his upper thigh, his legs positioned so that Patrick could see through the leg opening of his shorts to the black briefs that he was wearing underneath.

"I'm not really sure I follow all of your arguments," Baffi told him, a little while later, when they were each reading over what the other had written.

"Yeah... I'm sorry... I don't think what I wrote is very good," Patrick stuttered.

"No, you have a lot of good ideas... maybe I can just make a few suggestions..."

"Sure," Patrick said, thinking he would agree to anything Baffi suggested right now if it would hasten the pace of this afternoon and allow him to go home and jerk off in the privacy of his own bathroom.

But then a minute passed in silence, as Baffi tapped the capped end of his pen against his temple, and then just when it seemed like he was going to launch into his critique, he stopped himself and shook his head, as if chasing away bad thoughts.

"You don't think this is a waste of time, do you?" he said finally.

"I don't think Mrs. Ansen really gave us a choice," Patrick answered.

"No. The whole campaign. Running for class president. My father says all politicians are liars and fakes, so why would I want to be one of them. But... I don't know... I really want to try to make our school better for everyone." And all over again, and as much as he hated that this kept happening, Patrick's thought's went skittering in at least three different directions—*always* this was Baffi's power over him. He wondered if the sincerity he thought he heard in Baffi's voice was real or just another part of his act—if, in fact, he was just using Patrick to *practice* sounding like a politician. He wondered if this father that Baffi had just referenced was a kind of tyrant like Patrick's own.

He wondered, most of all, if Baffi—in his weird and impossible-to-figure-out Baffi way—might actually now be trying to open up to him.

"Has your dad always hated politicians?" Patrick asked, hopeful that this admittedly pointless question might lead to some sort of legitimate *conversation* between the two of them.

Baffi flashed one of his perplexing smiles—half-cocky, half-bashful, like a jaded movie star in the presence of an overzealous fan—and said nothing.

It was thirty minutes later, the two of them dutifully working on revisions, when Patrick heard the front door open and then the clacking of heels on the foyer floor. He looked to Baffi, expecting some sort of reaction, but Baffi only hunched down further over his legal pad. A few seconds after that, there was a plump, black-haired woman standing beside them.

"Nice of you to clean the place up before I get home," she said, looking to the now-empty Coke cans and pizza plates on the coffee table. She spoke with a thick Italian-American accent, not unlike Patrick's own mother: *you* was *yah*; *before* came out as *b'faw*. It was hard to tell, though, if she was genuinely angry with them or just teasing.

Patrick hurriedly stood up from his seat to greet her, figuring Baffi would do the same. Baffi just carried on scribbling on his legal pad.

"Since my son is too rude to introduce us, I'm Betsy Baffi," she said.

"I'm Patrick," he said. "I'm running against Marco for class president."

"Another bullshit artist like my son, huh?" she said; and still Patrick couldn't tell if she was being cruel or playful.

"Mom, *please*," Baffi finally spoke up.

"You invite a friend over, and you can't even manage to put some clothes on?"

Baffi sighed and rolled his eyes and otherwise ignored her.

"This kid would walk around naked if I let him," she said, turning back to Patrick, inexplicably winking at him.

"*Enough*," Baffi snapped.

Patrick watched Betsy's red-painted mouth tighten into a puckered frown. For a moment Patrick thought she was going to scold Baffi.

But then the moment passed, and Betsy shook her head and smiled at Patrick—a smile he thought contained a weird plea for commiseration, as if she were asking him, *Can you believe what a pain in the ass this kid is?*—and then silently left the living room and retreated to the second floor of the house.

From as far back as he could remember, Patrick Francis Monaghan had been a voracious reader of books. Fiction, preferably. Novels instead of short stories, which too often left him frustrated and wanting to know more about the characters. A regular visitor to the Great Kills Public Library, he was particularly attracted to tales where plainly delineated cause produced unequivocal effect and the distinctions between good and evil were unambiguous. (His three favorite novels, up to this point, were *The Stand*, *To Kill a Mockingbird*, and *Brave New World*.) More recently, he had become intrigued by the process taught by Mrs. Ansen in English class, of breaking down a story and diagramming its components: exposition, rising action, turning point, climax and denouement. He had developed a habit of trying to process the events of his own life in terms of this framework.

And so, for the past few weeks, Patrick had been thinking about *this* story, his present circumstance, *The Mysterious Mr. Baffi* he thought he might call it, if he ever put pen to paper; and in this instant he was convinced that they had arrived at *the turning point*—which of course was his favorite part of any story. The critical information had all been revealed, and now he understood the character of Baffi. This boy who at first seemed like everyone's friend was in fact all alone in the world—an only child, regularly dismissed by his father, probably embarrassed by his mother, tired of having to defend himself against their small-minded views of the world.

Counting the days—just like Patrick—until he could escape to college and be surrounded by people who actually "got" him.

Now, *finally*, Patrick realized why Baffi had engineered this whole "friendly competition" in the first place—because he must have sensed how much the two of them had in common, and this was his way of making a connection.

Of course. *Duh.* Turns out that the handsomest boy at Staten Island Tech wasn't so complicated after all.

It was only that—just like Patrick—he wasn't very good at making friends.

"Your mom seems nice," Patrick offered, settling back into his seat on the couch.

"I can't stand her," Baffi answered, and there was a swiftness and coldness in his voice—almost like a blade slicing through paper.

"Well... um... do you want to look at each other's revisions?" Patrick asked.

"Honestly, I'm getting a little bored with this," he said. Then he smiled a more devious version of the familiar Baffi smile and added, "I think we've done enough to keep Ansen happy."

"You know I've been thinking about your idea, and I think that we *should* vote for each other," Patrick said, hoping that maybe this would be enough to cinch an actual *friendship* with Baffi—something that suddenly felt more important to Patrick than anything else in the world.

Baffi shrugged in a way that Patrick thought was mean, almost like he was dismissing him with a *whatever*.

"I mean, I'm definitely willing to do it if you are," Patrick told him.

Baffi rolled his eyes just as he had at his mother, and climbed out of the chair, and bent over to pick up his legal pad, giving Patrick one last view of the Baffi ass—Patrick was sure of it now, it was sublime, glorious, a reason to rise out of bed in the morning, proof of the existence of God—and then Baffi uprighted himself, and arched his back in a stretch, and as unabashedly and unceremoniously as if he were reporting his intentions to tackle his chemistry homework, he announced, "I think I'm gonna go jerk off."

At first, Patrick thought he couldn't have possibly heard correctly. But the recording device in his brain replayed the words, and that's *exactly* what Baffi said. Patrick's next thought was exultant—he had been wrong about Baffi to start, and now he realized that he was *even more* wrong than before. It wasn't *just* that Baffi felt a kinship with Patrick. Everything that had happened between them these past four weeks had in fact been building to *something else*. Baffi liked boys, just as Patrick did. Baffi liked Patrick. But he couldn't bring himself to admit that, so he had instead struck up this "friendly competition," which was really just an excuse for the two of them to get to know each other, and then he had brought Patrick to his house and paraded in front of him in his skimpy shorts, and now he had just told him that he was going to jerk off.

How totally obvious. Baffi wanted to hook up. Maybe not full-blown sex, which Patrick didn't think he was ready for anyway, but definitely some fooling around.

He just blurted it out.

In his almost feverish state induced by this unbelievably *hard* hard-on burning in his pants, in his rush to speak up after so often cursing himself for failing in critical moments to say what needed be said, he didn't second-guess himself.

He didn't think about the many times he had overheard Baffi talking with his jock friends, with an ease that no one else would have confused for performance, about the girls he wanted to "go with."

He didn't have other male friends, so he didn't even know that this was the way boys their age sometimes talked to one another, boasting about how often they beat off, making a weird game of it, he who is the crassest and least self-conscious about his bodily functions wins.

He never considered the possibility that if this was his life as a horror movie, now would be the moment everyone in the audience groaned and shouted at the screen: *Get out of the fucking house.*

The three most ill-advised words of Patrick Francis Monaghan's first fifteen years. The moment they were spoken they could of course never be taken back.

"Can I watch?"

THINKING BACK ON IT LATER that night, because of course he couldn't fall sleep, Patrick could only anticipate retribution. Baffi would whisper the story of what had happened to two or three people, and those people in turn would whisper it to others, and soon there would be no whispering at all, everyone would know that Patrick Monaghan was such a fairy that he had actually asked Marco Baffi if he could watch him jerk off. All the effort, all through his adolescence, making certain his voice didn't go too high, that his wrist stayed ramrod straight, that he didn't shriek when a gym class volleyball came towards him—a million different things he was careful *not* to do, all so the other kids might think him quiet or bookish or unfriendly, but would *never* suspect he might be gay—all of it would be rendered worthless. Patrick would be greeted each day by a rainstorm of insults and mimicry, and what would make it all worse was that on some level he would believe he *deserved* this punishment.

Because he was too stupid, too much of a pathetic, lovesick faggot, to see what would have been obvious to anyone—that *of course* this handsome, charming, unimpeachably *heterosexual* soccer player didn't want to hook up with him.

Upon hearing Patrick's request, Baffi had made a face like he was smelling a particularly noisome fart. "You want to watch me jerk off?"

Immediately realizing his error—this epic, thunderous miscalculation, oh dear God, what had he just done?—Patrick looked away from Baffi and began sputtering a halfhearted defense: "I just meant… I've always been curious about how other guys do it… how it compares… "

"No, you can't," Baffi said flatly. "That's not a normal thing to ask someone."

"OK," Patrick said. He needed to get out of there, to run as far away as possible. Yet he didn't move. *He couldn't.* He first had to figure a way to twist off the couch without having to stand up and reveal to Baffi the boner tenting the front of his pants.

"I'm sorry… I didn't mean to…" Patrick tried to add, but then Betsy Baffi was back in the living room, asking if the boys wanted a snack, and Baffi was telling her no, Patrick had to get going, and all Patrick could think to do was to use his arms to lift his butt off the couch and spin himself in place and fling himself away from them—how strange and probably hazardous that move must have looked to them, like a gymnast trying to dismount a pommel horse from the sitting position—yet miraculously he landed on his feet, his back turned to both Baffis. He even managed to croak out a thank-you when Betsy said he was welcome to come over any time he liked.

That following Monday Patrick walked into math class and saw Baffi whispering to two boys sitting next to him, who looked up at Patrick and glared. He waited for the word to slip from their mouths, low so that the teachers wouldn't hear, *faggot, faggot, faggot*. But nothing. In the hallways, he kept glancing over his shoulder, expecting at any moment that Baffi would appear and crush him against the nearest wall. Still nothing. At the special sixth-period assembly, they both delivered their final speeches to the sophomore class—Patrick's confused and halting; Baffi's of course engaging and effortless—and afterward Baffi was guileless and even goofy as he vigorously shook Patrick's hand and proclaimed in front of everyone, "May the best candidate win!"

Voting took place at the end of the assembly. Patrick wasted no time, upon stepping into one of the makeshift, cardboard-and-wooden booths constructed by Mr. Lorenzo's shop class for today's election, in casting his ballot for his rival. He felt nothing other than a kind of grimly comic inevitability—just like in the W.W. Jacobs short story that he had read in Mrs. Ansen's class last year, about the bereaved couple who wish with a monkey's paw to bring their deceased son back to life, only to have the son's corpse begin knocking at their door—when the announcement from the principal came over the loudspeaker at the end of ninth period. The votes had been counted and recounted and recounted again, they were expecting it to be close, but they never expected *this*.

Marco Baffi had defeated Patrick Monaghan, seventy-four votes to seventy-three.

Mrs. Ansen found him a few minutes later at his locker, where he was taking an inordinately long time to gather his books. She said, "I shouldn't tell you this, but the reason I kept forcing the two of you together was that I was hoping you would see how he operates—and maybe figure out a way to beat him at his own game. Don't get me wrong. Marco is a very bright and likable boy. But he doesn't have substance inside of him like you do, Patrick. I hope you'll run against him again next year."

Baffi never did tell anyone about what had happened between them, at least so far as Patrick knew. He went on to choose Joey Aventino—one of the jockiest, most obnoxious boys in the school, a friend of Baffi's from the soccer team—as his vice president; and he ran again for class president junior and senior years, each time unopposed. And though every once in a while Patrick would get it in his head that he should seek out Baffi and clear the air, he never could bring himself to do it. What would he say? Where would he even begin?

Indeed, other than a few teacher-facilitated classroom discussions, they didn't speak again until graduation day. Patrick saw him standing alone, at the far edge of the soccer field, where the commencement had just concluded. A part of Patrick was still scared that Baffi remained angry about what had happened and would react to any sort of entreaty with violence. But another, stronger part of him—for better or worse—had never been very good at letting things rest. He excused himself from his parents. He figured it was now or never.

"I know we ended up going our separate ways," he said. "But I just wanted to say I'm glad we got to compete to be class president and get to know each other a little bit. Good luck in college."

"Yeah," Baffi mumbled. "You too."

"You know, I did vote for you that day," Patrick told him. "I said I would and I did. I've always wondered, though: Did you vote for me?"

Baffi opened his mouth, and it looked like he was going to say one thing, but then he shifted in place and shrugged his shoulders and plunged his hands into his pockets. Then he smiled one of his melting Baffi smiles and said to Patrick instead: "My folks are waiting, so I should probably get going."

1 9 9 2 - 9 3

The first two hours of waiting were the worst. Outside of the hospital, the Fort Worth police erected wooden barriers along South Main and Allen Streets, sluicing the rapidly descending members of the local, statewide and national media into an overflow parking lot across the street. Inside, Nora and Oscar were dispatched to a private waiting room: dirt-scuffed linoleum floor; two pale green vinyl sofas; Styrofoam cups and lukewarm water-cooler water. A nurse visited first, with a stack of admittance forms and her halfhearted apologies... *I know this is a terrible time... it's ridiculous to have to bury you in paperwork... maybe when Mr. Monaghan gets elected, he can go after the insurance companies...* The president of the hospital turned up next, a ruddy, well-fed fellow in his late forties, trailed by a baby-faced young man wearing a bow tie and skinny jeans. The president stayed only long enough to make a few bland assurances about how Patrick was presently in the hands of *the finest trauma team in North Texas*, before leaving them with his protégé, who introduced himself as Dustin, the hospital's "media liaison." He wondered if they had any objections to his scheduling a press conference at 2:30 p.m. to be led by the hospital president.

"Best to be out ahead in these situations," he said, as if gunshot victims of would-be political assassins were treated in this hospital every few days.

Nora glared at him. "But what can we *tell* them? Is Patrick going to be OK?"

"*Extremely critical* is what we're saying," Dustin answered. "That's not good, but it's better than *deceased.*"

A stultifying tension soon settled into the room. Nora stared at the floor; Oscar at the wall. Neither of them wanted to say a word, or do anything really, for fear that it might jinx their friend's chances. As the clock crawled past 2 p.m., Nora reached for her iPhone, less out of purpose than habit. It was buried at the bottom of her briefcase, on silent since just before Patrick took the stage to deliver his speech. She found the phone presently lit up with an incoming call, a producer from MSNBC trying to reach her. She hit the ignore button, but then checked and saw that her voicemail box was already full, and that, in the last ninety minutes, she had received hundreds of texts and emails.

It was enough to snap her out of her paralysis. This was no time to be passive; no time for silly superstitions about jinxing Patrick. As with every other aspect of this campaign, the aftermath of the attempted assassination of Patrick Francis Monaghan was going to have to be *managed*.

She located the nurse in the reception area and handed her back the stack of unmarked medical forms. "Find someone on my staff to take care of this," she said, and walked away without waiting for an answer. She then tracked down Dustin in his office and told him that in fact *she* would be coordinating and leading the press conference, at which she also expected the mayor of Fort Worth, the chief of the city's police department, representatives from the Dallas field office of the F.B.I., and the highest-ranking doctor on staff at the hospital who wasn't presently operating on Patrick to be in attendance—could he start making those calls and make sure they were all here ASAP? She next called her assistant, who got Marilyn Monaghan booked on the next flight out of Newark, and then she called Marilyn herself and did what she could to comfort her.

"He's going to pull through this," Nora said. "You and I both know he's indomitable."

Finally Nora tapped out an email to a producer at CNN and said that if he could have a remote crew and a makeup artist outside the hospital within the next fifteen minutes, she would be willing to go on with Wolf Blitzer. She would give them five minutes, exclusive, but, please, no questions about the possible motives of the alleged gunman, or about what the shooting might augur for the future of the campaign.

"The second it lapses into tasteless speculation," she declared, "the interview is over."

A half hour after that she was standing in one of the hospital's empty conference rooms, posed in front of a jerry-rigged green screen onto which a picture of the Fort Worth skyline would be projected on-air, a tiny plastic earpiece tucked too loosely inside her concha. She would be on live in thirty seconds, though at present she was having a hard time concentrating. Her mind kept circling back to the last thing Patrick had said to her, just before he bounded onto the front porch of the Stockyards Museum this morning. He'd been behaving oddly, even by the standards of these extremely odd last few days, and when he said it he sounded so sweet and subdued—two words she *never* associated with Patrick.

"I just want to say that if I've held you back in any way," he had told her, "if your commitment to me has in any way prevented you from being the person you wanted to be, I never meant for that. I've always just wanted you to succeed."

It came out of nowhere, and of course she brushed it aside. "Stay focused on your speech, Patrick," she answered. And though she acted like she was annoyed, she was secretly grateful when his phone started ringing a second later. He got distracted, and she got distracted by his distraction, and so she didn't have to think too hard about what he had just said, or wonder why he had chosen just this moment to say it.

"Nora, you're on in ten," the voice in her ear said, breaking through her reverie.

Because what *could* she have responded, when what had always characterized their friendship was the tendency on both their parts to contain their unruliest emotions within the square frames of emails; when the truth which she never would have admitted to Patrick was that he had tapped right into the unresolved dilemma of her entire life?

"Nora, are you there...?"

It wasn't like she didn't have her chances to cut him loose over the years; wasn't like she didn't willingly pour so much of herself into him, again and again. But it wasn't, either, as if she ever felt she had any choice—from the moment she met him, she knew she *needed* Patrick in her life, every bit as much as he needed her in his. In the end, she supposed, all she could do was laugh about it, and cry at the same time, just as she and Suzie had done that very last night at college, all of them in Patrick's dorm room, Patrick passed out on the bed, Steve sleeping on the floor, Nora and Suzie holding each other tight, not wanting to squander their very last hours at Dartmouth to something so commonplace as sleep.

"Nora, you're on in three... two... one... "

Leave it to Suzie to sum it all up so succinctly: "It's like the most beautiful and tragic love story ever told all rolled into one. Two lost and wandering souls meet and discover that they are perfect for each other—and then never get to have sex."

THEY ACTUALLY MET, PATRICK WOULD often hasten to explain, *before* the first day of college, on "Trips," the three-day hiking and kayaking expeditions that all incoming freshmen went on before orientation properly commenced. Nora Melissa Meacham from San Antonio, Texas, was set to be roommates with Suzie Brown, the Spence girl who sat in front of Patrick on the chartered bus from Penn Station to Hanover and peered in between the seat backs to talk to him all six hours there. Suzie made the introductions that afternoon, after the buses deposited everyone at Mount Moosilauke Lodge. A few hours later, Patrick and Nora locked upon one another as partners when it came time for square dancing, even though Suzie made it clear that she wanted Patrick as *her* partner.

"He's one of the few guys here who's actually taller than me," argued Nora, who had long blonde hair and a reedlike frame and stood just over six feet—and who even at eighteen took a quietly insistent approach to conflict that usually resulted in her getting her way.

Patrick and Nora danced and made jokes and asked questions about each other in between the hokey songs; and then the next morning, Patrick made a beeline for Nora's breakfast table, and they picked up their conversation right where they had left off. They were assigned to separate trip groups and wouldn't see each other again until orientation, but the very last thing Patrick said to her before they departed was that they should plan to meet for dinner as soon as they both got to campus.

He never imagined that Nora would think he had just asked her on a date.

Those first few weeks were a rush; a privilege he didn't know what he had done to earn: Was there really someone in this world with whom he so readily *clicked?* Nora had been the valedictorian at Northside High School, what she termed "the second shittiest school in the San Antonio Independent School District," and she had spent the previous summer in Austin, interning in Governor Ann Richards' office. Her plan was to double-major in government and philosophy, with the longterm goal of entering public service. Observing the governor up close, absorbing the woman's most steadfast lesson, Nora had come to believe that the greatest threat to the future of American democracy was the lack of women and minorities in positions of political power.

"A government must be a reflection of its people," she told Patrick late one night in September, "but ours is becoming an oligarchy made up of the hegemonic elite."

Patrick was in awe of Nora, at once intimidated and inspired by the intelligence behind her pronouncements. (Had she really just used the words *oligarchy* and *hegemonic* in the same sentence?) For his own part, he had no idea what he wanted to do with his life. He worried that the adult professions he might most enjoy—journalist, say, or book editor, or National Public Radio talk show host—were either exceedingly low-paying or deeply elusive or both; and the last thing he wanted was to end up confirming his parents' hectoring, high-school-educated worldview, that places like Dartmouth were pretentious and overpriced, no different, truly, than those restaurants in New York City that charged you forty dollars for a plate of food and still sent you home hungry. (His parents had only begrudgingly allowed him to come here, after he agreed not just to take out his own loans, but to pay back the loans that they would be forced to take out, too.) Listening to Nora, though, he understood that the one thing he couldn't do was think small. He had to believe as she did, that the world should be forced to expand in order to contain them, and never the other way around.

Talk, talk, talk—it might be cheap, but sometimes it makes you feel like a million bucks. Their conversations started each evening at one of the dining halls, Thayer or Home Plate, and then continued as they made their way to Baker Library to study, or to Spaulding Auditorium to watch a movie being shown by the Dartmouth Film Society, and then the conversation would just keep going, even after they retreated to their separate dorm rooms—Patrick to Mass Hall, to the two-room double he shared with a boy from Connecticut named Andy Curran, whom he and Nora had nicknamed "Snot Raggedy Andy"; Nora all the way to the River Cluster, at the far western edge of the campus—where they would compose messages to one another on BlitzMail, the intra-campus email system. Those emails lighted the nerves in their extremities, so excited were they when they heard the familiar bird chirp or wind chime—depending on which control-panel sound setting they were currently employing on their Mac II Classics—announcing that a new one had arrived.

Dear Patrick (began one such email, received late one night in October):

I'm sorry I got so quiet tonight. You asked a perfectly ordinary question when you asked me what my family is like. But whenever I'm asked about them, my instinct is to dissemble. It's probably because I feel like I'm surrounded by these kids whose entire lives are almost parodies of overachievement—they were first in their class at Deerfield, and their fathers teach at Harvard, and their mothers host fundraisers for Bill Clinton—and so inevitably I want to be able to compete. (As I might have already mentioned to you, I'm the most competitive person you will ever meet.) The problem is I can't compete. My background simply doesn't measure up.

Here's the honest answer to your question: My father is nine years younger than my mother, and they married when she was 35—the only reason he asked, I think, was because a wife and a kid would keep him from getting drafted into the Vietnam War, and the only reason she said yes, I think, was because she was starting to fear that he was the only man willing to have her. In 1977, when she was eight years old, my sister Natalie drowned in the swimming pool in our backyard. At the time I was in the house taking a nap, and this detail always makes me very sad. Can you imagine sleeping through your sister's drowning?

My mother claimed it was my father who was supposed to be watching them, and of course he said vice-versa. They divorced when I was eleven, and since then, my mother has struggled with her weight—she's diabetic and nearly four hundred pounds now—and my father has lost thousands of dollars gambling. My aunt is the one now paying for me to be here, though I've promised to pay her back, every penny with interest.

So that's what my family is like. I hope you don't blame me for not wanting to tell you all of this right away, and I hope you believe me when I say that you're someone I want to be COMPLETELY honest with.

Nora

Nora (began his reply sent the next afternoon):

I'm sorry it's taken me all day to answer you. It's just that your message gave me so much to think about, and I needed time to come up with a worthy response.

So your family isn't perfect. You're a little bit ashamed of them, and I'm guessing you also feel guilty for feeling that way, because, after all, they are your parents, and what makes you so special to think that you're somehow better than them.

All I can say is: At least one person on this campus knows exactly *how you feel.*

My father retired on disability last year after twenty-five years driving a truck for Coca-Cola. My mother works as a checkout clerk at Pathmark—a job she accepted over a slightly more glamorous-sounding one at Macy's, because it paid twenty cents more an hour. My sister got married when she was twenty-one and then eight months later had a baby. My brother dropped out of Brooklyn College and now works as a bank teller. Try explaining all of that to the kids here, as I made the mistake of doing with my roommate Andy, and they will look at you like you're an alien.

I'm sorry to hear about your sister. On the one hand, I can't possibly relate, and it would be insensitive for me to even try. But at the same time I *think* I understand how you feel. Nothing particularly tragic happened in my own parents' lives—or at least nothing that I'm aware of—but they also never seemed entirely there for me. I don't know how to explain it, and it's probably as much my fault as theirs, but at some point I just stopped talking to them about the things that were important to me.

Here's something to think about though: I used to envy kids whose lives seemed perfect, and whose parents are role models. Reading your Blitz, though, I started to wonder if we're the lucky ones. We're here because we worked to be here, and (unlike the Andy Currans of the world) we'll never be willing to rest on our laurels. We know what we're fighting against—and isn't that half of any battle?

As I said, something to think about. Maybe we can continue this conversation over dinner. Meet at the Hop at seven?

P.

FINALLY, FINALLY, *FINALLY*, HE'D DONE it. And it felt every bit as good as he imagined it would. This was what he had been searching for his whole life: a person who saw the world as he did; a person who felt the feelings he felt.

A person whom he could proudly declare his *best friend*.

And though Patrick wasn't quite ready yet to share with her his deepest secret, he nonetheless sensed himself getting closer. He would speak the words that he hadn't be able to speak to anyone else, and *of course* she wouldn't reject him. She would be nothing but supportive, because that's just the kind of person she was, decent and humane and open-minded. She wouldn't care in the least that Patrick was gay.

He truly believed this conversation between them—this *best friendship*—could carry on forever.

Until one Tuesday afternoon in the middle of November, when he was eating lunch by himself at the Hop, just before his Introduction to Film Theory class. Suzie didn't say hello; didn't even ask him if she could join him. She just sat down across from him and started talking.

"Before you find true love, you first have to have your heart broken, and you also have to break somebody's heart," she burst forth. "Otherwise you're just not mature enough to be in love."

"Is this some kind of riddle I'm supposed to answer?" Patrick responded.

"You are driving Nora absolutely crazy," she answered. "And I'm not saying this because I'm trying to cause trouble with you two—I am so *not* in the business of drama—or because I'm jealous that she's going to your house for Thanksgiving even though *I* asked her first—that's fine, no big deal—but you *can't* keep doing this to her, Patrick, acting like you're going to make a move and then not doing anything, I mean, *every single person* in the freshman class thinks she's your girlfriend."

Suzie finally paused to take a breath and then added: "How do you think she feels having to explain to people she'd *like* to be your girlfriend, but she's not?"

Patrick looked across the table at his best friend's roommate and told himself not to panic. Suzie was a plain-looking girl, with thick brown hair that tended to frizz and lips so thin that when she smiled you only saw teeth. From their earliest interactions as a trio, Patrick sensed that she was a little jealous of Nora—of her stature, her beauty, the instant attention she commanded when she entered a room—and thus understood that this outburst might easily just bullshit. Maybe she was just stirring things up and hoping to drive a wedge between him and Nora, because what she envied most of all was that Nora had found a best friend at Dartmouth and she still hadn't.

Yet at the same time Patrick had never heard Suzie sound so determined and oddly *earnest*—she usually just labored to come off as jaded and above-it-all, in her Upper East Side, *Oh-yeah-I-tried-heroin-when-I-was-thirteen-but-it-wasn't-really-my-thing* sort of way—and of course Patrick also couldn't pretend the thought hadn't previously occurred to him, that Nora might be carrying some kind of torch for him.

"I'm sorry... I didn't realize..." he mumbled.

"That's what I keep telling her, that you're just totally clueless, or that you are one of those high-functioning autistics—I forget what they're called—they don't process normal human interaction, but they can do math and other stuff—but she thinks you don't find her attractive and she's not your type, because you're always making jokes about her height, and because you went to see some stupid Polish movie together and afterward all you could do was talk about how hot Juliette Binoche was."

Patrick pushed his lunch tray aside, finding that he no longer had an appetite. Perhaps Suzie was laying it on a little thick here, raising the stakes the way they all did that freshman fall, because it was the first time they were getting to be grownups. But he knew she wasn't making it up. He did sometimes make light of Nora's height, whenever they passed an especially short guy on campus, Patrick would point and whisper to Nora, "There's another one you could take in a fight." But he assumed Nora was in on the gag; that she took great pride in forcing men to look upon her as a formidable adversary.

And, yes, guilty as charged, they had indeed gone to see *The Double Life of Veronique*, and after he gushed over the film's lead actress. But that hadn't meant anything, either, it was just this hard-to-die habit of his, he'd been doing it since junior high school: Turns out the easiest way to stave off rumors about you being gay is to make vague noises of attraction for women you have no chance of encountering in real life.

"Nora's beautiful," Patrick said now. "That's not it. That's not it at all."

For a minute neither of them said anything. Suzie reached for one of Patrick's French fries, twirled it between her fingers and nibbled at it before placing it back on

Patrick's tray half-eaten. Then she stood up and gathered her book bag and announced that she was going to be late for her next class.

She was ten feet away before she stopped and turned back to him and said, loudly enough so that everyone at the surrounding tables could hear: "Two things, Patrick. First this conversation never happened. And second, just fuck the girl. That's what she wants."

OH, THE HIDDEN PERILS OF being eighteen and a virgin—he'd never so much as kissed another person, hadn't even come close—and perhaps overly susceptible to all those speeches he had listened to during those first few weeks at Dartmouth, from the dean of freshman and the college president, imploring their class to *Think outside the box* and *Challenge your preconceived notions of how a life is supposed to be lived*. For weeks after that talk with Suzie, he carried on as before. Nora traveled with him to Staten Island for Thanksgiving, and they spent a long, lazy weekend sleeping late and watching movies and Patrick did nothing to disabuse the notions of his family that she was his girlfriend. Back on campus, they were inseparable the last weeks of the first quarter, studying for their finals in adjoining carrels in the stacks at Baker, making late night runs to EBAs for pizza.

But all that time he was thinking about what Suzie said; thinking about the boundaries of human sexuality and how to push beyond them.

He was applying his own peculiar brand of logic: *If being gay is not supposed to limit me in life or deny me opportunities because of others' prejudices, then why should it stop me from having a girlfriend?*

The night in question was the second Saturday of the winter quarter, cold and cloudy, with whipping winds that sent tiny snowflakes somersaulting through the valley air. Nora had wanted to stay in; catch up on her reading for government class. Patrick wore down her defenses over BlitzMail; convinced her to get hot chocolate with him at Rosey Jeke's. It was and it was not premeditated. He knew his roommate Andy would be out, probably all night, drunk in the basement of the fraternity he planned to pledge in the fall. But Patrick didn't recognize until they were finishing their hot chocolates that the weather was affording him an opportunity.

"It's too cold to walk back to the River," he ventured. "Why don't you just sleep in my room tonight?"

It unfolded much as he had pictured it in his head. She followed him up to his third floor room in Mass Hall. He gestured for her to take a seat on his bed. He retrieved two cans of Fresca from the mini-fridge and then settled onto the bed beside her. He put R.E.M.'s *Automatic for the People* on the CD player, and then they talked and talked and talked, and when they had finished their sodas and the CD had played through twice, Patrick finally worked up the nerve to speak the line that he had been silently rehearsing for weeks.

"I think it's okay for friends to hook up."

"Um…"

"So they can figure out if they might want to be more than just friends." He had rehearsed that line, too.

"Yeah… I… I guess I agree with that."

He stripped off his sweater and T-shirt and then shifted his body and pressed his back against the wall so that they could both lay down on the bed. Nora took off her own sweater, but kept on her bra and lay down beside him. First her hair got pinned beneath his elbow. Then she accidentally poked him in the eye, which set off fits of giggles in both of them. But finally they relaxed into a comfortable-enough pose, legs and arms touching, Patrick's right shoulder wedged against the side of Nora's left breast.

And there they remained, frozen like statues, saying nothing for the better part of fifteen minutes.

He tried. In his mind he made an immense effort. He pictured himself touching her breast over her bra and then leaning in closer and pressing his mouth to her lips. Her back would arch up so that he could slip his hand beneath her and unhook her bra, and then they would turn on their sides facing each other, and her breasts would press against his chest and then—what? would they make out for a while? or would she reach for his dick? he wasn't quite sure about this next part—but ultimately their jeans would come off, and then his boxers and her panties, and then his penis would enter her and that might be weird—he had never expressly asked, but he was pretty sure she was also a virgin, and he knew all sorts of painful and bloody things happened when girls lost their virginity, and, come to think of it, he didn't have a condom, so they were probably going to have to work out some sort of alternate solution—but whatever, *eventually* it would be over, and then they would have had sex. He imagined an entire cinematic love scene in his head, complete with candles he didn't own and mood music he didn't have playing, and because he needed a little inspiration, he also imagined that he was presently in bed next to Alex Panagakis, the Greek boy from his freshman seminar, with his black eyes and hairy arms and chin that looked sculpted out of marble.

Just fuck the girl.

Easier said than done.

"This is weird, Patrick," Nora finally said.

"Yeah."

"It's just that… I'm a little confused right now."

"I haven't wanted to rush things… because our friendship means a lot to me…"

"You aren't making any sense," Nora said, her voice clipped and cool.

Patrick inhaled, slow and deep. He was so scared of screwing this up. In Nora, he had found a treasured friend; filled a void he'd never fully realized was empty. Yet his fundamental evasion now threatened to divide them. He knew he had the power to fix this. He only had to speak the two words that he had heard himself saying at least a million times in his head. Nora would understand at once that his not wanting to be her boyfriend had *nothing* to do with her physical attractiveness—*of course* she was gorgeous, not to mention brilliant, who *wouldn't* want to date her?—and she would be grateful for his honesty and quickly forgive him for this stupid little episode of him talking her into bed.

Then they could go back to being *best friends*.

"Nora, I…" His mouth cottoned up.

"*What*, Patrick?"

No. He wasn't yet ready. Irrational though they might be, his fears were still his fears. He thought about how once he said it there would be no taking it back. Once Nora knew, soon *everyone* on campus would know, and even though his classmates were all supposed to be politically correct and *respectful of each other's differences*, they would nonetheless look at him a little funny. This would become the means by which they would identify him—*there goes that "gay guy…"*—even though he wanted to be known for so much more; and if everyone on campus knew, well, then it would only be a matter of time before he would have to fess up to his parents, and just the thought of how *that* conversation might go—his mother's tears, his father's scowls, so much fucking disappointment—was enough to make him taste bile.

He couldn't do it. Not yet. Sorry Nora.

"Maybe we can just take it slow," he offered, after the silence had turned agonizing, "and see how things develop, and then… after a few more weeks… if we think we should be boyfriend and girlfriend… then we can talk about it again…"

Dear Patrick:

First I should apologize for ignoring you for so long. Suzie kept telling me to just get over it, but it's been hard for me. You have this way about you—I don't even think you realize it about yourself. You are funny and charming. Quick, in every sense of the word. I know you don't mean to, but sometimes you make the rest of us feel as if we're racing to catch up with you. And so the more time we spent together… well, I started to think that I had finally caught up with you, and you were interested in making me your girlfriend. And I wanted that, Patrick. I'm not ashamed to say that I would have liked that.

But then I realized I was wrong. And that made me so mad. You know me, Patrick, I don't like to lose—especially when I don't understand what I should have done differently to win.

I've been thinking about this, though. Whatever your reasons for not wanting us to date, I can't act like they are illegitimate just because I feel differently, and I can't pretend like I have some claim over you to know what those reasons are. And the truth is, Patrick, I miss you.

Can we be friends again? These last few months have been busy, and there's so much I want to tell you about. I hit it off with my political theory professor from winter term, and she wants me to think about eventually doing a senior fellowship with her. I also started dating Steve Stollen. (Do you remember him? We all met on the Freshman Trips..) I'm not sure he's the love of my life, but it's been a nice distraction from schoolwork. In fact, I think you would like him. Maybe we can all meet up at Thayer one night this week.

Nora

Patrick sat at the desk in his dorm room, staring at his computer screen, reading this first-in-seventy-two-days communication from Nora, filling with outrage and contempt, like a ship taking on too much water. He couldn't fucking believe this.

For one thing: Did Nora not understand that the whole reason he tried so hard to be witty and charming in her presence was because he had been trying to catch up with *her*?

And for another: Steve Stollen? Of all fucking people? He was built like a utility pole, soaring and solid, and when they first saw him at Mount Moosilauke, he was wearing a tank top that showed off his crew rower's arms and his pumped-out Superman chest. But then they ended up at the same picnic table with him at dinner, and for one thing he had weirdly-shaped ears and too much nose hair, and for another, he was dumb as a box of rocks, he'd had *nothing* contribute to their conversation, for fuck's sake, he stared in confusion when Patrick used the word *bustling* to make a joke about what growing up on a Minnesota dairy farm must have been like.

Was she *that* fucking desperate that she'd be willing to date Steve Stollen?

Over the next two hours, Patrick wrote and deleted at least twenty different replies to her email. There were so many things he wanted to say to her; so many different ways he believed he'd be justified in lashing out. He wanted to suggest that she should try some fucking empathy, because as much as she was hurt by Patrick's actions that night, her months-long silence had devastated him; wanted to tell her she was slumming it by dating this ridiculous oaf; wanted to confront her with what he suspected was the real truth behind all of this—that she had chosen Steve Stollen only because she knew it would annoy Patrick.

He ended up telling her none of these things. Because what he wanted most of all was his best friend back. He wanted to resume the conversation that his life at Dartmouth didn't seem complete without.

I'm free tomorrow night if you guys are.

How easy it proved. How effortlessly they put water under the bridge. Within an hour of dinner that next night they were caught up on everything they had missed in each other's lives. Steve Stollen, to his considerable credit, had the good grace to smile and say very little. The three of them met for dinner again the following night, and the night after that Steve had crew practice, so it was just Patrick and Nora—just as it used to be. The emails were soon being volleyed back and forth, sent as fast as they could be written. Patrick guessed that Nora was attracted to Steve because of his gargantuan size, or his admittedly enviable triceps, or maybe a big guy like him just had a really big dick. (Girls, Patrick believed, *always* ended up dating the wrong guys for precisely such superficial reasons.) But there was no need to point out the obvious to her. She was smart and self-aware. She would figure it out soon enough that she could do so much better. And until then Patrick could take assurance that his own selfish interests in the matter—his basic human need to have Nora as his friend—were being met.

Alas, Patrick Francis Monaghan had never been one to leave well enough alone.

He had to find a way to break them up.

HE WAS ONLY EIGHTEEN YEARS old—still prone to see human conflict in absolutist terms; still possessed of the conviction that there was a road map for his own life ascribed in the pages of the novels he loved to read. He just so happened to be taking a comparative literature course that spring, "The Histories and Practices of Noir." *Red Harvest. The Bride Wore Black. The Postman Always Rings Twice.* Immerse yourself in enough of *those* dark, deceit-fueled worlds, and the paranoia proves infectious. He convinced himself that Steve Stollen had to be doing *something* wrong; that somehow he was keeping secrets from Nora. Those not-particularly-surreptitious glances at other girls. The arbitrarily scheduled crew practices that caused plans to be cancelled at the last minute. That general air of vapidity that Patrick sometimes suspected might be an act. It all added up to a damning case report, a *profile*, like the ones used by the FBI to track sociopaths. Steve was exactly the type of guy—quiet and mild-mannered and bereft of an interior life—capable of wholesale duplicity.

He took to following Steve. Nothing too serious—it wasn't like he wanted this to end with Steve taking out a restraining order. One Sunday afternoon he positioned himself a few tables away from Steve in the 1902 Room at Baker, just to take inventory of any girls who might come by to say hello while Steve was studying. (None did.) A few days later he followed Steve at a polite distance—thirty feet at least, no way Steve could have known Patrick was behind him—as he made his way to the Dartmouth

Boathouse, just to make sure he really went to crew practice when he said he did. A week after that Patrick ventured inside Theta Delt, where Steve was planning to pledge in the fall, and where that night they were having an open party. Nora always refused to accompany Steve to the frat—*patriarchal, misogynist, a factory for date rape and substance abuse, etcetera, etcetera*—and so Patrick figured that here, almost certainly, he would witness some kind of misdeed. He watched from a corner of the sticky-floored, low-ceilinged basement, lurking behind a beam so that his mark wouldn't see him. He was disappointed—no, actually he was crushed, like a kid on Christmas who doesn't get the present that he'd placed at the very top of his wish list—when Steve spent his entire time there talking to a handful of his crew friends and then left after just an hour.

OK, so probably not the best idea. Naïve of him to think that Steve would broadcast his indiscretions publicly. In fact, Patrick had pretty much decided to retire the whole private investigator routine when—one afternoon in the middle of May—he was making his way back to campus from Rosey Jeke's. He met Nora there every Thursday for coffee, though this week she had mysteriously failed to show.

He followed his usual route through the rear parking lot of the Hopkins Center, down the concrete pathway that led past the Loew Auditorium. He was coming up on the little octagonal space just outside the doors of the Loew. A steel grate in the ground there mysteriously spewed steam, and the only light came from the gassy green neon of the letters L—O—E—W over the doors—at night it really did look as if you had wandered onto the set of an old-fashioned film noir, with everyone cast in obscuring half-shadow.

Except presently it was the middle of the day, and from a distance of fifteen feet there was no mistaking who was standing there, not John Garfield, not Fred MacMurray, but Steve Fucking Stollen, and he was hunched over not Lana Turner or Barbara Stanwyk but Suzie Brown, Nora's roommate and so-called friend, and, *oh my God*, the two of them were making out, kissing, hooking up, whatever the fuck you were supposed to call it, *that's* what they were doing, lips, mouth, tongue, hand on ass, the whole bit. *No, no, no, NO!* Patrick moved sideways behind a brick wall, out of their line of vision, but where he could still see them. They kissed, pulled away, kissed again. The colossal Steve, a full foot and a half taller, had to bend at the knee to meet Suzie's face.

Patrick could hear the coffee he had just finished drinking gurgling in his belly; felt weak in his bowels at this sight. This was *so much worse* than anything he might have previously imagined of the contemptible Stollen. Mercifully the kiss lasted only a few seconds longer. Steve leaned down again and whispered something in Suzie's ear, and then the two of them parted in opposite directions, Suzie back to campus, Steve towards Patrick. Patrick had to scurry and hide behind one of the cars in the parking lot so that Steve wouldn't see him. As he passed, Patrick saw an insufferable smile crawl across his face—he looked so smug and so preening.

He raced back to his dorm room and to his computer to fix this once and for all.

Dear Nora:

I hope everything is OK—you never showed up at Rosey Jeke's. I need to see you. I have something to tell you, and it's not very good news, but I'd rather you hear it from me before you hear it from anyone else.

Patrick

I know what you have to tell me. Don't bother. I don't think we can be friends anymore.

Huh? I don't think you understand.
[No response.]

I saw Suzie and Steve making out outside the Loew this afternoon. It was horrible. I'm sorry to have to be the one to tell you. I had a bad feeling from the start about Steve. I only wish Suzie hadn't gotten herself corrupted by him. She's better than that.

You stupid, self-absorbed idiot! You saw Suzie and Steve putting on a show for your benefit. Steve said you had been following him around campus and that you were trying to gather evidence to convince me to break up with him. I told him he was being paranoid. But he said he was going to prove it to me, and now he just did.

Are you SURE? Because I saw them kissing and they seemed to be liking it.

I was standing inside the doors watching them. We set you up Patrick, but I never thought you'd fall completely into our trap.

Oh… shit…

You don't want to go out with me, but you don't want me to go out with anyone else, either, so basically I'm left with no option other than to live my life according to your whims. I can't do this anymore, Patrick. I'm sorry, but I can't. It's over between us.

IN LATER YEARS, HE WOULD sometimes feel a measure of regret that he'd never displayed any true integrity in the matter—his admission, finally, was born out of sheer desperation. It was his final and only hope of winning Nora's forgiveness.

He first tried every way he knew to say he was sorry. He found Nora studying on the lawn in front of Sanborn House, and then stood there absorbing the entertained stares of the students all around them, as she shouted at him, "Go away. I won't listen to your lies." He next sought the counsel of Suzie, who was obviously on Nora's side, but who was at least willing to hear him out. She accepted Patrick's apology for having thought she might actually betray Nora by hooking up with Steve—"I've told you a thousand times, *I don't do drama*"—but offered him little hope otherwise.

"Honestly, Patrick," Suzie told him, "you bring out her feminazi side. She's decided that you're one of these guys whose mission in life is to find new ways to dominate women. I don't know how anyone recovers from that sort of reputation."

He even swallowed every last ounce of pride and tracked down Steve Stollen one afternoon, working on a final paper in the computer lab. He confessed to everything; said he didn't know what had come over him, other than pure, puny selfishness—he hadn't wanted to share Nora as his best friend.

Steve shrugged his broad shoulders and said, "No hard feelings on this end, man, but I can't help you with Nora. That's between you and her."

He sent the email on the very last day of the school year, after his books and clothes were all packed up.

One last digital communication. The year was 1993, when, at least for a little while longer, technology still had the power to make us *more* human.

Dear Nora:

I'm gay. In the history of letters written by boys trying to win back the girls who have broken up with them, I imagine that line has never been employed before—but there you have it, and it's the truth, and my hands are literally shaking right now as I type this. I've known since I was a little kid, even if I've kept trying to find new ways around it.

I lied to you. I strung you along. I disrespected your relationship with Steve. I bear full responsibility for all of that, and I understand if you can't forgive me. But you have to understand something, Nora. If there was a button that I could press that could magically make me be turned on by women, I would press it, and I would want to be your boyfriend, frankly, I think I'd want to be your husband. It's all messed with my head so much, because I keep thinking: What if there's only one soulmate for you on the planet, and what if my soul mate is you?

But I can't fix it or change, I just have to accept it and admit it: I'm gay, and I've always been gay, and I will always be gay. I hope this at least sheds some light on my actions these last nine months.

Patrick

The reply came back fifteen minutes later.

Oh, Jesus, Patrick—you are unbelievable. Why didn't you just say something from the start?

OK, well, to be honest, it's not like the thought hadn't crossed my mind, and of course Suzie's been telling me that I need to give you another chance, and I guess this does explain things. I can't pretend that I'm not still angry. But I'm in Texas this summer working on the Ann Richards campaign, and I'll probably be too busy to talk on the phone—three months of Patrick decompression time will probably be enough time for me to get over it.

Nora

P.S.—Seriously, though, Patrick, sometimes you make things so much harder than they need to be.

1997-98

On September 6, 1901, just after four in the afternoon, in the Temple of Music in Buffalo, New York, a self-proclaimed anarchist named Leon Czolgosz, inspired to action by a speech he had heard Emma Goodman deliver a few months earlier, twice fired a .32 caliber Iver-Johnston revolver at President William McKinley. One of the bullets missed—it is presumed to have deflected off a metal button on McKinley's jacket—but the other struck the President in the abdomen. A sort of tragicomedy of errors ensued: McKinley was raced to the hospital, but a suitable surgeon could not be located; a gynecologist named Matthew Mann ended up being tasked with the doomed assignment. Unable to pinpoint the exact location of the bullet—he had no access to an X-ray machine—the doctor poked around inside McKinley's guts for a few hours before eventually deciding to stitch the President back up. (Mann was of the belief, as he would later write, that "a bullet once it ceases to move does little harm.") Eight days later, his stomach and pancreas devoured by gangrenous infection, William McKinley died. He was the third sitting President of United States to be assassinated.

The good news, or at least it seemed at first, was that the bullet that struck Patrick Francis Monaghan hadn't taken nearly as circuitous a route as the fatal McKinley bullet, which an autopsy later revealed had journeyed through the President's stomach and colon before coming to rest in the lining of the abdominal cavity. This bullet struck Patrick high in the abdomen, just below the rib cage, and then passed through the lower right lobe of his liver and into Patrick's stomach; it was now lodged in the serosa of the stomach's greater curvature—manageably extractable, as these sorts of surgical procedures go. But when the surgeons took a closer look at the intraoperative CT images, they realized the news wasn't good at all. The bullet was in fact pressed up against the left gastroepiploic artery. There seemed a fifty-percent chance that the extraction would result in aortic rupture; and if that happened, there would be a seventy-percent chance that Patrick would die on the operating table.

Still, it wasn't as if they had any choice in the matter; if the story of President William McKinley and Dr. Matthew Mann taught the medical profession anything, it was that once a bullet enters a stomach, it's going to have to come out. For forty minutes, the surgeons worked with deliberation and deeply steady hands, and the nurses followed their instructions with silent efficiency—this really *was* regarded as the finest trauma center in North Texas. But as the bullet was being extracted from Patrick's stomach, it took with it a piece of the serosa—think of it like the hairs on your arm getting yanked away when you rip off a Band-Aid—and the serrated edges of the now flattened slug tore through the gastroepiploic artery. The instant it happened, the lead surgeon let out a soft, baleful sigh and said to the room: "Fuck."

The junior surgeon on the team was eventually dispatched to deliver an update to the family and friends, as the others worked furiously to cut out the section of the artery that had ruptured and piece it back together with a stent graft. This doctor's name was Patrick also—Patrick Kim, a Korean-American originally from Astoria, Queens, not so far from Patrick Monaghan's old neck of the woods in Staten Island. A gay man in his early thirties, Dr. Kim had actually been following the Monaghan campaign closely in the *Fort Worth Star-Telegram*. Not that he'd ever admit as much to anyone at the hospital, but truth was he had more than once looked at the candidate's picture in the newspaper and thought to himself that he and Other Patrick might make a cute couple.

Dr. Kim entered the private waiting room expecting to encounter at least a dozen or more members of Patrick's entourage—hyper-alert, Type-A sorts who he assumed would drop not-so-subtle hints that if the patient didn't pull through, they wouldn't hesitate to sue everyone and their uncle for malpractice. He found only Nora, sitting by herself on one of the green vinyl sofas, calmly typing on her iPad. This tall and graceful woman listened without interruption to his explanation of the setbacks in the operating theater, her calm but faintly imperious stare making him feel like he needed to tell her more than he originally intended. When he finished, she didn't break down in tears or ask for further clarification, the way the friends and family members usually did after he delivered to them discouraging news.

She simply asked, "Does it matter that he's a fighter?" Her tone betrayed not a trace of sentimentality.

"I'm sorry?" Dr. Kim asked.

"I've always assumed it's all nonsense, all that business about the will to live. But then I thought maybe that was just me being cynical, and maybe there *is* medical research to back up the idea that people who are fighters have a better chance of pulling through something like this."

"Well… I don't know… I mean… it certainly couldn't hurt."

And Dr. Kim could see right away that his answer had disappointed her, because her placid expression collapsed into a withering frown; and before Dr. Kim could come up with something better to tell her—sixty seconds knowing her, and *already* he felt guilty that he wasn't performing up to Nora Meacham's standards—she turned away from him and back to her iPad.

She said as if to dismiss him, or maybe just to herself: "That's the one thing no one can deny him—he fights for the things he believes. Even when he picks the wrong battles, he fights them with all his heart."

NORA ASSURED HIM IT WAS a triumph, a great stroke of luck, an offer that Patrick would be crazy to turn down; and Patrick *didn't* turn it down—it wasn't as if, in the spring of 1997, potential employers were handing out entry-level positions to a double major in English and women's studies whose only notable "internship" had been working nighttime security at the Snug Harbor Cultural Center in Staten Island. But damned if he was going to roll over in gratitude, like a puppy dog getting his belly rubbed, just because he'd landed an editorial assistant job at the prestigious literary imprint of the second largest publishing house in the country, not when they were paying him $20,700 a year, hardly enough to keep up with his school loans, much less move out of his parents' house. His indignation only multiplied in his first few months on the job: when he spent three weeks working at a table in the photocopy room, because a proper cubicle hadn't yet been identified for him; when instead of reading manuscripts of groundbreaking new fiction, he spent his days answering phone calls from agents and other editors and his boss Dick Leonard's wife Bessie reminding Dick to bring home a bottle of wine for dinner; when instead of mentoring him and accelerating his rise through the ranks, Dick mostly ignored Patrick, or cast suspicious, sidelong glances at him, leaving Patrick to constantly worry that his fly might be unzipped or that his shirt was stained with ketchup.

"It's just a bunch of pretentious bullshit," he complained to Nora, during one of the many telephone conversations that got them both through those post-collegiate years. She had moved back to Texas after Dartmouth, much to Patrick's disappointment, in the hopes of making inroads in the political scene there.

"But you're at the center of it all," Nora countered. "You're meeting all the important writers."

"They're all nitwits! Mediocrities!"

Patrick knew he was being a brat. Problem was: He couldn't imagine any other way to be. First of all, he was exhausted from commuting nearly two hours each way to work from Staten Island; second, living at home meant that there was no hope of him doing what young people working in the city were supposed to do, like staying out late and meeting potential boyfriends. What made all of this worse was that every time he tried to imagine a way out of his current mess, he felt at once overwhelmed by the multitudes of options for his future and already defeated. With what sort of money was he supposed to travel through Europe and Southeast Asia, as half of his Dartmouth classmates now seemed to be doing? How was he supposed to find the time to write thoughtful essays of literary criticism that might get published in *Harper's* or *The New York Review of Books?*

"This is just the dues-paying part of our lives," Nora assured him.

He asked of her and the gods: "How come no one ever told me that being twenty-three would suck this much?"

It was in this mercurial and prone-to-feel-slighted state that Patrick, late on a Friday afternoon at the end of February 1998, looked up from his desk to find pale, bespectacled Dick Leonard holding out to a slim, softcover galley. This was weird. The only things Dick usually handed him were restaurant receipts so that Patrick could complete Dick's expense reports.

"FSG is putting it out this fall," his boss said, softly enough so that Patrick—as per usual—had to lean forward to hear him. "It kills me that this isn't ours."

Patrick gingerly accepted the book and stared at the cover. Right away he was dubious. He had never heard of this book's author, and the galley itself was suspiciously thin. Patrick had spent the previous six months powering through three dense, lockbox-sized novels—Pynchon's *Mason & Dixon*, DeLillo's *Underworld* and Wallace's *Infinite Jest*—and in reading them he had come to the determination that *this* was the only brand of literature that truly mattered. He wanted stories that were sprawling, unruly, uniquely engaged with the American condition—not the more straightforward tales of good versus evil that he had preferred as a teenager, and certainly not the allusive and painstakingly manicured novels about silently suffering souls that Dick Leonard seemed to exclusively favor in his acquisitions. Patrick considered the title of the book presently in his hands: *The Hours*. Allusive and painstakingly manicured! No doubt filled with silent suffering!

He knew in an instant that he would hate it.

"I really think it's something you might identify with," Dick Leonard told him.

Patrick was skeptical, but hardly stupid. This was the first novel his boss had ever passed along to him, and of course he understood it was a test. And he knew what would be expected of him if he hoped to *pass* this test. Dick Leonard would want his own opinion parroted and his ego flattered. Patrick saw the virtue of playing along, too. If he satisfied Dick with an enthusiastic report on *The Hours*, Dick might be compelled to seek out Patrick's opinion on other books, and little by little, Patrick's place here would solidify. Eventually he might even secure that elusive promotion to assistant editor and a raise to $27,000 a year.

Alas, Patrick Francis Monaghan simply wasn't wired to just play along.

As he held the galley in his hands, he told himself there was another option: he could use this novel to stake his own claim in this rigged industry. If trudging through the Pynchon, DeLillo and Wallace volumes had taught him anything—and, Jesus, those were long fucking books, and with Pynchon you had to read the sentences six times and you still had no idea what the hell he was talking about—it's that you have to think big, go for broke. Patrick determined he would read *The Hours* that weekend and come back on Monday and explain to Dick Leonard why he was wrong about this novel; why he was wrong about so many of the bloodless works he regularly unleashed on an undiscriminating reading public. He would prove to the staid, stay-the-course executive editor that he—Patrick—was the rare twentysomething with actual vision.

A vision for literature!

A vision for life!

And if Dick Leonard didn't appreciate Patrick's incisive criticism—if it inspired a streak of vindictiveness in his usually milquetoast boss and Dick ended up making his assistant's life miserable? Well, then fuck Dick Leonard, and fuck this stupid job, and fuck this whole world that refused to make a place for him. At least he would be able to say he had gone down swinging.

"I'll give it a look over the weekend," he said brightly.

He started it late that afternoon on the ferry back to Staten Island. It occurred to him, after about twenty pages, that it probably would have helped had he actually read *Mrs. Dalloway*—or really any Virginia Woolf, a staple of his women's studies classes at Dartmouth whose books he found mystifying—but whatever, he got the gist; and halfway through it began to dawn on him *why* Dick Leonard had passed along the book; and near the end, reading the passage where the character with AIDS hurls himself out of an apartment window and commits suicide, Patrick literally howled in protest.

He didn't merely *hate The Hours*. He was insulted and offended by it and above all infuriated that Dick Leonard would think that Patrick might *identify* with such a book.

Patrick finished reading *The Hours* late Friday night. The first thing he did upon waking the next morning was reach for the novel again. He ignored phone calls that afternoon and evening from Nora. On Sunday he left his room only to use the bathroom and even then he carried with him his copy of *The Hours*. When his mother knocked on his door that night to ask him if he wanted dinner, he screamed at her, "Don't bother me, I'm working"—an outburst that in turn drew his father to the door to tell him that he couldn't speak to his mother this way, and back and forth this argument went, until finally Patrick screamed, even louder than before, "This is my career at stake, I can't worry about your stupid dinner," and his parents finally gave up and went away.

By the time he arrived back in the office on Monday morning, forty-five minutes before anyone else in editorial, he had made his way through the novel three times, dog-earing pages, underlining passages, inking tiny little exclamation points into the margins. He was waiting outside the office of Roberta Stein when she arrived for a work a little after 9:30 a.m.

"I'D LIKE TO LODGE A complaint of sexual harassment against Dick Leonard," Patrick burst out.

Roberta Stein, the longtime head of human resources at the imprint, was the first person Patrick had met with when he interviewed here; and throughout the hiring process she had struck him as warm and encouraging, yet also unwaveringly professional—he assumed she would be the ideal person with whom he could share his concerns. Which only made Patrick that much more furious, when Roberta's initial response was to start laughing.

"That's a new one," she said.

Patrick stood stock still and took a deep breath—as much as he wanted to, he knew it would be a mistake to erupt into an epic tirade against the fecklessness and self-satisfaction of all publishing professionals. Instead, he calmly told her: "I'm not making a joke."

"What are you talking about?" Roberta answered, still grinning, as if in expectation that he was going to burst out any second now with a *Just fooling... gotcha!* "Dick is one of the gentlest, most respectful people I know."

"He gave me this," Patrick said.

Roberta took the book from Patrick and gestured for him to take a seat. She began flipping through the pages, taking note of the hundreds of markings he had made in the margins. When she looked back up to him, she wore the wide-eyed, *oh shit* expression of a horror movie character who has accidentally wandered into the lair of a serial killer.

Fuck. This was so not unfolding the way Patrick had imagined when he rehearsed all of this in his head this morning in the shower.

"He gave me this book," Patrick hastened to explain. "He said, 'I really think this is something you might identify with.' Those were his exact words."

"Patrick… um… it's very common for editors to share books with their assistants.…"

"No, no," Patrick sighed. "It's… it's a gay book…"—and here he felt a twinge of shame, for lowering his voice on the word *gay*, five years after coming out to Nora, three years after his first hookup, with a Dartmouth '98 named Randall Kirk—a skinny chess prodigy with psoriatic arms, that romance had lasted all of three dates before Randall said, sorry, it wasn't quite working for him—and *still* Patrick had trouble saying the word *gay*—"… Dick told me it was something I would *identify* with. So obviously he thinks I'm gay. And he's basing his perceptions of what I can and can't do on these… these… *suppositions*. That seems to me the very definition of sexual harassment."

Roberta looked across to Patrick, no longer grinning, but obviously very confused. "I haven't talked to Dick," she said, "but I'm guessing he wanted to draw you into his editorial process and give you a better sense of—"

"It's not just that it's a gay book," Patrick cut her off. "It's that it's a bunch of gay clichés. Do you know what it's about? There are three interlocking parts. There's Virginia Woolf in the 1920s, and she's going crazy, and then there's this repressed lesbian housewife in the 1950s who's reading *Mrs. Dalloway*, and then there's this other woman in the present day who's throwing a party just like the character of Mrs. Dalloway, and that alone would be insufferable enough, this ridiculous gay male obsession with anguished women—seriously, why do gay writers think they have *any* insight into the female psyche? what could they *possibly* know about women if they've *never even had sex with one?*—but what's really infuriating is that there's also this gay character, he's the son of the 1950s housewife, and he grows up to be a poet, and of course he has AIDS—what gay novel would be complete without some sad sack dying of AIDS?—and he commits suicide, throws himself out a window in fact—sorry to ruin it for you—and of course that's the most obnoxious cliché of all, the gay martyr, God forbid somebody write a book with a gay character who doesn't have to die for our sins."

"Patrick, I fear we're veering into literary criticism here," Roberta interjected. "Dick gave you a book he thought you would like, but it turned out you didn't like it. That's not sexual harassment."

Patrick shook his head furiously side-to-side. No, no, *no*—she still wasn't getting it. "What he thinks about me is *wrong*. I'm not the kind of person who likes *The Hours*. And if he's making decisions about my career based on those misperceptions… well, that's not right. And it's part of a much larger problem. This whole industry just keeps indulging people's uncomplicated, sentimental views of the world, and we publish books that perpetuate these myths, that all gay men are obsessed with their mothers, and they're all pathetic walking tragedies dying of AIDS.

"But where are the books about gay doctors, gay lawyers, gay car salesmen? Where are the books about gay people leading complicated loves against the backdrop of American history? Where's the gay Augie March; the gay Rabbit Angstrom; the gay *World According to Garp*? That's what we should be publishing."

"Garp dies at the end," Roberta said. "He's a martyr, too."

"That's not the point," Patrick muttered.

"Well, maybe those books haven't been written yet. Maybe you're the person who should write them."

"You're not *listening* to me," Patrick snapped.

For a minute or so, neither of them said anything. Patrick considered the walls of Roberta's office, lined like every other office in this building with books, ones that he had already read by Fitzgerald and Wharton and Mailer, ones that he still hadn't gotten around to but which were high on his list by Kundera and Kadare and Byatt. When he had first interviewed with Roberta, the sight of all these books plunged him into a memory of his youth: as the boy who would always sneak a paperback into his pants pocket and then absent himself from birthday parties and family dinners and find a quiet corner to read. At a place with so many books, he had thought, surely he belonged.

But now, less than a year later, Patrick was coming to realize that he didn't belong here at all. This was just another place where the rules were long since prescribed; where truly original thinking and bold leadership would never be encouraged; where—despite the human resources handbook's insistence upon "equal opportunity" and "fairness"—you were judged and put into a box because of your sexuality. He knew, of course, that Dick Leonard hadn't *technically* harassed him. But as Patrick thought about the books around him and then turned his attention back to Roberta, her clenched jaw and downturned nose suggesting nothing but disapproval, he believed more fervently than ever that Dick Leonard deserved some sort of censure.

To assume that you know someone just because you understand him to be gay; to imagine that you can recognize the kind of literature that will move him; to be one of those heterosexual do-gooders desperate to assuage your own liberal guilt by being "down with" gay people, a lover of novels and films and stage plays that illuminate their battles against disease and discrimination… all of these might be perfectly human impulses, but to Patrick they were not forgivable ones.

"I read the employee handbook before I came here this morning," he told Roberta. "It says I can lodge a complaint of sexual harassment and that an internal investigation will be conducted."

He paused and then added: "I'm lodging a formal complaint."

For weeks nothing happened. Patrick didn't make mention to Dick that he had read *The Hours*, and Dick didn't ask him about it. Just as before Dick remained courteous of Patrick, yet indifferent—entire days passed when the only request he made of his assistant was to see if Patrick could get his lunch reservation switched from noon to 1:00 p.m. As for the sexual harassment charge, Patrick assumed that Roberta had decided to pretend as if the whole thing had never happened—and for this he was grateful. Now that the initial sting of reading *The Hours* had worn off, Patrick had come to realize that he had grossly overreacted. One misjudged literary recommendation hardly meant that Dick was trying to impede his advancement in the company. The fault had been Patrick's, for bottling up all his frustrations; for failing to make peace with the fact that adult life was never going to be like his life at Dartmouth, idealistic and filled with boundless possibility.

But then, just when enough time had passed that he thought Roberta almost certainly must have decided to let the matter drop, just when he began to forgive himself for the slandering of a genuinely kind-seeming man, Patrick received a call one Friday afternoon instructing him to report to the eighth floor.

He arrived to find Roberta Stein sitting in the center chair on the far side of the oblong conference table. To her left sat Dick Leonard, his hands neatly folded, his head cast down. To Roberta's right was Martha Mayborne, a thick-hipped woman with a nest of silver-blonde hair, Dick's boss and the publisher of the imprint.

"Please take a seat, Patrick," Roberta said.

Patrick's heart went racing.

"First, I want to assure you that we took your complaint very seriously," Roberta began. "We have a zero tolerance policy at this company for any form of harassment. The results of our investigation"—and here she looked down and began reading from the single piece of printed paper resting in front of her—"are as follows: A formal reprimand has been issued to Mr. Leonard and placed in his employee file. He has been warned that if anything like this happens again, it will result in his immediate termination."

Oh fuck. What embarrassment had the fever-tempered, oh-so-full-of-himself Patrick Francis Monaghan sent down upon them all? Patrick cast a furtive glance across to Dick, but Dick was looking down at his hands—all he could see were the veiny creases in the man's forehead. In that instant Patrick realized how wholly *wrong* he had been. Here was a man who had spent his entire life with his nose in a book—a man who saw it as one of life's great pleasures to be able to share with others a novel he admired. Dick hadn't been testing Patrick in giving him *The Hours*. He had only been seeking out a connection—connecting the best way he knew how.

Patrick had to find a way to take it all back.

"Dick, please go ahead," Martha Mayborne said.

Dick Leonard raised his head slightly, but couldn't quite bring himself to look Patrick in the eye—he directed his apology at the younger man's chin.

"I'm sorry for my inappropriate behavior, Patrick. It won't happen again."

Patrick felt heat in his cheeks; sweat pooling in his armpits. He had to fix this. Not to get overly melodramatic, but he thought that if he didn't get that formal reprimand removed from Dick's file, every plan he had for his own future—his steadfast conviction, from as far back as he could remember, that his life would *matter*—would consequently be thrown into jeopardy.

"I feel like there's been a misunderstanding," he blurted out. "I never meant for this to happen, I never wanted—"

Martha Mayborne immediately cut him off. "Thank you for your apology Dick. Patrick, you can return to your desk now."

The email came over a month later, sent from Martha Mayborne to the entire staff.

Subject: Bittersweet news

It is with great sadness that I write to tell you that Dick Leonard, our peerless executive editor, has decided to retire. I tried my hardest to persuade Dick to reconsider, but after nearly three decades on the front lines of the good fight for serious literature, Dick must now turn his attention…

Patrick didn't even finish reading the email before bounding into Dick's office.

"Please don't do this," he implored. "Please don't quit because of me."

Dick looked up from the manuscript he was reading and took off his glasses. He smiled benevolently at Patrick and said, "Can you please call Bill Buford's office, and tell them I can't do lunch on Monday? See if they can reschedule for Thursday."

It was announced that Dick's final day would be June 15th, three weeks hence. As the date drew nearer, Patrick agonized to find a solution. First he sent a long email to Roberta Stein and Martha Mayborne, cc-ing Dick, explaining that the complaint of sexual harassment never should have been made, and requesting that the formal reprimand be removed from Dick's file and replaced with a document that articulated that Dick Leonard had *never* committed sexual harassment and most certainly never would. Except neither Roberta nor Martha responded to Patrick's e-mail, and Dick gave no sign of having ever read it.

Next he decided he had to quit, and he even began drafting his resignation letter— perhaps his absence from these offices and the promise of an entirely new assistant might be enough to compel Dick to stay. He told himself this was the right thing to do; that in fact this entire incident was proof that he had no place at all in a traditional corporate environment—so it made sense to extract himself now rather than later. He stalled on the second sentence of the letter. He was terrified of not having a job, especially considering that it had taken him a year after graduation to find this one; terrified of not having any money, especially now that he had finally saved up enough for a deposit on his own apartment. He had worked way too hard these last two years to just willingly place himself back at square one.

Finally, on the night of June 14th, he determined that he would beg his boss' forgiveness; get down on his hands and knees if that's what it would take. He thought that maybe if he came clean to Dick about being gay—about the shame he had felt since he was a little boy now being compounded by the shame he felt over not yet having found the courage to come out to his parents—then maybe Dick would understand why he had lashed out and see that there was no reason he should feel like he needed to resign.

But when Patrick arrived for work on Friday morning, he found not Dick Leonard but three guys from maintenance packing up boxes of books in his office.

"Where's Dick?"

"Didn't he tell you?" one of the men answered. "Decided to move his retirement up a day. Said he hadn't worked a Friday in June in years and didn't see the point in starting now."

In the weeks that followed, as Roberta conducted a search for Dick's replacement, Patrick was assigned to fill in for the other assistants on their days off. Having succeeded in alienating virtually the entire editorial department—they all found him moody and churlish; and he suspected that by now the rumors had gotten out, that it was his fault Dick had quit—he spent most of his days in silence, turning over the events of the last few months in his head. He was particularly tormented by the words Roberta Stein had spoken to him, when he had advocated for a new kind of literature.

Maybe those books haven't been written yet.

Maybe you're the person who should write them.

He tried. He truly did. He typed the dedication page first, before he even had an idea for a story: "To Dick Leonard, who I hope now understands why a foolish young man did what he did." Then he wrote every day, before and after work and sometimes at his desk. First he attempted an autobiographical coming-of-age story, and next a futuristic thriller, and then a sweeping historical fiction based on the life of the painter

Thomas Eakins, who in college Patrick had read was likely bisexual. But nothing seemed to take—the words themselves looked unconvincing and contrived to him the moment he got them down on paper—and after six weeks he decided he would never have it in him to write a novel and gave up.

In August, insult was added to injury: the early trade reviews for *The Hours* were all glowing, and there was even scuttle that it might win this year's Pulitzer Prize. Had Dick Leonard been right? Had Patrick been wrong—not just in his firmly held opinion of *The Hours*, but in his even more firmly held opinion of himself as someone destined for greatness? By then, he had been reassigned as the assistant to Phyllis Lowry, a onetime titan at the house, now nearly eighty, whose eponymous imprint had published only two volumes the previous year. But Phyllis paid him even less attention than Dick ever did—for days at a stretch he sat at his desk and did nothing.

"I've turned into dumbest cliché of all," he whined to Nora, on the phone one night in October. "The rudderless post-collegiate."

"These things take time. You just have to keep your nose to the grindstone."

Easy for you to say, Patrick thought, but at least had the decency not to speak aloud. Nora had recently landed a well-paying junior position at a political consulting firm in Dallas—the very work she had dreamed of doing all through Dartmouth.

That autumn seemed a kind of prison sentence. He was nervous all the time; bleary-eyed because he lay awake at night inventorying all the mistakes he had made. He started losing weight, more than ten pounds—his yearning for *something* to happen to him was so palpable that he felt it as an appetite-squelching ache in his gut. But *nothing* happened, each day went by just like the one before it, and he didn't know what he was good at, all he understood of himself was that he wanted desperately to be influential and important, he wanted his ideas to be heard and debated around the world—and what was *really* crazy was that some days he wished he could call Dick Leonard, because, well, Dick was smart and accomplished and had thirty years of experience and what Patrick really needed right now was some advice.

THE LIGHT ON THE PHONE started blinking one afternoon in October, though Patrick hadn't heard it ring or been away from his desk long enough to have missed a call. Dick's voice—as per usual—was so soft that Patrick had to jam the headset against his ear just to make sure he heard the voicemail.

I was wondering if you might come to the apartment this evening for a drink. Six o'clock. No need to return the call unless you can't make it. See you shortly.

Patrick imagined a different, earlier version of himself being annoyed as all fuck: that Dick still thought he could order him around; that Dick would (correctly) assume that he had no other plans for a Thursday evening. What he instead felt in that instant, though, was an overwhelming, almost ecstatic sense of gratefulness—like a man on the verge of drowning given a hit of oxygen. Finally a chance to fix this. Finally he could at least apologize to Dick and alleviate some of this paralyzing guilt he felt.

He left the office at 5:30 p.m. The subway trip uptown took twenty minutes. Dick's building was sixteen stories of gleaming limestone, with a navy-blue-and-white-striped canopy that extended onto the sidewalk from ironwork-latticed entry door. A doorman in a gray vest and suit pants pulled open the outer door for Patrick, who stepped inside and up three stairs, into a wide, marble-floored lobby.

"Mr. Leonard is expecting you—I'll take you up," a second doorman said —though of course Patrick barely heard him, because by now he was completely bewildered and his heart was pounding uncontrollably. All the times he had directed messengers to take manuscripts to Dick's apartment, how could he never have put two and two together and realized that his boss lived on *the* Fifth Avenue, across from *the* Central Park, in a building of multi-million dollar apartments.

Dick was standing in the hallway when Patrick steeped off elevator. He shook Patrick's hand, but said nothing as he led him into the apartment. They made their way through a long hallway, its walls lined with framed photographs of Dick standing next to the likes of Toni Morrison, Stephen King and John Irving, and then past an open set of French doors, a room that Patrick saw in a blur was lined floor-to-ceiling with books. They arrived finally in the living room, where a row of four windows looked out onto the park and its yellow and orange treetops dappled with just-set sunlight.

"Rest assured, it was all inherited," Dick Leonard said. He then chuckled and excused himself to the kitchen.

In an instant, the ache that had gripped Patrick's stomach for most of the last six months returned. As he stared out the windows, all the way across to the lights beginning to come on in the apartment buildings on the other side of the park, he understood with renewed clarity how completely he had bungled things with Dick. Here was a man who lived the very finest kind of life this city offered, a life so different from the one Patrick had lived all these years in Staten Island. A man of influence who had surrounded himself with great thinkers and cultural icons, just as Patrick longed to do. Fate had put into his path a true mentor, and Patrick had mowed him down.

And isn't *that* the surest guarantor of failure? When you declare yourself too good for your teachers? When you think you know better than *everyone*?

"I'm so sorry for what I did," he burst forth, as soon as Dick returned from the kitchen, a glass of red wine in each hand, a book discreetly tucked under his arm. "I'm sorry I forced you to quit."

Acting as if he hadn't heard him, Dick handed Patrick a glass of wine and then gave him the book, a yellowing and brittle hardcover with its dust jacket removed.

"I was hoping you might read something," he said. "Read it aloud if you would. Page two hundred forty. Start with the first sentence at the top."

A thought flashed in his head that this was weird: Had Dick invited him over for some kind of *reading*? But by now Patrick was too embarrassed to do anything other than what he was told. He didn't pause to look at the binding; couldn't tell from the header the name of the author or the title. He simply turned to the requested page and began reading.

"There is something ludicrous and at the same time poignant about many stories involving homosexuals. Inside the leather trappings and chains and emblems and fascist insignia of homosexual 'toughs,' there is so often our old acquaintance the high-school sissy, searching the streets for a man he doesn't believe he is. The incessant, compulsive cruising is the true, mad romantic's endless quest for love. Crazier than Don Juan, the homosexual pursues an ideal man, but once they have made a sexual conquest, the partner is a homosexual like them, and they go on their self-defeating way, endlessly walking and looking, dreaming the impossible dream."

Patrick broke off, puzzled and actually a little bit insulted. He closed the book and considered the spine. "What *is* this?"

"A review of a movie called *The Sergeant* by Pauline Kael," Dick explained. "Published in *The New Yorker* in January 1969."

"It's kind of…"

"Homophobic? Obnoxious? I reread that review sometimes in memory of my father. He was a very successful lawyer, a partner at his firm—his money bought us this apartment. He had a massive heart attack and died when he was just fifty-two years old. Had he known what was coming I'm pretty sure he would have destroyed the box of diaries and photos that I ended up stumbling upon in his closet. I have no idea if he ever acted on what he felt, or if he ever cheated on my mother. But from what I found in that box, there was no mistaking.

"A year after he passed away, I saw that movie, *The Sergeant*. I suppose it was terribly melodramatic. Rod Steiger becomes obsessed with a straight man and then eventually kills himself because he can't have him. A gay martyr story, you'd probably term it. But sitting in the theater, seeing the emotions my father must have felt all those years expressed on the screen—the fear, the loneliness, the complete inability to just be *himself*—I wept. I wept for him as I couldn't seem to do at his funeral.

"And then, a week or two later, I read that review in *The New Yorker*. This bastion of journalistic sophistication, famed for its hip film critic… and she *belittled* the movie. She didn't look upon the Rod Steiger character as some towering figure out of Shakespeare, the way I saw him—the way I suppose I saw my father. She just saw him as this pathetic homosexual cliché. And I wondered what it must have felt like for my father, when he read things like that—this was back when *The New York Times* reported on the raids of the queer bars in their trademark fashion, with glee masquerading as opprobrium. It's probably no coincidence that a few months later I started at the publishing house. I think that's when I realized the great power of words. I saw the harm they could do, and I wanted to counterbalance that."

Hearing all of this, Patrick felt embarrassment, pummeling sadness—he tried once again to beg his former boss' forgiveness. "I'm sorry, Dick. I realize *The Hours* meant a lot to you. I never should have done what I did."

"I didn't ask you here so you could apologize," Dick said. "No one took you very seriously. That whole formal reprimand business was mostly staged for your benefit."

This puzzled Patrick—and for a moment he felt a flash of the familiar Monaghan indignation—but before he could object, Dick started up again.

"To be honest, you taught me something, Patrick—in your decidedly abrasive way. To some extent, you're right. It's the toxic waste of social progress, this expectation that the members of minority groups must all think the same way and share the same opinions; that there can't be healthy dissension among the ranks."

"Yes, *yes*, that's exactly my point," Patrick said, speaking very fast, partly because he had gulped too much wine, but mostly fueled by this mixture of elation and regret he felt swirling inside of him. How smart Dick Leonard was! How stupid Patrick had been not to try to learn from him while he had the chance!

"I want people to respect and understand me as a gay person," he added," but not *define* me as one. Is that too subtle a distinction to understand?"

"For a lot of people, probably," Dick told him. "Not for me. I understand why my giving you that book angered you the way it did. But what you should never forget, Patrick, is how incredibly privileged you are. *The New Yorker* doesn't publish articles like that anymore. There are anti-discrimination laws in place now. There finally seems to be a cure on the horizon for this odious disease that has killed so many of my friends. I can only imagine my father looking down upon the gay men of your generation with such *envy*. And it's only going to get better. I know as you're struggling to figure out who you are that's hard to believe, but trust me—it's all going to change so quickly, and you'll be even more privileged to see the changes in your lifetime.

"And I guess what I'm telling you is that you can never cast off history in your headlong rush into the future. You can never forget those who weren't nearly so privileged."

THEY BURIED THE HATCHET. Dick poured them second and then third glasses of wine. They had the sort of getting-to-know-one-another conversation that they both acknowledged they should have had when they first started working together. Eventually, light-headed from the alcohol, Patrick worked up the nerve to ask Dick how he had known that Patrick was gay when he had never told anyone at the office. Dick didn't laugh, didn't regard the question—as Patrick feared he might—as juvenile and narcissistic. He stared into his wine glass and answered: "Truthfully, you reminded me of my father. You even look a little bit like him. He struggled to contain his frustrations, but he wasn't always successful—and then this normally stoic man would suddenly explode with such rage."

It was after 8:00 P.M., and Patrick was very close to drunk, when Dick stood up and said, "I didn't mean to keep you so long." Patrick unsteadily followed Dick back down the long hallway to the front door. Twice he had to touch the wall beside him—the one lined with photos from a literary life lived long before Patrick Francis Monaghan ever came along—to stop himself from stumbling.

He was slightly slurring his words when he asked Dick: "If it wasn't because of me, then why did you quit?"

In the grey and brown shadows of the unlighted hallway, his former boss's pale face seemed to lose even more of its color, like an apparition fading from sight. "Oh... I... for some reason... I thought you knew ... from the email that Martha sent out..."

"I just figured you were embarrassed," Patrick said, and the instant he said it, he realized how stupid it sounded.

"My wife Bessie..." Dick began.

Patrick shook his head. He didn't know. Worse than that, two-plus hours here, and he hadn't bothered to wonder: Where *was* Bessie, whose daily phone calls to Dick always used to annoy him so much?

"Rapid progression Parkinson's. It happened even faster than the doctors said it would. She passed away in September."

"Oh my God, Dick, I'm sorry, I didn't know, how could I have not known—"

Dick Leonard stopped Patrick with a gesture of his hand and opened the front door for him to leAvenue "No more apologies," he said, neither warmth nor scorn in his voice. "I find they have very limited value. I was very lucky, Patrick. For nearly thirty years, I had what my parents never had, what so many people—straight or gay—never get to experience: a person who I knew was absolutely perfect for me."

He gave Patrick a winsome smile and added: "I hope you are one of the lucky ones, Patrick. I honestly do. I hope one day you get to experience the glorious good fortune of realizing that the world doesn't have to revolve around you."

2003

A LITTLE AFTER 5:00 P.M., THE doctors thought they had lost him. The procedure to stent the gastroepiploic artery was slow-going though hopeful—the site of the rupture was such that the surgeons thought it could repaired without any loss of vascular potential. But after nearly five hours in the surgical theater, Patrick's blood pressure started fluctuating wildly, until it commenced a steady decline that the doctors could do nothing to counter. As the medical team debated what to do next, the heart-monitoring machine entered flatline. For fifteen agonizing seconds, the surgeons and nurses stood silent while the anesthesiologist pumped adrenaline and atropine into the patient's bloodstream. Nothing, and then nothing, and then finally the line on the monitor started to tremble. A few minutes later, as Patrick's blood pressure settled at 100/65, the lead surgeon let out a halting half-chuckle and said: "I think we're going to be able to bring him out of this."

By this point, of course, the assassination attempt had been seized upon with uncontained relish by the media. On the cable news channels, especially, there were teary-eyed interviews with bystanders; alarums from both the gun control advocates on the one side and the Second Amendment nuts on the other; and—inevitably, inappropriately—debates over what the shooting might mean for this closely-watched Senate race. To their credit, the anchors all remembered to speak of Patrick in the present tense—but, even then, it was too much for Oscar to bear. He turned off the television in the waiting room and forbade any updates that didn't come from official sources or that began with the phrase, "CNN is reporting..." Later he took to pacing: up the fluorescent-lit hallways; down the unswept, unpopulated stairwells. The challenge of this savage and interminable day—that he must show *nothing* to the hordes of reporters and law enforcement officials and hospital staff, *nothing* that might foment rumors that could undermine the campaign—had created a nervous energy that desperately needed to be released.

No one knew, but he supposed everyone knew, or at least everyone in the know knew: the reporters and Washington pundits following the campaign; the staffers on their opponent's team. Nonetheless Nora had insisted, for the entirety of the eighteen months that Oscar and Patrick had been dating, that the campaign's official stance was that Patrick remained single. Oscar argued with them both on the matter, but Nora's reasoning always seemed to win out. "You win elections by *simplifying* your narrative, so that even a junior high schooler could articulate what you stand for," she insisted. "A boyfriend is too complicated."

So he dutifully stayed silent, out of allegiance to the man he loved, out of respect for this campaign which he believed in so fiercely. But of course every so often the resentment burned and bubbled up in his chest, like a too spicy meal that sends you reaching for the Pepto: How could they honestly campaign for equality—for every man and woman's right to live an open, unabashed life—when Patrick was still keeping secrets of his own?

The irony, of course, was that Oscar knew more of those secrets than anyone. He couldn't really remember why Patrick had decided to share all he did, a year or so earlier. Perhaps it was just that they were in that hazardous early phase of a relationship, when lovers unwisely convince themselves that the path towards greater intimacy includes a complete inventory of each other's sexual history. (Imagine the awkwardness when Oscar—who listened to Patrick's confession the way most people first read *Ulysses*, thinking surely this can't keep carrying on, only to realize you're barely through the first section—quietly explained in response: "Well, I was with my first boyfriend two years, and my second boyfriend for fourteen months, and then there were a couple of other romances that didn't really go anywhere, and you're exactly the fifth person I've ever slept with.")

Yet he never judged Patrick, or at least not as harshly as Patrick judged himself; and the more he came to know his boyfriend, the more he sympathized with the central contradiction of the man's adult life—that just because at some point the world stops denying people their humanity, it doesn't also mean the world hands them an instruction manual on how to live an unselfconscious life.

Besides, Oscar being Oscar, he eventually found a way to use Patrick's peccadilloes to the campaign's advantage, crafting what turned out to be arguably the candidate's most widely talked-about speech. It had been delivered the previous August to a group of college students at the University of North Texas in Denton. It had been bold and uncompromising—if Oscar did say so himself—in tackling a topic Democrats normally shied away from: the limits of free speech and the scourge of Internet pornography. It sounded, quite frankly, like something you might have heard thirty or forty years prior, from the likes of Jerry Falwell or Jim Dobson.

"We are undermining our ability to make meaningful connection to other people," Patrick proclaimed. "We are teaching an entire generation that sexuality is directly linked to commodity." He then went on to call for greater regulations on the production and distribution of online sexual material, and said that pornography should be discouraged in the manner of cigarette smoking, with onerous "sin" taxes and harrowing warning labels depicting the ravages of STDs.

"You see, I told you it was a good idea," Oscar said, as Patrick left the stage— conveniently ignoring the fact that the students who had shown up expecting to cheer for promises of better access to federal tuition grant programs sat stone silent for the entirety of Patrick's speech.

"Did we *really* need to open that can of worms?" Patrick responded.

Oscar smiled and repeated only what he had been saying to Patrick for months: "Trust me, if it ever comes out that you hooked up with two hundred men over the course of a single year, you are going to need *some* kind of leg to stand on."

PATRICK FIRST HEARD ABOUT THE website from Antonio Dominguez, a voluble, unreservedly bitchy marketing manager in his mid-forties, who sat in the cubicle next to Patrick's at the Dallas Convention and Visitor's Bureau. It was late on a Friday afternoon, and Patrick had just asked Antonio if he wanted to head out together that night to "The Strip," the stretch of gay clubs along Cedar Springs in the Oak Lawn section of the city. Patrick hated venturing alone into that strobe-lit, heartless universe, with its supercilious college kids and screechy drama queens and spray-tanned meatheads all looking for cause to reject you, even if you weren't interested in them—and so he regularly recruited Antonio to serve as his wingman and glad handler.

"Honestly, I think I'm just going to stay in tonight and type someone up."

Patrick blinked uncomprehendingly at his co-worker.

"Gay.com," Antonio clarified. "You don't have to deal with the crowds and the smoke and those little twinks who think they are God's gift to faggotry."

"You go on there and find dates?" Patrick asked, still not quite understanding.

"I wouldn't exactly call them dates," Antonio answered. "More like hookups. He comes to your place, you go to his. No fuss, no muss." Antonio then laughed as he always did, much too loudly, so that the other members of their department—three grim-faced, gray-haired women in their fifties, upon whom Antonio had secretly bestowed the nicknames Sue Ellen, Pam and Miss Ellie—all looked up from their desks and scowled.

"Is that... *safe?*" Patrick asked, not really sure if he was asking whether safe sex was practiced during the ensuing encounters, or if it was safe to allow a complete stranger into your apartment with the expectation that you would soon be having sex.

"It's just a bunch of guys who want to get off—how dangerous can that be?" Antonio answered, and then he laughed even more boisterously than before. As one, Sue Ellen, Pam and Miss Ellie shushed him.

DALLAS, TEXAS. Fifteen hundred miles from where he grew up. Even farther from anywhere he ever imagined himself landing. A not-quite-middle-American, not-quite-Southern city, sweltering hot, unaccountably crowded considering that it barely had any zoning laws and presumably you could site new houses and skyscrapers *anywhere*, so why did everyone still choose to be right on top of everyone else? Where you never saw anyone reading a book on the DART train, unless it happened to be the Bible. Where the men of his generation, gay or straight, all drove white Ford F150 pickups or black Escalades, even if (or *especially if*) they only earned twelve dollars an hour working at the Ralph Lauren store in Highland Park Village.

Nora was the one who persuaded him to move here, though of course by then he needed little persuading. He had been laid off from the publishing house in the summer of 1999, after Phyllis Lowry retired and Roberta Stein gently but unequivocally told him that there wasn't any other place to put him. Patrick, nearly twenty-six, found himself waiting tables at an Italian restaurant in Staten Island and *still* living at home with his parents. Nora promised him a couch on which he could crash, for as long as it took him to find his own apartment. She said her boss knew someone who might be able to get him a job writing promotional materials for the Dallas CVB.

He thought it would be a renewal of those luxuriant days in college, when all day long and deep into the night they would just carry on *talking*. But business was booming at Nora's firm, and she was regularly dispatched to work on campaigns all across the country, sometimes for weeks at a stretch. When she was in town, she was consumed with errands or dinner dates with potential boyfriends—they rarely saw each other at all.

So he was feeling bored and sorry for himself that night when he logged onto Gay.com and created his own profile. His motives, he told himself, were pure—he was only satisfying a kind of journalistic curiosity about a popular new trend about which he knew little. He certainly didn't intend to do what Antonio apparently did and *type someone up* for a sexual encounter.

He filled in all the required fields, listing his age and weight and height, turn-ons and turn-offs and HIV status. He spent the longest amount of time choosing a screen name, MrMorrisTownsend, after the male character in Henry James' *Washington Square*, and then he spent a few minutes fantasizing that there might be someone in the chat room who would be well-read enough to get the reference. He debated but finally decided against posting a digital photo of himself, out of fear that Antonio would see him online and possibly tell their co-workers.

And what he discovered within moments of entering the Dallas chat room was a cavalcade of sheer imbecility. He clicked on some of the screen names, which in turn brought up online profiles and pictures—disembodied torsos and dimly lit faces and, in one instance, a still of Brad Pitt in *Thelma and Louise*. He tried to follow the group conversation, but it was senseless, free-associative, riddled not just with typos and bad grammar, but with the sort of knowingly effeminate phraseology that gay men used to refer to other gay men—*gurrrl* and *queen* and *Mary*—and that always set Patrick's teeth on edge. What was Antonio thinking? This website was not a viable alternative to meeting men in person. This was just a spectacular waste of any intelligent person's time.

He was about to click off Gay.com entirely when a private message popped onto his screen.

Mustang1971: *Looking?*

Patrick clicked on the name to bring up his profile, but this man didn't have a picture and most of the information fields had been left blank. Still Patrick was curious.

MrMorrisTownsend: *Not sure.*

Mustang1971: *U should let me come over and suck you off. 32yo, 5'11", 170#*

And then, when Patrick hesitated for nearly a minute:

Mustang 1971: *DDF. VGL. No reciprocation needed. Just really in the mood to suck a guy off.*

Could it possibly be *this* easy? Patrick knew that his lack of sexual experience was a problem—that it wasn't normal or especially healthy for someone in his twenties to go years between dates, or for those dates to rarely lead to a second or third meeting. He suspected that his lingering unease about his sexuality was at the root of the problem—a kind of reverse pheromone that his body emitted that turned other men away. But the thing that no one seemed to understand, certainly not Nora, who shrugged unhelpfully when he had tried to explain it to her, was that finding a potential boyfriend was *hard*. He despised the bars on Cedar Springs, especially when he didn't have Antonio standing there beside him. All of Nora's friends in Dallas to whom she had introduced him were straight. Where was he even supposed to begin?

MrMorrisTownsend: *Do you have a picture?*

It wasn't like he was signing some sort of unbreakable contract. He told himself he was just having a conversation.

Mustang1971: *Sure. Email address?*

As soon as he opened the email, his stomach did somersaults—the shame duking it out with the elation, like he was fifteen years old once again, staring at the Umbro-clad rump of Marco Baffi for the very first time. The first picture was a headshot, Mustang1971 with his unkempt hair and a squinty gaze smiling into the camera; Patrick thought he looked like the actor Josh Hartnett. The other picture was a shot of Mustang1971's reflection in a mirror, cropped at the top at his chin, revealing a smooth and tapered torso, and then cropped at the bottom just below the waist, offering a teasing glimpse of pubic hair.

Mustang1971: *Did u get?*

MrMorrisTownsend: *Yeah, you're hot man.*

Mustang1971: *Give me ur address.*

MrMorrisTownsend: *I don't have any pictures to send you.*

Mustang1971: *That's OK, man. Your stats sound great.*

Patrick pictured himself opening the apartment door to someone who would turn out not to be interested in sex at all, but would instead turn instantly violent. He pictured himself opening the apartment door to someone who would turn out to look nothing at all like Josh Hartnett, he would be overweight and pushing fifty and the flesh of his finger where he would have just removed his wedding ring would be paler than the rest of his hand. No—he couldn't do this. No matter how lonely he felt; no matter how ardently he craved the heat of another's body. He didn't want to be that kind of gay person—that *cliché*—the faggot whose sexual proclivities define all of his interactions with the world.

Mustang1971: *Come on man, what do you say?*

Patrick thought about it for another minute and then typed out his address and pressed ENTER.

FOURTEEN MINUTES. After it was over, he catalogued the things that he might have done instead in that time—watched half of a rerun of *Cheers*, say, or brushed his teeth and showered and fallen asleep. He marveled that it only took fourteen minutes for him to betray all of the ideals that he held for himself—until finally he realized that it actually took even less time than that, just the second or two that elapsed when he typed the letters www.gay.com into his Internet browser.

A wave of relief had washed over him, when he opened the door and saw that Mustang1971 looked almost exactly as he did in his picture. Patrick stepped aside to allow him through the door and then pointed to the sofa. He figured they would first talk and get to know one another before deciding if they wanted to take things further.

But Mustang1971 didn't move toward the sofa. He stood in the entryway, looking to the door just beyond the living room, which led to Patrick's bedroom.

"Is this OK?" he asked

"Is what OK?"

He gestured the length of his body with his hand.

"Yeah, totally," Patrick mumbled nervously.

"So you want to do this?" Mustang1971 asked, looking toward the bedroom.

As it was happening, he struggled to stay focused. He was awake to the unavoidable pleasure, a warm mouth and wet saliva on his organ. But he also found himself distracted: by the rustle of the springtime breeze through the magnolia tree outside the window; by the stray strands of dust, like the cilia of a human cell diagrammed in a biology textbook, that he saw had gathered in the corner of his carpeted bedroom floor. Eight minutes along, no closer to orgasm than when they had started, he thought to apologize.

"I'm sorry it's taking me awhile."

Mustang1971 stopped sucking him only long enough to say, "No, I love it"—his eleventh, twelfth, thirteenth and fourteenth words he had spoken to Patrick that evening. Patrick had been keeping a running count.

Yet those words proved to be the right ones. The hint of boundless insatiability in his voice, like a glutton piling his plate high at the buffet line; the idea that Mustang1971 was never any happier than when he was devouring another man's cock; the thought that Patrick was the one doing *him* a favor—it was enough to bring climax within reach. Sensing Patrick's arousal, Mustang1971 redoubled his efforts, until a minute or so later Patrick hips buckled and he exploded into the stranger's mouth.

"Thanks," Mustang1971 said, dressed again and standing at the front door. Fourteen minutes from arrival to departure.

"Maybe we can do it again sometime," Patrick ventured.

Mustang1971 shrugged his shoulders and struck an apologetic, yet uncompromising note as he said, "I have a one-and-done policy." Then he passed out the apartment door and into the blackness of the night. Patrick never did get his first name.

Those next six months he felt as he had as an adolescent, first discovering the intoxicants and disgraces of masturbation: This thing that heretofore he had gotten through life without could now never again be forgotten, its evidence stuck to his fingers or dried into his boxer shorts or clinging stubbornly to the basin of the toilet bowl. Each orgasm was a thrilling shock—had he *really* just made that happen?—followed almost instantly by regret and guilt and bargaining: *Please God, just don't let anyone find out, and I promise I'll never do it again.*

Two weeks went by after that first encounter with Mustang1971 before he found himself driving thirty minutes to Desoto, to meet up with a twenty-two year old in torn sweatpants who had garishly-colored tattoos of skulls and crosses on both arms. The day after that he bought a digital camera and took photographs of himself—disembodied shots of his legs and torso and ass and cock; one of his face in shadow, so that if it ever ended up in the hands of someone he knew in real life, he could plausibly deny that it was him—and posted them to his profile. Suddenly there were twice as many offers as before.

Of course there was shame and self-recrimination; eviscerating monologues that he carried on in his head. *You are becoming the most odious of all gay clichés. The bathhouse dweller! The glory hole attendant!* There were mistakes and misjudgments, too. He broke his own hard-and-fast rule, never to invite someone over without at least a photograph of his face, and he opened his apartment door one night to find a squat, pockmarked man, at least ten years older than he had advertised online, and because his powers of empathy were sometimes too pronounced—how would *he* feel if he turned up at a stranger's door only to be coldly rejected?—Patrick went through with the hookup anyway. Three months along, he began to feel a fiery stab in his prostate every time he ejaculated; an itch at the head of his penis that made him constantly feel as if he had to pee. The diagnosis was humiliating—chlamydia!—delivered in monotone by his purse-lipped, heterosexual male general practitioner, who reminded Patrick that it was important to use condoms when he "fiddled around."

Yet when Patrick realized how easy it was to make the disease go away, just two pills a day for a week, he decided there was no reason to beat himself up. He became expert at combating his guilt—or at least holding the force of it at bay. He told himself that this was just what it meant to pursue romance in the digital age—no different in spirit, really, than the sock hops and ice-cream socials the men and women of his parents' generation would have once attended. Surely among the hundreds of strangers who lurked in the DallasCitywide1 and DallasCitywide2 chatrooms there might actually be one with whom he could make a meaningful connection.

And because he didn't do drugs or drink excessively or eat fast food—he had no other vices to speak of, or at least none of which he was aware—and because the hookups only rarely got in the way of work—two or three times he turned up late, and one morning he claimed to have the flu, after an SMU student invited him over to his dorm room and asked to be fucked while blindfolded—he carried on.

He told himself that none of this was bad.

THEY HAD BEEN CHATTING ONLINE for weeks, but each time Patrick pressed for a meeting, he came up with an excuse or disappeared from the chat room entirely. Tonight, however, when Patrick propositioned him, PocketNerd quickly typed a response: *Well, I am a little buzzed from happy hour ...*

He showed up just twenty minutes later. To be honest, he was too short for Patrick, barely five and a half feet, and skinnier than the guys Patrick usually went for. But he had a sweetly disjointed smile and sleepy brown eyes and almost as soon as he entered Patrick's apartment that Thursday night in November, he made his way to the bookshelf in the living room and started pulling volumes off the shelves, *The Magus* and *A Passage to India* and *Sabbath's Theater*, asking Patrick what he thought of this one or that one.

His name was Jace Hopkins, born and raised in Arlington, Texas. He had majored in English at Rice and was presently working in the press office of the Dallas Mavericks—the only thing he loved as much as books, he said, was sports. He was thinking of applying to business school, with the longterm goal of landing a job with the Cowboys franchise. He was twenty-seven years old but his friends all told him he acted like he was a senior citizen—because he hated loud clubs and his favorite thing to do on Friday nights was cook gourmet meals. He said that, dorky as it sounded, he hoped one day to meet the right guy and enter into a civil union and adopt kids and cart them to soccer games on the weekends.

All throughout his life, Patrick Francis Monaghan had often been guilty of thinking too much, too fast, usually on the basis of incomplete information—so why should now be any different? Listening to Jace talk, Patrick found himself remembering his freshman fall at Dartmouth, and those conversations with Nora that would send electrical currents shooting through his veins. Now it was happening again, except this time with a guy, and the possibilities of this filled him with such excitement that he thought he might actually start trembling. Patrick even started wondering if maybe there had been actual *purpose*, subconscious but very much real, behind his countless hookups these past nine months. Perhaps he had been sharpening his eyes and instincts, so that when he did finally find himself in the presence of a man of true character, he would be able to recognize him instantly.

"I was thinking," Patrick said, after they'd talked for two hours, "maybe we shouldn't hook up tonight."

Jace turned his head sideways and answered neutrally: "Oh."

"It's just that I don't want to spoil things, I don't … " Patrick began, but then immediately doubted himself. Had he just been wildly presumptuous in saying that? Was Jace even attracted to him?

"Are you sure?" Jace asked.

"I'm never really sure about anything," Patrick said, and then immediately regretted saying it, because he knew it sounded so callow.

"How about we strike a deal? I agree to a second date with you this weekend, and you agree to make out with me right now."

And though he didn't know if it was the right thing or the wrong thing to do—didn't know if the only way to true intimacy was to build up some anticipation with another person before you got naked; didn't know if making out with Jace would obviate the magic of these past few hours or consecrate it—he nodded to Jace, and then Jace flashed him a flirty grin, and seconds later Jace was kissing him, and Patrick was kissing

Jace back, and soon they were on his bed, and the clothes were off, and just like their conversation it was all so startlingly *effortless*, so entirely intoxicating, and after ninety minutes of lovemaking, after asking Jace if he wanted to sleep over and delighting when Jace said yes, after sighing with such contentment and saying "Me too," when Jace said to him, "I never thought I'd meet someone like you on that stupid website," Patrick fell into an easy and dreamless sleep.

HE KNEW THE RULES, AND he had every intention of following them. The biggest mistake he could make now was to scare Jace away.

Give it two days, preferably three. Four if you're playing it cool.

But what if you really just can't wait to see him again? What if you want him to know that you think he might be "The One"?

Patrick brooded about it at work the next day. He tossed and turned in bed that Friday night. On Saturday morning, he started to dial Jace's number, but then forced himself to stop—*too soon, still too soon*—and then spent the next few hours staring at the display window of his cell-phone, willing Jace to call *him*. At 8:45 p.m., approximately thirty-six hours after Jace left his apartment, Patrick decided he couldn't wait any longer.

It went directly to voicemail.

The next ninety-six hours were unendurable. He replayed in his head every moment of their encounter, trying to figure out what he might have done wrong for Jace to deny him a return phone call. He cursed himself for having ever agreed to a hookup —now there was no mystery, no fantasy, *nothing* to compel Jace to ever want to see him again. He repeatedly logged onto Gay.com to see if Jace was online seeking out someone new. (He wasn't.) At work, tasks that normally might have taken him a few minutes dragged on for an hour or more. All he could think about was how Jace was just like every other slick player in this slick fucking city, interested only in getting off and getting out, another Mr. One-and-Done.

Until Jace finally called him, late on Wednesday evening, his voice sleep-slurred and apologetic. He had been traveling with the Mavericks in Portland, where one of the players had been arrested for D.U.I., plunging Jace into a four-day, round-the-clock public relations firestorm. He'd only just gotten back into town this evening.

The second date when it finally happened on Saturday was a tonic; a benediction; a silencing of his demons; another of the most perfect nights of his life. They ate at Mi Cocina and drank two rounds of strong margaritas and then went to see a movie at the Magnolia. Later they walked over to Borders and wandered the fiction aisles, recommending titles to one another. At some point, a thought entered into Patrick's mind, and he balled up his fists and closed his eyes tight as a means of holding onto it—like a little kid gripping the string of a helium balloon in fear that it will float away.

The thought was: *I think this must be what it feels like when you're falling in love.*

"What are you doing?" Jace asked.

"Nothing," Patrick answered, opening his eyes, exhilarated that Jace was still standing there in front of him.

They went back to his apartment, where Patrick suggested they have a beer and watch *Saturday Night Live*: No use rushing to the bedroom, since it was clear they were headed there anyway. Patrick felt wonder; a kind of lucidity—like when you learn the definition of a new word and you start seeing it everywhere. The word whose definition he now understood was *boyfriend*. For once, he didn't feel anxious or unsure of himself, the way he had ever since moving to Dallas. Even when Jace excused himself to the bathroom and stayed there for nearly ten minutes, Patrick didn't second-guess the situation. If anything, he took it as a good sign that this soon in their relationship Jace wasn't being precious or coy; that he didn't care if Patrick knew that sometimes he might have to take a shit.

Except when Jace finally returned from the bathroom, he took a seat at the table just off the kitchen, and not on the couch next to Patrick; and then he shook his head when Patrick held out to him an opened bottle of beer.

"You feeling OK?"

"I'm fine."

"Do you want to sit here?" Patrick offered, patting the empty space beside him.

"Honestly, it's none of my business," Jace said, "and it's probably my own fault for thinking that this was something different, but I saw a used condom in the trash can in your bathroom."

At first Patrick didn't understand. He assumed it must have been stuck to the bottom of that soap-scummy, plastic trash bucket for months.

"I'm sorry, that's gross," he said. "I'm not the best at keeping the place clean."

"It looked like it was pretty recently used."

"What do you mean?" Patrick responded, and only then did it dawn on him.

"Well, it definitely wasn't there the last time I was here."

A few different options presented themselves. Patrick could lie and insist to Jace that the condom was an old one, or he could try to summon up a sense of self-righteousness he didn't feel and tell Jace that it was a little bit weird for him to be paying such careful attention to the contents of his trash can. But in that instant he thought it made the most sense to tell the truth; to put faith in the feelings he had for Jace and trust that they would be enough to carry them both past this bump on the road to boyfriendhood. Because in all honestly he didn't think that what had happened the previous Tuesday night was a betrayal of Jace or a sullying of this thing they had started together. It was just that he had been feeling so skittish and doubtful, waiting for Jace to call him back. He'd needed to do *something* to calm himself down. But it certainly as if he was going to *continue* hooking up with other men now that he and Jace were going to be boyfriends.

Before he could explain this, though, Jace started up again.

"I know we just spent one night together, and maybe this is my issue, because I just can't accept this is how relationships go these days, and you're not supposed to take them seriously for a long time. But… I don't know… you didn't seem glib to me."

"No… no … it was just some guy I met in the chat room," Patrick tried to protest. "It didn't mean anything. You hadn't called me back, and I thought—"

Jace cut Patrick off with a sharp, breathy sigh—a sound like the summertime wind in Dallas, just before the blackening sky unleashes a torrent of golf ball-sized hail. "It's that stupid fucking website," he said. "I'm an idiot for thinking I could meet someone worth dating on there. It's just a stock exchange for people, buy or sell or hold for the next time you're horny. All my friends think I'm a prude, but I can't understand how they don't see that it's destructive."

He paused and then added: "People are not stock prospectuses."

"But that's how I feel, too. I hate going on there."

"No, Patrick, you don't. You can say you hate it, but you don't. If you hated it, you would have been able to wait more than four days after our first date before having to fuck another guy." And then Jace stood up and started to make his way to the door.

Patrick knew that he should stop him from leaving. Beg his would-be boyfriend's forgiveness. But he just sat on the couch, silent, dumbfounded. Was this what adult life was always going to be: hopefulness that never comes to anything; a series of exasperating, game-losing fumbles just inside the one-yard-line?

Jace hesitated when he got to the door—and Patrick thought this might be a signal from him. Maybe he didn't really want to leave, any more than Patrick wanted him to go.

Just say something. Anything. You can still salvage this.

But what Jace said next rendered a future between them impossible. They were words that, no matter how deeply rooted in the truth of Patrick's life these days, he simply could not bear to hear.

"I thought you were different, but I guess I was wrong. You're just like everyone else."

And then Jace opened the door, and he turned back to cast one last disappointed glance in Patrick's direction before walking out of the apartment for good.

What Patrick did finally say he said only in his head, and of course by then it was much too late.

I am different—different, and just like you. I know that I don't always succeed in living up to my own standards. I know that I'm a risk that no one would ever want to take on. But I want so much to be exactly the man you thought I might be, and shouldn't that count for something?

Can't you please just believe me when I tell you I'm trying my best to figure this all out?

THE FALL WAS FAST AND vertiginous, and he knew he was falling as he fell, but that only seemed to make him fall faster.

Who knows how much further he might have fallen if not for that phone call from Nora?

An hour after Jace left his apartment that night, Patrick logged back onto Gay.com. Within minutes he had arranged for another hookup. He drove forty minutes to a house in Lewisville, where he discovered that the man who lived there was someone he had hooked up with in his own apartment seven months prior. His skin had the glassy sheen of heated cooking oil, Patrick's memory of their initial encounter was dismal—yet he had sex with the man anyway.

Over the next month there were fourteen more individual encounters, a threesome and also an orgy, ten bodies all flailing in the half-darkness of a two-room "suite" at a La Quinta in Grand Prairie. There was even another diagnosis of Chlamydia, though this time Patrick didn't wait until finishing his antibiotics course before he started having sex again. He was sleeping, at most, two or three hours a night. He skulked through the office each day, a stinging in his belly from the cups of coffee he drank one after the next. There wasn't anything he wanted to do, unless it was hunt for a new hookup; wasn't anywhere he wanted to be, least of all inside his own skin. The holidays drawing nearer, he called his parents and told them he couldn't afford to fly home and would instead spend Christmas with Nora, and then he called Nora and told her that he would be celebrating Christmas in New York with his family. He kept vigil in front of his computer, and it was 4:15 p.m. on Christmas Eve, the ranks of DallasCitywide1 attenuated, when he saw the username Mustang1971 turn up in the chat room.

His never-forgotten first.

Mr. One-and-Done.

MrMorrisTownsend: *What's up? Looking?*

Mustang1971: *Trying to get a group together for a special party tonight…*

Maybe it would have ended that night regardless.

Maybe Patrick would have been sickened by the sights he saw.

Maybe he would have felt all used up, depleted of spirit and seed.

Or maybe it really was as Patrick would come to believe: that Nora—the one person in this world who knew and still believed in his best self—was nothing less than his savior and guardian angel.

Patrick would never know for sure, one way or the other. The only thing he could claim with certainty was how he felt in those minutes before the call came through. So tired like if he closed his eyes he might never wake up again. Sorry for himself, yet ice-cold inside—like he wasn't even worthy of his own tears.

The party took place at a high-ceilinged McMansion in Plano, though to whom the house actually belonged Patrick never did find out. The furniture was all cleared out of the living room, save for a halfheartedly decorated Christmas tree. The music was a techno remix of Sarah McLaughlin's *Possession* played on a continuous loop. There were fourteen men in attendance, not counting the two who were skinny and tweaking, with pimples on their shoulders and blond hair that hung into their faces—the "party bottoms" positioned on all fours on the floor.

All these thoughts, bottled up and bouncing off one another, like bumper cars in his head. He was remembering that from as far back as kindergarten all he had really wanted to believe was that he was special—smarter than his classmates and family members; destined for achievements that would inspire such envy in all of them. He was thinking that his presence at this Christmas Eve party probably didn't qualify as such an achievement. He was wondering if twenty-nine was too young for him to raise a white flag in surrender, or in fact much too old—because for three decades now he had felt under siege, and at some point you have to say enough is enough, only a fool or a masochist would possibly keep fighting.

He was thinking, thinking, thinking, the curse of his waking life, thinking that he was horny, thinking that he wanted to get off, thinking that he preferred the second of the two party bottoms, but why bother discriminating, thinking that at this very moment in Staten Island his family would be unwrapping their presents at the annual Monaghan Christmas Eve celebration, and thinking that maybe it was time for a present all his own.

All the other guys here are doing it, so why not you, Patrick?

What the fuck's so great about being different?

He was unbuttoning his shirt. He was perhaps no more than thirty seconds from taking his turn.

He would chalk it up to fate; tell himself that it probably could have been predicted. She was always keeping an eye out for him, even during those stretches when they argued or drifted apart—so why should this night have been any different? Indeed, long after he deleted his Gay.com profile, and then relapsed and created another, and then—after a year of weekly visits to a therapist—finally stopped himself from going online to find men, Patrick never bothered to ask Nora why she called at the precise moment she did. His atheistic tendencies notwithstanding, he chose instead to view her intervention as evidence that maybe some kind of celestial force or higher power really was paying attention to and guiding the universe.

"I'm sorry I've been such a lousy friend lately," she told him, after they had exchanged hellos and Merry Christmases. "I hate myself for this Patrick, but there was something about having you in the same city—I think I've been afraid that if I spend too much time with you I'm never going to have a chance at a normal husband and family."

It usually drove Patrick crazy when people used the word *normal* to basically mean *not gay*, but presently he didn't think of correcting her. He felt much too elated and relieved just to hear her voice on the line. "I've been doing a lot of shitty stuff myself lately," he answered.

"It's so confusing to me, that I can feel so confident at work, and yet when it comes to my friends and my personal life, I'm always doubting myself."

Patrick told her, "I think that happens a lot with people like us—people who feel like exiles."

Nora exhaled through her nostrils, a laugh desperately in search of mirth. "It's funny you use that word. A few weeks ago, I told one of my coworkers that I sometimes feel like an exile, like I'm on the outside looking in at everybody living life correctly. He mocked me. Said I get paid way too much to call myself an exile."

"Fuck that douchebag," Patrick said; and this time Nora's laugh seemed to contain at least a modest measure of joy.

"God, I've missed talking to you Patrick," Nora said.

"You know, I can be at your place in twenty minutes," he answered.

"I thought you were in New York."

"No," he answered, and the music and the noises of the men fucking and the thumping of his heart all faded away, and the only thing he could hear was Nora's breathing on the other end of the line. "I'm right here in Dallas."

2 0 0 8

The man who never should have been President endorsed John Sherman for the Republican nomination of 1880, in exchange for Sherman's support for his own bid to become United States Senator from Ohio. Fortunes rise: Sherman, then Secretary of the Treasury, found himself in a deadlock at the National Convention in Chicago against Ulysses Grant, running for a third, non-consecutive term, and James Blaine, a United States Senator from Maine. Attention among conventioneers soon turned to a possible compromise choice. A former seaman and seminarian, born into penury, who went on to serve eight terms in the House, James Garfield claimed the nomination and eventually won the Presidency without quite abandoning his central doubts: that his ascendancy had taken place too quickly; that it wasn't yet his time.

Fortunes fall: On March 5, 1881, Charles Guiteau—convinced that a pamphlet he had written in support of Garfield was responsible for the man's victory—was granted a meeting with the President, who turned down Guiteau's request for a diplomatic post to Paris. On July 2, the vengeance-seeking Guiteau ambushed Garfield at the Baltimore and Potomac Railroad station, shooting him in the shoulder and the back. That second bullet, inoperably lodged behind the pancreas, was the one that killed him, though it took eighty days. We can only speculate as to whether, during that long and poisonous decline, the President cursed the failed candidacy of John Sherman; cursed the sixteen delegates from Wisconsin whose switched votes at the convention shifted the momentum his way; cursed his own ambition and cried to the heavens: *Why the fuck did I ever leave Ohio?* James Garfield was the second sitting President of the United States to be assassinated.

At 8:21 p.m. the trauma surgery team at John Peter Smith Urgent Care Center stepped away from the operating table. The bullet had been successfully extracted from Patrick's stomach, and the gastroepiploic artery had been stented and seemed to be functioning normally. But out of one set of woods, they would soon be deep into another: the possible infections that might spread through his bloodstream; the possible permanent damage to the internal organs. The doctors could not say with any degree of certainty whether he would make it through the night.

By this point, nearly nine hours since the story first broke, the television news coverage began to take its inevitable next turn. Enter the cable news talk show hosts and their soundbite-ready guests, those Chicken McNuggeteers of the early twenty-first century, who processed the spare parts of any saga, added appropriate amounts of sugar and salt and bitter, and served them up to viewers for fast consumption. Rachel Maddow devoted the opening of her show to monologue, her voice periodically breaking as she compared the shooting of Patrick Monaghan to the assassination of Robert F. Kennedy in 1968—"quintessential American populists who strived to unite a nation that may simply prefer to remain divided." A few channels further along, a porcine and bespectacled "Fox News analyst" resorted to that strange brand of commentary unique to this Age of Irony, commentary that insists the subject isn't worth commenting on at all.

"He got famous on a reality TV show?" this man squawked. "Was there *anybody* out there—even among the Democrats—taking his candidacy seriously?"

Which isn't to say there wasn't someone out there trying to place Patrick's achievements in useful context—only that you had to know where to find her. All that afternoon, Rebecca Lowenthal assumed one of the big names would call her for an interview, Anderson Cooper or Chris Matthews or at least Nancy Grace, whose show she had done three times previously. The only person she heard from was the producer of an hour-long radio show that aired live each evening on the NPR affiliate in Boston. All these other Johnny-come-latelys, from *New York* magazine and the *Times* and *Texas*

Monthly—the people who had only paid attention to Patrick *after* Rebecca helped to make him famous—were being trotted out as experts, but Rebecca, to her considerable irritation, had been forgotten. (Forgive Rebecca: Fifteen years working in New York City magazine publishing will make you competitive over *anything*, even the fleeting media exposure to be gained at the expense of someone else's near-murder.)

Still, she agreed to do the radio interview, and not out of some desire to satisfy her ego, or to set herself up just in case one of the big publishers might be interested in a book on the subject. (Or at least not *entirely* for those reasons; truth was, she did already have a call in to her agent.) For Rebecca, going on the radio to talk about Patrick was mostly about her conviction that she told a more compelling version of his story than anyone had ever told—more compelling than Patrick could ever possibly tell himself. Every would-be legend needs a balladeer, and for whatever reason—maybe because she also still felt remorse about the things she had included in that profile that she had promised him she would leave out—Rebecca was now determined to sing Patrick's song.

Interviewer: *You say that your article had a major impact on both of your careers?*

Rebecca Lowenthal: *I certainly don't take credit for Patrick's rise in politics—that was all Patrick and Nora Meacham, his campaign manager. But no one knew who he was before that article was published. And it was my first major piece for* Rolling Stone, *where I'm now managing editor. I've told Patrick many times since that I owe him a great debt, though I don't think he feels the same way about me. I know he hated what I wrote.*

Interviewer: *What did he hate about it?*

Rebecca Lowenthal: *He didn't want me to do the story in the first place. Even though he was on a reality TV series at the time, he hated the idea of a journalist following him around all the time. "Journalists capture things that cameras can never see," I remember him saying to me. But I think what most upset him was that I wrote about his relationship to his family.*

Interviewer: *His father had just passed away at the time, right?*

Rebecca Lowenthal: *Yes—and that's the great unresolved relationship of Patrick's life. To this day, I'm still not sure if he's ever resolved it for himself.*

Loud and (Mostly) Proud
Is Patrick Monaghan the Gay Voice of His Generation?
By Rebecca Lowenthal

Rolling Stone, June 20, 2008, pp. 78-82, (cont. 136-140).

Here he goes again, once Patrick Monaghan gets started, there's usually no stopping him, today he's talking about Eddie Murphy, the legendary comic actor of Beverly Hills Cop, The Nutty Professor *and* Dreamgirls *fame, a man, it's probably worth mentioning, Monaghan has never met. But that won't stop the breakout star of the A&E reality series* Dallas Three Ways *from delivering one of his bravura, impromptu mini-lectures on the subject of Murphy's history of homophobic stand-up comedy.*

"I was thirteen years old when my brother brought home a copy of Eddie Murphy's Delirious *and played it for my father—loud, like you would play a rock record," Monaghan explains, over lunch last winter in the Deep Ellum section of Dallas.* "It starts with a bit about Ed Norton wanting to have sex with Ralph Kramden on The Honeymooners. He makes fun of people with AIDS. He just keeps using that word—faggot, faggot, faggot—and I shuddered each time I heard it, like bullets were being fired inside our house. My father and brother just laughed and laughed.

"Eddie Murphy made the mockery and hatred of gay people mainstream," Monaghan continues. "He made it enjoyable. At this moment in history when we were finally starting to see sympathetic portraits of homosexuality in the culture, like Robert Preston in Victor/Victoria *or Billy Crystal on* SOAP—*Murphy reassured America that gay people were every bit as disgusting as they feared, and then some. He eventually apologized, said he didn't realize the hurt his words caused. But I'm not sure people understand the damage he did—how he singlehandedly shamed millions of young gay men into staying in the closet. I'm not sure something like that is ever forgivable."*

Unless you are a devotee of slightly disreputable reality television, chances are you've never heard of Patrick Monaghan. (Eddie Murphy certainly hasn't—through his publicist, the actor declined to comment on Monaghan's statements.) But last fall, over the course of ten episodes of Dallas Three Ways—*which follows the thirty-four-year-old Monaghan and two other gay men, both ten years his junior, as they navigate Dallas' viscid social scene—*

Monaghan unexpectedly transcended the show's sometimes silly trappings. He's someone who might legitimately be proclaimed as the voice of an entire generation of gay men, born in the 1970s and '80s, who came of age after the AIDS crisis and who have seen extraordinary strides in the battle for equal rights—but who still struggle with the shame and self-hatred that bedeviled previous generations.

What makes Dallas Three Ways so compelling is that Monaghan is working through his internal contradictions in front of the camera. He is one part Oprah-esque spirit healer, one part Dick Cavett-like pop intellectual, one part Real Housewives-style emotional train wreck. In one episode from the first season, Monaghan—who is tall and dark-haired and seems to develop a five o'clock shadow somewhere between nine and ten in the morning—pleads with his co-stars to join him at a rally in support of same-sex marriage, even though both want to spend the night at a gay club. "You have to resist this idea that's taken hold in the gay community," he tells them, "that we're somehow compromising our identities by wanting to adopt these traditionally heterosexual institutions." In response they roll their eyes and march out of the room.

In another episode, he awkwardly suffers through a conversation with a waitress at a restaurant, who assumes that he's straight and begins flirting with him. Monaghan never bothers to correct her.

"Something about having to say those three words in public—'I am gay'—still causes me a twinge of embarrassment," he confesses later in the same episode.

"He's a hot mess, but there's also real soulfulness there," says Doug Dunbar, the twenty-six-year-old Dallas native who created the series. "And that makes for great television."

Fuck, fuck, fuck, why, why, WHY? Why had he agreed to this article?

Patrick sat in the green room of the show's production facility on Hamilton Avenue, waiting for the crew to light the studio so that he could film his weekly "confessional"—an hour-long interview with the supervising producer about the events captured on camera over the past seven days. But the studio crew was running late, so Patrick had decided to do what he had been putting off all morning and finally take a look at Rebecca's article. It had been posted online overnight and already the emails and texts were pouring in, complimenting and congratulating him. He generally hated reading about himself—even the favorable articles felt strangely inconsiderate, like someone talking about you as if you're not in the room even though you're standing right there—but he wouldn't be able to avoid this for much longer.

Except now he saw it was *far worse* than he had feared. Rebecca had portrayed him as someone both wildly pretentious *and* completely neurotic; as just another gay joke for people to laugh at.

How could he have ever fooled himself into thinking it might come out otherwise?

Nora was the one who had convinced him, to cooperate with Rebecca on the article, and of course to try out for *Dallas Three Ways* in the first place. Those were blurry and bruising years for Patrick—it sometimes felt to him as if a sheen of Texas haze was blanketing his very being. Even after he deleted all of his online profiles, he went through a phase where he was convinced he had contracted HIV and insisted on getting tested monthly, no matter that the results always came back negative. Then, in January 2006, he was laid off from the Convention and Visitor's Bureau as part of a cost-reducing purge of ten percent of the staff; and after trying and failing to find something in a similar field, he eventually had to take a waitering job. Nora learned that they were casting for the reality show through a friend at the Dallas Film Commission, and then she made a few introductory calls on his behalf. He agreed to a first meeting with the producers mostly because he was scheduled for fewer than usual hours at the restaurant that week—and he knew it was best to keep busy, even with nonsense, lest he end up going online and getting himself into trouble.

It wasn't like anybody tricked him. As the interviews and auditions progressed—the process dragged on for three months, a long stretch of silence followed by days of frantic meetings, followed by more silence, and then more meetings—he grasped what the producers were after. Patrick's proposed co-stars were Logan Taper, a delicate-featured scion of oil and gas billions, who drove a sky-blue Ferrari and was presently trying to launch his own society magazine, and Gabriel Vasquez, a muscular Dominican torn between a career as a fashion model and one as a classical violinist. Without actually coming out and saying so, Doug Dunbar obviously wanted him to serve as their "gay uncle," alternately disapproving and envious of his younger friends. Patrick signed on regardless. He needed the money, fifteen thousand dollars for eight weeks of filming. He told himself that, just maybe, this might be a chance to become the person he had long wanted to be: a gay man who lived and led by example.

He struggled through those first weeks of filming, standing in defenseless silence as Logan and Gabriel—who despised him from the instant they all met, for reasons Patrick assumed had solely to do with appealing to the constantly-rolling cameras — mimicked him and called him "a dried-up, over-the-hill queen." But one night during filming, as the three of them were returning to the Turtle Creek penthouse apartment they were sharing together for the duration of the production, after a debauched night at S4, where both Logan and Gabriel had hooked up with separate men in the bathroom, Patrick sensed a kind of opening—almost like he were playing a chess match and now saw a combination of moves that would lead to victory. He wasn't being snide or condescending; wasn't trying to get back at them for how shitty they had been to him these last few weeks. Quite the contrary, what made what he said to them so arresting was that it came from a place of earnestness and sympathy.

"It's not that I think you should be spending your Friday nights digging wells for arid villages in Africa," he told them. "And I admit that half the time I look at you guys and I feel a measure of envy. But you have to believe me when I tell you that what seems like such fun now will leave behind this toxic residue. You will end up having such little respect for the men you meet, and even less for yourself. I'm not trying to moralize here. I'm just trying to make you see that you can both be so much better than this cliché of gay promiscuity."

His co-stars were struck silent—this all unfolded in an elevator jammed not only with the three of them but also a camera man, a sound woman and a field producer—and Patrick wasn't at all surprised when he got a call from Doug Dunbar the next morning.

"I need you to do more of what you did last night."

"More of what?" Patrick asked, though he knew what Doug's answer would be.

"You're their truth-teller *and* their shoulder to cry on—you're like a gay, non-religious Joel Osteen—and most of the time they're going to hate you, but every once in a while you will wear down their defenses, and they'll realize the insight of what you're telling them. And *those* are the scenes that will make us all rich and famous."

Even in this moment of triumph, though, Patrick couldn't quite get past the idea that he was still trafficking in bullshit. How could it possibly be any different, when the scenarios on *Dallas Three Ways* were all manufactured by the producers and the arguments among the cast members were all artfully assembled in the editing room? In the weeks that followed, Patrick lectured his castmates about the failings of the Democratic candidates for United States President to advocate for marriage equality; about his fears that the gay men of Logan and Gabriel's generation were far too glib about condom use; even about his longstanding contempt for *Queer Eye for the Straight Guy* ("*It's the kind of gay minstrel show that sets back the cause by two decades!*") Yet for as much sincerity as he poured into his on-camera performance, he knew in his heart it was just that—a *performance*, being shaped by people over whom he had no authority or control.

Nonetheless he signed on for another season. For one thing, they were willing to quadruple his fee. For another, he thought it might buy him some time to figure out a proper next step—perhaps there was a way to parlay the notoriety he'd gained on *Dallas Three Ways* into more substantive work, a blog or a book or a radio show.

But he also told Nora that he had to draw the line *somewhere*. He wouldn't allow a reporter from *Rolling Stone* to trail him around for weeks. There was no way she could accurately portray the man he believed himself to be; the man he wanted others to see him as—not when he still regarded himself as a work-in-progress.

"She thinks you might be this generation's Larry Kramer," Nora argued. "Why *wouldn't* you want her to write that?"

"If Larry Kramer was dead, he'd be spinning in his grave that you just said that."

Yet it was one thing to begrudgingly allow himself to be persuaded by Nora and sweet-talked by Rebecca, so that finally he just said, *Fine, go ahead, worst case scenario it at least gets my name out there*; and at first it was bearable, even entertaining, Rebecca talked faster than anyone Patrick had ever met, and she started at least fifty percent of her questions with the phrase "One last question..." But at some point this woman turned into the proverbial houseguest who won't leave; the more time and information he afforded her, the more she claimed to need of him; and now the finished article had been published, and it was just like watching himself in a new episode of *Dallas Three Ways*, waiting to see how material he never should have offered up in the first place would be used against him.

"Almost there. Just give us five more minutes. Sorry."

Patrick looked up to see Ben Lewin, this season's supervising producer, at the door of the green room. He nodded at Ben and let out an anxious sigh, and then looked down again to his iPhone. He skimmed through the next few paragraphs of the article, the boilerplate biography. He arrived at the middle section. He clenched his jaw and scrolled forward.

Let's see how much worse this was going to get.

ON A SATURDAY EVENING IN *April, Patrick Monaghan stands by himself in the living room of a three-story, 8000-square-foot mansion in Dallas's elite Highland Park neighborhood. His cast mates on* Dallas Three Ways, *Logan Taper and Gabriel Vasquez, are huddled together on the opposite side of the room. Filming for the second season of* Dallas Three Ways *has been carrying on for nearly a month: Last week, Monaghan movingly counseled Tapper after the man Tapper had been dating sent him a text message breaking up with him; just yesterday, in the middle of the NorthPark shopping mall, Monaghan successfully persuaded Vasquez to boycott Chick-fil-A because of anti-gay statements the company's owner has made in the past.*

Yet the tension and cattiness that animated season one of the series has thus far been in short supply.

Or at least it has been until now. Because as the cast members stand in their separate corners, waiting for the cameras to roll, Taper and Vasquez keep whispering in each other's ears and casting snide glances in Monaghan's direction—like two schoolyard bullies egging one another on for a playground fight.

This house where tonight's shoot is taking place is owned by Patsy Reardon, a twenty-four-year-old commercial real estate heiress. The party she is hosting here is in honor of her "best new friend" Vasquez, celebrating the launch of his newest modeling venture, as the face and body of an underwear line called Southern Boyz. The expensive artwork on Reardon's walls—including original paintings by Rothko, LeWitt and Hockney—has all been taken down and temporarily replaced by framed, black-and-white images from the Southern Boyz campaign, some of which feature Vasquez wearing no underwear at all.

A little after eight, the hundred or so invited guests begin to arrive. Look closely and you might recognize many of the faces from the first season of Dallas Three Ways, when they drifted through the backgrounds of gallery openings and charity dinners. (Almost every episode of the show features some sort of large-scale social event where all the cast members converge and usually get into a shouting match.) The cameras are already rolling as they step inside. There are three four-person crews—consisting of a cameraman, a boom microphone operator, a sound recordist, and an assistant producer—following all of the action. The ringmaster of this circus, meanwhile, sits hunched over a video monitor in a maid's room off the white-on-white kitchen. His name is Ben Lewin, an affable, twenty-eight-year-old New Yorker serving as this season's supervising producer.

"All I can tell you is that there's definitely going to be some drama tonight," Lewin says to me, an impish smile on his face.

For the better part of an hour, nothing seems to happen. Taper and Vasquez entertain separate groups of partygoers, who exaggeratedly laugh at their jokes and do an altogether unconvincing job pretending that they're not conscious of the camera crews hovering mere inches away. For his part, Monaghan keeps drifting off to a lonely corner of the living room, taking doleful half-sips from a gin and tonic.

But then the assistant producer assigned to Vasquez, acting on instructions coming through his earpiece from Lewin, begins twirling his finger at Vasquez, and then pointing to Monaghan on the other side of the room.

"Do it now," he silently mouths to Vasquez.

Vasquez strides toward Monaghan, the camera crew following behind. The crew assigned to Monaghan begins to fan out so as to allow this enemy gaggle into their midst.

And suddenly Vasquez is right up in Monaghan's face, and everyone else at the party has gone silent.

"I want to know what gives you the right to poison people against me," Vasquez demands of Monaghan.

"Whatever you think I said, I can assure you I didn't say," Monaghan answers.

The crew members draw in tighter, pushing Monaghan and Vasquez further into one another's personal space. "So you haven't been going around telling people I'm some wannabe supermodel?" Vasquez responds.

Monaghan puts up his palms, a gesture that's meant as a plea for calm. "What I said to Logan was that I wished that an incredibly gifted classical musician like you would pour his soul into his art—and not buy into this lousy cultural obsession with zero body fat and six-pack abs."

"So now you're saying I'm just a dumb slut?" Vasquez says.

Monaghan is about to protest further. But before he can say anything, he is bumped from behind by one of the sound men and pushed into Vasquez. Whether the bump is intentional or because the heavyset man has lost his balance in such close quarters is impossible to say.

What happens next is a frenzy of overreaction that will only be made fully comprehensible in the editing suite. Vasquez, who is drinking some sort of orange-hued cocktail, gives Monaghan a hard push with his free hand. Monaghan's arms go flailing. Vasquez next makes like he's going to punch Monaghan, at which point the camera crews part so that Taper can enter the scene, in order to restrain Vasquez and tell him, "Dude, it's so not worth it." From another corner of the living room, Patsy Reardon begins shouting, "No pushing. No fighting. Those lamps are worth twenty thousand dollars."

And then, just when Monaghan has finally steadied himself, just as he's again trying to make peace, Vasquez tosses the remainder of his drink into Monaghan's face, with deadly aim, and then Vasquez storms across the room with Taper by his side. The camera crews remain tight on Patrick, to record his half-embarrassed, half-perfunctory reaction—he looks like the poor sap assigned to the carnival dunking station at the end of a long day on the job. The "drama" has been delivered, and the last thing that can be heard before the murmur of the other party guests rises up again is Reardon loudly pronouncing to anyone who will listen: "That better not stain the carpet."

IN THE STUDIO GREEN ROOM on Hamilton Avenue, Patrick looked up from his cellphone and allowed himself the start of a smile. Had he been too hasty in his initial judgment of the article? Was it possible that Rebecca had actually done right by him? He thought that in this section she had put forth a clear-eyed analysis of *Dallas Three Ways* without resorting to the usual elitist bluster about reality shows that they are all distraction and tawdry spectacle. He liked, too, her descriptions of things—especially the way she compared him to a man in a carnival dunking tank. She had deftly conveyed to readers that Patrick was *conscious* of the joke, in on it and mostly above it, even if sometimes he was inevitably the butt of it. (There's no way to maintain *complete* ironic distance when someone throws a blood-orange margarita in your face.)

He could barely even remember how that silly argument with Gabriel had started. He was pretty sure that, like so many of their on-camera feuds, it was engineered by the producers, who the day before that party probably told Logan, *Get him to say something about how he thinks Gabe's modeling is stupid*, which definitely *wasn't* what Patrick said to Logan, but who knows how it all got translated back. The specifics, by now, hardly mattered. In the eight weeks since, there had been at least a dozen more petty blow-ups and near fistfights just like that one. Doug Dunbar had made it clear that was what he wanted for the second season, and Patrick, Logan and Gabriel were all guilty of behaving accordingly.

But it wasn't *just* illusion and farce. *That's* what he liked about this article, Rebecca's grasp of an elusive contradiction—she understood that reality television could be manipulated and more than a little fake, and yet still allow its participants to speak certain truths. When Patrick gave voice to his ideals and argued with Logan and Gabriel on camera, he wasn't just trying to create "good television." He genuinely wanted his co-stars to listen to him. He believed that if he had had someone speaking to him in this fashion when he was in his early twenties—explaining to him which battles are worth fighting and which are merely wastes of your energy; forcing him to realize that sex and sexuality are two vastly different things—then he might have saved himself so much time and trouble. Of course, Logan and Gabriel usually just laughed at him or fought him bitterly. But the point was that *sometimes* they listened; and the larger point was that even when they refused to listen, there were millions of people watching at home who nonetheless heard. They saw on their television screen an articulate, entertaining, thirty-four-year-old gay man communicating to them a way to look upon the world.

Just then there was knock on the door of the green room. Ben Lewin popped his head inside and said, "We're ready for you, Patrick."

Today was the final day of shooting for the second season. These new episodes wouldn't begin airing for another month, but editing on the first two was already complete. Apparently the network bosses were thrilled. "There's a feeling that we might be able to take the leap from cult hit to cultural phenom," Doug Dunbar had emailed him. A week from today, he was scheduled to fly to Los Angeles to meet with potential agents and talent managers. It was time, Nora insisted, to "broaden the Patrick brand."

Maybe Nora had been right all along. Maybe Rebecca's article was *exactly* what Patrick needed: a framework; a packaging; a case made on his behalf that he never would have had the perspective or the sheer, shameless chutzpah to make for himself.

Maybe he *could* be the gay voice of his generation, and maybe he could ascend to such a height by way of a reality television show.

Patrick asked Ben Lewin for a few more minutes. He needed to finish reading the article.

He had gotten into a series of arguments with Rebecca during the course of her reporting, over questions about his family. The first time the subject came up, midway through their initial meeting, Patrick told her he wouldn't talk about them. Rebecca responded by turning off her tape recorder and threatening to kill the story right then and there. He relented, by recounting to her a handful of childhood anecdotes. But when she asked him how he had gone about telling them he was gay, he shrugged and said, "There really isn't a story there." In the interviews that followed, he rode out her periodic temper tantrums each time he declined to share his mother's and siblings' contact information—and eventually she stopped asking. But then, three months along, just when he assumed she was finally finished—because how much longer could this possibly go on, she was writing a three-thousand-word profile, not a three-volume biography?—Rebecca called him and said that his mother had invited her to dinner at his childhood home in Staten Island.

"It will give me the color the piece is still missing."

Patrick was livid with Rebecca for going behind his back; livid with his mother for ignoring what he had said to her a dozen times—*if a woman from* Rolling Stone *calls, tell her that you are unable to talk and then hang up the phone.* But he was also outmaneuvered, especially once his mother dug in her heels and refused Patrick's demand that the invitation be rescinded. What else could he do but book a ticket to New York to join them? It had happened just last month. It had been his first trip home since his father's funeral.

"Since you're probably going to find out anyway, I should tell you that I didn't come out to them until just before Dallas Three Ways premiered," Monaghan tells me, as he steers a rented Chevy Impala along Hylan Boulevard, one of the main thoroughfares on Staten Island.

"I used the show to tell them that I was gay."

Today is Mother's Day. We are headed to Eltingville, a neighborhood of semi-attached, two-story houses with concrete-paved fronts, where Monaghan lived until his mid-twenties. Yet as we turn from Hylan Boulevard onto Richmond Avenue, Monaghan begins talking much faster than before. A man so confident on television turns into another man entirely— jittery and inarticulate and desperate to be anywhere but here—the instant he draws within a mile of his family.

"He's the guy who tells everyone else how they should live as a means of camouflaging his own emotional retardation," Logan Taper previously described Monaghan to me. "You should ask him how long his longest relationship has been. He won't say, but I'd guess two weeks is his record."

Monaghan—who indeed deflects questions about past romantic relationships—says he struggled all through his twenties to confess his homosexuality to his parents. His father, James, was a delivery man for Coca-Cola. His mother, Marilyn, was a homemaker and later a grocery store cashier. Church-going Catholics, if not exactly fire-and-brimstone types, they had long assumed that their son was dating his best friend, a Dallas-based political consultant named Nora Meacham.

But in early 2006, James Monaghan, then only sixty-two, was diagnosed with Stage III prostate cancer. Radical surgery and three months of chemotherapy did little to halt the spread of the disease. Late that summer, the younger Monaghan flew home. Throughout the visit, he was wracked with uncertainty: Was it crueler to allow his father to die without ever having truly known his adult son, or to add turmoil and regret to the man's last days by coming out to him now?

On his fourth morning there, after a night spent twisting and turning in his childhood bed, Monaghan came to a decision. Terminal illness did not absolve his father for the hurtful remarks and casual homophobia that his son had internalized over the years. It also didn't absolve Patrick of the burden of what he knew to be an inescapable truth: that only when a gay person is open to everyone about his sexuality can he hope to be fully human. Shortly after breakfast, he knocked on his parents' bedroom door, determined to finally confess. When there was no answer, he knocked again and entered. He found his mother lying beside her husband, very softly sobbing. James had passed away an hour earlier.

Patrick recalls, "I remember my mother saying to me during the wake, 'He wished he could have stayed alive long enough to see you and Nora get married.' Hearing that just sent me even deeper into the closet."

Nevertheless Monaghan carried forth with the shooting of the first season of Dallas Three Ways, knowing that its premiere would force matters to a head. At Meacham's insistence, he eventually mailed his mother a rough-cut DVD of the first three episodes so she wouldn't be blindsided when the promos started airing. On his way home from the post office, he pulled over to the side of the road, opened the car door and vomited.

Marilyn Monaghan called him the next evening. She told Patrick she was proud of him. She said, "You were so handsome and funny."

"Is there anything else you want to talk about?" he asked.

"I don't usually like reality shows, but this one is interesting," his mother said; and then she never raised the subject of Dallas Three Ways with him again.

"It's a series of paradoxes that are enough to make you want to weep," Monaghan explains to me now. "My family can know and even accept that I'm gay, and yet carry on overlooking the matter—so that it's this elephant that squeezes all the air from the room. And I can tell myself that I have nothing to be ashamed of, and yet still feel as if I'm an embarrassment to them."

An hour or so later, we settle down to an expansive Southern Italian feast, served on both the dining room table and a second collapsible table that extends into the living room. Gathered here are Patrick's siblings and their spouses; his three nephews and two nieces; his Aunt Marcie and Uncle Al; two of their kids and their spouses, and three of their kids—twenty-one people in all. At the head is Marilyn Monaghan, sixty-five, a large and unshy woman who speaks with a thick Brooklyn-Staten Island accent.

I point out that she sounds nothing like her accent-neutral younger son. She shoots me a mordant look and says, "He goes off to college and comes back at Thanksgiving talking like somebody new."

The dinner with Monaghan's family is sweet, unruly, a little claustrophobic. There is affectionate ribbing of the reality star; stories of his childhood mishaps. Timothy Monaghan, who looks like a sharper-angled facsimile of his younger brother, beams with unmistakable pride when he explains that, at a restaurant just a few weeks earlier, he was mistaken for Patrick by a fan of Dallas Three Ways.

But there is a noticeable shift in the mood when I ask them if they are aware that some people are starting to regard Patrick as a culturally influential gay figure. Bodies tense up. Everyone suddenly seems to be staring at his or her plate.

"I'm not sure that's something they really think about," Monaghan leans over and whispers to me.

And later, after everyone has left, while Monaghan is in the kitchen cleaning dishes, his mother leads me into the now-denuded bedroom that belonged to Patrick when he was a boy and pulls out a stack of old family photo albums. And it's then that I fully understand her son's dilemma—why, even if Patrick Monaghan does turn out to be one of the most important gay Americans of the early twenty-first century, he may never feel like a man in full.

"To tell you the truth," Marilyn says to me, lingering over a picture of a seven-year-old Patrick wearing a blue blazer and white pants on the day of his first Holy Communion, "I'm glad his father passed away when he did, thinking Patrick was going to settle down with Nora. That's not a disappointment he would have enjoyed. I'm proud of my son. Don't get me wrong. But honestly I wish I could be proud of him for something else."

Marilyn then opens another photo album and flips to a picture of Patrick on the day of his college graduation, in cap and gown, his mother and father on either side of him. They are all looking in different directions—presumably more than one person was trying to snap a picture at the same time.

She says, "You tell me he's a big deal in your world, and it's not that I don't believe you. But I don't see that. I still see a boy who ran away from his family; a boy who didn't want anything to do with us. I see a boy who's always been very good at breaking his mother's heart."

"Is everything okay Patrick? You seem a little out of it."

Patrick shifted in the canvas seat of a wood-framed director's chair, trying to make himself more comfortable. These weekly confessionals were usually the easiest part of the filming process—you quickly got a sense of what the producers wanted you to say, and then you said it—but today he was having trouble stringing even a simple sentence together.

Six thousand words, twice as many as Rebecca Lowenthal had initially promised. Posted online and soon to be in print. A *Rolling Stone* profile—the ultimate stamp of cultural approval. It would be linked to and blogged about and no doubt lead to dozens more media requests. It would set him apart from all those other flash-in-the-pan reality sensations, who were lucky to score a photo and three hundred words on their latest adulterous dalliance in *Us Weekly*.

So why did this hurt the way it did?

He wasn't necessarily angry with his mother. Surprised that she felt so bitterly towards him; chagrined that she didn't know to be more guarded in the presence of a quote-hungry journalist. But how could he be angry with her for only speaking the truth as she knew it; for not going along with Patrick in his attempts to rewrite entire chapters of his history?

Nor was he angry with Nora, for pushing him to do the story in the first place. He suspected if he were to explain it to her she would shrug off his disappointment altogether. *She has made you a part of the water-cooler conversation in a way the reality show alone never could have done,* she might say—a point he would have a hard time disputing. Besides, Nora wanting him to be featured in *Rolling Stone* was just Nora being Nora, always seeking out a competitive edge. How can you begrudge someone such consistency, especially when it's you they're trying to help get ahead?

Honestly, he wasn't even angry with Rebecca Lowenthal. Dismayed that she had included the story of his father on his deathbed, even after her repeated assurances that it would remain off the record. Annoyed that she had ended the piece on such a damning note, and given credence to Logan's assertion that he was a hypocrite. But he respected Rebecca for trying to craft the best profile she could; and he certainly couldn't gainsay the conclusions about him that she had drawn.

"I'm sorry, can we start again?" Patrick said to Ben.

The person he was angry with was himself—a feeling by now in his life he knew quite well. For buying his own hype. For telling himself that he might yet find his place in the world while surrounded by video cameras and boom microphones. For believing that authenticity and artificiality can and should be brought into closer alignment.

He wasn't now disavowing the experience of the last few years. He was still pretty sure there was something of value about *Dallas Three Ways* and his onscreen persona, however contrived both might be. He believed he was closer than ever before to solving the daunting riddle of his life.

But he still didn't have it quite figured out. What Nora and Rebecca didn't understand—and what Patrick was only just now processing—was that the most sensational words and provocative ideas mean nothing if they aren't also wedded to *action*. There's a fine line between having a platform from which people might hear you and having one from which they will be commanded to pay attention. He had to proceed now with caution. He had to find a way to place himself on the right side of that line.

"OK, first question," Ben Lewin said, his voice emerging from the blackness behind the camera. "Do you think Gabriel and Logan are getting too close for comfort, or do you think they might actually make a good couple?"

Patrick stared at the camera lens. He shrugged and looked off to the side.

For the first time in awhile, he found that he had nothing to say.

They all remembered

AS THE CLOCK DREW NEARER to midnight, as the doctors and nurses who spent the day trying to save his life left the hospital for their homes and collapsed into their beds exhausted, as the news of the assassination attempt spread far beyond the borders of the United States—there were reports on the BBC and the Press Trust of India and the Xinhua News Agency and Al-Jazeera, *everyone* around the world was asking the question of what the shooting of one man in Texas might say about the foundering dream of America—all of these people remembered.

In truth, they had never stopped thinking of Patrick Francis Monaghan. He had never been as alone in the world as he sometimes feared.

In San Francisco, Cal Coombs, now sixty-two, came to the news late, having spent most of the afternoon and evening being interviewed by a film crew for a documentary about men who had been diagnosed with HIV in the early 1980s and were miraculously still alive. He had made the connection a year or so earlier, after reading a story about Patrick in the *San Francisco Chronicle*: This guy running for Senate in Texas was the same little boy who had stared at him so strangely and insistently that hellish afternoon at Anthony's cousin's house in Staten Island. They had joked about it later, after returning from the humiliating and failed trip to New York—they had gone to plead with various members of Ant's family to help pay for an experimental drug trial—while Anthony was still strong enough to sit up in bed and breathe and laugh. *That poor little boy*, Ant had said to Cal, *was in love with you.*

In Indianapolis, where he has was now an executive vice president in charge of sales and marketing at Eli Lilly and Co., Marco Baffi thought of telling his wife of his history with Patrick—it would certainly account for why he had been snappish with her and their two young daughters all night. Many times over the years he had thought about the wrongs he had once committed against Patrick: first signing up to run against him for class president when it was clear that the job meant everything to the kid; and then later never having the courage to tell Patrick that what had happened at his house that afternoon was really no big deal. He certainly hadn't meant for Patrick to think that he was coming on to him—though in retrospect it was obvious how Patrick would have seen it that way. And he certainly hadn't meant to be such a jerk to him in the years that followed—only that Baffi had been having a lousy time of it himself, with his father in the throes of a nervous breakdown from which he never did fully recover and his mother working two jobs and still unable to pay their bills. But how to explain all of *that* to his wife, who would probably look at him like he was crazy—theirs had never been the sort of relationship where Baffi felt comfortable discussing his *feelings*. So instead he said nothing. He watched the television news coverage of the shooting. He wondered if in another version of this story he and Patrick might have ended up best men at each other's weddings; godfather to the other's children; oldest and dearest friends.

In Saint Paul, Minnesota, Steve and Suzie Stollen—that kiss had indeed started something, though Suzie dutifully waited two years after Nora had broken up with him and then properly secured her friend's permission before chasing after him for herself—twisted and turned in separate bedrooms. The gap that had opened between them when they learned that Suzie was unable to have children had widened and become unbridgeable in recent years. Come this weekend, Suzie would tell Steve that she had consulted a lawyer and would soon be moving back in with her parents in New York. And now this horrible news about Patrick, their old classmate, their beloved friend—by senior year, all really had been forgiven, and the four of them would hang out together all the time—shot in the stomach, fighting for his life in a hospital in Texas. The golden age of their youth, most certainly, was over.

On the Upper East Side of Manhattan, Dick Leonard sat at the computer in his study, typing out an email to his newest assistant, a young Bowdoin graduate named Henry McKee. In 2002, Dick married a second time, to a retired art historian named Alice Owens. They spent three years traipsing through Europe, taking long walks in the Berkshires, and seeing virtually every production at the Metropolitan Opera, before coming to the conclusion that retirement was for the birds. At which point, Dick decided to borrow a couple of million against the apartment and launch an independent publishing house. Hearing what had happened to Patrick today, he inevitably wondered if he might have the inside track on a sure-fire bestseller—a heart-rending memoir of struggle and survival—and he wanted Henry to put together some notes for a proposal. He sent the email, ignoring Alice's objections that he was being an ambulance chaser and, for God's sake, shouldn't he at least wait to see if Patrick lives. But the way Dick saw it, first of all Patrick still kind of owed him one for subjecting Dick to those idiotic charges of sexual harassment; and second, to judge by his memories of that prickly little bastard, there was no way a single bullet was going to be enough to take Patrick out.

In San Antonio, Texas, Jace Hopkins—director of communications for the Spurs basketball organization—had never told any of his friends or colleagues about the relationship he had *almost* started with that reality TV guy now running for the Senate. Unbeknownst to Patrick, Jace had been volunteering on weekends in the Bexar County field office of the Monaghan campaign and even shook the candidate's hand three months earlier, though Jace's hair was thinner now, and he had put on twenty pounds since they'd last seen each another, and Patrick was too distracted by the scores of other volunteers swirling around him to make the connection. Now Jace scanned the latest headlines about the shooting on the Internet, and he grieved—not necessarily for what might have been between them, but for the way life makes it so difficult to ever know if you chose right. Doubt, Jace thought ruefully, is truly the only thing you get to carry with you to the grAvenue

In her offices at *Rolling Stone* in New York, Rebecca Lowenthal was flipping through her Rolodex, trying to find someone who could write for her the definitive story of the assassination attempt. At Dallas-Fort Worth airport, Marilyn Monaghan was stepping off the plane and then seeking out a taxi that would take her to the hospital.

In the private waiting room at John Peter Smith Urgent Care Center, Nora and Oscar were now slumped onto each other's shoulders, a blanket draped over them by one of the nurses, asleep but just barely, each dreaming a version of the same dream: It is Election Day, and the sky in Texas is an iridescent cerulean dotted with pillows of white, and all precincts are reporting except one, and only a handful of votes separate the two candidates. Astonishingly, improbably, gloriously, it might still go either way.

They all remembered Patrick Francis Monaghan.

They held their breath and waited.

PART THREE
RUN FOR YOUR LIFE

FOUR DAYS BEFORE

Patrick Francis Monaghan steps out of the thick iron entrance door of the Hotel Icon, onto the red-brick sidewalk of Main Street in downtown Houston, lightheaded because there is no food in his stomach. He opens his eyes as wide as the already-blinding sun will allow and looks across the street, expecting the bus to be parked there. According to Nora it arrived from Tennessee early this morning, gassed up and ready to go—forty-five feet long, eight feet wide, and eleven and a half feet tall, detailed in the fashion of their campaign posters, bright red with blue-outlined white lettering. Except the bus isn't here. He looks left and then right and across the street once again. He sees a taco shop, a dry cleaner, an Edible Arrangements—but the curb in front of these shops is empty.

He turns back to Nora, herself just out of the door, trailed close behind by three of her countless assistants whose names he has long since stopped trying to remember. He knows it would be wisest to stay calm, take deep breaths. But he can't help feeling like his peevishness is justified. Why should he have to stand here and wait when he could still be in his hotel room; when of late even just fifteen minutes extra sleep in the morning could mean the difference between an agonizing day and an at least bearable one? This bus that will take him from city to town to rural outpost on the final stretch of the campaign—forty-one stops are scheduled for these next thirty days—this bus whose lease is costing the campaign $140,000 and change, not counting who knows how much in gas and tolls, for the price of this fucking thing they could have purchased a brand new Mercedes S-Class and just sped off into the sunset—*still* isn't ready to roll.

"Where is it?" he barks.

Nora gestures with her eyes and chin, all the way to the far end of the street.

"Oh no… no, no, no…"

"Obviously it's not what we were expecting."

"You've got to be fucking kidding me," Patrick says, loud enough so that all three of Nora's assistants look up from their cell-phones and gape at him.

"I think the light is deceiving…"

"Jesus Christ… it's…"

"… because it's so bright out here…"

"It's *pink*."

In truth it is pinker than pink, a screaming blur of it, Pink Panther pink from roof to rims, so assaultingly pink that even the words printed on the side of bus in white—**MONAGHAN 2014: Turning Rejection Into Acceptance**—are tinted pink, albeit a sicklier shade.

"Once we're in better light, it will look fine."

"*Where?* In what light won't it look *pink?*" Patrick hears the words coming out of his mouth; knows they sound shrill and mocking. He does nothing to contain himself.

"Patrick, please—"

"That bus is a fucking joke."

Nora looks across to the bus, winces at the sight of it. This only enrages Patrick more. "They will see that bus from a mile away and say, 'Here comes the faggot in the pink bus,'" he carries on.

He is in a frenzy now. He will accept nothing less than a compete surrender on her part; a prostration at his feet; a promise that this pink fucking bus will be hastily returned to Tennessee and a full refund secured.

Silly Patrick—who is he fooling? This is Nora he's shouting at. *His* Nora: his best friend; his toughest critic; his walking, talking bullshit detector.

"For Christ's sake, Patrick, it's just a stupid bus," she snaps back. "A means of getting from point A to point B. It is *not* a symbol of your entire persecuted existence."

"I'll rent my own car! No fucking way I'm getting on that bus!"

"Try keeping a little perspective for once in your life."

"My perspective is being blocked by a giant pink bus!"

Nora looks down at the ground, takes a deep breath — is she going to back down? Nope. Turns out she is just digging deeper into her well-stocked arsenal to launch a counterattack.

"I just got off the phone with Washington," she announces to him, low and cold. "The President will no longer be joining us at Wednesday's speech."

Patrick stops sputtering and turns away from the pink bus and looks to her. In an instant, all the fight has gone out of him. "Seriously?"

"His staff doesn't want him wasting his time on a race that—and I'm quoting here—'the party has zero chance of winning.' The President is disappointed with the way this one turned out." She pauses and adds: "Their words, not mine."

"Oh... wow... "

"And don't even get me started on yesterday's tracking polls, Patrick, because compared to those numbers, that hideous pink bus right there is *the greatest fucking thing that's ever happened to you,* your port in a fucking storm, you should be counting your blessings that you at least have someplace to hide while this entire campaign turns to shit."

SHE NEVER TREATED IT AS a joke; never saw it as anything less than possible. She severed more than a few professional ties along the way—to her it was the only appropriate response to those who might dare to suggest that she was engaged in some sort of lark or folly. Nora Melissa Meacham didn't do larks or follies, and anybody who didn't understand that didn't know shit about her.

She was going to win this thing, with or without their help.

In the one respect she had always considered herself more fortunate than Patrick, in that she had never really questioned what she wanted to do with her life. She figured it out that summer between freshman and sophomore year, in Austin, where she had a front-row seat to the annihilation of her political heroine. The slurs and slanders poured forth daily that summer from Bush and his pit bull Rove. No one in the Governor's camp understood how to combat them, and a certain fatalism began to gather, like humidity in the air before a rainstorm. Her only real surprise, at the end of her fourteen-week internship, was that the polls were still so close, when it was obvious to Nora that Ann Richards was going to be obliterated.

Yet even on the losing side, Nora thrilled to the strategy and gamesmanship. The work appealed to the very essence of this young woman, who clung to a core of optimism, even as many times as she had been taught the same lesson growing up, that the arc of most people's lives bends toward defeat. It was on the Richards campaign that she first realized that the assertion of one's ideals is *always* going to be a battle—and that sometimes you have to fight dirty. Back on campus that fall, watching the voting returns on the television in the common room of Mass Hall, Nora felt less pity for the loser than scorn. The Richards team could and probably would blame Bush and his well-heeled heavies; argue that the white male elite of Texas had conspired to eliminate from their power circles this tart-tongued woman whom they regarded as an interloper. But God, how Nora hated crybabies; and, frankly, maybe had the now-deposed Governor's advisors listened to a few more of Nora's suggestions—she might have been a lowly intern, but that didn't stop her from regularly typing up five-page memoranda offering her unsolicited advice—they might have been able to staunch the bleeding and turn things around. Listening to the Governor's defiant (and, Nora believed, fundamentally clueless) concession speech that night, she began to envision a future for herself in politics, identifying and blazing paths of victory where others just saw dead ends.

Right out of Dartmouth, she landed a job working for the longtime incumbent Democrat United States Congressman who represented Austin. Her boss hadn't faced a serious challenger in years—these days, he barely even bothered to campaign—and she had little interest in the week-to-week routine of writing self-serving press releases. But shuffling back and forth between Austin and Washington D.C., she made some useful connections; and in her nearly two years there, the suspicions Nora first harbored on the Richards campaign were usefully confirmed. She came to realize that most of the people involved in politics—the elected officials pumped up on their own egos; the sycophants and hangers-on hoping for a cushy appointment; the fundraisers and consultants always looking ahead to the next contest—weren't especially intelligent, or at least not in a way that Nora valued. They knew nothing of the political theory she had spent four years at Dartmouth studying—the notions of agonistic pluralism espoused by William Connolly, say, or the "radical democracy" championed by Ernesto Laclau and Chantal Mouffe—and they certainly couldn't imagine such theories being practiced in any real world setting. They saw things in black and white, or perhaps red and blue: Only a certain kind of candidate could be run; only a previously successful strategy could be attempted. They would have thought Nora mad if she even dared express her conviction that the political future Ann Richards had hinted at was within reach: a future where women and gays and blacks and Hispanics all elbowed their way into office; a future where a candidate's perceived "flaws" might actually be the thing that could get him or her elected.

She had little doubt she could run rings around all of these buffoons, given the proper opportunity.

She got luckier with her second job, in Dallas, as the junior member of a twelve-person political consulting firm run by a retired United States Court of Appeals judge named Tom Tharp. Those first few years there she did everyone else's grunt work, recording notes at meetings, proofreading reports, only occasionally getting asked to share her opinion. But she worked her way up. She volunteered to spend weeks at a stretch on the road; studied polling data and census reports the way Christian converts pore over the New Testament. In 2004, her strategy recommendations proved instrumental to a pair of victories in United States Congressional races, in Tulsa and south Texas, both places where a Democrat never should have stood a chance. Two years after that she was the lead consultant on a campaign that nearly toppled the popular incumbent governor of South Dakota—a race that so effectively raised the loser's profile that he ended up being offered a regular contributor's spot on MSNBC.

But still it wasn't quite enough—not for the ravenously competitive Nora Melissa Meacham. Arrogant and entitled as she knew it sounded, she wanted to one day be regarded in the same exalted terms as Kenny O'Donnell or Lee Atwater or James Carville, American political operatives whose ideas helped change the course of history. Instead, at age thirty-three, having recently attended her tenth-year Dartmouth reunion with Patrick—where they encountered millionaire hedge fund managers and tenure-track university professors and even a Tony-winning actor—Nora felt *stuck*. Tom Tharp ran his firm as a kind of benign dictatorship, making it clear to all new hires that opportunities for advancement would stop short of partnership. Her most audacious strategies, meanwhile, were usually naysaid or watered down, until they came to resemble a million other strategies that had worked for former clients.

She considered opening up her own firm, but couldn't see it working out—fact was, there weren't really *any* potential clients out there willing to take the risks she longed to put to the test. Besides, she had already proven to herself that she could excel at her job. What she wanted now was that thing that all creative-minded and ambitious people are chasing after, whether novelists or architects, painters or political consultants: the butterfly-in-the-stomach-inducing challenge that she had never attempted before; the masterpiece that would make her name.

Maybe she wouldn't have felt these yearnings so acutely if she had had some other outlet, spiritual or romantic or otherwise. And, indeed, on this count, she knew she was wholly responsible for her situation—she had willingly *chosen* the way of the workaholic. But for long stretches of her twenties and early thirties, her career at least served as a kind of escape from everything else she couldn't seem to make right in her life. For one thing, it had gotten so that she could barely speak to her parents without consequently sinking into a week-long depression. Her mother lurched from one health crisis to the next, and complained bitterly about the infrequency of Nora's visits home. Almost every time she phoned her father, now living in a single-room-occupancy hotel, the conversation ended with a request for cash. (She filled out the Western Union transfer slips—$200 here, $500 there—without any illusions that the money would pay for something other than a bottle of Gordon's gin and another failed bet at Retama Park.) Her love affairs, meanwhile, usually ended in calamity. She had a hard enough time to begin with finding men in Dallas whom she regarded as independent and serious-minded—she couldn't believe how many of them worked for their family's accounting firm or car dealership. When she finally relented to follow Suzie's advice and not dismiss someone "just because you don't like his résumé," she ended up in a two-year relationship with the unctuous manager of a high-end steakhouse who turned out to have been cheating on her the entire time. (Though she never told anyone, Nora learned of his deceptions after contracting

Chlamydia from him.) In 2003, she *thought* she found the right guy—an assistant professor of microbiology at the University of North Texas, six-and-a-half feet tall and handsome in a nerdy sort of way. But he would immediately clam up the moment she made even the most throwaway reference to marriage; and the longer the relationship carried on, the more frequently he would cut her down over obscure bits of trivia she didn't know or the occasional grammatical errors she might make. ("I thought you said you were *smart*," he would say.) She wasn't especially surprised when he announced that he had taken a job at UC Davis, not far from where his ex-girlfriend now lived.

In the months that followed that breakup, Nora sometimes blamed herself for the fact that she was still single, because all these years she had done nothing to coddle men who might find intimidating an Ivy League-educated, financially secure, six-foot-tall woman. More commonly, she saw the problem in sociological terms—she knew a number of other women her age who had been strung along in just this fashion, only to find themselves cast off and barreling towards forty. Could it be that an entire generation of men had misinterpreted the message of the feminist movement and now assumed that a culture that extolled a woman's equality also exonerated a man of *any* responsibility?

Most of all, though, she spent night after semi-sleepless night marveling at the depths of her own naïveté: Back when she was at Dartmouth, she never questioned that *of course* she would eventually marry and have children, because that's just how it worked out for *everyone*.

That was when she finally decided she had to stop implicating Patrick in her romantic failures; when she realized that holding him at arm's length was less about self-preservation than this nagging worry that others might regard her as some sort of fag hag. By then, he was mostly estranged from his own family, and he wasn't dating anyone either. They resumed the pace of their interactions in college, talking at least once a day, emailing back and forth a dozen times. They spent almost every Friday and Saturday night at her place, cooking dinner and drinking wine and watching movies.

And though she was conscious of the fact that she might actually be making matters worse for herself—that Suzie was probably right when she told Nora that she was using Patrick as a shield against potential suitors, so that she wouldn't have to put herself out there and risk getting hurt again—she also didn't really care. More than a best friend,

Patrick had become a kind of lifeline for her. Yes, he could be difficult, exasperatingly mercurial, occasionally ridiculous—who else could be sent into an apoplectic fit if she dared order the wrong romantic comedy from Netflix? ("These Kate Hudson princess fantasies you love so much teach young women that the greatest goal in life is to be innocuous!") But he listened to her as nobody did, leaning in with his whole body, always *hearing* every word; and this sense of dislocation she so often felt—that somehow her life wasn't *rooted* to anything; that it was like she was trying to run a race from a starting block made of quicksand—was something only he seemed to understand. And when their conversation circled back to the subject to which it always circled back—to this question of how they might go about realizing all of their still-unfulfilled promise—it was a succor; a caesura; a way to make the disappointment go away.

"Maybe I should look into graduate school and consider teaching," Nora might say, because Patrick was also the only person with whom she felt could indulge her vulnerabilities.

"We need to embrace the fact that we're never going to fit into already established frameworks," Patrick would answer right back. "We need to think of ourselves as entrepreneurs of our own lives."

She was the one who encouraged him to audition for the reality show—she knew from the start that he'd be a natural. For a while, she even had a good time acting as his unofficial manager and mused about moving with him to Hollywood and helping him launch a show business career. But she knew that wasn't quite right—probably not right for Patrick, and definitely not right for her. Entertaining as he was on the show, she couldn't see him continuing in television without turning into some kind of self-parody. And as exasperated as she often felt at her own job, she still loved the *idea* of the work too much to even consider doing something else.

So she stewed. She treaded water. Sometimes she felt sorry for herself. Mostly, Nora being Nora, she brought the full force of her intelligence to bear on the problem. She didn't know what; didn't know how—only that she had to work with what she had, and what she had was a sense of purpose. Nora Melissa Meacham took things *seriously*. She didn't do larks or follies. Her short-sighted colleagues, her piece-of-shit boyfriends, her desperate and hopeless parents could all take away a lot from her—but no fucking way was she ready to concede defeat.

SNAP, SNAP, SNAP, BICKER, BICKER, bicker, all fucking day, snapping and bickering, they've entered into this spiral, this *echo chamber*, there isn't anything one can say to the other without setting off an argument that in turn sets off two or three more arguments. They finally agreed to disagree over this monstrosity of a campaign bus, and Patrick enjoyed a solid thirty minutes of silence as they cruised out of downtown Houston, but then it started up again, at brunch with the Greater Woodlands Suburban Business Alliance and Chamber of Commerce, she was furious at him there for referring to them in his remarks as the "Greater Houston Suburban Business Alliance"—*The Woodlands are* NOT *Houston, it's like greeting people in Fort Worth by saying, "Hello Dallas," what the* FUCK *were you thinking?*—and then at a luncheon with the Woodlands Junior Women's Club, she snapped at him as they were walking through the front door— *Do not under any circumstances call them* The Junior League *or you might as well chuck this election altogether*—but of course he screwed that one up, too, he kept saying "Candy" when the club's vice president was actually named "Cassie," and Nora tore into him yet again, as soon as they were back on the bus, and of course he reviles these meals that just keep blurring one into the other, he looks at the plates of food in front of him and sees his very existence staring back him, a desultory slab of salmon and a cluster of broccoli steamed so long it's turned to mush, and in between the events they are supposed to be working on Wednesday's speech, the "Major Speech" that is supposed to turn everything around, but of course Nora is shooting down every one of his ideas—*not a big enough pronouncement, not a bold enough stance*—and she's only succeeded in tightening and twisting the knot that has taken up permanent residence in his gut in recent weeks, because he is also wracked by the fear that he has made a terrible mistake, the worst mistake of the mistake that is his entire fucking life.

"Patrick, are you even listening?" Nora says presently.

"How about I just read the Gettysburg Address," he snaps at her, "and hope that nobody calls me out on it?"

"Do *not* raise your voice," she hisses. "There are reporters on this bus."

"Yes, our vast media entourage," Patrick answers. In fact there are only three reporters following them on this latest leg of the campaign, one from the *Dallas Morning News*, the other two self-employed bloggers. What was once an eccentric-sounding Cinderella story that over the summer attracted the attention of national newspaper and magazine writers—*The Gay Guy Running in Texas!*—has now turned into the uninspiring, deeply uninstructive tale of another Southern Democrat, all-but-certain loser.

"One more stop, and then you're done for the day," Nora says.

One more stop! How could he possibly forget? They are cruising north along Interstate 45 to Huntsville, "the death penalty capital of the world," where Patrick is set to tour the Texas State Penitentiary. And lest anyone think traipsing through the gray and bleach-smelly execution chamber where triple homicide offenders are injected with pentobarbital isn't depressing enough, later they will stage a press conference in front of the gates of Captain Joe Byrd Cemetery, the parched plot of land where executed prisoners whose bodies family members prefer not to claim are buried. There he will reiterate his platform plank about the need to phase out capital punishment in Texas; and though Patrick doesn't see much point in campaigning among prisoners who aren't even allowed to vote, he will say precisely what Nora wants him to say. She is insistent that there is support to be won from employees of the Department of Criminal Justice— the largest employer in the county, go figure!—many of whom apparently believe the death penalty is being utilized too frequently.

"Patrick, I know you think I've become some kind of royal ballbuster," Nora says. "But everything I'm insisting upon is for the sake of this campaign."

"It's just that this has stopped being fun," Patrick answers.

"I never promised you uninterrupted fun."

He understands she is trying to calm him; that he should have the decency to at least meet her halfway. But he does not want to be calmed. All the bickering and all the snapping, all day long, have left him in no mood to be conciliatory.

"Just for one day," he says, "I would love it if you didn't condescend to me."

"Please don't, Patrick. Not here."

"Have you ever asked yourself *why*, Nora? *Why* my success has become your singular preoccupation? Do you ever wonder that maybe there's something a little *strange* about it?"

He is aware as he is saying it that he is breaking a kind of unspoken covenant between them. She has been forced to defend herself throughout this campaign— against former colleagues and clients; against Suzie; even against Oscar—they hint in their smug, not-so-subtle ways that the psychic scars here run deep, that she is still romantically hung up on him, and that he—out of narcissism, or maybe just some weird kind of self-hatred, because all these years later he still probably wishes he wasn't gay—allows it to carry on. It has been Patrick's job to stand beside her in united front, to remind her that their critics don't know shit about why they are doing what they are doing.

Or at least that *was* Patrick's job, until he opened his big mouth a few moments ago and took the side of the opposition.

Her spine stiffens against the seat back. She stares at him, unblinking and impassive. She says nothing.

He can think only of Caesar in the instant of Brutus' betrayal, the shock commingling with a bone-weary resignation.

Et tu, Patrick? Is that how little you think of me?

"Nora… I'm sorry… that was callow… "

Nora continues to say nothing.

"I'm sorry, I'm exhausted, I lay awake at night wondering if this whole campaign is a mistake. For so long I've wanted to have an impact… and I *love* that you want me to have an impact and think I can… but it's hard, Nora, it's been so much harder than I ever realized it would be… and I snapped… I'm sorry, Nora, I just snapped."

Still she says nothing. She holds her gaze; defiantly refuses him pardon—*of course* that's what she does, this is Nora we're talking about, this is what he's always been in awe of, her steel will, her unwavering confidence—except now it's being turned against him. Nora maintains her silence even as the bus rolls to a stop.

Why does he do what he does next?

They will all have their theories.

Nora will tell him that it was a deliberate act against her: another *fuck you* from a candidate over whom she's lost all control. She will say to him that she's sick to death of him acting like a spoiled, self-absorbed diva.

Oscar will tell him that he thought it was tender and sweet, if admittedly ill-timed. He will say to Patrick, "I think I know what you were trying to tell me, and I can tell you right now my answer will be yes."

One of the bloggers on the bus, who will post on the incident in detail, will actually speculate that Patrick might have been under the influence of the Sauvignon Blanc that had been flowing freely at the Junior Women's Club luncheon, "... so strange was the candidate's half-galloping stride as he made his way across the parking lot. He moved the way a man might if his leg has fallen asleep and he is trying to power through the numbness."

Only Patrick can explain the truth, though, which is simply this: Nora's silence has always had the power to drive him to distraction and caprice. He goes a little crazy when he doesn't have his best friend to talk to.

He is regretting what he said to Nora, ashamed that he has hurt her feelings, but at the same time a wave of indignation washes over him, because why *shouldn't* he be able to hurt her feelings when she keeps refusing to even listen to him? That's when he looks out the window of the pink bus, and the first person he sees is Oscar, sent ahead to Huntsville with the advance team early this morning, standing just inside the entryway to the courtyard that leads to the facility's administrative building, in the middle of a disorganized circle of corrections officers and prison officials and local press and photographers. Oscar is laughing, no doubt being polite in response to some stupid joke the sunburned man in the too-tight khaki suit standing beside him has just made; and the late afternoon light reflects off his dark brown skin and for a fleeting moment Oscar appears incandescent to Patrick, like an angel taken earthly form, and all at once he decides he wants to hold Oscar and kiss him, his boyfriend's warm touch will pull him out of the meta-fiction of his life, this soul-squelching, identity-transforming thing known as a United States Senate campaign, and bring him back to Earth, back to Patrick.

A hug and a kiss will restore him.

He bounces out of his seat and makes his way down the aisle. He steps off the bus, moving a little too quickly. He sees the puzzled expressions on the faces of the prison officials, worried that he might stumble. He is desperate to reach Oscar, who sees him, and smiles, and then sees him coming closer—much, much too close for a public event—and frowns. Patrick carries forth, almost in a sprint now, and he crashes into Oscar, so that Oscar's only choice is to open his arms and embrace him, reflexively *catch him* in order to prevent his own nose from being smashed, like Patrick is some sort of human football that's been abruptly thrown in his direction.

Oscar's instinct, at least, is to turn his head to the side, away from Patrick's open mouth. Which is to say: It could have been much worse. Because what the two dozen or so people gathered outside the Walls Unit see this afternoon is not a full-on kiss between an increasingly paunchy forty-year-old white man who has just stepped off a giant pink bus and the handsome African-American campaign staffer twelve years his junior so much as a kind of slobbering of Oscar's cheekbone, followed by what looks to them all like some sort of college wrestling move, Oscar grabbing Patrick by the sides of his shoulders and then giving him a hearty shake and setting him on the ground upright.

"Ready to tour the prison," Oscar says brightly, as the hiss-clicks of the photographers' digital cameras sound all around them.

OF COURSE IT WAS A risk that might easily render her a laughingstock of her profession and squander whatever cultural capital Patrick had earned as the star of *Dallas Three Ways*. Certainly she was a little bit guilty of delusions of grandeur, thinking that she might be able to ameliorate this restlessness they both felt in one swoop. She fully anticipated that *everyone* was going to second-guess and mock them, even those who professed to be in their corner. There was in fact an unusually bitter phone call with Suzie, whom she first bounced the idea off, a few weeks before proposing it to Patrick.

"It's like some adolescent fantasy you never grew out of," Suzie said.

"This isn't a joke," Nora came back at her. "Please don't talk to me like I'm some sort of silly person."

"There is no such thing as a *shared destiny*—you can't keep indulging that myth," Suzie argued; and it went back and forth like this, until Nora did something she had never done before and hung up on her closest female friend. What use was there trying to logically explain what for Nora far transcended logic. It would have been like trying to describe the motorized car to a buggy driver, or the personal computer to a 1940s schoolboy: Some ideas are so brazen-sounding—and yet for their progenitors so fundamentally *attainable*—that all you can do is bring those ideas to life, and then let the haters eat your dust.

The way it unfolded was this: In 2008, not long after Rebecca Lowenthal's article in *Rolling Stone* was published, as ratings for *Dallas Three Ways* were soaring, when everyone including Nora was expecting him to re-up his contract, Patrick quit the show and no manner of money or perquisites could get him to change his mind. By then, Nora had worked on enough campaigns to occasionally wonder if her own natural assets (a knack for seeing patterns in numbers; a willingness to keep fighting in the face of certain defeat) and Patrick's (an unselfconscious inclination to place himself at the center of attention; a hard-held set of sometimes contradictory ideologies that nonetheless seemed to speak to this crazily bifurcated age) might actually be exquisite complements. A wave of suicides by gay teenagers, many of whom had been bullied in their schools, crystallized these initially fanciful musings. The passage of Proposition 8 in California proved to be a tipping point for her: Was Patrick really going to be a mere spectator to this great debate of the early twenty-first century, when it was obvious to Nora that he was born to be in the middle of this and so many other arguments?

She presented her findings to him on Christmas Day in 2008, when it was just the two of them at her house. She had spent countless hours staring at maps and poring over voting returns, and she was convinced she had identified a loophole. An alligator-shaped state legislative district in Fort Worth, stretching from the half-gentrified south side of downtown to the green and hilly neighborhoods surrounding Texas Christian University, had emerged in the three most recent election cycles as the second farthest left-leaning legislative district in a predominantly Republican county in the entire country. The Republican State Senator who had represented said district had already made it known that he would not be seeking re-election. The seat would be up for grabs in November 2010.

"You want me to become a State Senator?" Patrick said to her, at first just as incredulous as Suzie had been.

"It's a way for your voice and your message to be heard," Nora answered. "A serious platform—isn't that what you keep saying you want?"

"I'm not even sure I know what a State Senator does."

"It's not just a bunch of lawyers and career politicians," she told him. "It's a lot of ordinary people like you trying to have an influence—businessmen, schoolteachers, Iraq war veterans."

"I'm a gay atheist who's not only pro-choice but who thinks abortions should be dispensed like the free cups of water those nice people on the side of the road hand out to marathon runners. I don't see a lot of people in Texas voting for me."

"I can get you elected."

"What about shopping a book proposal?" Patrick countered. "Or we talked about recording a pilot for a radio show."

"I know it doesn't sound especially glamorous," Nora said. "I agree that it's the tortoise's way forward. But I've spent a lot of time thinking about this, Patrick. The tortoise will win the race."

After the initial skepticism wore off, Patrick admitted that he was intrigued: Hadn't he once made an estimable freshman class president at Staten Island Technical High School, before Marco Baffi came along and wrested away the position? Wasn't he always arguing to Nora that the reason the country was so politically divided was because there were no longer any truth-tellers for people to rally behind, only barely discernible versions of the same feckless equivocator?

Hadn't the thought occurred to him, too, if not quite so specifically worked out as Nora was presenting it to him now—that it would be pretty cool to run for some kind of political office and have Nora as his campaign manager.

"I mean, if Arnold Schwarzenegger can be governor of California, I suppose it's not totally outside the realm of possibility..." he said, after Nora explained it and explained it again, the conviction in her voice deepening each new time she flipped through her stack of Excel spreadsheets.

"Promise me you'll at least think about it."

While he was thinking, Nora went about laying the groundwork. She established residency in the district for Patrick, using her own money to rent him a house on Ryan Avenue, a drafty two-story with cracks running through the windows and a backyard sinkhole into which rats, squirrels and possums regularly plunged. ("Do State Senators have the power to get dumps like this condemned?" Patrick asked.) On weekends, without telling him where she was traveling, she flew to Boston, Portland, San Francisco and Key West, for meetings with wealthy gay men who had contributed to campaigns she had previously worked on. She delivered to them a carefully-refined pitch: The hard-fought battles for marriage equality in California, New York and elsewhere were certainly essential and worthy of their donations, but a commensurate effort needed to be made in the red states. She had a candidate, she told them, whose Texas-based story would reverberate all around the country and maybe even the world.

Next, after promising to pay for the repairs to the windows and hire an exterminator, she persuaded Patrick to actually move into the Fort Worth house; and then she called in a favor from a reporter at the *Fort Worth Star-Telegram*, who agreed to interview the former reality television star. She coached her candidate-in-the-making on exactly what to say: that Fort Worth seemed to him a more approachable and humane city than Dallas; that he felt the seeds of real social progress being sown here, and he wanted to be a part of it. He was to *hint* at a possible political future but make no firm commitments.

"You let the public and press think they are the ones compelling you to run," Nora explained. "You act like the idea never would have occurred to you independently."

And Patrick, though still deeply skeptical, couldn't deny that he was curious to see how this might play out.

She turned out to be right about everything. A week after his two-hour lunch with the reporter, the resulting article turned up on the front page of the paper's Metro section: "A controversial reality TV star settles in Cowtown." Patrick groused at first. "Only in a backwater is 'controversial' a synonym for the word 'gay'!" But the article portrayed Patrick just as Nora hoped, as deeply earnest in his belief that his celebrity could be used to serve a greater public good. With an accompanying photograph of him standing in front of a newly-opened coffee shop on gentrifying Magnolia Avenue, arms crossed confidently across his chest, Patrick looked and sounded like a plausible candidate—which to start was all she believed she needed.

After that she dragged him to Austin, to meet the state party leaders and assorted Democrats in the lege—a dozen meetings over dinner at Truluck's or drinks at the Four Seasons, and always Nora paid the tab. None of the legislators they met seemed especially ecstatic about the idea, but they all found Patrick charming and intelligent, and they knew and respected Nora's track record. Perhaps figuring that he would never have a chance regardless, they pledged that if she did decide to run him, they wouldn't stand in her way.

In the end, the hardest convincing she had to do was convincing Patrick himself. By then the reruns and marathons of *Dallas Three Ways* had run their course and his public profile was quickly diminishing. Yet he clung to the hope that new offers would be forthcoming, from talk show producers who would want to audition him for a hosting gig, or perhaps from book editors who might offer him a contract to author some sort of memoir. Nora had to keep making her case: she insisted that *this* was the grand gesture he had been searching for his whole life; *this* was his chance to bring his public and private selves into union. With Suzie Brown's voice whispering its warning in her head, she nonetheless invoked the myth of a "shared destiny."

"Don't you see how much *sense* this makes—the two of us finally joining forces to conquer the world?" she asked.

"It's not that I don't like the idea," he said. "It's just that it doesn't feel as organic to me as it does to you. I mean, when I was a kid, I never said, 'When I grow up, I want to become a State Senator.'"

"It need not be forever. But this is the biggest thing you can do right now."

"And if I get halfway into a campaign and realize it was a really bad idea?"

"Then you call it quits, and we chalk it up to a worthwhile but failed experiment."

"But that's the thing," he said. "I don't want to keep throwing away years of my life on failed experiments."

"Don't you see, Patrick," she answered, and this was what finally seemed to win her the argument. "Those years are going to happen anyway, regardless of whether you throw yourself into the game or stay on the sidelines trying to figure out the perfect next move."

He called her a little after eleven that night, and when she picked up, he said, "This is Patrick Francis Monaghan, your next State Senator from Fort Worth." The next morning, she requested a leave of absence from her job, shrugging off an obnoxious lecture from Tom Tharp about how "Ivy League political theory is *never* going to work in the real world," and then she set about building a small campaign team.

The Democratic primary ended up being a cakewalk: Patrick had name recognition, good looks, and novelty appeal; and his campaign war chest of $1.2 million—eight times greater than the next-best-funded candidate—more than made up for the fact that he wasn't especially well-versed on what were expected to be the major issues of the next legislative session. (Patrick tried to read the policy papers that Nora's team prepared for him, but he said they reminded him of his periodic attempts to wade through *Anna*

Karenina, all arcane legal terms and convoluted relationships, and he would doze off after three or four pages.)

The general election proved trickier. His Republican opponent was a potbellied good ol' boy in cowboy boots and Wrangler jeans named William Landry, the owner of a popular burger emporium on whose sprawling patio up to a thousand people gathered on Friday afternoons for happy hour. Landry hammered Patrick on the carpetbagger issue; claimed that he wasn't "real Fort Worth" and was interested only in advancing his own celebrity. Nora decided they would counter with a strategy that Patrick feared would be too quaint, too "tortoise-like" in this era of major media buys. She insisted that he trust her and, more than that, he trust in his own charisma; and then she accompanied him door-to-door, church supper to Kiwanis Club meeting, as he smiled and shook hands and ultimately introduced himself to approximately ten thousand voters.

Eventually they caught the break they needed, the proverbial October surprise—though Nora regarded it as anything but a fluke. ("Fortune favors the brave!" she cried.) Two weeks before Election Day, while introducing Landry at a Chamber of Commerce luncheon, one of the Republican's supporters referred to Patrick as "the sissy from Dallas." The *Star-Telegram* reported that Landry "laughed uproariously at the slur," a characterization that the candidate vigorously denied—until a video clip surfaced on YouTube, showing him indeed laughing so hard that he induced a twenty-second coughing fit. The day after that, the *Star-Telegram*'s traditionally conservative editorial page published an unexpected endorsement of Patrick. ("We can't afford to elect someone who lies in the face of incontrovertible evidence, and who encourages hateful speech at his events…") When Landry finally apologized, nearly a week after the incident, Nora responded with what she considered their knockout blow, delivered via Patrick's Twitter account: "An apology that consultants and op-ed writers pressure you to make is no apology at all. Sorry @WillyLandry—too little, way too late."

Patrick won by a healthy two-thousand-vote margin, which prompted Nora to observe: "This is why the architects of the political correctness movement in the 1980s were right. Being P.C. isn't about undermining our freedom of speech. It's about neutralizing those who speak from a bully pulpit."

She was gleeful. She had been right about *absolutely everything*.

Patrick stared back at her, a broad, lopsided grin on his face. He usually loved this sort of debate—indeed, the one and only course he and Nora took together at Dartmouth was Introduction to Semiotics, in which they both earned As—but this time he had nothing to offer in response. He instead seemed merely awestruck that he had actually *won* and was now expected to, um, legislate.

"So what happens next?" he asked, and then burst out in exhilarated laugher.

"Do you want to know what I *didn't* tell you today?" Nora says, sitting on the nearest of the two double beds in his hotel room, her chin jutted toward him like an accusation. "Do you want to hear about the *humiliations* I spared you, so that you could keep your head clear and go out and campaign?"

It is nearly midnight, the end of his worst day yet on the campaign trail. Everything that could have gone wrong since he jumped off the bus at Huntsville did. The tour of the facility took twice as long as scheduled, and the air-conditioning must have been busted—or maybe they just liked to make the inmates suffer—because by the time they got out of there they were all soaked with sweat; and then there was a mix-up among Nora's assistants, each thought the other had reserved a block of rooms in Bryan, and by the time they realized the mistake, there weren't any rooms in Bryan to be had—it was homecoming weekend, A&M versus Tech!—and their only option was an America's Best Value Inn twenty miles southwest on Highway 21.

By now, he most certainly *doesn't* want to know what bad news Nora spared him this afternoon.

"What I didn't tell you," she carries on, "is that the tracking poll that came in this afternoon has you down twenty-three points, four points worse than yesterday, which was two points worse than the day before. Keep hemorrhaging support at that rate, and you will be the first person in American history to lose a Senate race by unanimous decree.

"Then while you and Oscar got to eat a nice, normal dinner—"

"Oh, whatever, we ate at the Macaroni Grill—"

"—while you were having dinner," Nora raises her voice over the interruption, "I was on a conference call with our fundraising committee chair, who shared with me the encouraging report that contributions have slowed to a trickle. If we don't find new money soon, we're not going to be able to make any ad buys in the final two weeks."

"And you expect to solve these problems by yelling at me?"

"I won't let this campaign become a joke, Patrick," Nora snaps. "The gay reality TV guy whose avowed atheism we do our best to play down? That already *sounds* like a joke—a sitcom that would be cancelled after one episode—and I've worked my ass off, grabbing people by the throat just when they start to chuckle and telling them, *You better not fucking laugh*. But then you throw in the black, twenty-eight-year-old campaign staffer who the candidate kisses in public just prior to commencing a tour of an execution chamber? That's a joke even to me. That's something lower than a sitcom."

Patrick stands against the door of the room. This argument has been roiling for nearly an hour, and always it keeps coming back to this, his folly at Huntsville. Nora is angrier than he can *ever* remember seeing her, which in turn makes Patrick want to throttle her. He's willing to acknowledge that the kiss appeared eccentric to those gathered there this afternoon; and, true, the last thing the campaign needs right now is the press corps speculating over whether or not Patrick has come unglued.

But, *come on*, it was a silly little mistake, and at that it was a mistake of the heart. He was feeling anxious and lonely and wanted a hug from Oscar. For *that* he has to beg her forgiveness?

"So having a boyfriend is a joke now?" he says. "*That's* what we want this campaign to represent? It's OK to be gay, so long as you don't give people a mental image of two men kissing?"

"Oh, please, Patrick, spare me the entitlement. You do *not* get to have your cake and eat it too."

"I'm not asking for—"

"You want to know why your romance"—and here she places the word "romance" in air quotes, which only makes Patrick more furious—"with Oscar is a joke? It's because for twenty years you've talked about not wanting to be a cliché. But then at every other turn you embrace the cliché. You go chasing after a guy in his twenties, who's got a body like Tyson Beckford's, and who *also* happens to be on your payroll. Cliché atop cliché atop cliché. You wanna know something—when I interviewed Oscar, he told me he had a *girlfriend*. I never would have hired him if I knew he was gay. *Never*. Because I know you, Patrick. I know your propensity towards hypocrisy."

Part of Patrick wants to keep fighting. He believes it a kind of moral obligation—to himself! to Oscar! to all of gay society!—to do so. She has just done precisely what straight people have been doing for generations, dismissing a relationship between two grown men as some sort of silly, horny affectation—something lesser than a "real" relationship. She has implied that, even now, at age forty, his sexuality is something for which he should feel a measure of shame.

But he stops himself. Nora's charges against him have given him pause.

At every other turn, you embrace the cliché.

I know your propensity towards hypocrisy.

He has heard these criticisms before, of course: from his cast mates on *Dallas Three Ways*; from Jace Hopkins, the man he let get away; from Nora herself, way back when they were in college. They say he has a tendency to talk out of both sides of his mouth; that his actions don't always match his words. All through this campaign, his critics have been saying basically the same thing: that he isn't serious about a commitment to public service; that he's in this only because he wants to be famous.

Yet listening to Nora now, he realizes something he hasn't grasped previously. Yes, he wants his cake, and yes, he wants to eat it, too—guilty as Nora has charged. But what of it? Isn't this the most commonplace of impulses—not just to want it all, but to also elide the necessary sacrifices to get it all? Who but the insufferably pious doesn't sometimes yearn to *fudge it*; to cut the occasional corner? Isn't a tendency towards hypocrisy what makes us *human*? And thus if he is battling for equality—the right as a gay man to be viewed as no better or no worse than the next guy—then isn't this a tendency actually worth *clinging* to?

"What I've been arguing for all along," Patrick says now, speaking the words slowly, still trying to make sense of this in his head, "is the right to *not* have to be a paragon. I want the privilege of getting to screw up without having that screw-up being defined in terms of my sexuality."

"You don't get that privilege four weeks before Election Day."

"When Bill Clinton fucked Monica Lewinsky in the Oval Office," Patrick continues, "they said he was drunk on power, or that he was a womanizer, or that he had a self-destructive streak. No one ever blamed his philandering on the fact that he's heterosexual. No one ever said, 'This is exactly the reason straight men should never be taken seriously.'"

"But that's just setting the bar low and then congratulating yourself for meeting rock-bottom expectations," Nora answers. Her voice is softening; the tensed-up muscles in her shoulders are relaxing—her familiar physiological responses to settling into a debate with her best friend.

"But why *should* the bar be set any higher? Don't we need to evolve beyond the point where I'm expected to play the gay version of Sidney Poitier in *Guess Who's Coming to Dinner?*"

"Progress takes time, Patrick. The idea of a gay United States Senator is still something new to most people."

"But that's the argument the majority *always* makes when it wants to stem the tidal wave of change. *We have to proceed cautiously. Don't upset the apple cart.* It's just a more polite way of keeping people in the same boxes they've been kept in forever."

They might have carried on like this for hours. As strained as the day has been, as much bickering as they have done, they are also conscious of the fact that this is *exactly* the kind of conversation that first brought them together, winding and unanswerable, each one of them slicing off and savoring tiny slices of nuance like that last wedge of pumpkin pie on Thanksgiving that no one wants to be so greedy as to finish.

But just then there is a loud rapping at the door, which Patrick turns to open. Oscar is standing there, holding out to Patrick a single piece of paper. His hand appears to be shaking.

"Oh, thank God, you're both here," Oscar bursts out. "You need to read this. It's from the FBI. I think we need to cancel the Fort Worth speech immediately."

HE WAS NEVER ESPECIALLY GOOD at policy-making, not in the Texas Legislature, which met for just eighteen weeks every other year, and where back slapping and horse trading carried on among sexagenarian white men whose first or last names invariably seemed to be Earle. He had his share of second thoughts, especially during those initial months on the job, when he could tell from their strained smiles that his fellow lawmakers—Democrat and Republican alike—weren't taking him very seriously. But eventually something in his brain clicked, and what Nora had been saying all along—that he should think of his political career as a kind of spin-off of his reality television show—began to make sense to him. Winning a place in the State Senate didn't resolve the central dilemmas of his life, of how to make his voice heard, and what precisely his voice should say. But it did offer him the platform that Nora had promised; and with a little bit of creativity and imagination, he could make that platform singular. He was the junior-most member of the minority party—no matter how many asses he kissed and tedious meetings he endured, he was *never* going to be able to exert that much influence. What he could do, though, was start a few arguments; ruffle some feathers; piss off the standard-bearers of the status quo. It was, after all, something he knew how to do brilliantly.

He began issuing press releases, as many as five or six each week, usually written by himself, on subjects like abortion rights and creationism-versus-evolution in junior high school textbooks—arguing that Texas had become a national embarrassment by allowing the dialogue on social issues to be hijacked by uncompromising religious zealots. He gave interviews to anyone who asked, in which he criticized by name virtually every one of his fellow State Senators for being corruptible and in the pocket of big business. He staged rallies with Texas-based celebrities like Ruth Buzzi and Sandra Brown in attendance, calling for new regulations on the use of growth hormones in cattle farming or increased funding for programs serving the mentally ill—legislation that had zero chance of finding any traction.

And on the very last night of the 2011 session, more than a little bit amazed at how much *fun* he had been having, he strode into the Senate's green-carpeted chambers and commandeered the speaker's lectern and filibustered, Jimmy Stewart in *Mr. Smith Goes to Washington*-style, to prevent a vote that would massively slash public funding for the arts. Once again, it was mostly grandstanding—the funding cuts would come up for another vote in a special legislative session a few weeks later, and then Patrick would be powerless. But the filibuster nonetheless landed him on the front page of all of the state's major dailies—the political columnists wrote that they hadn't witnessed anything quite so enjoyably *theatrical* on the Senate floor in years—and it filled Patrick with a sense of professional gratification that he had never known before. It wasn't merely that he was good at this—from as far back as high school debate team, he had known he had a knack for public performance. It was that he was good at undermining the majority's confidence in its hard-held views; good at forcing the traditionally unapologetic to defend themselves. And unlike when he was starring on *Dallas Three Ways*, this time he thought what he was doing might actually matter to rest of the world.

Again he caught an extraordinary break; fortune favored his brand of bravery. In July 2011, an assistant manager at the Lowe's on the north side of Fort Worth named Kyle Newsome was barred by police from entering the hospital room of Sheldon Breaux, his lover and housemate of the past two decades whose liver cancer had now commenced a shutdown of his vital organs. Newsome and Breaux had had the foresight to arrange for living wills, each citing the other as the person to whom all medical decisions should fall in the case of incapacity. But Breaux's living will was now being challenged in court by his father, an eighty-six-year-old retired Baptist preacher from Nacogdoches; and the first judge to consider the case—whom Patrick had actually met a few weeks earlier at a charity function, where the judge shook his hand too hard and then wolfishly smiled and said, "So you're the one with the unusual lifestyle," stretching out the word in his courtly Southern style, pronouncing it *un-YOU-za-wah-lah*—sided with Breaux's father, issuing an injunction against Newsome barring hospital visitation.

When the story first broke, Patrick was at DFW on his way to a weeklong solo getaway to Provincetown. He considered turning off his phone, ignoring the texts and emails that were suddenly pouring in. For one thing, Newsome and Breaux didn't actually live in his district; for another, there was still a part of him, no different from when he was in his twenties, that even while insisting upon equal treatment for everyone bridled at having to frame the modern gay experience in terms of the sorriest stories. There was also the not inconsiderable fact that, even now, seven months into his tenure as State Senator, he still wasn't a hundred percent sure: Was this *really* the adult life he imagined for himself—as the man in the middle of others' business; the *politician?*

His hesitation did not last long. Within minutes he was in his car heading back to Fort Worth; within just a few hours, he had organized a press conference and secured the pro bono services of a team of local lawyers. By the next afternoon, he had gathered forces from around the state for a thousand-person protest in front of the judge's home in Tanglewood. The fact that Kyle Newsome wanted nothing to do with any of this—the attention, he said, would only cause him grief at work, where no one knew he was gay—did nothing to slow Patrick down. Like many a great politician before him, he embodied a certain brand of paradox: He could be conscious of his exploitation of others' anguish, and yet never doubt the fundamental righteousness of that exploitation.

A video of Patrick speaking at the protest, his voice quavering with disgust, instantly went viral. The interview requests poured in, from the *Washington Post*, NPR, *Good Morning America*, *The View*. Three days later, when the controversy landed on the front page of the *New York Times*, Patrick had the money quote: "When will the hatemongers lay down their weapons against us and admit their inevitable defeat?" He felt a swelling sense of triumph—if perhaps a little too much glee for so somber a scenario—when an appeals court threw out the injunction and the entire lawsuit, allowing Kyle Newsome to once again enter Sheldon Breaux's hospital room, albeit just twenty-five minutes before Breaux passed away.

Was it Nora—back at her old job, but increasingly restive and eager to return to this game—who first put the thought in his head, or was it the bloggers on the political websites who came to basically the same conclusion: that after two decades of running bland and conciliatory candidates in the doomed hopes of winning over the political middle, perhaps it was time for the Democrats in Texas to unleash a polarizing firebrand, the post-Ann Richards messiah who'd been promised for years but who heretofore had failed to materialize? Neither Patrick nor Nora could say; and they wouldn't be able to recall, either, the moment it stopped becoming something that they mused about half in jest and started becoming something they took very seriously. What was evident to both of them, though, was that by now Patrick's doubts about a political career had faded, and Nora's conviction had only redoubled. Yes, yes, yes—*of course* it made sense. Two decades after first pledging to one another that they would make an enduring mark on the world, they had finally found that which they perhaps didn't realize they had been searching for all along: a means of collaboration.

How could they have *ever* allowed themselves to sink into depths of self-pity in the past?

The race of their lives was far from over!

The tortoises were just now picking up steam!

On February 27, 2012, the weather so balmy that they were eating lunch on the patio of at a tiny Italian restaurant within walking distance of Patrick's rental house, Nora said: "Would you be opposed to my putting together an exploratory committee for a United States Senate run?"

Through a mouth of half-chewed gnocchi, Patrick answered: "Well, Texas is hot as hell most of the time, and I've always regarded myself as pure and delicate as a snowball—so I can't see why we wouldn't have some kind of chance."

THREE DAYS BEFORE

The sound is a just-discernible click, followed by a deafening, hollow boom, finished with a soft, almost sensual little hiss, like air escaping the puncture hole in a tire—even though he's wearing protective headphones, Patrick once again flinches. He looks across to Mitchell Tomlin, his regional campaign manager for south central Texas, clutching in his right hand the just-fired Taurus .twenty-two3 Remington revolver. Behind Mitchell's plastic safety goggles his rheumy green eyes are wide with a little boy's delight.

"You're next," Mitchell pipes up, shouting because after an hour inside this indoor, bulletproof glass-enclosed range none of them can hear each other speak. He holds out the revolver to Patrick, who is expected to load it and then shoot a series of gaping holes though an already shredded black-and-white paper bullseye twenty-five feet away. The specific message the campaign is trying to project to the handful of reporters and photographers gathered with them here, or so sayeth Mitchell, is "a post-Gabrielle Giffords, post-Newtown message of strict gun control that nonetheless pays heed to the inviolability of the Second Amendment." The broader strategy, or so Nora has contrived, is to "butch Patrick up"; to show Texas voters that he's not some liberal pansy when it comes to guns.

Patrick thinks it would have been a lot easier—and probably just as effective—had he just done what most hopeless cases do on Sunday mornings and gone praying for a miracle at church.

"The metaphor seems too pregnant," Oscar says to him, after Patrick fires off his ten shots, burning the stretch of skin between his thumb and forefinger. It is just the two of them today—Nora is already on her way to Waco, where she plans to hole herself up in the hotel and work on Wednesday's speech.

"What does *that* mean?"

"It's what my creative writing professor in college used to say about my short stories. A politician goes begging for votes at a shooting range at the same time he's receiving anonymous threats on his life. It's too on the nose. My professor would have demanded a rewrite."

"Well, that's where we're lucky," Patrick says, "because metaphors are constitutionally prohibited in Texas."

The threats have in fact been pouring in for months now: pencil-scrawled, unsigned missives mailed to the campaign's Fort Worth headquarters; a bass-voiced phone message that might have been confused for a late-night radio deejay's long-distance dedication, were it not also for the promise that "if he keeps talking 'bout ho-MO-sexuals gettin' married, that faggot gon' get himself hurt"; a mimeographed image of Patrick, with a bright red "X" and the letters "RIP" Magic Markered over his face, taped to utility poles throughout Amarillo. Agents from the Dallas field office of the FBI have dutifully investigated each of these threats and many more—and shrugged them off as the handiwork of harmless septuagenarian cranks or Fox News-addled shuts-in or perhaps just very bored teenagers, but of no serious cause for concern.

Until last night, that is, when the FBI reached out to Oscar, recommending that Wednesday's speech at the Fort Worth Stockyards Museum be cancelled immediately. They offered few details of what they said was an ongoing investigation; said only that "recent intercepted communications" hinted at a planned attempt on Patrick's life there. Nonetheless the urgent tone of their warning was enough to terrify Oscar, who couldn't believe that Nora and Patrick didn't agree with him.

"It's too vague to be credible," Nora told Oscar last night. "The FBI is just covering their asses."

"At the very least," Oscar countered, "we need to move the speech inside."

"Major speeches happen outdoors, for everyone to see and hear—*not* in a hotel conference room."

"So you'd rather he get shot for the sake of ceremony?"

But Nora just shook her head at Oscar, like he was a little kid in the grocery store who was *never* going to get that box of sugary cereal, no matter how loudly he pouted, and said, "This is our very last chance to turn things around."

"This isn't a joke," Oscar says to Patrick presently.

"Just think of the publicity we would generate," Patrick answers, smiling mischievously, "if there actually were an attempt on my life."

"Stop being so fucking glib," Oscar exclaims; and now that the gunfire has finally ceased, and the two dozen or so people squeezed into the shooting range have all removed their noise-canceling headphones, everyone hears this outburst and they all look in Oscar and Patrick's direction.

Oscar, realizing his mistake, moves closer to Patrick and adds in a whisper: "You can't allow her to send you into a war zone."

"Not here," Patrick says, smiling wide for the reporters and photographers, who are suddenly reaching for their just-packed-away notebooks and cameras, in the vague hope that this waste-of-time photo-op might yet beget some kernel of juicy gossip.

"I'm not being melodramatic."

Patrick says nothing as he tries to move them in the direction of the exit.

"It's crazy to me that people think I'm being melodramatic just because I don't want you to die."

HE CAME RECOMMENDED TO THEM by one of Nora's old Dartmouth professors, currently the chair of the political science department at Indiana—one of their graduating Ph.D. students had just completed his dissertation on the modern-day intersection of sexuality and politics and was looking for some real-world campaign experience before he entered the academic job market. His credentials were certainly impressive: valedictorian of his public high school in Milwaukee; *summa cum laude* at Wesleyan; co-author while still in grad school of a paper published in the *American Political Science Review*. Nora and Patrick even read the chapter of his dissertation on the Larry Craig scandal — ... *a* spectacular blurring of the line—or, in this case, the bathroom stall wall—between public and private, straight and gay, hetero-normative and homo-progressive...—and cheerfully agreed that it was something they might have come up with back in *their* school days.

They flew him to Fort Worth in August 2012 for two days of interviews. Nora liked his ideas about how Democrats in red states should be exploiting the widening divisions within the Republican party, but she worried he wasn't really invested in the campaign and would be using them merely as fodder for his next scholarly paper. Patrick acknowledged her concerns, but couldn't help but be flattered when Oscar told him that the Monaghan 2014 campaign would one day be viewed as historically significant, a "game change" in the parlance of the moment.

Wasn't that *exactly* what they needed, someone who never even questioned the rightness of his candidacy, someone who saw what they were trying to do in truly epic terms? (Besides, there were considerably worse things that being the subject of a scholarly paper, weren't there?)

All through that fall, it was just the three of them—poring over polling numbers; playing out possible strategies; researching and drafting an issues platform. Almost immediately Nora and Oscar butted heads. She found exasperating his tendency to want to debate even the tiniest and most inconsequential-seeming campaign decisions; and she flat-out reviled the way he would name-drop political theorists as if they were people she had never heard of—even though (as she liked to remind Patrick) *she* had been referencing those same political theorists since Oscar was in grade school. Patrick ran interference when he needed to; told Nora that she was being much too rash when, on Thanksgiving Day, she announced her intentions to fire Oscar. He felt no real allegiance to Oscar at this point, but he nonetheless suspected that having two similarly stubborn yet otherwise contrasting personalities on the team—Nora was always too tightly wound and prone to wage battle; Oscar took a more passive-aggressive approach to things, telling people what they wanted to hear and then going off and doing whatever he pleased—would ultimately prove valuable.

Of course he thought Oscar was gorgeous. That would go without saying—who *didn't* find Oscar Douglas Davison gorgeous? Chestnut-colored skin. Eyes a shade darker. A body that looked like a feat of modern engineering, broad in the shoulders, narrow at the waist, dense in the legs—he had captained the cross-country team at Wesleyan, and had never stopped running, six miles each morning. He was easy with his smile, quick with a sarcastic joke. His laughter had a kind of heat to it, warming you when you were melancholy, inspiring filthy thoughts if you had consumed even one glass of wine. And he was *smart*, that was what excited Patrick the most, he had studied every book of political theory ever written, and always he was reading, newspapers or magazines or blog posts, and he had an opinion on everything he read, usually nuanced and impossibly articulate. Sometimes Patrick would sneak glances in the younger man's direction, following Oscar's eyes as they skittered across the screen of his laptop. How could he *not* be turned on by the fact that Oscar was always so absorbed in whatever he was reading that he never even noticed Patrick staring at him?

Nora called him out on his crush, a few days before Christmas. "I feel like your energies could be better spent elsewhere instead of drooling over him." He brushed her off while privately fuming at the censure. He had already pledged to Nora that he would remain celibate for the duration of the campaign, lest he give the press the opportunity to portray him as some kind of promiscuous gay cliché. In which case, there seemed to him vastly unhealthier ways to express his pent-up sexual frustrations than fantasizing about and occasionally flirting with Oscar. Besides, he could fantasize and flirt until he was blue in the face and bluer in the balls. Oscar was straight, and—as Marco Baffi had once taught Patrick, forcefully enough so the lesson had never needed to be repeated—no good ever came of a gay man hitting on a straight one.

He learned he had it all wrong on an icy morning in early January, when Nora was in northern California trying to line up a new set of campaign benefactors. Oscar had recently returned from a Christmas visit to Milwaukee. Patrick was bored and just making polite conversation. Did Oscar see his old classmates when he returned home? Had the guys on the football team all become used car salesmen? Was the girl he took to the prom now married with three kids?

"I took a boy to the prom," Oscar corrected him, a rapacious glint in his smile.

"Oh… for some reason… I thought…"

"I lied to Nora in my interview and told her I had a girlfriend," Oscar said. "I got the sense that she didn't want you to be seen as some sort of queer ideologue who hires a bunch of gay people for his campaign."

What intrigued Patrick was that Oscar wasn't in the least manner apologetic or embarrassed—the way Patrick himself always was when called out on his own dissembling. What Patrick found plainly fascinating, as Oscar kept talking to him on that long, lazy morning, was how *different* this young man's adolescence had been from his own. He came out his junior year of high school. His parents shed the inevitable tears, but pledged their acceptance and support. There was the occasional bullying and name-calling, but a lot less than you might imagine—perhaps, Oscar speculated, because he was one of the more popular and athletic boys to begin with, but also because he didn't think it was all that cool anymore, even in a poky, middle-American town like Milwaukee, to ostracize classmates because of their sexuality.

"Only twelve years between us, and yet it seems like a lifetime's worth of difference," Patrick said; and Oscar just shrugged and smiled sweetly.

Even still a romance was hardly predestined. The official declaration of Patrick's candidacy was drawing nearer. He was conscious of all the work that would need to be done in the coming months. He didn't have the time for seduction, and neither—he told himself—the interest. Celibacy, he had concluded, wasn't just the right thing for the campaign; it was also the right thing for his soul. These next sixteen months were going to be a reboot of sorts; a once and for all purging of the sexual hang-ups and anxieties that still sometimes plagued him.

But then one day in June, they were all sitting at Patrick's dining room table, trying to compose the speech in which he would announce his candidacy. Patrick suggested starting with an anecdote about the name-calling he had endured in grade school—"The Ballad of Peppermint Patty," he called it—"sentimental and maybe these days overly familiar, but I promise you I can make it effective."

Nora instantly shot down the idea, said that it would be a mistake "to go too gay too soon," a characterization that Patrick declared "puny and insulting," and back and forth they went, the seeds of their future, nonstop bickering being sown right here, and it must have carried on like this for an hour, turning unnecessarily personal at every turn, until finally Oscar—with the stentorian aplomb of a Supreme Court justice announcing his decision after a long deliberation—broke through the clatter and quieted them both.

"Patrick is at his most affecting when he talks about his vulnerabilities, and when he allows others to share in those vulnerabilities. So why would we ever want him to be anything less than his best self?"

Late the same night, Patrick couldn't stop himself from texting: *Thanks for sticking up for me. It's always so nice when someone actually "gets" me.*

Oscar's answer shot right back: *I've had a lot of fun these last few months trying to figure you out. I'd like to figure out more.*

Patrick's answer to that: *Please don't take this the wrong way, but I think you're totally fucking hot.*

"She's become obsessed with this speech beyond all reason," Oscar says, shifting his body further into Patrick's ever-diminishing personal space. "It's becoming her Waterloo."

"This is our very last chance to turn things around," Patrick answers, aware but no longer caring that he is parroting what Nora said last night.

"A speech she still hasn't written! A speech for which she has no new ideas!"

Patrick turns and looks out the window of the pink bus. He swallows what if he let it out would be a thunderously loud burp. Lunch had been at Dixie Chicken, home of the best chicken-fried steak in these parts, or so Mitchell had proclaimed, just before ambushing a half-dozen unwitting A&M students, promising a free lunch in exchange for twenty minutes of their time to hear what the Democratic candidate for United States Senate had to say about entry-level job creation. Except now the chicken-fried steak—the batter translucent with grease, the cream gravy the texture of toothpaste, God how he hates chicken-fried steak, the vilest of this state's endlessly vile culinary traditions—is repeating on him; and of the six students he dined with, three had no plans to vote, and the other three were officers of the Aggie Young Conservatives. That indignity (barely) endured, they are now headed to Waco for a private dinner with big money donors—private dinner and big money in Waco being $75 a plate in the party room of a Hoffbrau Steaks—and then on to Waxahachie and Dallas tomorrow. The promise that he will get to sleep in his own bed in Fort Worth on Tuesday—the night before Oscar is convinced he will be murdered—is perhaps the only thing right now keeping him from sinking into total despondency.

"She believes in me body and soul," he says to Oscar, though he stutters on the word "believes." Truth is he isn't sure how much Nora believes in him anymore. Truth is he isn't really sure about anything. He is struggling with this feeling; this awful, dirty secret that he can't share with anyone. *He doesn't want to do this anymore.* He is tired of the voters he meets, with their blind faith and "traditional values"; tired of listening to himself talk, trying to persuade these unpersuadables. Most of all he is tired of the arguments, between him and Nora, and between him and Oscar, and especially now between Nora and Oscar. The two of them have become so devoted to their competing myths of "Patrick Francis Monaghan" that they have forgotten there is an actual human being whom they are arguing about. He can't see how his relationships with them are supposed to survive four more weeks of this.

"Sometimes people can love you and want you to succeed and still end up leading you astray," Oscar says. "You understand that, don't you?"

"I do."

"I'm not trying to make a power grab here, Patrick. But I'm honestly not sure she's the right person to be leading this campaign anymore."

"I respect your feedback," Patrick says. "But I agree with Nora on this."

A few minutes pass in silence. Patrick hopes that the matter is settled. His nerves are frayed; his energy depleted—he needs his boyfriend to recognize this and give him a little peace and quiet. (Space would be nice, too. *Move the fuck over, Oscar.*)

Oscar has other plans.

"I love you," he whispers, leaning in still closer to Patrick.

"Now isn't the time."

"Do you understand that? I love you."

Patrick slumps down in his seat and squeezes as close as he can to the window—anything to put even a centimeter of physical distance between them. He tries to ignore Oscar's shifting beside him, the elbow that keeps jutting into his stomach. Except this annoying pantomime carries on for a good thirty seconds, until Patrick yet again snaps.

"What the *fuck* are you doing?"

"Patrick, open your eyes and look at me."

Patrick contemplates closing his eyes tighter, realizes that would be childish. He turns and sees Oscar holding in his open palm a small, sprung-open jewelry box. There is a thick band of rose gold tucked into its plush velvet middle.

"I love you, Patrick, and I want to marry you."

Patrick's eyes narrow in confusion; his mouth opens but no words come out. He is aware that Oscar is not just watching his expression, but *memorizing* it, so that it will be part of the story that he can one day tell their grandchildren, *You should have seen the look on his face, your Grandpa Patrick was so shocked, but then he broke into this giant grin and said,* Yes!

Except Patrick does not break into a giant grin; does not instantly accept Oscar's proposal. He can only think to himself: *I need this like I need a fucking hole in my head.*

"Patrick, I want to marry you, and have a family, and build a life with you."

Patrick says only what he has been saying for months now, whenever Oscar insists on discussing their relationship: "I think we're going to have to wait until after the election to talk about this."

THE SEX WAS FRENZIED, BREATHLESS, maniacal, marathon. The sweat poured off their bodies, turning the white sheets of Patrick's bed cloudy gray with moisture. The orgasms built slowly, deep in their guts and their balls, and then reverberated into the farthest reaches of their extremities. The first time Patrick assumed it was because they had both been working around the clock, and it had been months since either of them had gotten laid—all that stored-up energy had turned unstable and combined to create a kind of nuclear fission. But the second and third and fourth and fifth times were exactly the same, he loved the way Oscar kissed him, patient and insistent, like Patrick's mouth was a puzzle that could be solved by considering it from every angle, and Patrick was enraptured by Oscar's form, the V-line of his torso, the bulbous curve of his ass, the erection that gloriously resisted deflation, and Oscar seemed just as inspired by Patrick, just as *bewitched*, so that almost immediately they understood that there was nothing they would be embarrassed to do in each other's presence, nothing they wouldn't try at least once in their relentless pursuit of making the other one come.

So that, after a week, Patrick could smell Oscar on his own skin; could taste the sour mint and heat of his breath in every one of his own breaths.

So that, after a month, when they should have been working on Patrick's stump speeches, they were huddled in a corner of the newly-opened campaign headquarters on Magnolia Avenue, just out of earshot of Nora, daydreaming together about weekend getaways they might take to Houston or New Orleans.

So that, after two months, when Oscar brought up the issue of gay marriage—*Do you ever wonder if you could make a bigger statement by giving your tax dollars to a state that actually allows you to marry, instead of staying in Texas and fighting a possibly unwinnable battle?*—Patrick wasn't entirely weirded out. He knew this wasn't merely theoretical; and that, of course, it was *way* too soon to be having such a discussion.

But he also thought to himself: Well, *maybe*.

"Break it off, or I'm going to have to fire him."

By then it was October 2013, and technically speaking they still hadn't ever gone out on an actual date. Instead Oscar turned up at Patrick's house every night after dark, left each morning before sunrise, always parking a block away just in case Nora—who had recently sold her condo in Dallas and moved to Fort Worth to be closer to headquarters—happened to be driving by. They regularly got into arguments over it: Oscar told Patrick he needed to come clean to Nora; that he couldn't keep asking him—Oscar—to participate in a "half-closeted existence."

As it turned out, and as Patrick probably could have predicted, Nora had known all along.

"How did you find out?"

"I'm not blind," she told him. And then, with a studied calm that revealed nothing of her own feelings about the romance, she pronounced: "I don't like to issue ultimatums Patrick, but for this campaign to succeed, we need people to take your sexuality *for granted*. They have to see it as this no-big-deal part of who you are. But—I'm sorry, Patrick—a twenty-eight-year-old black boyfriend just rubs your sexuality in their faces."

"But I think I might be falling for him," Patrick said.

"You can fall all over him after the campaign is over."

He stewed over it for weeks. He felt all the predictable indignation: how *dare* she force him to ask her *permission* about something as primal as loving someone? He even started to wonder if perhaps she was jealous of him for having found someone while she remained single. The self-described most competitive person Patrick would ever meet, Nora would obviously never be able to bear so stark an imbalance in their best friendship.

Yet Patrick didn't ignore Nora's orders. Quite the opposite, he set about breaking up with Oscar. He began pleading exhaustion when Oscar wanted to come over to his house; and then he declared headquarters "professional space" and labored to avoid situations where it was just the two of them alone in the same room. He told himself that his actions had nothing to do with his complicated history with Nora and his longstanding habit of following her orders to the letter, and everything to do with his own doubts: that as hot as Oscar got him, and as smart as he found him, there nonetheless seemed something *off*, like that picture frame that stubbornly hangs crooked on the wall even though the leveler asserts it should be square. The problem, Patrick was increasingly convinced, was their age difference, those twelve years that might have been a lifetime. Oscar hadn't known the anguish Patrick had known as a closeted teenager; hadn't known, as an adult, the self-consciousness that Patrick still struggled with. Instead he had arrived, with virtually no real effort on his own part, at a place Patrick had been working towards all his life. Maybe Patrick loved Oscar, and maybe that love had the potential to deepen over time. But he nonetheless hated the way Oscar unwittingly made him feel, like a man's birth year is akin to his IQ—a number that says how far he'll be able to go in life before he crashes into the brick wall of circumstance.

He even tried explaining all of this to Oscar, when Oscar finally demanded to know why Patrick was being so cool with him.

Only problem there: Oscar refused to allow Patrick to break up with him.

"Honestly, Patrick, it's like you're trying to act out this heterosexual marriage with her that both of you want but know you can't hAvenue"

"This isn't about Nora."

"Oh, fuck that, this is *all* about Nora. She's made it her life's mission to keep you single. A gay man who doesn't actually have sex with other men—she's taken every lovelorn straight girl's fantasy and made him incarnate."

"That's not fair, Oscar! Apologize right now!"

"No—*you* apologize. We fuck like a house on fire—like *two* houses on fire, like a goddamned forest fire that leaves a thousand acres scorched—and we make each other laugh, and we're invested in each other's success, and you're going to tell me there's something *wrong* with all that?"

"I don't know," Patrick murmured, and truly he didn't.

"How about we fuck one more time, and then you decide?" Oscar said, and there wasn't a note of seductiveness in his voice, it was all scalding hot fury, and he didn't wait for an answer, he just started taking off his clothes, and within seconds they were naked on Patrick's bed, kissing and grabbing, feverish and *sweating*, Jesus could these two sweat, and Patrick was apologizing to Oscar, he didn't want to break up, he didn't know what he had been thinking, he would tell Nora to mind her own business, which of course he didn't actually do, he lied and said it was over between them, and a month later she found out that they were still together, and this time she *did* fire Oscar, but Patrick overruled her and hired him back, and then Nora stopped talking to Oscar and began only communicating with him via email, and Oscar took to ignoring Nora altogether and deleting most of her emails without even reading them, and on and on this went, until finally Patrick couldn't take it any more and brokered with Nora what he hoped would be a peaceable solution.

"We keep our relationship under wraps for the duration of the campaign, you pretend not to see anything, and *everyone stops fighting*. It will be our very own 'Don't Ask, Don't Tell' policy."

That didn't really work either.

From a distance of a hundred yards, Patrick can see there is some sort of going-on here tonight, a long line of cars are all trying to gain entry into the parking lot, which so far as Patrick can discern from his seat on the pink bus is already two lanes deep with idling vehicles. *Fuck.* Two hundred miles, five hours on one-lane highways, and now they are stuck, fifteen minutes and running, an impossibly distant quarter mile from their destination. He so fucking hates his life right now.

"It's a wedding," a member of his security detail, finger in ear, chin pressed to clavicle, calls out from the middle of the bus.

Patrick rises to his feet, leans across the aisle and peers out the window. A flaxen-haired college kid in a white dress shirt and khaki shorts is standing near a wooden lectern, furiously scribbling on squares of blue cardstock paper while also dangling three sets of cars keys from the pinky of his left hand. Patrick sighs and settles back into his seat. He senses this is going to take awhile.

"We're going to circle around and take you through the kitchen entrance," security goon number two says, after another ten minutes have passed.

"Can't we just get off here and walk?"

"The situation is too volatile, Mr. Monaghan."

"What are you talking about? It's a wedding, not a death metal concert."

"Just bear with us a couple of minutes longer."

Patrick knows that you aren't supposed to fight these guys. Nora instructed him on the point early on. You hire a head of security, even though most of the time he will come up with excuses not to actually travel with the campaign and instead subcontract the work to a half dozen beefy, buzz-cut fellows at least twenty pounds above their fighting weight, ex-military most likely, or who knows, maybe ex-World Wrestling Federation, who will walk in front of you, or behind you, or at your sides, or occasionally all around you in what they love to remind you is called "the six-point diamond formation"—but you will put up with it, you will in fact thank them as often as possible, and above all you will *follow their instructions.*

Except Patrick is in no mood to follow orders that he considers patently stupid, not now, not after five hours on a bus with Oscar, who first kept pushing for him to cancel Wednesday's speech, no matter how many times Patrick begged him to give it a rest, and who then went and stuck that ring in Patrick's face—a proposal! of marriage! Patrick has a hard time even acknowledging that's what it was because it seems so plainly lunatic, what on Earth was Oscar thinking, for Christ's sake, were gay men even supposed to exchange engagement rings, wasn't that just some hetero thing?—and of course Oscar wasn't exactly pleased with Patrick's nonplussed reaction, and so he scowled and muttered the word "douchebag" under his breath and went off to sit by himself in the middle of the bus, which is where he is now, sulking.

"This is ridiculous—pull over," Patrick declares, after the bus has circled around the perimeter of the hotel, only to find that the kitchen entrance is presently blocked by a catering truck.

"Just waiting on instructions for a secure parking place, Mr. Monaghan," security goon number three says.

"Open the door," Patrick shouts to the driver, standing up and making his way to the front of the bus.

"Sir, please sit down."

"Open the door right now," Patrick repeats; and his command contains such force that the driver promptly obliges.

"Patrick, wait," Oscar says, hurriedly gathering his iPad and three cell-phones and chasing after him.

But by then Patrick is off the bus, past the bottleneck of idling cars, through the parking lot, into the revolving entrance door of the hotel, and finally inside the lobby; and though Patrick doesn't exactly regret his decision—*anything* to get away from his goof troop of security men, if only for a few seconds—he is definitely taken aback when he suddenly finds himself trapped in place and surrounded by wedding guests, at least two hundred of them, far more men than women, all crushed together in boisterous, backslappy clusters. Never one to feel claustrophobic, Patrick nonetheless finds it unnerving that there are so many people here that he can't identify a clear path to the front desk.

"This time the metaphor is so pregnant she's going to pop," Oscar says, when he finally catches up to him a minute later.

"What's happening?" Patrick says. Plump and pinkish faces are swirling all around him. He is starting to feel flushed and dizzy.

"A gay wedding," Oscar explains. "Though according to the manager, the hotel staff thought it was starting an hour from now, so the ballroom isn't ready. One of the grooms is fuming that they did it on purpose, because they didn't want a gay wedding reception here in the first place."

"A gay wedding," Patrick repeats, not entirely comprehending.

"If you ask me," Oscar says, "they already got their revenge. This lobby looks like a daddy bar on Dollar Jell-O Shots Night."

In the next instant, all four of the security goons from the bus are standing next to them, saying they really need to get Mr. Monaghan to a secure location. They begin clearing a path for Patrick, stiffing up their backs, spreading their arms out wide. Patrick feels Oscar's hand on his shoulder, gently pushing him forward.

Later, at least five eyewitnesses will confirm that Oscar wasn't completely losing his mind, that from the way the man slowly reached his hand into his tuxedo jacket pocket and then swiftly brought it back out, and from the way the light glinted off the sterling silver of the case, it really did look alarming. A couple of these eyewitnesses will add that, the way they saw it, what Oscar did was brave and heroic.

That's the sort of guy, they will say, *I'd want on my campaign team.*

For his own part, Oscar will insist that his actions warranted no apology or defense, it was total fucking chaos down there, and, besides, what was he supposed to think, given the threats they'd been receiving?

Nora will of course fume; grit her teeth; shake her head in disgust.

Patrick will shrug; say nothing; see no possible reward in taking sides.

In the instant, though, there is no time for analysis or a determination of who is right and who is wrong. A mere ten seconds elapse.

Oscar senses movement from behind, a baldheaded man coming towards them at an angle, and he cranes his neck back, because the man is moving too fast and something about him just looks *weird*; and that's when he sees the man reaching into the pocket of his jacket. Oscar registers the potential for violence: this man has placed himself just behind Patrick, inside of a five-foot gap where the candidate goes unblocked by security. Oscar hears a strange sound from across the lobby, a high-pitched shriek—is it laughter, or is it screaming?—and he turns in that direction but sees nothing. He looks back to the baldheaded man, even closer now, and just then he sees the gun, shining and cylindrical and mere inches from Patrick's ear.

Oscar yells, "Get down," and with both hands he shoves Patrick forward; and then he spins on his heels and throws his body at the baldheaded man, and the two of them collapse in a pile to the floor. He hears the gun unloose from the man's hand and clink against the tiled floor. He braces himself for the inevitable discharge.

"Get the gun, get the gun," Oscar shouts.

And then the room goes quiet, and Patrick is grabbed from beneath his arms and scurried to the elevator, and though he doesn't quite understand what's just happened, he's starting to piece it together, and the very first coherent thought that pops into his head is, *Oscar just proved himself willing to take a bullet for me*, though that thought is followed just as quickly by a countervailing one, *What the fuck am I supposed to think about that? Is this superhero routine of his now supposed to make me want to say yes to his proposal?*, and the very last thing that Patrick hears, just before the elevator doors close, is a high, out-of-breath voice that breaks through the stunned silence, rising up in self-defense and also accusation.

"It's a pen," the tuxedoed man buried beneath Oscar's body cries. "I just wanted an autograph. Please don't arrest me."

TWO DAYS BEFORE

Breakfast in his hotel room the next morning, his silk-draped, textured-wallpapered, taupe-carpeted prison—a Hilton in Waco, a Sheraton in Sweetwater, an Intercontinental in Austin, he can no longer tell the difference. In another hour they will head to the offices of the *Waco Herald-Tribune*, and then on to Waxahachie and Dallas, but for now it is one more plate of $21 eggs Benedict, one more $12 pot of coffee, one more morning briefing from his campaign manager, who fifteen minutes after turning up at his door still hasn't uttered a word to him. She just keeps staring down at her iPad, running her finger up and down the screen, periodically grimacing and shaking her head.

"*What?*" he asks finally.

"I'm trying to put a positive spin on all of this," Nora says, her voice more rueful than angry. "But I'm not sure it's possible to spin a steaming pile of shit."

"Would it help if I got you a pair of rubber gloves?" He is trying to be a little silly; hoping to make her smile. He has to find a way to defuse the tension of these last few days.

Nora finally looks up from her iPad. She is not smiling.

"Do you realize that right now we are on the path to becoming the *Ishtar* of electoral politics—the flop that becomes its own noun? For decades hence, the phrase "Monaghan 2014" will cause people to snicker."

"Oh, come on, it can't be *that* bad," he says, still trying to be cheerful.

"The *Houston Chronicle* is reporting that you and Oscar were openly arguing all day yesterday," she continues, "and they are quoting an anonymous campaign source saying that there is now dissension among your senior staff. And I'm assuming that anonymous source is Oscar himself, trying to undermine me—"

"—Oscar wouldn't do something like that—" Patrick tries to interject.

"—and on top of that I've just finished reading an interview on the *Dallas Voice* website with the autograph seeker who Oscar decided was your killer last night. Turns out that it was Harland Moore, who owns a huge advertising agency in Dallas, and who—wait for it, Patrick—actually donated ten thousand dollars to your campaign last month. Except now Mr. Moore says that he can no longer support your candidacy, because—let me quote for you here—'Monaghan didn't even have the good manners to reach out to me with an apology.'"

Nora pauses for a few seconds and then asks, "Should I carry on?"

Patrick shakes his head no.

She carries on anyway.

"Let's see, there's also this choice email from a reporter at the *National Enquirer*, who says that he's in possession of—quoting again—'a sexually explicit video where Mr. Monaghan can clearly be seen in the background'—whatever the hell that means—and, yeah, fine, it's just the stupid *National Enquirer*, but ever since the John Edwards scandal, a lot of people start to wonder if their lies might actually be true, and while I'm adding insult to injury, I'll also tell you that the *Texas Tribune* is reporting that Karl Rove's Super PAC is financing a massive ad buy for your opponent."

Patrick's eyes have opened wide; the roof of his mouth has gone dry. Karl Rove and Harland Moore and last-minute ad buys and leaks from within the campaign—already he's forgotten most of what Nora has just said to him.

All but the one phrase: *A sexually explicit video.*

He knows at once to what she is referring. He even remembers the man who had been doing the videotaping, with his pale skin and hard, concave belly; remembers telling himself to steer clear, because even if he was stupid and sex-hungry enough to bring himself to the party, he still had enough of his wits about him to know he didn't want evidence of his attendance caught on camera. Yet somehow he *did* end up on video, and now someone is trying to sell this video to the *Enquirer* for fifty thousand or a hundred thousand or whatever the going rate is these days for the ruin of a man's reputation. His fantasy of getting to quit the campaign will in effect be granted. He will be ridiculed by the newspaper columnists and Sunday morning talk show pundits; demonized by conservatives as a creep and a deviant and *the worst possible example for our children*. This life of which he thought he could finally be proud will instead be reduced to a punch line of late-night talk show hosts' stupid, puerile jokes.

But *how*? If this is his fate, then he demands some kind of explanation. How had he been positively identified, when the image quality of a homemade video from 2003 couldn't be very good? Who has been in possession of the video all this time—and who had watched it and put two and two together, that one of the men onscreen was a younger version of the man presently running for United States Senate?

"Honestly, at this point, it might be better if you did get shot," Nora says. "At least then you'd be put out of your misery."

"What did the email from the *Enquirer* say?" Patrick asks, staring at the congealing lemon-yellow egg on his plate, thinking he might throw up.

"I'm sorry," Nora says, when she sees that Patrick is now red-faced and watery-eyed, as if someone just beaned him in the nuts. "That was a stupid joke to make."

"Did he say he's actually *seen* this video? Or is he just chasing down a rumor about it?"

"I don't know… it's just some stupid… "

And then Nora's voice trails off, because she realizes what Patrick is telling her.

"Can I see the email?"

"Oh, Patrick, please not that… "

"Just let me see it."

"Please don't tell me you have a sex tape. Anything but that."

THE STATE PARTY DIDN'T WANT him; indeed, seemed to hope that the announcement of his candidacy was just some dopey publicity stunt. The chair of the national Democratic Senatorial Campaign Committee sent ALL CAPS emails to Nora and left hectoring voicemails accusing them of being rogues and traitors. There was even a call from the White House, not the President but close enough: *The Republicans are going to win this regardless of who we run—but we can't have someone as far to the left as Patrick dragging down all the other Democrats on the state ballot.*

Nora sloughed off their cynicism, told Patrick they could all go fuck themselves; and for his part Patrick—who had always responded with such energy to the faith Nora placed in him—matched her righteousness and then some. Even on the bad days, even as their bickering became more pronounced, even as his relationship with Oscar emerged as this sore spot between them, he held fast to a core belief: Nora had been right about everything thus far; of course she would be proven right again.

"The base is exasperated—a Democrat hasn't occupied statewide office in two decades—and that's when strange things start to happen," she told him, one night in March 2014, two months before the primary. "We just have to get you into a one-on-one race, and then hope a few things break your way."

The primary battle was bruising and protracted. Six candidates, yet no clear frontrunner. A public pledge from all involved not to make it personal, though phrases like *dilettante* and *tabloid celebrity* kept getting lobbed at him from five different directions. Without conspiring to do so (or at least Nora said she didn't *think* it was a conspiracy), his competitors all settled on a common meme in their campaign literature, which the editorial pages of the newspapers all parroted: that Patrick Monaghan was simply *unelectable* in the general election—*unelectable* being the latest synonym for *gay*.

Again, they had the advantage of money—at least three times as much as the next best-funded competitor, mostly courtesy of a dozen or so out-of-state donors, gay doctors and lawyers and investment bankers and even a recently-out-of-the-closet pop music legend, who hosted black-tie fundraisers on Patrick's behalf and paraded him before their well-heeled friends as if he were some sort of exotic or endangered creature, *Homosexualis Texas Politicus*.

Even still, Patrick only managed to finish a distant second behind Carol LeMarsh, a State Senator from Amarillo and a former high school principal—the moderate white woman the Democratic Senatorial Campaign Committee had thrown its weight behind. Eight million dollars drained from their coffers—it was said to be the most expensive primary campaign in Texas history—not to mention fifty-one consecutive days on the campaign trail pressing the flesh, posing for innumerable cell-phone pictures, and smiling wide as blue-haired matrons told him that they would never approve of his "lifestyle," but might consider supporting him if he pledged to vote to repeal Obamacare—all for the ignoble status of also-ran.

Except it wasn't yet over. If Patrick sank into despair that night in mid-May, beating himself up over his perceived failings, thinking of all he might have done differently, Nora held tight, waiting for the final numbers. The rules stated that if no candidate received more than thirty-three percent of the vote, there would be a runoff between the top two finishers. A little after midnight, they learned that Carol LeMarsh had fallen short with thirty-one percent, compared to Patrick's nineteen—not the greatest result in Nora's political consulting career, but still something to work with. She insisted to Patrick that this grandmotherly and hopelessly vanilla woman was far more vulnerable than anyone realized; that—because ever since the near flame-out and resurrection of Bill Clinton in 1992 the narrative of "The Comeback Kid" had become the most popular narrative in all of American politics—their second place finish was actually *preferable* to their competitor's first-place non-victory.

"We got you in a one-on-one race," she told him. "Now let's see if we can engineer a few breaks your way."

Moving quickly, Nora publicly challenged the other side to a series of three debates, knowing that LeMarsh saw herself as the unbeatable front-runner and wouldn't want to debate at all, but hoping to use the pressure of the press to get a counteroffer. The LeMarsh campaign ended up agreeing to a single debate, to be aired live on Texas public television on May 31st. Next she pulled Patrick off the campaign trail, holed him up for nine days in a suite at the Worthington and drilled him for hours at a stretch, on the childhood obesity epidemic and hydraulic fracking; on the rising threat of ISIS and the importance of speeding up the confirmation process for federal judiciary appointments; on every possible legislative issue a United States Senator might reasonably be confronted with and a couple of hundred more. Determined not to go down without swinging, Patrick did exactly what Nora asked of him, he learned his lines, and then he learned what those lines meant, and he learned to evince passion and conviction even for subjects for which he had no natural affinity or interest. He understood without her having to explain it the central tenet of all political performance—that always you must fake it until you make it.

His moment arrived. Standing backstage at McFarlane Auditorium on the SMU campus in his twenty-six-hundred-dollar Tom Ford suit and seven-hundred-dollar Gucci lace-ups, Patrick looked virile, commanding—and certainly a hell of a lot younger than his sixty-two-year-old opponent wearing off-the-rack Macy's. "Slicker than grease," Nora said, as she personally applied one last brush of powder to his forehead, just before he stepped onto the stage. Yet when Patrick opened his mouth, he wasn't slick, he was all substance, insistent but never bullying, grandiose but not pretentious, he talked rings around Carol LeMarsh, he called her out on contradictory statements on abortion rights and food stamps programs that she had made over the years, he asked her to explain her positions on subjects about which she obviously hadn't been briefed, and Carol seemed altogether blindsided. In ninety gloriously one-sided minutes, Patrick made *her* look like the attention-seeking dilettante—the unelectable one.

The momentum shifted, if not cataclysmically, still enough. The newspaper editorialists speculated that perhaps they had underestimated Patrick; that maybe this runoff would be closer than originally predicted. A fresh wave of donations poured in via the campaign's website, this time from the previously untapped category of middle- and working-class Democrats offering up $50 or $100 a piece. With just twelve days remaining until the runoff, Nora hastily commissioned a pair of attack ads that devastatingly strung together LeMarsh's worst moments from the debate, and then she spent literally every last cent in the campaign's bank account, another four million in all, blanketing each of the state's twenty media markets.

"I think you're going to pull this out," Nora told him, on the morning of the runoff; and though she didn't sound especially jubilant—she wasn't one to count her chickens before they'd hatched and the hatchlings had been court-certified—Patrick had never seen her happier.

"I feel like I owe you a debt I'll never be able to repay," she added. "You've been my living experiment. You've allowed me put all of my theories into practice."

The feeling was mutual. Patrick couldn't help but think what an incredible *privilege* their friendship had turned out to be. Fuck those who didn't get that, or who insisted on trying to fit them into a puny, condescending framework, that she was romantically hung up on him, or that his love for her was a vestige of his self-hatred. The truth was that she understood his personality better than anyone, that for all his mulishness and tendency towards indignation, he was also at heart a people-pleaser, a dogged populist who believed that if people would just listen to what he had to say, *of course* they would be compelled to agree, and he understood like no one else what made *her* tick, that she didn't give two shits about what people whispered about her, didn't care if after this campaign was over she ended up blacklisted from politics and had to go to work at Starbucks, so long as she could say she had tried to achieve something that no one else before her had. She was the most ambitious and competitive person he would ever meet, and unlike everyone else they knew—friends and enemies alike—he would never ask her to apologize for that.

Twenty-two votes. Recounted automatically by machine, and then—after LeMarsh challenged the results in court—by hand. They pulled it off against all odds. They pulled it off without the endorsement of any of the state's major dailies. They pulled it off despite the fact that, as effectively as he debated the finer points of eminent domain for gas drilling and public-private financing schemes for the building of new sports arenas, Patrick never did put forth a persuasive rejoinder to those who called him unelectable in the general election.

"Did you ever think we would get this far?" he asked her, early on the morning of July 1st, a full two weeks after the runoff, when they finally got the call they had been waiting for from the state certification board.

She answered, "Oh, Patrick, we're going to go so much farther than this."

"THAT'S REALLY WHAT THIS STREET is called—Justice Way?" Patrick asks brightly, as the pink bus makes a sharp right off Story Lane. Nerves are predictably frayed; it's been nothing but silence these last two hours—he's just trying to inject some desperately needed levity into the atmosphere. "Do you think we're going to meet Captain America manning the metal detectors?"

He gets no takers. From opposite seats two rows in front of him, Nora and Oscar turn and stare quizzically in his direction, before turning their attention back to their iPads.

The request for the meeting had come over while they were sitting in the conference room at the *Waco Herald Tribune*, making their case to the bored-seeming members of the paper's editorial board—one of ten such interviews Patrick has scheduled over the next week for endorsements he's probably never going to get. All of Nora's and Oscar's respective gadgets started buzzing at once, but of course the FBI wouldn't tell them anything over the phone; said only that it was best if they could all meet face-to-face. They cut the Waco interview short, cancelled a lunchtime rally scheduled in Waxahachie and headed straight to Dallas. But no one's been talking, the whole two hours here, and Patrick has no idea if he should be annoyed at this wrench thrown into their schedule, or merely terrified that he is about to be told the details of his own impending assassination.

They step off the bus, Nora and Patrick and Oscar. Waiting for them in the parking lot is their head of security John Stone—a good solid name, Patrick has always thought, if you are going to open your own security firm, though of course you took one look at *this* John Stone—with his distended gut and wrinkled shirt and hair as white as untrammeled snow—and suddenly you didn't feel so secure. The four of them proceed into the lobby of the FBI building, where they are met by an agent in his late twenties, one Christian Mangiano—dark-eyed and thick-necked and built like a fucking tank, Patrick is pretty sure he catches Oscar checking him out—who leads them to a conference room, where two others—Special Agents Jeff Coleworth and Emily Baker—sit at a long, glass-topped table. Their expressions are so solemn that Patrick doesn't know if he is supposed to laugh or nod thoughtfully when Special Agent Baker—a round-eyed brunette in her early thirties—instructs them to call her, "Emily, or just M, like in the James Bond movies."

"Most of the threats we get are nonsense," Coleworth begins, when they are all finally seated. He speaks in a monotone drawl, pausing between virtually every word; and of course Patrick is having an impossible time concentrating, not just because Coleworth talks so slowly, but also because he bears an unnerving resemblance to Patrick himself—tall, fortyish, dark hair flecked with silver on the sides, ten extra pounds all discernible around the middle. This whole fucking weird thing just keeps getting weirder.

"Usually it's just somebody who's knocked back a few too many before logging onto Facebook," Coleworth continues. "But about a month ago we started coming across message board comments, with references to a *tornado brewing* that would *restore order to the great state of Texas*. There were also a lot of specific details about your schedule; speculations about when and where you might be most vulnerable to attack."

"So you're saying we should cancel the Fort Worth event?" Oscar interjects, with perhaps a bit too much hopefulness in his voice.

The very next instant, Nora counters: "We are *not* canceling Fort Worth."

Coleworth looks back and forth between them, uncertain whom he is supposed to address, before finally looking to Patrick for guidance. Patrick smiles humorlessly and stares off in a different direction, like a parent incapable of quelling his toddlers' temper tantrums on a transatlantic flight.

"We tried to trace where these messages were coming from," Coleworth picks back up, "and we ran into all sorts of dead ends. Fake email accounts, altered IP addresses. This was obviously someone who knew how to cover his tracks. Or maybe it was more than one person."

"For a little while, we thought it might be a group we've been monitoring up near Wichita Falls," Special Agent Mangiano offers. "One of these neo-Klan organizations that pop up now and again."

Mangiano then stops himself and turns to Oscar and makes a "no offense" gesture with his palms. The scowl that Oscar has worn for the past twenty-four hours since Patrick sidestepped his marriage proposal only darkens.

"And then we got a tip," Coleworth says. "We're still not sure who it was from. Maybe it was your guy just bragging about himself in advance. Sometimes these assassin types like to do that. But the tipster said that Patrick was going to be shot in Fort Worth on Wednesday exactly sixty seconds into his speech. Really specific stuff. That's when we decided to reach out to Oscar over the weekend."

"I don't understand—now you're saying it's definitely just one person?" Nora asks. "Have you found him?"

"We found him, yes!" Coleworth proclaims, and then takes a long, cryptic pause. A good twenty seconds pass before Agent Mangiano mercifully takes over the narrative.

"He got sloppy. We were finally able to trace one of his blog posts to a public library computer in Lubbock. We pulled all the security tapes. A librarian was able to identify him as Oliver Welch, a sixty-four-year-old retired schoolteacher. We checked his name against the recent 4473 filings, and it turns out that he purchased a .40 caliber Glock twenty-two about a month ago at a gun show in Plainview. We think that's the weapon he was planning to use on Wednesday."

Coleworth burps out a chuckle and says to Patrick: "Trust me, that's not a gun you want to get shot with."

Patrick realizes he is expected to laugh along with this, but instead bares his teeth in an open-mouthed grimace and brings his head back, as if Coleworth has just hocked a loogie in his direction.

"Anyway," Mangiano continues, "that was enough to get us a warrant. We went into the house this morning. There were clippings about the campaign everywhere. We even found a map of the Fort Worth Stockyards that seemed to mark out an escape route."

"And what's *really* crazy," M says, her first contribution to the briefing, "is that he's *gay*. Divorced with two kids—came out of the closet at age fifty-eight—"

"—that may also explain why he took early retirement," Mangiano offers. "The kids at the school were apparently very cruel towards him—"

"High school kids can be such little shits," M observes.

And then Mangiano again: "Oh, and get *this*. He's also a registered Democrat—donated five hundred bucks to Obama in each of the last two Presidential campaigns."

There is another long moment of silence, and then all at once they are all talking.

Nora: "Did you *arrest* him? Where is he now?"

Oscar: "Are you *sure* Patrick is safe? Do we still need to cancel Fort Worth?"

And John Stone, who still seems to be a few beats behind the rest of them: "In addition to my team, we're bringing in a dozen off-duty police officers on Wednesday morning for an assist."

All except for Patrick, who slumps down in his chair, his heart pounding wildly in his chest. He feels confused, abandoned, almost *spurned*, as if has been wading through a labyrinthine spy novel, following its every arcane twist and ambiguous motivation, only to arrive at a passage that his brain simply cannot process—and now the whole saga is jelly in his head.

A sixty-four-year-old gay Democrat had been plotting his assassination.

The metaphor is both too pregnant and a hideous miscarriage.

This story that he can no longer follow is the story of his own life.

"He was arrested for intent to commit murder and threats to injure the person of another over the Internet," Coleworth resumes. "The lawyers are figuring out what else we can throw at him. Meantime, we'll do our best to keep it out of the press—Mr. Monaghan's name is redacted from the indictment. The takeaway here, though, is that the threat has been eliminated. Full steam ahead on Fort Worth."

Nora is the first to her feet, reaching across the table to shake the hands of the federal agents—she displays not even a trace of the anger she's carried with her since this morning, after learning of the videotaped sex party Patrick attended a decade ago.

John Stone stands up next, murmuring something about how he is still planning to have a larger-than-normal security presence at Wednesday's event, "just to show these people we're not going to be intimidated," and then Oscar stands up, his lips pressed together in a valiant-but-doomed effort to stave off a disappointed frown.

Only Patrick remains seated, hands gripping the sides of his chair. He fears that if he doesn't hold onto *something*, he might end up slipping into some kind of oblivion.

"This doesn't make any sense," he says. "Why would someone whose equality I'm campaigning for want to kill me?"

But by then it is much too late, too *loud*, everyone is exchanging business cards and clapping one another on the shoulder, bidding farewell and heading towards the door.

Not a single person gathered here has heard him.

"Patrick, are you okay?" Nora asks, and without even waiting for his answer, she's out of the conference room and on to their next stop.

WAS IT A CASE OF that which goes up eventually having to come down, and thus entirely unavoidable? Was it a matter of hard numbers and rudimentary political science—and the fact that, despite a much-ballyhooed influx of left-leaning Latino voters, a Democrat in Texas was only going to be able to get so far in a statewide contest?

Or was it instead as Patrick feared a kind of comeuppance, his just desserts for allowing Nora to sell him on his own hype? Was this karma's way of telling him that he had no business in politics after all?

No one could possibly say. It might have been all of those things or none of them. The only certainty was the unraveling itself, swift and initially imperceptible, like the tickle at the back of your throat that a few days later lands you in the emergency room with a possibly deadly strain of flu.

It started like many political downfalls, with a surfeit of hubris. High off their come-from-behind triumph in the primary, Nora decided on a strategy for the general election based on the strategies she previously employed against William Landry and Carol LeMarsh—a strategy that relied perhaps a bit too much on the ineptitude of the other side. They would challenge their opponent aggressively on social issues, coming out in favor of everything from taxpayer-funded HPV vaccinations for teenage girls to a repeal of Texas' restrictive abortion access laws. They would fashion Patrick as a fearless minority-interests voice willing to speak up for what was right, even if he risked alienating the undecided middle. Their opponent would inevitably do what Republicans of late were always doing in the face of such fearlessness—lash out and say something inappropriate about gays or women or minorities. Once he or she was revealed to be an intransigent ideologue—not merely conservative, but *bigoted* and *retrograde*—Patrick's all-inclusive brand of liberalism would suddenly seem a lot less threatening.

"It worked for the Democrats in Missouri and Indiana in 2012," Nora told Patrick, "and maybe we can make it work again here."

What they never expected was that the Republicans—after an even more protracted primary process than the Democrats that went unresolved until the third week of July—would choose their own renegade candidate. A forty-four-year-old naturalized citizen, born in Mexico City and educated at Yale and Stanford Business School, Andrew Cisneros was the founder and CEO of a hugely successful gas and oil exploration company in Midland—the only political neophyte among the eight men and women competing for the Republican nomination, and the one Nora had long assumed would have no chance. Estimates of his net worth ran as high as $400 million, and he made no apologies for his willingness to spend his own money to get elected—instantly mitigating whatever financial advantage the Monaghan campaign might have enjoyed. From a purely visual standpoint, the news was even worse. They had been assuming the

Republicans would put forth another of the craggy, aging linebackers or cotton candy-coiffed grande dames they loved so much—for Christ's sake, this was the same party that had launched the likes of Kay Bailey Hutcheson, Rick Perry and George W. Bush into national prominence—someone Patrick could stand next to, just as he had stood next to Carol LeMarsh, and instantly prove himself the obvious choice for anyone who wasn't still living in 1954.

Alas, Andrew Cisneros was only four years older than Patrick, and, frankly, looked four years younger, with a thick head of dark hair, a strong, square chin, and a mischievously angular arch to his right eyebrow. Even Patrick had to admit it: The guy was smoking hot.

From bad to worse to *total fucking disaster*: On August 8th, Andrew Cisneros delivered a speech before the Chamber of Commerce in Abilene, proclaiming himself as nothing less than a champion of gay equality. "Texas must not remain on the wrong side of history," he said. "I will do whatever I can to change our current, exclusionary laws denying gay men and women in our state the right to marry." A week after Cisneros' speech, the *New York Times* published a front-page article on the race, the headline of which sent Patrick's heart sinking—*Conservative Texas Embraces a Pair of Modern Politicians*. The thrust of the story was that regardless of whether Texas elected its first gay candidate to national office or its first Mexican immigrant, history was about to be made. The campaign narrative they had spent years crafting and burnishing was in an instant rendered worthless. Suddenly running a gay Texan for the United States Senate didn't even seem all that original.

Seriously, what good was progress if it progressed so quickly that you couldn't even exploit your own oppression?

The last week of August, they conducted a round of internal polls, and Nora said it was some kind of miracle that they were only down by twelve points. Thank heaven (literally) for small favors, but apparently large swaths of evangelicals were stewing over Cisneros' speech in Abilene and would sit out this election entirely, otherwise the margin would have been even wider.

"We're going to have to try to win this thing on the issues," Nora said, staring forlornly at the spreadsheets of polling data.

"Even though most Texans agree with him on the issues?" Patrick asked.

"I haven't figured that part out yet."

She decided a few days later, against Patrick and Oscar's objections, that their only option was to go negative. She had employed this strategy with some of her former clients at Tom Tharp's firm, with varying degrees of success, and though she said it always left her queasy, she was convinced they had no other choice. She hired four private investigators, three in the United States and one in Mexico. One of them located an old girlfriend who had dated Cisneros at Yale, and who claimed that he paid for an abortion after getting her pregnant—a helpful if hardly devastating ding against a practicing Roman Catholic running on a pro-life platform. While Nora was trying to figure out which news organization she should leak that story to, there also emerged a former domestic employee who claimed that Cisneros had paid her off the books and then fired her after she skipped work to take her chicken pox-stricken child to the doctor. Even better news: this woman was living in the United States illegally. It hardly mattered that the ex-employee's story didn't hold up to scrutiny; that, in fact, she seemed to have missed work at least a dozen times before she was terminated. They could nonetheless portray Cisneros as both a heartless elite making misery of the lives of the underclass *and* an abettor of illegal Mexican immigration.

"This is a man whose past actions do not match his present words; a man who will do anything and step on anyone in pursuit of his own self-interest," Nora had Patrick say, in mid-September, at a speech in El Paso; and though Patrick worried they were in danger of turning themselves into the very bullies they claimed they wanted to neutralize, it was hard to argue with the results. A week of similar speeches and attack ads later, internal polling showed that they had closed the gap to nine points.

The first of two scheduled debates took place on September 30th, in Anderson Hall on the campus of Rice University. Nora's plan for the evening was that they should double down on the attacks; try to further undermine the support of Cisneros' base. She coached Patrick to use a light touch but hit him hard on his employment of illegals; to find "a graceful way" of reminding voters about the abortion he'd paid for "without actually using the word 'abortion.'"

She even instructed him to raise the issue of same-sex marriage and point out that

Cisneros' position was at odds with the Republican party's national platform.

"That's ridiculous," Patrick protested. "I'm not going to attack him for *not* pandering to hate-mongers."

"Think of yourself as the mean girl in high school trying to bring down the popular cheerleader," Nora told him. "You want to float a few rumors out there—that this guy has no ideological integrity; that, who knows, maybe he's secretly more liberal than *you*—and then hope the rumors catch wind."

Patrick's heart simply wasn't in it. He didn't doubt that Nora knew what she was talking about; concurred with her argument that sometimes one was justified in hitting below the belt if that's what it took to defeat an ill-intentioned opponent. ("And never forget," she said, "*all* Republicans are ill-intentioned!")

Yet this approach felt to him banal; the path of the ordinary when they had both always regarded themselves and each other as special. One of the reasons he had quit *Dallas Three Ways*, even after they offered to up his fee to $100,000 per episode, was that it had come to embody the thing he hated most about contemporary America—this frenzy of the punitive, where everyone belittles everyone else's honestly-made mistakes solely to exalt their own middling achievements by comparison. Only now his own campaign wasn't all that much better, tarring someone over actions that were barely problematic to begin with. Patrick was plagued, too, by an encroaching sense of disillusionment about his best friend: Had Nora become her own kind of cliché, one of those would-be revolutionaries who in their twenties rail against the rules, but who in their thirties uphold those same rules as the only way things can possibly be done? Was she now so corrupted by success—not necessarily financial recompense or press attention, none of which especially fazed her, but the *winning*, the trumpet blare of it, the steady and elating validations these last few years that she was *right*—that she had lost sight of her core ideals?

He still thrilled to the idea of this life he had stumbled into. Truth was he had never *really* known what he wanted to be when he grew up—only that he wanted people to pay attention to him, and that he wanted to be able to fight back when he witnessed injustice. That's exactly what he had been able to do in the State Senate, and that's what he was *supposed* to be doing as a candidate for the United States Senate.

But what if the fundamental injustice he faced now was the compromise of his own humanity? Was the voice with which he could commandeer others' attention in effect getting drowned out by the silence he had forced upon Oscar about their relationship? Would victory really be worth it if, in the exchange, he ended up feeling even more inauthentically 'produced' than when he was on the reality television show?

He got through the debate fine. He dutifully lodged all of Nora's requested attacks. At one point, he caught his opponent flat-footed when he raised the question of whether Cisneros had used the excuse of the Great Recession to lay off hundreds of workers that his company could have easily afforded to keep on. But Patrick also knew he sounded perfunctory and unusually tentative, in glaring contrast to Cisneros, who mostly coasted through the proceedings with the unrufflable ease of someone who regards victory as a foregone conclusion.

The first poll following the debate, published by the *Dallas Morning News*, had Patrick a full sixteen points behind Cisneros—whatever ground had been gained over the last month was gone and then some. The political blogs that Oscar and Nora constantly checked, with their red- and blue- and grey-shaded maps, all changed Texas from dark pink, meaning a likely Cisneros victory, to solid red, meaning Patrick had no fucking chance. That was when Nora declared they needed to change tacks yet again. Patrick would deliver a "Major Speech" in Fort Worth on October 8th—a speech of such moral conviction and literary eloquence that it would find an immediate place in the political history books. She would pull every string she could and call in every outstanding favor and try to get the President to be there with Patrick—so that all the world would see how *serious* he was about winning.

And that was when all the frustration and uncertainty and faithlessness that he thought he had finally surmounted in his life began swimming once again to the forefront of his consciousness, like the sediment that gets shaken up from the bottom of a bottle of salad dressing, and Patrick Francis Monaghan found himself wondering how unforgivable a betrayal it would be—to Nora, to Oscar, to Democrats in Texas and around the country, to the gay men and women who had invested so much hope in his run, mostly to himself—if he pulled out of the race entirely.

SHE IS RAGING AND UNAPPEASABLE, her body is pitched forward at the edge of the chair, her fingernails are pressed into the armrests, so that any instant now he thinks they will tear through the upholstery and unfetter the white acrylic stuffing inside. Ten minutes ago, she turned up at the door of his suite, her iPad held out in front of her and in between her fingers, like a baby's soiled diaper. The reporter from the *National Enquirer* had finally emailed her a link to the rumored video—a three-minute, twenty-second clip that he claimed to have just stumbled upon buried in the bowels of XTube, an online pornographic video sharing site. She watched it and discovered that indeed, *there's Patrick*, visible from 1:55 to 2:12, and again from 2:50 to 3:01, hovering in the background, fully clothed, thank God, but paying rapt attention to the main event, a skinny, likely doped-up boy, no older than nineteen or twenty, performing fellatio on a gray-haired, potbellied man probably three times his age.

"It's not even plausibly deniable," she seethes. "It's so evidently *you*, Patrick. How could you enter into a campaign knowing that something like this was out there?"

"It was eleven years ago," he tries to reason with her. "People didn't think back then about videos ending up on the Internet."

Nora shakes her head at him, slow and baleful—the head shake since time immemorial of those who can't bear to listen to any more of your bullshit.

"Do you ever think about the impact your actions have on other people?" she asks. "Or is that too selfless a concept for you? Do you realize the ammunition you've just handed to opponents of marriage equality? Turns out the guy campaigning for the right to marry another man also likes to attend gay orgies and videotape them. Classy, Patrick—*really fucking classy.*

"I'm sorry, I didn't—"

"Have you considered what this does to *me*?" Nora cuts him off. "Do you think other politicians will be lining up to work with the consultant who tried to run a gay porn star for Senate?"

"I'm not a gay porn star," Patrick answers churlishly, knowing that it sounds ridiculous, but unable to think of anything else in his own defense.

A long silence ensues, three or four minutes as each stares away from the other. Patrick's thoughts, already doleful in recent days, turn still gloomier: He begins to wonder if, more than the end of the campaign, more than an irreparable tear in the fabric of his public identity, the emergence of this video also marks the end of his friendship with Nora. For twenty-two years now, he has cherished her as his greatest champion; the person who saw his potential long before he recognized it himself. But he is coming to realize that he was naïve to think that her devotion was not unconditional. She might have allowed him to become more famous than she would ever be; might have stood by silently as he was showered with praise for ideas that had been hers to start—yet all of this wasn't simply out of generosity or affection. She enabled his rise in part because that's what *she* wanted; because it dovetailed with her own ambitions. And what she will *never* allow is for Patrick to undermine her vision of herself. That is the one thing in this world that Nora Melissa Meacham doesn't forgive.

There is a knock at the door. "I thought your boyfriend needed to know about this so I forwarded him the email," Nora says, rising to answer it; and before Patrick can even take measure of her motivation in bringing Oscar into this—does she think he might be able to devise a strategy for weathering the crisis, or is she trying to destabilize their relationship, by forcing Oscar to breathe in a long, musky whiff of Patrick's dirtiest laundry?—Oscar is striding into the room, his laptop already open.

"This is probably a minority opinion," he says, settling himself onto the couch next to Patrick, "but I don't think it matters that much."

"Oh, God—of course you're going to defend him," Nora sneers.

"People my age won't blink twice over this," Oscar says. "There isn't a college kid in America who hasn't used a cell-phone camera to film himself having sex."

"College kids don't vote. Old people do."

"I say we own it. Emphasize that only consenting adults were involved; that Patrick had no idea the video would ever be made public. We say that there are cynical forces out there trying to use this thing to create a smokescreen, to distract people from the real issues, etcetera, etcetera."

"Are you insane or just—"

"I drafted a statement if you guys want to take a look," Oscar says.

"—or just a complete fucking idiot?"

"Don't talk to me like that," Oscar comes right back at her.

"I'll talk to you however the fuck I please."

And in the next instant they are both shouting.

"You want Patrick to be a different person entirely," Oscar says. "That's your problem. You want him to be the candidate that's in your head, not the person he actually is."

"Please just shut up, Oscar."

"You're only willing to support him and be a friend to him if he's living his life *on your terms*. So long as you're the one calling the shots, and he never makes things too difficult or uncomfortable for you."

"Fuck off, Oscar."

By now Patrick barely even processes what they are saying, can only vaguely follow the rising and falling inflections of their voices. His eyes are closed. He is remembering that night eleven years ago, that strange and sinister party in Plano, those fourteen uncoupled gay men who saw no better way, or perhaps had no better opportunity, to celebrate Christmas Eve. He is thinking of that entire chapter of his life, as harrowing as it was undeniably intoxicating. What he is embarrassed to acknowledge to himself—and would certainly never admit to Nora or Oscar—is that sometimes he feels nostalgia for those ignoble days. He has been faithful to Oscar these sixteen months, has never so much as smiled at a good-looking stranger. But he has never really known if his fidelity is rooted in genuine love for Oscar and a commitment to his own dignity, or if he's only mastered the recovering addict's art of excising all manner of temptation from one's life. Which is to say: He doesn't know if he's a grown-up man, or a scared, self-destructive boy who's learned to put on a good show. He wonders, too, if this is a gay thing or if straight men struggle with these same contradictory impulses—this urge to be both prisoner and warden of one's desires; to be both locked up and set free at the same time.

The argument between Nora and Oscar carries on. Patrick wants to side with Nora, because that's what he has been doing for years. Patrick wants to side with Oscar, out of loyalty to a lover who even though he has every right to do so now refuses to judge him. He wants to fire Nora off the campaign, explain to her that—as thrilling as their collaboration has been—it's time for them to make their way through life separately. He wants to tell Oscar that, as much as he feels pressure to marry him—because if you stand before the whole world and ask for the right to marry, you damn well better be ready to say "I do" if and when the right is finally afforded—he fears their relationship is doomed.

Mostly he wants someone to explain to him why, even after he thought he had things figured out, he still so often feels like he's doing everything wrong.

"Patrick, are you *sleeping?*"

He hears Oscar's voice, interrupting his reverie.

"We're trying to find a way to salvage your reputation, and you're sleeping," Nora says.

"Enough," Patrick announces, opening his eyes and standing up from the couch.

"Enough, *what?*" Oscar asks.

Patrick looks to Oscar, and then Nora, and back to Oscar, and then down at his shoes. He says nothing. He shakes his head. He doesn't know.

He is sick to death of never knowing.

THE DAY BEFORE

PATRICK WAKES EARLY AND FIRES off text messages to Nora and Oscar: He is not to be disturbed under any circumstance. He sits at the desk in his hotel suite and opens his laptop. Over the course of thirteen hours, he writes two speeches. The first is familiar, but uncowed and optimistic: He makes a pledge to go positive in these final weeks of the campaign and challenges his opponent to do the same. He proposes sweeping legislation that would hold teachers and principals nationwide professionally culpable for violent bullying that takes place in their schools. He ends with a mantra that he hopes might get picked up as a kind of catchphrase: *This election is closer than you think, it's closer than you think, it's closer than you think…* It takes him only about two hours to write and edit and email this speech to Oscar and Nora.

The second speech takes much longer. He procrastinates; paces at least a hundred times the perimeter of his suite. Each sentence is an anguish that demands a little piece of his soul when it's finally set down on the page. He doesn't finish writing this speech until nightfall, at which point he checks out of the Adolphus and climbs onto the pink bus to make the forty-minute trip to Fort Worth. He does not share this second speech with anyone. He will not know, until the moment he steps before the lectern in front of the Fort Worth Stockyards Museum on Wednesday morning, which speech he is going to deliver.

My fellow Texans, I stand before you today, three weeks and six days before you will go to the polls to choose the next United States Senator from the great state of Texas. My message to you today will surprise most of you. I can only try to explain, and to offer up a bit of context to what has been the most difficult decision of my life.

How do we live?

How do we know when we've found enduring friendship, or true love, or when we're doing the work that we were placed on this Earth to do?

We're told to trust our gut in these matters—but what if our gut has let us down one time too many, and we're no longer feeling so trusting?

These are the questions I've struggled with since childhood. I suppose they're questions everyone struggles with—yet some are more fortunate than others. Some people had parents who did it just right, whose lives provided a blueprint for making all of the right decisions. Some people have a profound belief system and take solace that God will make the proper path apparent to them.

I've never considered myself one of the lucky ones. My parents did their best, but how could they be expected to provide a blueprint for a boy who was so unlike them, and whose secret of being gay would be such an inevitable disappointment to them? My faith in a higher power, meanwhile, has never been very strong. I can't reconcile what seems to me a very obvious contradiction: that the churches and religious sects that foment shame and make gay people feel as if they are outcasts do so in the name of the same God who is supposed to have created me.

So I've puzzled through. I've tried to make peace with this sense of dislocation that gay adults often struggle with—this feeling that our places in the world have been permanently undermined because we grew up internalizing others' beliefs that we are lesser. Yet there is nonetheless something about rejection that is like grief. It burrows deep inside of you and forms itself to match your DNA. So that you feel as if you are the only one who has ever felt these feelings. So that you think that no one can possibly understand what you are suffering through.

I want to share with you a brief history lesson. I know none of you came here to be lectured to. But only by looking at the past can I hope to make sense of my decision for you *today.*

In 1983, Gerry Studds, a Democrat from Massachusetts, became the first openly gay man in the United States House of Representatives, though hardly by choice. He was forced out of the closet when news surfaced of his affair a decade earlier with a seventeen-year-old male Congressional page. Mr. Studds, who died in 2006, insisted that the relationship was a quote-unquote "private matter."

Four years later, it was Barney Frank's turn. He did come out by choice, in an interview with the Boston Globe. "I don't think my sex life is relevant to my job," he said, "but on the other hand I don't want to leave the impression that I'm embarrassed about my life."

Two steps forward, one step back. We've heard those phrases repeatedly over the past three decades, as recently as 2013 from Jodie Foster, and from Anderson Cooper the year before that. *It's a private matter. One's sex life simply isn't relevant to a person's work.*

As if.

As if one's sexuality can possibly be separated from who one is, what one believes, how one looks upon the world.

As if straight people somehow do the same. As if they don't stand before an altar and declare their private love public when they marry.

As if it's okay to be a gay person, and even remain in Congress, so long as you first apologize, and assure the world that you'll keep your dirty business out of sight.

I don't blame Gerry Studds or Barney Frank. I don't blame Steve Gunderson of Wisconsin, who was outed on the House floor in 1994 by a fellow Republican, and who later issued a statement saying, "It's one of those things that isn't dignified with an answer." I don't blame Jim Kolbe of Arizona, who in 1996 was outed by activists enraged by his votes against gay and lesbian issues, and who in response tried to argue, "That I am a gay person has never affected the way that I legislate."

These men were puzzling through. Their willingness to try to bring into union their public and private selves—even as all eyes were watching; even as many others wanted to see their careers destroyed—has made it possible for the likes of Tammy Baldwin of Wisconsin and Jared Polis of Colorado to win places in Congress, and for me to stand before you today as the Democratic nominee from Texas for the United States Senate.

Yet one thing has not changed. Gays and lesbians are still being asked to apologize for who we are. We are still expected to promise that we aren't trying to promote some sort of pernicious "homosexual agenda." We are still expected to assure parents that we are not here to turn their boy scouts into sissies or their tomboy daughters into bull dykes. We are still encouraged to keep lovers and even spouses from public view; to deny our most commonplace predilections—even something as inconsequential as a fondness for Broadway musicals—lest others regard us as "too gay." We have never not been asked to apologize.

Today I am announcing that I am ending my campaign for the United States Senate. There have been many times in political history when the underdog believes that a more powerful statement can be made by bowing out of the race entirely. When you feel as if a system is rigged, I believe there is integrity in saying, "I won't play a game according to rules that are fundamentally unjust." I'm certainly not calling into question the possibility of a fair election. But I am calling into question an entire culture that makes it impossible for people like me to succeed without also having to deny on some level who we are.

In the coming days, some lousy stuff is going to come out about me. What makes it particularly lousy—at least for those of you who supported me and believed in our message of defying rejection and cynicism—is that the central allegation being made against me is true. My advisers suggested two equally plausible scenarios for weathering this scandal. I could deny and insist that a smear was being orchestrated by my opponents, or I could cop to the indecency, plead youthful pusillanimity, and hope for forgiveness.

Yet those are not choices. They are compromises dictated from on high, from the media and the political pundits, from the Bible thumpers and reality TV competition hosts—all of these people whose job it is to ridicule the rest of us for our missteps. So I'm choosing, instead, a third option. I'm not denying, and I'm not apologizing. I'm asserting my right to have done things that others might find distasteful. I'm standing before you now as a deeply error-prone human being who isn't going to keep pretending that he's got it all figured out.

The simple fact is that I haven't lived a life that lends itself to contemporary politics. Until now I told myself that that's what the system has been missing: People who find their path to greatness by wrestling with their demons. But it's foolish of me to pretend that that's what American voters want. What voters want is a certain unimpeachability in their elected officials—movie stars like Ronald Reagan, good ol' guys like George W. Bush, wealthy and accomplished businessmen like my opponent, Andrew Cisneros—men who are never expected to apologize. Men who represent the myth of what America is supposed to be, and not the muddy reality in which most of us struggle to find our footing.

To the countless volunteers and donors, to the people who poured so much of their hope and energy into this campaign, I extend my deepest thanks and sincerest wishes that it might have turned out differently.

But I won't apologize. I will never again apologize for being Patrick Francis Monaghan.

THREE HOURS BEFORE

They begin arriving much earlier than expected, before John Stone's team has even cleared and secured the area. This many people, still three hours before the rally's scheduled start time, is surely some sort of encouraging sign.

Perhaps the Monaghan 2014 campaign isn't down for the count quite yet.

They have already settled into the just-set-out chairs—close to the front; better to see and hear everything—when they are rounded up and shooed away, told that they must wait in a line on East Exchange Avenue until security has established a proper entry checkpoint. They will eventually have to pass through a metal detector and be wanded and patted down—all for the privilege of getting back to the very seats they occupied hours earlier. Yet none of them complain. For this chance to be witnesses to a moment that will go down in history, they will do whatever is asked of them.

There are five of them to start, from near and in some cases very far. They are all strangers to each other and to the adult Patrick, though in a few cases not for much longer.

There is the girl nervously bouncing on the balls of her feet, long hair hanging into her face so that it's impossible to get a good look at her. The security guards are willing to take her word that she is here with her parents' and teachers' permission. They are less persuaded by her explanation for the screwdriver buried at the bottom of her backpack, which she says she uses to open her locker that's always sticking at school. They tell her they are going to have to confiscate it, or she will not be allowed entry to the speech.

There is the man who is in his early twenties, pallid and freckled, his teeth all crooked, his eyes kind of ferrety. He's obviously hopped-up on something, coke or meth or who knows what; and almost immediately he starts to make a nuisance of himself, entering the now-secured grounds and then leaving, entering and leaving again. The guards have got enough to worry about without this dirtbag causing them trouble—next time he comes back, they tell one another, they are going to deny him re-entry.

There is the man who will turn the heads of the two female security guards, though for reasons hardly suspicious in nature. Blue-eyed. Red-bearded. Muscles on top of muscles. No wedding band on his finger, and, Jesus, who wouldn't mind waking up next to *that* each morning? This man has never trusted politicians; regards them all as crooks and liars; blames them—in fact—for the deaths of at least a dozen men he considered brothers. But having recently finished his third tour in Afghanistan and having begrudgingly accepted a medical discharge from the United States Marines, under Section 6203.3, this man now finds himself with perhaps too much time on his hands. He has been thinking that something really needs to be done to drastically change the direction of the country.

There is the woman who is here from New Jersey, the one so high-strung and self-conscious. She has already tried writing letters to his campaign headquarters; sent emails via the "Contact Us" link on his website—and thus far she's received not even a token acknowledgement in response. Lately she's barely been sleeping. She'd be the first person to admit to you that she's looking like a bit of a mess. But trust her on this, she's not crazy, she's not some sort of pathetic, pining groupie; and sure it's a long shot, but she can't not try, she just needs to get close enough to him and then hope the rest works itself out. She just needs a minute of his time.

And there is the man who is here from Connecticut—bald-pated; heavy-lidded; a body made of Dr. Pepper and donuts—who has travelled here by Greyhound bus. Despite the long journey, this man feels focused and energetic as he slips off the security line and along East Exchange to the opposite edge of the museum's perimeter.

This man is thinking about all the explanations they will put forth that will be wrong: that he is a paranoid; a homophobe; a disenfranchised wingnut boiling over with rage. The truth is that he's never been this quietly, calmly logical about *anything*. This man is thinking about all they will never know: that in the previous six months he identified four other political rallies around the country as sites for his possible mayhem; that just before getting on the bus, he read and reread what Jared Loughner posted on MySpace on the morning of *his* shooting.

"The literacy rate is below 5%," Loughner wrote. "I haven't talked to one person who is literate. I want to make it out alive. The longest war in the history of the United States. Goodbye. I'm saddened with the current currency and job employment. I had a bully at school."

Pure fucking genius. This man wishes that he could come up with something similar, something that at once grieves for and mocks our collective hopeless cause.

All of these people have gathered here. Five at first, and then dozens, and then hundreds more. All of them waiting and hoping and anticipating a speech from Patrick Francis Monaghan that will change everything.

TWO HOURS BEFORE

Something is wrong, every inch of him aches, his lower back is a knot, his mouth is paper dry. He turns his head to the side, finds that his neck won't rotate to the full forty-five degrees, turns his head back and hears a worrisome pop. He fears he might have come down with some kind of flu.

Fuck. This is so *not* how he wants to start this day—this day he thinks might be his very last as a candidate for United States Senate.

After fifteen minutes on his back, staring at the hairline cracks in the ceiling, he finally manages to plant his feet onto the floor. He lumbers through the underfurnished, dusty rooms of his house. (And, yes, five years later and he's *still* renting this dilapidated monstrosity, but of course he's always too busy to go house hunting, and Nora insists it doesn't matter, voters don't care where you live, *stop being such a baby, Patrick, the house is just fine.*) He hears his cell-phone ringing, though from where within the house he can't quite determine. Figuring that it's Oscar, he decides to let it go to voicemail.

They got into another fight last night, Oscar called just as Patrick was walking through the door, wanting to come over with a bottle of wine. "It's been so long since it's been just the two of us," he said; and of course Patrick's admittedly brusque answer—"It's been even longer since it's been just me"—didn't go over so well. There followed twenty minutes of tense silences alternating with bitter, name-calling outbursts.

"I know you feel overwhelmed right now, and you think there's no room in your brain to consider the future of *us*," Oscar finally told him. "But now is *exactly* the right time. Think of the message you'd be sending: that as much as this campaign is about fighting to improve voters' lives, you're also running for *your* life—for your freedoms and your God-given right to love and be loved. Can you not recognize how *powerful* that message would be?"

All Patrick could think to do was sigh and quietly tell Oscar: "I'm hanging up now. We'll talk about this later."

Presently his cell-phone rings again. He remembers that he left the phone on the desk in the spare bedroom he uses as his home office, but by the time he gets there, he has missed the call. When he looks at the screen, he does not recognize the number.

Patrick stares through the window over his desk and looks onto the back yard. A nearly century-old pecan tree stands at the northeast edge of the property. Planted by the original owner, and now soaring at least seventy feet into the sky, it has long been the one thing about the house that he loves—this tree whose crooked, gray-barked limbs stretch in every direction and whose dark brown-shelled nuts always fall to the ground with such unadorned purpose each October and November. This living thing that without doubt lives and carries forth and *belongs*.

He closes his eyes and begins nodding his head. He is sure of it now. It is not the flu he is suffering from—it is the fundamental fallacy of his candidacy. If he doesn't bow out of the race today, this illness will spread and worsen, like a cancer, into his lungs, so that he won't be able to breathe, and into his brain, so that he won't be able to think.

By Election Day it will drive him mad.

Just then his cell-phone rings again. This time he sees that it's Nora.

"The driver is outside your house," she says, before he can even say hello. "He's been calling you for the last fifteen minutes."

"What time is it?" Patrick asks.

"Don't tell me you overslept," Nora says, and again she's about to lose her temper. "Come on, Patrick, please stop fucking everything up."

"You're looking a little yellow this morning. Were you out partying last night?"

He is seated on the edge of a hotel bed, itchy in his new Paul Smith suit, eyes closed, lips pressed together in a pucker. He would like to offer up some sort of retort to Jenny—the "licensed cosmetologist" the campaign pays $200 an hour on days when Patrick is expected to appear in front of television cameras—and explain to her that in fact he *is* feeling a little feverish, and quite frankly any second now he's probably going to have to bolt to the toilet to take a massive, liquidy shit. But Jenny is presently pressing a synthetic pie-shaped sponge, slathered in cool, taupe-colored foundation, over his mouth and along the sides of his nose.

"Are you excited for Election Day?" she continues. "I know everyone says you're a long shot. But you've definitely got my vote, and I finally got my boyfriend to register, so he's going to vote for you, too. It doesn't matter to us who a politician sleeps with, so long as he does the job he says he's going to do."

And as she tells Patrick all of this, she circles a bristly brush doused in beige-colored powder around his lips and cheeks and forehead; and Patrick makes the mistake of opening his mouth—he has been conditioned like Pavlov's dog to say "Thank you" whenever someone says they plan to vote for him—and flecks of the dust instantly coat his tongue. The gurgle that has emanated from his belly for the past hour only worsens.

Ten minutes later, Jenny is futzing with his eyelashes when the door of the suite opens, and Nora bursts through, followed right behind by Oscar. They are disconcertingly matched in gray power suits and pale pink shirts and self-satisfied expressions.

"This is brilliant," Nora says to Patrick, holding out to him a thin stack of paper. "Oscar wrote it. He was right, and I was wrong. It kills me to admit that, but it's true."

"I would never have been able to get it right if I didn't have you to spar with," Oscar says to Nora, his tone—or is Patrick hearing things?—a little flirty.

"No offense against what you sent us yesterday."

"That was good, but this—"

"—*this* is what a major speech is supposed to read like. I know Oscar's been telling us this for the last year, but until I saw the words on the page, I didn't get it."

"You hear that, Patrick?" Oscar says. "She's giving us permission to come out of the closet."

For a few moments, Patrick is genuinely heartened: He hasn't seen Nora or Oscar this energized in who knows how long; has never once witnessed such harmony between them. With Jenny hovering next to him, waiting for this interruption to end so that she can tweeze the last few stray hairs between his eyebrows, and with a dozen or more of their staffers and security guards gathered already at the Stockyards Museum, he is touched by the idea that he is surrounded by a *team*—a cheerleading squad of sorts that has refused to give up on him. He even starts to wonder if he might be able to use the faith these people have placed in him as fuel, so that he will have the strength to eradicate all of his doubts and go out there today, deliver this purportedly brilliant speech that Oscar has written for him and carry forth with the campaign.

Maybe he has been too hasty in deciding to drop out of the race. Maybe he might yet turn out to be the ultimate Comeback Kid.

But gradually the awareness settles upon him, and he realizes what is likely written on these pages. Oscar, no doubt well intentioned, but nonetheless a bit deviously, has composed a speech that reveals their romance to the world. Patrick's stomach clenches at the thought of it, and in the next instant his bowels loosen. He rises from the bed and points to the bathroom, taking the stack of paper along with him.

He reads through it twice. It is indeed honest and fearless and unusually affecting. It speaks openly of the disagreements among the senior members of the campaign staff, particularly on the issue of "how gay might be 'too gay'?" It talks about how Nora and Oscar struggled to find a way to make Patrick "more palatable" to voters—"as if a human being is akin to a new flavor of Ben and Jerry's, something that can be tweaked and focus-group-tested before being introduced into the marketplace." It builds to a climactic confession, with Patrick telling the world that he has been dating his deputy campaign manager for the past sixteen months. It concludes with these stirring words: "The battle for human equality commenced by our founding fathers and carried forth by the likes of Abraham Lincoln, Susan B. Anthony, Dr. Martin Luther King, Jr., and Harvey Milk is the essential American battle. But as long as any of us feel compelled to hide parts of our lives in the closet for fear of others' reprisal then the battle is far from over."

Patrick rises from the commode, washes his hands. He looks into the mirror, blinks furiously in hopes of stopping the tears that are forming in his eyes. He does not know why he is crying. He presses his hand against the right side of chest, feeling for the other speech tucked inside his suit jacket pocket.

"What do you think?" Oscar asks, the instant Patrick emerges from the bathroom.

"It's brilliant, right?" says Nora.

"And I think it puts us in a good position," Oscar adds, "for when that business with the *National Enquirer* breaks. It makes it clear that you're not going to allow people to shame you for who you are and for the mistakes you've made in the past."

"Really sharp stuff, Oscar," Nora tells him, and again these two erstwhile enemies exchange tender smiles.

Only Jenny notices that something might be wrong; that Patrick is blinking and turning away from them.

"Are you okay? You look like you're—"

"I'm fine... "

"Wait, are you *crying?*" Nora asks.

"Did the speech actually bring you to tears?" Oscar asks, playfully ironic, but of course probably secretly hopeful that Patrick will say that it did.

"No... no... it's the makeup. It must have gotten in my eyes."

Jenny's sympathy is instantly gone. "I do *not* get makeup in my client's eyes."

"No... no... I'll be fine..." Patrick stammers.

"You have twenty minutes to make changes before we have to load it onto the Teleprompter," Nora says.

"No... it reads great."

"Are you *sure* you're okay?" Oscar asks. "You're looking a little yellow this morning."

"That's what *I* told him," Jenny adds, on top of him now, dabbing at the bridge of his nose with a tissue, trying to make sure that the makeup doesn't run.

THE JOURNEY FROM THE HOTEL to the Fort Worth Stockyards Museum is approximately two hundred yards of sidewalk, a leisurely two-minute stroll, past Fincher's White Front Western Store, where a brown mannequin horse looks down onto the street below from its perch on the building's second-floor balcony; past Cowtown Coliseum, where a rodeo is scheduled for seven this evening; past a large placard advertising "The World's Largest Honky Tonk," where Pat Green will be performing on Friday night. John Stone would prefer Patrick make this trip by car—still unnerved by Monday's meeting with the FBI, he says there's no compelling reason to have the candidate exposed like this in broad daylight. But Patrick decries this plan as preposterous—he's not about to act like visiting royalty in his adopted hometown. They finally strike a compromise. Patrick will be surrounded by six of John Stone's men, in six-point diamond formation, who in turn will be escorted by a pair of Fort Worth police officers. The result is this veritable *phalanx* that takes up the whole of the sidewalk, at the center of which are Patrick and Nora and Oscar and Alison Bennett, the campaign staffer in charge of coordinating today's event. Alison is the one presently briefing him, though between her rapid-fire delivery and the fact that the tallest and thickest of the security goons keeps inadvertently stepping on his heels, Patrick is having a hard time understanding what she's telling him.

"… security checkpoint at the east end of 28th Street… lectern at the top of the museum steps… seating on the pathway that leads to the steps, and then on the east and west sides of the lawn… a green room for you inside the museum… what else, what else, what else?"

Patrick tunes out Alison altogether, cranes his neck to the sky. The sun looks like the stamp of a bingo blotter, bright yellow and wet. It is hot out here, at least ninety degrees, hotter than it has any right to be in October; and of course he is sweating, fuck is he sweating, in mere moments his shirt will be soaked underneath his arms, and the thought of this—the sweat mixing with the white chalk of his stick deodorant, creating a cakey goo in the black hair of his pits—causes his stomach to do a flip. He is about to raise an alarum to Nora, tell her that he needs to get into the air-conditioning immediately. But right then everyone comes to an abrupt halt.

"Hold," the heavyset police officer at the front of entourage commands.

Through the thin spaces between the bodies that catacomb him, Patrick can see across the cobblestoned street, to the tourists milling in front of the shops and restaurants in this heavily trafficked corner of town. He can tell they are staring back at him, wondering no doubt what is going on over there.

What makes that *guy such hot shit that he needs a ten-person escort?*

He smiles as he imagines himself shouting back to them: *Nothing! Nothing makes me special! The attention being paid me is not commensurate with anything I've accomplished in the past, or anything I might accomplish in the future!*

But his amusement over this little fantasy is short-lived. The pause in their procession carries on, for thirty seconds, and then a minute. This is starting to get weird.

"Is there something I'm not being told?" he asks Nora, who looks back at him and says nothing. She doesn't seem to have understood the precise nature of his question. He's not sure he understands precisely what he's asking himself.

And then, without any explanation, they all begin moving again.

Another long, disorienting minute passes. They are taking smaller, slower steps than before. Patrick registers the tension in the bodies of the men hired to protect him, their navy blue blazers stretched tight across their broadened shoulders, their unblinking eyes scanning the horizon.

"We haven't received any other threats, have we?" he asks Nora.

But Nora doesn't respond, doesn't even turn to look at him; and Patrick wonders if he actually asked the question, or only imagined himself doing so.

He must be seeing things. He must be hearing things. This is what happens when your mind reaches overload; when life as you are living it is simply *too much* and the entire system commences a kind of shutdown. In front of him and to the right, past the big, blockish head of one of the Fort Worth police officers, he catches glimpse of a man, bald and chalk-white pasty, in a black T-shirt too tight for his doughy torso. Patrick feels an inexplicable but overwhelming urge to draw closer to this stranger; to look into his dark eyes and take measure of any ill will he might intend. Except he can't. They are moving much faster now. Their pace has nearly doubled.

He hears it, though. He is absolutely certain he hears it. There are so many sounds competing for his attention right now—Alison is rattling off a new set of instructions; others just beyond their rectangle are pointing and spiritedly calling out his name—but this he hears as if it has been spoken into his ear. And though he wants to pretend he didn't hear it—because how could he alone have heard it, while Nora and Oscar and

Alison and John Stone and the security goons all heard nothing?—he *can't* pretend, he knows what he hears, he hears it like a secret whispered inside a cave that echoes and reverberates, louder and louder and louder, until it results in an avalanche.

"Run for your life, Monaghan," he hears. "You better run for your life."

How HE GOT HERE HE'S not quite sure, but Patrick finds himself in a dimly lit room on the basement floor of the Stockyards Museum—a replica of an old Texas schoolroom, with a dusty blackboard and too-small chair-and-table desks bolted to the distressed wooden floor. He is sitting at one of these desks, his butt half-hanging off the seat. In front of him are the two speeches, only one of which he will be able to deliver.

He insists on these few minutes of solitude before every major public appearance: to read through and practice his speech; to pump himself up by imagining himself speaking to the crowd. Except today he is in no mood for pumping himself up. He keeps flipping through Oscar's speech, mentally marking the words he would single out for emphasis. It's unquestionably the best speech Oscar has ever written for him, and Patrick imagines an earlier version of himself delivering it with a mixture of sincerity and fire that would be mesmerizing. But just as he starts to *yearn* for that earlier version of himself, just when he thinks he should just go out there and speak these words that might yet change everything, he looks to the other speech, his valedictory, *his bow out*, and then he curses himself.

How did he get to this point in his life where he barely even knows anymore how to make up his own mind?

There is a knock at the door, a sharp rap against the thick opaque glass that causes Patrick to startle. He looks up at the clock, and sees that he still has fifteen more minutes before he is expected onstage. He climbs out of the desk, annoyed and ready to scold, and just then the door opens, and he sees Oscar. His suit is perfectly pressed; his skin is freshly scrubbed and smooth—even in 90-plus-degree weather, Oscar is always so eminently *presentable*. Patrick feels his resolve against the interruption weakening—and even thinks for a moment that he wouldn't mind a quick make-out session with his beautiful boyfriend—but then quickly catches himself.

"What is it?"

"Patrick, there's someone here I'm hoping you can take a minute to meet?" Oscar says, and before Patrick can protest, Oscar enters the room, trailed by a girl, fourteen or fifteen by Patrick's guess. "Her name is Angela Walsh. She's a sophomore at Paschal. She was the very first person through the security line this morning."

He understands at once that it is some kind of ambush; that Oscar almost certainly has an ulterior motive in bringing her here. But as Angela Walsh steps forward, Patrick's irritation fades—and he instead finds himself a little spooked. She is on the pudgy side, with long brown hair and an excess of flesh in her face that drags her entire expression down. Senseless as it sounds, Patrick is certain that he has seen her before, a long time ago, possibly in his own childhood or adolescence.

"I know you're busy, Mr. Monaghan," she says nervously.

"No… no… it's a pleasure to meet you."

"I just wanted to come here and thank you…" she begins, but she is a shy girl, and cowed in his presence, and her voice trails off.

"Thank me for… ?" Patrick asks.

And then, as sometimes happens with teenagers who haven't yet found their footing but who are intelligent and ambitious and who have the good wits to force themselves into uncomfortable situations, it all comes out of her in a rush.

Now she reminds Patrick of Patrick when he was her age.

"You inspired me, Mr. Monaghan. I wanted to tell you that. You inspired me to come out to my parents and to the people at school. I've known I was gay since I was a little kid. But I didn't know how to tell other people. I guess I didn't feel *safe* telling anyone. But then in the spring I started following your campaign and listening to your speeches and reading about how *you* struggled to come out, and—I don't know—I guess I finally realized there wasn't any reason to be afraid.

"My parents haven't taken it well, so I'm living with my aunt now. And the kids at school have been awful. But I don't regret coming out. You made me realize something, Mr. Monaghan—that those of us who are gay are actually *lucky*. Because we *know* you can't live with secrets, whereas everyone else goes through life thinking that maybe they still can."

Patrick stands there stiffly, not knowing what to say.

"I just wanted to thank you for that," she adds; and then she twists and begins digging into her purse and brings out a cell-phone.

"I just thought that Angela was someone you should meet," Oscar says.

"And maybe... I could bother you for a picture..."

He poses with his arm around her, while Oscar snaps one horizontal shot and one vertical. Angela looks at the results of Oscar's photography and breaks into a girlish giggle.

Still Patrick cannot remember who she reminds him of.

Still he has nothing to say.

Oscar tells her to be in touch, and that when she's ready to apply to college, Mr. Monaghan will be happy to write her a recommendation letter.

Patrick shakes her hand, mumbles something about what an honor it has been to meet her. He watches them make their way to the door, first Angela, and then Oscar, who at the very last instant turns his head back and winks at him. The door clicks shut behind them, and Patrick collapses into the too-small seat of the desk chair and stares down again at the two speeches in front of him. He is due onstage in exactly nine minutes.

THE PHONE RINGS AS HE is being guided through a long corridor to the front doors of the Stockyards Museum, accompanied by Nora beside him and John Stone leading the way. In the distance, he hears the loudspeakered voice of the man who is introducing him, a former Mayor of Dallas. He is thinking about Nora, how he just tried to apologize for letting her down with this stupid sex tape business, and thank her for the sacrifices that she's made over the years on his behalf—though predictably she just shushed him and told him to concentrate on his speech. He is thinking, too, about his encounter with Angela Walsh. He understands now why Oscar brought the girl to him: to illustrate in the flesh that Patrick no longer has any choice in the matter. For *everyone's* sake—for Oscar's, for Patrick's own, for the sake of Angela Walsh and all the gay teenagers of America—their relationship *must* be made public.

He is thinking, albeit too late, of what he should have said to her back in the green room: *You are a member of the generation two behind mine, and one behind Oscar's, and one day soon you will leave us both in your dust.*

The wheel turns slowly, Angela, but gloriously it turns.

Yet through this considerable din—the noise from beyond the doors and Nora in his ear telling him to focus and the conversation with Angela he is carrying on in his head—Patrick somehow hears his phone, and he goes reaching into his suit jacket to see who it might be. The strangest thing about being a public figure is that, as many people as might have your number, only a handful feel as if they have the license to actually call. He tells himself this must be important.

Truth is he is perhaps longing for someone to talk to.

"Patrick, what's wrong?" Nora asks.

He looks at the screen, and recognizes the number, and though he usually sends his mother's calls to voicemail—if she is reaching out to him, he prefers to know exactly why before calling her back and engaging—this time he doesn't hesitate.

"Mom?"

"What are you doing?" Nora exclaims. "Turn off the phone."

"Is everything OK?"

"Tell her you'll call her back," Nora says. They are fifteen feet from the front doors of the Stockyards Museum. Patrick is expected to be standing at the lectern in fewer than sixty seconds.

"Patrick, are you there? I can't hear you."

"I'm here, Mom," he says, and then he holds up his palm to Nora and sharply shakes his head at her. *This will take as long as it needs to take.*

"Where are you? It sounds so noisy."

"Actually, I'm at a rally. I'm about to give a speech." And then he laughs. For the first time in he doesn't know how long, he finds all of this hilarious, Nora's steamroller ambition, Oscar's lovelorn attempts to make Patrick his husband, the hundreds of people on the other side of these doors who have taken time out of their day to hang on his every word—and on top of all that, an ill timed phone call from his mother. *Of course* it's funny, and for once he actually feels relaxed enough to laugh.

"Oh, I'll let you go," Marilyn says, though of course she sounds disappointed that he can't be bothered with her.

But he could be bothered! He *wants* to be bothered! Please, mother, the person who has known me longer than anyone: *Bother away!*

"No, go ahead, what's up?" he says, turning his back to Nora as she slices her hand back and forth across her neck in a *cut it off* gesture.

"Oh, Jesus, this will probably sound so stupid…"

"Tell me."

"All of a sudden, I had this terrible feeling that something was wrong, and I had to call and make sure you were all right. Just hearing myself say it out loud, I realize how stupid it sounds…"

"No, no, Ma,"—he never calls her *Ma*, he forced himself to stop when he was a teenager, because he thought it sounded so ethnic and working-class, these days he usually says the more proper *Mom*—"it means a lot to me to know that you still worry."

"I'll never stop worrying about you, Patrick. I know you hate when I say that, but that's just how I am."

"It's okay, Ma," he answers. "I'm safe now. But thank you for calling."

In the distance, Patrick hears the words booming from the loudspeaker: "And now… ladies and gentlemen… the next United States Senator from Texas…"

"I really have to go now."

"Go, go, I shouldn't have bothered you," she says, but this time she doesn't sound disappointed. Maybe Patrick is imagining things, but it actually sounds to him like she's proud.

"But after this campaign is over, maybe you and I—"

"Yes," his mother answers, a lifetime's worth of both hopefulness and regret in her voice.

"Maybe we can go on a trip together. Maybe you'll let me treat you to that trip to Paris you've always wanted to take."

"Yes. I would like that."

He hears the cheering of the crowd, anticipating his arrival on stage, and so he says goodbye to his mother, but not before saying something he cannot remember ever saying to her before, "I love you, Ma," and then he hangs up the phone, and begins sprinting the final fifteen feet down the corridor. He *runs*, both arms held high over his head. He no longer feels sick as he did earlier this morning. He feels energized and exhilarated and boundless. He thinks he could keep on running, for miles and miles, and years and years, to come.

He knows, in that instant, exactly what he is going to say.

THIRTY SECONDS BEFORE

THIS IS THE STORY EVERYONE knows; the story by which all the other stories are measured; the story of American innocence lost and unregainable.

This is the point on the circle where the story begins and also ends.

On the night of April 14, 1865, just before 8:00 P.M., Abraham Lincoln took his seat in the Presidential Box of Ford's Theatre in Washington D.C. Beside him sat his wife, Mary, and next to her Mayor Henry Rathbone and Rathbone's fiancée, Clara Harris. The play they had gathered to see was *Our American Cousin* by Tom Taylor—a fish-out-of-water comedy about a Vermont country bumpkin who travels to Great Britain to lay claim to his ancestor's estate.

But could a man and a President then so wholly *preoccupied* possibly engage with such distraction? Was Abraham Lincoln's mind on *Our American Cousin*, or on his wife sitting next to him, fretting as she was always so prone to do, this time over what Miss Harris would think of the fact that she clung so anxiously to her husband? Was he brooding about the war that raged on outside the theater, the end now in sight, victory for the North certain—but at what impossible-to-quantify future cost to a still young nation?

At some point before tragedy struck, was there at least a fleeting moment of perspective? Could he take comfort knowing that, as wracked by doubt as he so often felt, his was a life that had been *justified*—his time on this Earth would never not matter?

At approximately 10:15 p.m., deep into the third act of *Our American Cousin*,

John Wilkes Booth burst through the interior door of the Presidential Box and shot Abraham Lincoln at point-blank range in the back of the head using a Philadelphia Derringer pistol. The bullet entered the President's skull and then passed through the left side of his brain before coming to rest just above his right eye. The history books tell us nothing of his last thoughts, and maybe it happened so quickly that there were none: maybe he was laughing uproariously one second, and then it was blackness—and maybe *that* is its own kind of grace.

Maybe that was the one way he could die without regret.

In the immediate aftermath of the shooting, three doctors in the sold-out crowd worked to keep the President breathing, before a group of soldiers carried him to a boarding house across the street. Still more doctors were called, including the Surgeon General of the United States, Joseph Barnes, and he was the one who broke the hard news: There was nothing that could be done. Abraham Lincoln was pronounced dead at 7:twenty-two a.m. the next morning. He was the first sitting President of the United States to be assassinated.

On October 8, 2014, at 11:52 a.m., Patrick Francis Monaghan bounds through the front doors of the Fort Worth Stockyards Museum. He embraces and thanks the ex-Mayor of Dallas who has just introduced him, and then steps to the left side of the lectern and waves both of his hands in the air. He makes an eyeball estimate of the crowd. He thinks there might be as many as four hundred people here—not too shabby at all.

He scans the faces in the audience. Almost instantly he makes eye contact with Angela Walsh, beaming at him from the front row on the left lawn. He looks further down the same row and sees a bald, heavyset man in his late twenties, wearing a black T-shirt too tight for his fleshy torso and military camouflage cargo pants. Patrick knows that he has seen him before, but as with Angela back in the green room, his mind refuses to make the connection.

He turns next to the seats directly in front of him, and he sees a woman in the fourth row, fortyish or maybe older, her makeup applied unevenly, her hair a tangled mess. He wonders if she might be some sort of unhinged loony here to interrupt his speech. He keeps scanning faces and sees a man a few rows further back, seated on the aisle, barrel-chested and red-bearded, with eyes so crystalline blue that they pop from twenty feet away. He just as quickly looks away, for fear that he might induce an inappropriate stirring in his pants—but Patrick is nonetheless heartened. In the frustration and exhaustion of these recent months, at least he hasn't lost his heat-seeking capacity to find a cute guy in the crowd.

The clapping carries on, even as he gestures for the crowd to quiet down. They can see that he's relishing this—no, he's *loving* it, his spirits are soaring, and he's absolutely certain now which of the speeches he will deliver—and so they clap with even greater enthusiasm. He looks to his right, to the far end of the museum's front porch. Nora is standing out of view of the audience, twirling her index finger horizontally in the air. *Enough with the attention whoring,* she is telling him, *get on with the show.*

He thinks how lucky he is to have this person in his life who cares enough to keep his ego in check *and* keep him on schedule. Current rough patch notwithstanding, they are going to be best friends for as long as they are both alive.

He looks to his right, to the other side of the porch, and he sees Oscar, scrunching up his face and then shaking his head. Then he sees Oscar pointing into the crowd and opening his mouth to say something.

But Patrick doesn't think: *What's wrong with Oscar?* He thinks instead that as special as this man is—and as highly unlikely as it is that he's *ever* going to have such seriously *hot* sex with anyone again—Patrick just doesn't feel it in his gut. He is going to have to decline Oscar's proposal.

And as Patrick steps sideways to finally take his place behind the lectern, he sees flashes and colors and swirls of movement, almost as if he is watching a strip of film being run through a projector at three or four times the normal speed, a man he doesn't know or recognize is running across the lawn, coming toward him from the left, and other men in navy blue blazers—men he's pretty sure are on his payroll—are running from the opposite direction, and the people seated in the first few rows are leaping from their chairs, and something metal and shining is in his sightline now, yet he can't quite make out what it is.

It occurs to him that something has gone awry, but he can't imagine what; assumes it will be corrected momentarily. He hears the shouts of people all around him, all exclaiming the same word: *Stop.*

He doesn't understand.

Stop? he thinks to himself. *What are you talking about?*

No, no, no.

I'm only just now getting started.

PART FOUR
THE UNDECIDED

There was Martin Luther King, Jr., in Memphis, on the evening of April 4, 1968. James Earl Ray's bullet did its nasty business quick, striking King in the face and then shattering his jaw and tearing open his jugular—at least we can say the victim didn't linger and suffer. Two months later, on June 5, Robert F. Kennedy took his turn, in the kitchen of the Ambassador Hotel in Los Angeles. Shot by Sirhan Sirhan three times, in the head and chest, Kennedy remained conscious at first—the pronouncement of his death wouldn't come for another twenty-eight hours, after surgery to remove bullet fragments from the brain failed to halt the systematic shutdown of his organs.

There were those who were brought down by their rivals: Huey Long, on September 8, 1935, ambushed by Carl Weiss, the son-in-law of a judge whom the famously finagling Louisiana senator was attempting to gerrymander out of his seat; Harvey Milk, a member of San Francisco's Board of Supervisors, and America's first openly gay elected official, as well as George Moscone, that city's Mayor—both of them murdered by a former city supervisor named Dan White, on November 27, 1978. As recently as July 23, 2003, there was New York City Councilman James Davis, shot and killed by Othneil Askew, a closeted gay cop who tried but failed because of a procedural error to get on the ballot against Davis.

There were the ones that history has mostly forgotten: John Clayton, in January 1889, in Arkansas—he had just been elected to the United States Congress, and to this day the identity of his shooter remains an unsolved mystery; William Goebel, in February 1900, in Kentucky—still the only sitting state governor to be assassinated.

Hear enough of these stories and you think that of course Martin Luther King, Jr. had it right, in the aftermath of the John F. Kennedy assassination, when he said to his wife: "I keep telling you, this is a sick society."

There is not now nor will there ever be a cure for what ails us.

Yet even silenced, the voices of some of these leaders could still be heard—can *still* be heard—calling for justice and equality and *progress*, in opposition to an only slowly yielding America. The fights they died fighting were carried forth by others, brave and indefatigable men and women of all ages and colors and creeds and sexual orientations. These fights carry on *peacefully*, with words and ideas, not bullets and guns—even when others sometimes try to claim that the larger battle has been won and no further fighting is necessary. These fights justify lives already lived, and lives being lived now, and so many lives still to come.

And while "silver linings" would perhaps be the wrong term, not all of these stories end in tragedy—and a few of the wounded do rise again, their legends burnished, their purposes clarified and strengthened. On January 30, 1835, Andrew Jackson beat off with a cane his would-be murderer, Richard Lawrence, whose gun misfired twice at the President—would we expect anything less from that ornery statesman nicknamed "Old Hickory"? On October 14, 1912, Theodore Roosevelt, the manliest of all Presidential men, went ahead with a planned speech in Milwaukee, despite having just been shot in the chest by a saloon owner named John Schrank. On March thirty-one, 1981, Ronald Reagan survived John Hinckley's bullet with a broken rib and nary a hair out of place on his immaculately coiffed head—though three others were seriously wounded in the incident, including his press secretary, James Brady, who would spend the rest of his life in a wheelchair. On January 8, 2011, Congresswoman Gabrielle Giffords was one of nineteen victims of mass shooting perpetrated by Jared Loughner—and though six died that day, and Giffords suffered permanent vision and language loss, she like James Brady would go on to become a vigorous advocate for stricter gun control legislation.

And on October 9, 2014, just after ten in the morning, approximately twenty-two hours after taking a bullet to the stomach in Fort Worth, Patrick Francis Monaghan startled awake in his recovery room, opening his eyes wide and gasping. A national tragedy had been averted, though it would take another five days before anyone could say so for certain.

HE COULDN'T MOVE HIS NECK or his head; didn't know where he was, only that this couldn't possibly be heaven. He sensed that there were others surrounding him, and then he heard voices calling for nurses and doctors. He felt no pain—only a kind of floating imperviousness, almost as if he were submerged just beneath his ears in a bath of warm water. In the next instant there was a man in a white lab coat hovering over him—young and unshaven and quite possibly handsome—shining a dilating penlight into Patrick's eyes, asking him questions that made no sense to him, and to which he responded with a faint, passing gas sort of smile.

"He's going to be fine," he heard someone say, and that was the last of his three-hundred seconds of consciousness.

He woke again four hours later, and now he remembered more, and he understood also that he had been plunged into another crisis. Pain seemed to be coming from the wrong place, not necessarily his stomach (though that hurt, too), but his head and eyes and ears—a clenching tightness just beneath the surface of his face that he could only compare to a hangover. When he tried to inhale to settle himself, he discovered he couldn't expand his lungs. This time he was conscious for only two hundred seconds, though were Patrick to guess he would have thought he had been awake for at least an hour.

What he wouldn't learn until weeks later was that at some point early that afternoon the doctors had discovered that a staph infection, likely some bacterial vestige of the shrapnel from the bullet, was now needling its way through his bloodstream. He was intravenously administered a thousand milligrams of cephaloglycin, but Patrick—who had no drug allergies listed on his chart, because so far as he or anyone else knew, he wasn't allergic to anything—had a quickly life-threatening anaphylactic reaction.

The waiting that everyone thought was finished started all over again. It was decided that Patrick would be placed in a medically induced coma to buy his doctors some time to figure out an alternate means of combating the infection. Nora raised objections, after Googling this course of treatment on her phone: some of these medically induced comas in response to staph carried on for months, and sometimes the patient *never* came out of it. The doctors repeated ad nauseam those words she had come to hate, *We're doing everything we can*. But at least Oscar agreed with her, that in light of their screw-ups, the doctors couldn't entirely be trusted—and so the two of them spent those long, harrowing days following the shooting threatening every hospital employee they spoke to with malpractice suits and attorney general investigations. For her part, Marilyn Monaghan—who never once broke down in public, but who each night in the spare bedroom in Patrick's house called Laura and Tim in New York with the latest updates and then cried herself to sleep—listened to the two of them whispering back and forth at Patrick's bedside, but contributed nothing. When it came to doctors, she was of the belief, you just had to let them do what they said they had to do, and then place your faith in a much higher power.

And as it turned out the doctors were vindicated: They prescribed a new and more powerful cocktail of antibiotics, and the infection began to retreat. They brought him out of the coma on the morning of Tuesday, October 14th, though he slept another eight hours after that. When he finally opened his eyes for good at four that afternoon, he saw Nora sitting in a chair against the wall, scanning her iPhone. Except he perhaps overestimated his strength, because when he tried to lift himself up, a stabbing, off-the-charts pain shot from his belly into his torso and groin.

"Holy fuck, that hurts," he cried out.

"You're awake," Nora cried, jumping out of her chair. "Your mother just went to get a cup of coffee, she'll be back in a second… Oscar went home, but I'll call him right now… Oh, Patrick, you probably don't even understand why you're here… you're not going to believe what happened to you…"

"Shhhh, it's okay," Patrick said.

In fact, save for a few details, he now understood and remembered almost everything. He remembered that scraggly, mullet-headed man racing out in front of him, just as he was about to deliver his speech. He remembered hearing the two bullets being fired, remembered his mind drifting far afield from his body. He remembered, perhaps most vividly, the countless assurances of his safety from John Stone and those dimwits at the FBI in the days prior to the shooting.

Lying in his hospital bed and remembering all of this, Patrick was incredulous, appalled—Jesus Christ, they had almost allowed him to be assassinated. Where the fuck had the six-point-diamond formation been when he needed it?

"Did they at least catch the guy?" he spat out, and glowered at Nora, as if she were somehow to blame for the lousy protection; and later Nora would tell him that this was the moment when she could finally breathe easy. The bullet had made a mess of things, but it was obvious there would be no permanent neurological damage.

Patrick Francis Monaghan would soon be back to his old self, as much of a pain in the ass as ever.

THE AMERICAN PUBLIC WAS SHOCKED, dismayed, for a few days, deeply ashamed of itself. Coming just four years after the near-murder of Gabrielle Giffords, there was widespread hand-wringing that this time we had reached a tipping point: Isn't the ritual attempt to silence a society's most progressive politicians the surest sign of an empire in decline?

Alas, this spirit of reflection did not last long. Once it became clear that Patrick was going to live, the urgency seemed to fade from everyone's voices. When it next emerged that the only reason Patrick's would-be assassin was on the streets in the first place was because of a controversial "scared straight" program, which radically truncated the sentences of first-time felony offenders in the hopes that a brief stint in prison would be enough to compel them to put their lives back in order, the nature of the debate shifted entirely. This wasn't at all like what had happened in Tucson, the argument went, where an unhinged man had too easy access to assault weapons. This was a fluke of the criminal justice system; a dumb idea designed to reduce prison overcrowding that had instead run amok.

Stop saying such cynical shit about the future of our democracy. America is doing *just fine*.

As for the identity or motivations of the shooter, well, it was hard to draw any broader conclusions there, either. The son of an auto mechanic and a beautician, Curtis Huber—the twenty-four-year-old man who managed to fire two bullets from a ten-foot distance before being toppled by two members of Patrick's security detail and a brawny, red-haired ex-Marine who just happened to be sitting in the aisle seat of the sixth row—made it through high school, but only barely, and only because his staunch Baptist grandmother in Alvarado was then raising him. A handful of citations and arrests when he was a teenager, for marijuana possession and underage drinking, hardly augured a life of brutal violence. But ever since he was a child Curtis had suffered from assorted attention deficit and mood disorders—the doctors blamed it on his mother, who admitted to snorting cocaine and smoking weed throughout the pregnancy—and when his grandmother died at age sixty-one in a car wreck outside of Cleburne, Curtis seemed to come unstuck. He took to spending almost every night with Johnny Harrell, a fellow hamburger slinger at Sonic whose father was on Death Row in Huntsville, and together they drank vodka and Red Bulls, and did too much meth, and picked on the poor Vietnamese and Ethiopian immigrants who worked the cash register at the Shell convenience store off Interstate 35. One night at a shitty little bar in Venus, Curtis got into a fight with some guy he knew from high school, over something so stupid that later no one could recall what it was, and Johnny handed his friend a switchblade and said, "You should go take care of that fucker outside." Curtis was so high he barely even remembered stabbing his victim three times in the face and permanently blinding the man's left eye.

Five to fifteen years, though the public defender worked out a deal: If Curtis kept his nose clean, the judge would consider him eligible for the "scared straight" program. His release was approved a mere seven months later, without a single public hearing on the matter; and of course in his haste to thin the ranks at Dalhart, the judge failed to pay much heed to a psychiatric evaluation which warned that Curtis Huber was prone to paranoid thoughts when he failed to take his meds. Curtis had only been out of prison for a month when he turned up at the Fort Worth Stockyards Museum on the morning of Patrick's planned speech. When the federal investigators asked him why, he just shrugged and said, "I got sick of seeing him and his stupid ads on TV."

No grand conspiracy, no secret connections to neo-Nazi organizations, no underlying political motivations (in fact, Curtis told the investigators that he had no idea if Patrick Monaghan was a Republican or a Democrat, or gay or straight). Once the governor asked for and received the resignation of the judge who released him, everyone—the politicians and pundits and public alike—seemed satisfied and content to move on. Stop feeling so sorry for yourselves, gay people. He could have just as easily ended up shooting a straight dude.

The only unresolved question for the investigators: How did Curtis Huber manage to get past the barriers and metal detectors and the sixteen men John Stone had on site that day? Huber told them that he had arrived there with no knowledge of what security would be like, or if he would even be able to get a clear shot at the candidate. He said that he was actually kind of shocked when he saw he could hop an unguarded, chest-level metal barrier on the west side of the enclosed perimeter—unguarded because, at the time, the police officer stationed there was busy shooing away a doughy, bald-headed weirdo who seemed to be trying to jump the barrier himself. Content with this explanation, and presumably hesitant to open up a can of conspiracy theorist worms, the investigators never did bother to figure out who that other man was.

A FEW HAPPY ACCIDENTS; WHAT others but not Patrick—who had always revolted against such sentimental religious hooey—might term examples of "God working in mysterious ways."

The *National Enquirer*'s investigation of Patrick's sordid past landed with a woeful thud, like a would-be Hollywood blockbuster released against too-stiff competition. The report, in fact, went live on the *Enquirer*'s website only eighty minutes before the shooting, but just as it was starting to get passed around via social media—and just as a prominent conservative commentator was considering linking to it as the lead item on his blog—word of the assassination attempt broke, and in an instant the tabloid's work seemed unconscionably cynical: Was this dying man *really* going to be dragged through the mud for the sake of increased Web traffic? The *Enquirer*'s editors gamely tried to keep the controversy alive in the print edition the following Monday. *Texas Shooting Victim Linked to Gay Sex Tape!* The effort refused to take. In a week when "shocking" new photos emerged of Bruce Jenner dressing like a woman and sources close to Jennifer Garner hinted that she and Ben Affleck were headed for a split, enquiring minds just didn't seem to care that the nearly assassinated United States Senatorial candidate from

Texas had once been filmed in attendance at a fourteen-man orgy. The carefully worded non-denial that Oscar had scripted during those long hours in the waiting room (*deeply disrespectful... suspiciously timed...*) never even had to be issued, since not a single mainstream news organization reported on the *Enquirer*'s scoop or followed up with a question about it to the campaign.

Score one for Curtis Huber, who had at least succeeded in helping Patrick out of *that* pickle, by trumping one October surprise with another.

Perhaps even stranger: After two years of squabbling, Nora and Oscar finally found that they could and should be friends. It wasn't anything sudden. There were no formal declarations to let bygones be bygones; certainly no teary-eyed mutual apologies for all the slights and insults each had sent down upon the other. But as they waited with Marilyn Monaghan at Patrick's bedside, they found themselves frequently turning to each other for comfort and counsel. In that second week, when it became clear that Patrick was going to survive, they lingered over lunch in the hospital cafeteria, each telling winding, funny stories the other didn't know about the man they both loved—stories which usually concluded with the shared observation, *God, he can be such a* dick. Without even realizing it, they even started using phrases like *When we launch our next campaign*, almost like a couple on a third date talking about what they might do together on their fourth and fifth dates, taking for granted the likelihood of some sort of future together.

Would the Senate campaign carry on? By October 17th, with Patrick's condition now upgraded from serious to fair, that was what everyone wanted to know.

"We have to, don't you think?" Nora said to Oscar.

"I mean, it's ultimately Patrick's decision, but to me it's not even a debate," Oscar answered.

"Honestly, I'd like to see what kind of impact the shooting has on the polls."

"It's his decision, obviously, but I bet he wants to keep going."

They ran it by him the next afternoon, though the way they presented it was nothing if not leading. "We both think it would be a terrible message to send if you were to back down." Patrick thought about it for a minute, but couldn't see much of a reason to disappoint them; assuming they wouldn't ask him to hit campaign trail in a wheelchair—admittedly, a big assumption with these two—he figured two more weeks of Nora and Oscar's zealotry wouldn't kill him.

Back to work they went. They tried not to be crass about it. Last thing they wanted was for it to seem like they were somehow *exploiting* the assassination attempt. Nonetheless there were opportunities that wouldn't have been there otherwise. Nora, just out of curiosity, put out a few feelers to the Los Angeles talent agencies, and the response was swift and enthusiastic: A group of famous Texans past and present—Sandra Bullock, Marcia Gay Harden, Matthew McConaughey and Sissy Spacek among them—agreed to appear in a campaign ad for Patrick, which Richard Linklater volunteered to direct. (Let the opposition carp that Patrick was only interested in advancing his own celebrity and cavorting with Hollywood liberals. This was simply too good a group of Hollywood liberals to pass up.)

Meanwhile, Oscar released to the press the text of the speech that Patrick was supposed to deliver the day of the shooting, and then he offered up *himself* as an exclusive interview to *The Dallas Morning News*. The published article, which ran on the paper's front page on Tuesday, October 21st, did precisely what Oscar hoped it would do, and added another dimension to the saga, framing the assassination attempt as an almost-tragic love story that would now have a happy ending. ("We're like a gay Nicholas Sparks novel," Oscar bragged to Nora. "People are going to eat this up.")

Together Nora and Oscar then went about negotiating with producers for *The Today Show*, the *CBS Evening News* and *Anderson Cooper 360*, playing one off the other, to see who would win the rights to Patrick's first taped interview upon his release from the hospital.

"We get him on air, and viewers see him as the *ultimate* underdog story—like *Rocky* meets Gaby Giffords—and then I think we win this thing," Nora observed.

"You know, it might be even more powerful if the interview took place in his hospital room," Oscar said. "Think of *those* sympathy points we would win."

"I can't imagine Patrick would go for *that*, can you?"

"It can't hurt to ask…"

(They did ask. Patrick shook his head and frowned at them. They decided not to push it.)

On Sunday, October 26th, ten days before Election Day, with early voting already underway in most counties, the *Houston Chronicle* published the first statewide poll since the assassination attempt, placing Patrick five points behind his opponent. Another poll, conducted by the *Texas Tribune*, had it as a three-point race.

"They are saying that it's something unprecedented in American politics," Oscar reported, sitting beside Patrick's hospital bed that Monday afternoon. "The post-assassination-attempt bump."

"We just need to get you in front of those cameras, and it could tip it in our direction," Nora said, for approximately the fifteenth time in the past few days.

Patrick only smiled and said maybe. Keep Matt and Katie and Anderson on standby, and he'd see if in a few days he felt up to it.

He was more amused than annoyed in those days by Oscar's and Nora's renewed energy and their sudden spirit of cooperation—had he only known that this was what was required to get them to stop fighting, he might have taken a bullet in his stomach much sooner. He of course listened patiently to their regular updates and did his best to pretend that he still wanted to win. But in his head he had decided it no longer mattered. Removed from the day-to-day hustle for votes, and the struggle to hold a crumbling campaign together, he understood now that, win, lose or draw, this too would pass, one way or another. And it would leave behind the same bittersweet residue that he had tasted throughout his childhood and adolescence and adulthood—the taste of a half-charmed, half-damned life.

Plus, what could he possibly achieve as a United States Senator that could compare to what he had achieved already—the singular, enduring triumph of *not dying?*

Instead he found himself much more compelled, during that long convalescence, by the spectacular unreality of what had happened to him, and by his own wounded body. He had been shot and nearly assassinated by a violent, mentally unstable stranger—this had happened to *him*, Patrick Francis Monaghan. It was all so perverse and unfathomable that the only proper response seemed to be to make a joke of it. (*Whew, I really dodged a bullet there...*) If only it didn't hurt so much to laugh. If only it didn't hurt so much to do *everything*. He couldn't sit up in bed without sending waves of pain contracting through his body; couldn't walk ten feet without wholly exhausting himself. Worst of all were the days when he had to shit. Two and a half weeks after the shooting, he was still on a mostly liquid diet, not to mention a bevy of stool softeners, but the strain on his abdominal muscles would be so intense that he'd end up in tears.

Forty years old, he thought, *and I'm only just learning that the one thing a man should never take for granted in this life is the ability to take a dump in peace.*

Yet as much physical pain as there was, it hurt a little less every day; and near the end of his hospital stay, just before visiting hours finished on a Tuesday night, Patrick found himself sitting up in bed, pretending to read a magazine, but really just gazing across the room at Oscar, who was busy tapping out an email on his laptop. Certainly nothing had changed the fact that Patrick still thought he was gorgeous. In fact, it was precisely in these sorts of moments that he found Oscar the most irresistible: bespectacled; brow furrowed; lost to his brainy pursuits.

Nora was at the campaign office; his mother was at his house, getting the place ready for his return; the nurses never bothered them at this time of the evening—he could have easily gotten Oscar's attention and pointed to the sudden tenting of his bed sheets.

It had been, what, six weeks since their last coupling? Good God, would they have sweated.

But instead Patrick did nothing. He closed his eyes and allowed his erection to deflate; and when Oscar got up to leave for the night, he pretended that he was already asleep. Hooking up now, hot as it sounded, would only be cruel and confusing to both of them.

Later that night, though, Patrick masturbated, to thoughts of Oscar, and also to thoughts of Marco Baffi, and Mr. One-and-One, and Jace Hopkins, and even of that awful Christmas Eve party, a million different memories flooded his brain, a kind of greatest hits collection of his erotic life. His orgasm was explosive, voluminous, a whirling sticky mess—there was no way the nurse wouldn't know what he had been doing when she turned up in the morning to change the sheets. And afterwards Patrick could only grin and feel a perhaps ridiculous measure of pride. Broken as his body might be, he was still a man, flawed and restless and ruled by passion and very frequently horny.

That was all he would ever be, and that was more than enough.

He was discharged from the hospital on Thursday, October 30th. By then, he assumed their resurrected campaign would have finally run its course—how far could they possibly go without a candidate able to actually campaign? But the money that had been earmarked for traipsing around the state in that godforsaken pink bus had instead been funneled into radio and television ads, and in the aftermath of the shooting, donations had increased twentyfold over the previous month. The pundits all still insisted that he was within striking distance of Cisneros.

There were more than a dozen reporters gathered that final morning at the hospital. And though by now she had mostly given up on her daily entreaties that Patrick do some kind of television interview prior to Election Day, Nora couldn't resist making one last push.

"Let's just do an impromptu press conference, ten or fifteen minutes, and let them ask about the shooting. Honestly that alone might be enough to put you over the top."

For a few minutes, Patrick thought about giving her what she wanted. Why *not* embrace this strangest of the campaign's twists? Even if he had come to believe that winning or losing was beside the point, he was nonetheless still tickled by the idea of becoming a United States Senator. If the job was even half as much fun as the Texas State Senate had been, he'd probably get hooked—and, who knows, possibly even start contemplating a run for President.

But then he thought about it some more, and no. His days as a candidate were over.

Of course, that wasn't the end of it. Silly Patrick, still fooling himself, the essential lesson still not quite learned—regardless of what interviews he did or did not give, it wasn't like he had any real *control* over anything.

On November 2nd, the *Austin American-Statesman* and the Associated Press both published polls that had him trailing his opponent by a single point—pretty much a statistical tie. They said that the most dramatic political contest in recent American history was getting tighter by the minute; that all predictive models go out the window with a race like this, where there are no historical correlatives or precedents.

The next night, the night before Election Day, Patrick sat on the couch in his living room, in between Nora and his mother, Oscar in the armchair beside them, flipping between CNN, MSNBC and Fox News.

He could only smile and shake his head in disbelief. They all claimed it was going to come down to an estimated five thousand or so likely voters across the state, who at this late hour still said they were undecided.

PART FIVE
ELECTION DAY

9.19 a.m.

POTS AND PANS CRASH AGAINST the stovetop; the refrigerator door opens and then closes with a thud; the radio is turned up loud—or at least loud enough to drown out the occasional whirrs of the blender—and she is singing along to *Where Have All the Cowboys Gone?*, a song he has always despised. Patrick is presently in the living room, trying to pay attention to *The Daily Rundown*, but of course he can't hear a goddamned thing, and actually it's been like this for days now, a nonstop clanging and banging and chattering and singing, and everything she does is so *loud*, and all of it is undertaken with an outsized cheerfulness that he certainly doesn't remember from his youth. He's starting to fear this is never going to end, that he's been thrust into another reality show, some kind of bastard child of *The Golden Girls* and *Will and Grace*, about a widowed mother who moves in with her adult gay son.

"Can you keep it down, please?" he shouts churlishly.

"You need to eat breakfast and get ready," she shouts back. "Oscar said he'd be here at eleven."

It takes him nearly a minute to lift himself from the sofa and journey the fifteen feet to the kitchen. "You know, I was thinking..." he ventures, after gingerly dropping himself into a seat at the table. There's got to be a way of raising the subject of her returning home to New York without making her think that he isn't grateful. Maybe he should tell her that in order to heal psychologically he needs to be on his own again and feel like he's able to do things for himself, or maybe he could just point out that she's been away for nearly a month now and surely her grandchildren must miss her…

Hardly for the first time in his life, Patrick contemplates too long. Getting shot in the stomach has not altered his tendency to overthink a simple problem.

"I was thinking, too," his mother interrupts. "You know, I'm really glad that I'm not registered to vote here in Texas, because I honestly don't think I could vote for you in good conscience."

Patrick gapes at his mother, busy banging an omelet pan against the grate of the gas burner. She seems to have no idea that what she has just told him sounds awful.

"That wasn't very nice," Patrick can't help himself from muttering—but of course as the words are coming out of his mouth he regrets them. She's going to take offense that he took offense, and it's only going to lead to an argument. Is it his own fault or his parents'—because after all it's their DNA he's doomed by—that he can never just smile and act oblivious in the face of an insult?

"It's nothing *personal* against you, Patrick. Of course I want you to win. But I don't vote for pro-choice candidates."

"You're pro-life? Since when?"

She ignores this question and tells him, "You know, not everything is personal, Patrick. I don't think enough people of your generation realize that. Maybe if people did realize it then everyone wouldn't be at each other's throats all the time."

She winks at him and adds, "Maybe then somebody wouldn't have ended up getting shot like he did."

Patrick briefly wonders if she has just implied that he was the one to blame for the assassination attempt, but he decides to let that one pass. He is far more hung up on the confounding news that his mother could feel so strongly about abortion.

"How did I not know you're pro-life?"

"Well, I won't say it's because you don't call home often enough—though you don't," she says. "But abortion is one of those things that the people of my generation were taught to keep to ourselves, regardless of which side you were on. It's different now. Now everyone talks about everything."

"But especially as a woman, how can you deny someone else the right—"

"Oh, Patrick, I'm not going to get into an argument over abortion with you…"

"But you can't—"

"Your father would have voted for you," she cuts him off. "He would have moved to Texas just so he could register here. He would be out today knocking on doors. He'd probably slip a few of those undecided voters a twenty-dollar bill if he thought he could do it without you finding out."

"What do you mean?"

"He would have been so proud to have a son running for the Senate. He never got the chance to dream that big in his own life."

Patrick's mother places two breakfast plates on the table and sits down across from him. As she cuts into her omelet and sips at her coffee, Patrick considers the lines around her eyes and mouth, splayed like tiny pieces of cracked glass; her thick, curly hair, once black, now mostly grey. Without him previously noticing, she has passed out of middle-age—she will in fact be sixty-eight on her next birthday in February. Yet Patrick has a hard time thinking of his mother as old. He still sees her, he realizes, as he did when he was a boy, her thirties giving way to a not-so-youthful-sounding 40, when much like Patrick is now she would have still been struggling to define the adult she wanted to be.

"Don't you think Dad might have had trouble voting for a gay candidate?" he asks.

"I think if he were alive he would be calling you every week, asking when you were going to move back to New York and get married to Oscar in a state where you can be legally married."

Marilyn pauses and adds, "Not that I think Oscar's the right one for you, but that's another story."

"That doesn't really jibe with my memories of him," Patrick comes back, a little more testily than he intended. "Or with what you told Rebecca Lowenthal."

"You never gave him the chance to show a different side of himself," his mother answers, just as testily.

"I know that. And I regret that very much."

Marilyn Monaghan puts down her fork, shrugs and lets out a breath. "What do you want me to tell you, Patrick? That he was some kind of saint? No one's going to buy that line. But you never walked in his shoes, either. He had three kids and no money in the bank and he had a job that sent him home every night with a backache. And, unfortunately, your father wasn't the type to suffer silently."

"You don't see it," she adds, "but you and he are alike in so many ways."

"I don't think that's true at all —" Patrick interjects, but his mother talks over him.

"Eventually he stopped fighting against the whole world. You didn't see any of that, you had moved down here, and you didn't come to visit us very often. But that was when he started to realize that what mattered to him was his children; that at least with you kids he had created something that would live on. And you probably won't believe me—and don't you dare tell Tim or Laura I said this to you—but you were the one he would have been the proudest of. He would have seen you doing important things, and seen how other people respect you, and that would have made him so proud. He would have loved that you showed him there was a different way to live a life than the way he had lived his."

"I just wish you'd given him that chance."

"Why was that *my* burden?" Patrick's voice cracks, and he hates himself for this. He hates letting his mother know how much the fear of his parents' rejection paralyzed him over the years; hates displaying this vulnerability that has never really gone away. "Why didn't he have any responsibility to make me feel safe enough and loved enough to be honest with him?"

"Because life isn't fair," his mother says. "I know you'd prefer some complicated answer, but that's it: life isn't fair."

"Especially for a gay kid who watches his father kick his mother's gay cousin out of their house," he answers.

Marilyn Monaghan at first says nothing. From the way she looks down at her plate, her eyes half-closed as if in daydream, Patrick can tell that she too has never stopped thinking of that day.

"That was the last time I saw my cousin," she finally offers. "When he died, your father wouldn't let me go to San Francisco for the funeral. But even then, Patrick, what he did that day, it was about you kids. I'm not trying to excuse him. Turning his back on

Ant was something I never forgave him for. Family doesn't turn its back on family.

"But it was such a different time. It was seen as such a shameful thing to have a gay person in your family—stupid and wrong, I know, but that's how it was. And no one knew if you could get AIDS from shaking a sick person's hand or drinking from the same glass of water. Your father wasn't going to let anyone hurt you kids. He thought he was protecting you."

Ten minutes pass in silence. They both pick at their breakfast, but neither seems especially hungry. Marilyn Monaghan eventually stands and begins loading the dishwasher. Patrick thinks they have come to the end of their conversation.

It is only when he rises from the table that he looks to his mother and sees that she is standing stock still, gripping the edges of the kitchen counter, as if to steady herself in the middle of an earthquake.

"For whatever it's worth," she says, still facing away from him, "after I gave that interview to the girl at *Rolling Stone*, I called her and begged her not to use what I said about your father—that it was somehow better that he hadn't lived to see your television show. It wasn't even true—he *would* have been proud. I don't even know why I said it, other than I was probably angry with you.

"I'm sorry for that, Patrick. I probably should have said that to you years ago, I know, but I'm sorry."

Patrick considers all his mother has just told him. He supposes he could still choose to be angry: An apology doesn't change the fact that she said what she said to Rebecca in the first place, and that when she said it she must have on some level meant it. Knowing that his father was perhaps more complicated than Patrick imagined doesn't erase the worst of the memories, either. But he finds now that none of this hurts the way it once did. Perhaps he's finally gotten over it; or perhaps when he got shot, something that hurt even more came along to replace the original hurt. Either way, he's ready to move on.

Besides, he doesn't want to be *that* cliché, the petulant 40-year-old still whining about all the wrongs Mommy and Daddy did unto him.

"It's okay, Ma," he says, and with all his heart and soul he means it.

11:55 a.m.

He's a lanky, pimply kid, no older than sixteen, with a rubbery, outsized grin and a booming baritone voice: Patrick would bet good money that he's president or vice president of his high school's drama club. "Vote for Patrick Monaghan," he bellows, thrusting the flyer into Patrick's hands—but then he looks up and sees that in fact this *is* Patrick Monaghan, and he says, "Oh, my God, I don't need YOU to vote for YOU." Patrick laughs and shakes the boy's hand, and then he glances down at the flyer. It is in color and on glossy-stock paper. The headline in block letters reads: **PATRICK MONAGHAN: A NEW AMERICAN HERO.** The accompanying photograph is one he has never seen before, from the rally at the Fort Worth Stockyards Museum, his arms held high in triumph over his head—it must have been snapped just seconds before the shooting. While he's still debating the tastefulness of using this particular photo, he considers the two lines of text printed at the bottom of the page:

That you are here—that life exists, and identity;
That the powerful play goes on, and you will contribute a verse.

"They're the final lines of Walt Whitman's *Oh Me! Oh Life!*," Oscar leans in to explain to him. "In case you were wondering."

"*We* made these flyers?"

"Well... Nora designed it... and I helped... " he says, like he's worried Patrick might be about to throw a fit.

Patrick stares at the piece of paper in his hand a few beats longer, but then says nothing as he folds it into fours and slips it into the inside pocket of his blazer. He's certainly not about to confess to Oscar that he wants to keep the flyer as a memento. How shameless and how utterly wonderful! He really does love that his two dearest friends have finally joined forces, and he loves even more that they know no limits when it comes to laying it on thick.

He stops and shakes hands and takes pictures with each of the volunteers who step forth to wish him good luck. There are at least three dozen of them gathered in this parking lot across from Paschal High School, holding their **MONAGHAN 2014** signs, pimping for votes a legislatively-mandated fifty feet from the entrance of the polling station. The impromptu meet-and-greet eats away a half hour, but eventually they make their way across the street and to the front doors of Paschal. The security guys—there are three of them today—stick so close that Patrick can smell the bacon and onion on the breath of the one behind him. Just before they enter, Oscar looks up from his iPhone, which he has been checking all morning, and tells Patrick: "They're saying turnout is high, and that in Texas large turnouts historically favor the Democrats."

A minute or so later, behind the red curtain of the makeshift voting booth rigged from a classroom desk and a wobbly metal frame, he at long last considers the 2014 Election Day ballot. He looks over the other races first, for country commissioner and State Senate (his own seat from which he is stepping down) and a half-dozen judgeships. He starts marking his choices, careful not to color outside the squares. After four years in the State Senate and the last eighteen months campaigning, he has come to know personally all of the people he is voting for today. He suspects that most of them are going to lose—oh, the poor, demographically-challenged Democrats of Tarrant County who haven't enjoyed the popularity boon of attempted assassination—but he still feels a burst of enthusiasm each time he darkens a new square. America would be a better place, he has come to believe—more humble, more just, perhaps more joyful, too—if more people were willing to identify themselves as the underdog, and to come out fighting for lost causes.

Finally he arrives at his own race, printed at the top of the paper. **UNITED STATES SENATE (VOTE FOR ONE)**. Patrick smiles as he hovers his pen over the box next to his name.

He tells himself: *The votes don't need to be counted because I've already won. To have staked a legitimate claim in the competition was the victory.*

He's spent many hours these last few weeks thinking about this, and he understands now that he didn't write that speech bowing out of the campaign because he was in a bad mood that day, or because he was suffering through a temporary spell of disillusionment with Nora and Oscar, or because he needed to let off steam. He wrote it, essentially, because he believed it was the correct thing to do. You can only change a system from within so much before the system starts to change you, and when that time arrives, there is no shame or defeat in giving up and moving on.

He was right for politics for awhile, but he's not right for it anymore. His true fate is still out there, waiting to be discovered.

Actually, scratch that: His true fate is the fate he is living. And there are many more verses still to contribute to this powerful play of his life.

He moves his hand a half-inch to the right, so that the pen is now hovering over the box next to Andrew Cisneros' name. He holds it there. This is the right choice. His opponent won this thing fair and square.

But then Patrick stops himself.

Wait a minute. What the fuck is he doing? He has come to genuinely like and admire Andrew Cisneros—a handwritten note and a towering bouquet of flowers from him arrived in Patrick's hospital room the day after he awoke from the coma—and he thinks he'll probably end up being a much-needed moderate Republican voice in the Senate. But that doesn't mean he has to vote for him. If the vote is as close as Oscar is suggesting, then no way is he going to be the one who tips things Cisneros' way. Once in a lifetime is enough times to make *that* ridiculous mistake.

So instead Patrick sets the pen down and with a triumphant flourish pulls aside the curtain and steps out of the voting booth and feeds his ballot into the counting machine, swiftly and surreptitiously enough so that no one—not Oscar, not the guys on his security team, not the elderly polling place volunteers watching his every move so studiously—could possibly see that he has left the boxes for United States Senate blank.

1:14 p.m.

"I know the timing probably seems strange, but I felt I had to tell you this today," Patrick says, sitting next to Oscar in the back seat of the campaign SUV, which is still parked in the lot across from Paschal.

He asked the security guys to give them a few minutes, maybe walk over to Whataburger and treat themselves on Patrick, but their orders from John Stone are that the candidate is not to be left unattended. So the security guys are standing outside the vehicle, one each on the driver's and passenger's sides and a third behind the trunk, and of course it looks silly, and by this point—ten minutes into a conversation that so far has been mostly protracted silences—all of the sign holders and flyer distributors probably think he and Oscar are in here fucking.

In retrospect, probably neither the time nor the place for a breakup, but given the nature of his schedule today—and his hard-to-explain conviction that he had to do this before they learn the outcome of today's vote—it was the best he could do.

"It's not like I didn't know this was coming," Oscar says. "Seriously, Patrick, for future reference, when someone asks you to marry him, 'I'll have to get back to you on that one' is *not* an appropriate response."

Patrick starts to protest, that wasn't what he said, or at least not what he *meant*, but Oscar holds up his hand to quiet him.

"I told myself that when this happened I wasn't going to be pathetic and cry and ask you to reconsider. But, I don't know, Patrick… what makes you so certain things can't work out between us?"

"Would you hate me if I said, 'I'll have to get back to you on that one'?"

The joke does not go over well. Oscar frowns and looks out the window.

Patrick hastily apologizes, but struggles to figure out what else to say. It's not that he expected this to go easily—only that he perhaps underestimated how difficult it would be to avoid cliché in his explanation. He doesn't want to say to Oscar, "It's not you, it's me," but he also doesn't want to come off as a heartless dick—and beyond those he's not really sure of his other options.

Finally he takes a deep breath and says, "When I'm with you, the self-consciousness doesn't go away, Oscar. That's not your fault—it's not your job to make me feel unselfconscious—but it's there, and it's *never* going to go away. I'm always going to wonder if I'm just interested in you because the sex is great, or because it's a marvel to me that someone who looks the way you look would be interested in me. I'm never going to be able to stop thinking *why*, and just exist as your partner."

"But that's your *perception* of things," Oscar answers. "Your self-consciousness has nothing to do with the reality of how we work together as a couple."

"I acknowledge that I might be making the perfect the enemy of something very good, but…" Patrick doesn't know how to finish the sentence.

"Real life is not about finding your soulmate across a crowded room and living happily ever after," Oscar says. "You *choose* to be in love. You *work* at it. You understand that, don't you?"

Patrick shrugs and shakes his head—he realizes this approach isn't working. They've had many variations on this same argument before, and it usually ends with Patrick agreeing to carry on as Oscar's boyfriend.

"The generation of gay men before mine was ravaged by AIDS," he says softly, deciding to try another tack. "Tens of thousands of strong, healthy young men, and virtually overnight they were dead. I dodged that bullet. I was born in 1974, and that means I didn't have to die, because by the time I became sexually active people knew how to prevent the disease. And now, another twenty years go by, and not only do I get to live, but I also get to be accepted and taken seriously, and there are even twenty-six states and counting where I can legally be married.

"But I still remember what it was like in the '80s—all of those men who were mocked and reviled; whose shame got consecrated as disease. *That's* the source of the self-consciousness, Oscar. It's this fear of squandering the privilege I've been afforded. It's this change that's happened faster than my spirit can even process. I want to get married. I really do. But I want to do it right. I can't take it lightly, because I can't help but think that all these men first had to *die* so that one day I'd be able to have this basic human right.

"And if I feel an ounce of self-consciousness, Oscar, then I think that means I'm not with the right person."

"Jesus, Patrick, don't you think you're placing an unfair burden on the other person?" Oscar responds. "Don't you think you're holding *yourself* up to too high a standard? I mean, wasn't the whole point of your campaign that gay people *shouldn't* have to be paragons?"

There is a quick, startling rap on the window on Oscar's side. One of the security guys is pointing at his watch, staring back at them quizzically. They were due downtown twenty minutes ago.

"I think self-consciousness is probably a lot like cholesterol," Patrick says. "There's the good kind and the bad kind, and the challenge is to cultivate enough of the good kind before you give yourself a stroke."

"It's going to be awkward if you win today," Oscar tells him. "We'll have to issue a statement saying we broke up, all of ten days after announcing to the world our undying love for one other."

"First of all, I'm *not* going to win—"

"Yes, you *are*, Patrick. I know you don't believe it, but the momentum is all in your direction—"

"—and second, *you* were the one who released that speech, knowing full well that we weren't exactly on solid footing."

"That was the best speech I've ever written—no way was I going to lose it to history," Oscar says; and the mischievous glint that Patrick has always found so sexy flashes in his beautiful brown eyes.

Another minute or so passes. Oscar starts to say something and then cuts himself off. Patrick, too, can't figure out what comes next.

When they each finally determine what they want to say, they end up talking at the same time.

"Maybe I'll *never* not be self-conscious in a relationship—"

"I swore to myself that I wouldn't beg you to give this another chance—"

"—but I have to trust my instincts."

"—but I love you, Patrick, and I wish I could make you change your mind."

Patrick looks over to Oscar looking back at him. A thought floats into his brain—a memory of Suzie Brown sitting across from him at the Hop in the fall of 1992, when they were eighteen and away from home for the first time and thought that's all it took to be grownups. She spoke with such assurance when she said that before you could find true love, you must first have your heart broken, and you must also break somebody's heart. *Otherwise you're just not mature enough yet.* He remembers the heartbreak he felt that night in 2003, when Jace Hopkins fled his apartment after their perfect date turned sour. He suspects that Oscar feels much the same way now. And though he knows he's being silly—and that anyone who holds too close to heart an eighteen-year-old girl's advice on matters of life and love deserves whatever misery he gets—he nonetheless wonders if this means he has at last fulfilled Suzie's dictum; if, at age 40, *finally* he's mature enough.

"We should get going," he says. "Nora is waiting."

And as Patrick knocks on the window and waves to the security men that they are ready, and as Oscar reaches to check the newest texts and emails on his phone, they both seem to accept that they are going to have to leave it at that.

2:56 p.m.

Where is she, she's two hours late, not answering her phone and not returning texts, and they should have heard something by now—data from the exit pollsters, projections based on the early voting returns, *something*—and Oscar has been pacing and fuming and checking his watch constantly. He is convinced that like Pheidippides in ancient Athens Nora should be racing to them from wherever she's been all morning with news of their victory—though if it's even half as close as people are saying it is, Patrick doesn't understand how they'll know anything for certain until nine or ten o'clock tonight.

"Of all fucking days to disappear…" Oscar starts up again, and Patrick tunes out the rest.

They are presently standing in the center of an empty ballroom in the Worthington Hotel, watching as three large projection screens are mounted to vertical metal brackets. The party is set to commence at six o'clock this evening. One thousand invited guests will enjoy free drinks and canapés. The polls will close at eight o'clock. The plan is for Patrick to make only a fifteen-minute appearance to deliver his speech—most likely a concession, but at this point who the hell knows—before retreating to his suite.

"*Finally*," Oscar bursts out.

She is moving toward them without any urgency, trailed close behind by four junior staffers, one of whom is carrying a shiny black plastic garment bag over his shoulder by the crook of the hanger. Oscar's fists are balled up at his sides, and Patrick readies himself to play peacekeeper for the fight he knows is going to break out between them. But as Nora draws nearer, Oscar and Patrick are both rendered speechless. Her blonde hair is swept up and pinned behind her. She wears pale red lipstick, a dusting of blush, eyeshadow the color of rose champagne. She looks to him, Patrick realizes, as unaffectedly lovely as when he first met her twenty years ago at Mount Moosilauke.

"Va-va-voom," Oscar offers, and Nora breaks into a giggle.

"Just wait until you see the dress," she says. "Marc Jacobs on clearance."

"Love it," Oscar says, and there's not even a vestigial trace of anger in his voice, all is forgiven for her unexplained absence. Patrick can only marvel. The two of them are becoming something more than just friends. If he had to guess, he would say that the political consulting firm they are probably going to end up opening together will be called Meacham-Davison—if only because there's no way Nora will ever let her name come second.

"We're celebrating, right?" Nora says, "So I figured why not go all—"

Oscar doesn't let her finish. "What do you mean we're *celebrating*? What have you heard?"

Nora smiles an abstruse smile and turns to Patrick. "I need to talk to you privately."

"Oh, God, *what*?" Oscar says. "Please don't be coy. Not now."

"I need to talk to Patrick."

"I'll come with."

"Just me and Patrick," she says; and before Oscar can protest further, she instructs Patrick to meet her in his suite in fifteen minutes and spins on her three-inch, also-newly-purchased heels and disappears from the ballroom.

3:33 p.m.

His heart is racing, his hands are shaking, he is pitched at the edge of the couch in the sitting room of the Worthington's Presidential suite, watching Nora at the window on her phone, though to whom she is talking Patrick doesn't know. Five minutes this has carried on now, and she keeps holding up her index finger, an apologetic gesture of *just one more minute*, and then shooting him this mysterious smile—tender, affectionate, toothless—something more than Mona Lisa, something less than the Cheshire Cat—and he's pretty sure she *knows*, and maybe he's crazy, but each new time she smiles at him, Patrick thinks he sees evidence of his own victory.

When she hangs up the phone, she is going to tell him that all signs are pointing positive: Around nine o'clock tonight, the *Associated Press* will project that Patrick Francis Monaghan has pulled off one of the most extraordinary upsets in American electoral history.

He looks over to her again and catches her eye and *again* she smiles at him and this time he's certain. She was right about *everything*, and now he's going to become a United States Senator. He starts thinking about the victory speech he will deliver tonight, a draft of which Oscar has already scripted for him; starts thinking about his future office in the Capitol, wood-paneled and amber-lit.

Soon, like Nora, Patrick is also smiling, though his is more of a lopsided, absentminded grin—like the guy at the ballpark too busy enjoying his hot dog to notice that there's a giant mustard stain on his shirt.

Nora finally turns off her phone and shakes her head and says, "Not even close."

It takes a few seconds for the words to sink in, and even then he hopes she is talking about something else. "What do you mean?"

"Well, exit poll numbers are notoriously difficult to crunch, so I don't want you to *totally* give up hope," she explains. "But the number crunchers are all saying the same thing. My guess is that we'll lose by ten points. It *might* tighten up a little once they finish tabulating the early vote, but I'd be shocked if we ended up any closer than eight points."

"Not even close?" Patrick asks, and though he knows that he should feel otherwise—above all, he should feel *grateful* that finally it is over and that they got to the end without humiliating themselves—his dominant emotion right now is outrage. The familiar Monaghan indignation.

Not even close? What the fuck?

"What can I say? It's really hard to get a Democrat elected in Texas," Nora offers.

"But the polls had us neck and neck…"

"I didn't tell you or Oscar this because I didn't want to spoil everyone's fun," Nora says, "but our internal polls never had us closer than six points. I didn't really understand it myself. My guess is that sometimes the media roots for a tighter race than actually exists, and then nudges things in that direction."

Patrick tries to make sense of his disappointment. He didn't even vote for himself—it's not like he has any real right to feel this way. But, still, nobody likes to lose, even those who didn't want to win; and he imagines he would have enjoyed the rebuke he would have been able to serve up, to *anyone* who had ever rejected him, all the way back to kindergarten at P.S. 42 in Staten Island, where the other boys started calling him Peppermint Patty. He would have had the ultimate proof—Federally-mandated, court-certified proof!—that Patrick Francis Monaghan should *never* be underestimated.

A little external validation, Patrick thinks, never hurt anyone.

"We need to celebrate," Nora announces, and as if on cue—who knows, maybe it *is* on cue, maybe Nora in her cross-the-*t*'s, dot-the-*i*'s fashion has had someone positioned outside waiting for her to speak exactly these words—there is a knock on the door. A bellman enters with a bottle of Perrier-Jouet Grand Brut, plunged into a stainless steel ice bucket. Nora allows the bellman to pop the cork, but then hands him a five and says she'll do the pouring herself.

"Cheers," Patrick says, after she hands him a glass flute filled to its brim. He is trying—and failing—not to sound disconsolate.

"You were the one who wrote a speech announcing that you were dropping out of the race," she tells him. "You got your desired result, and you didn't completely betray hundreds of thousands of your supporters. That seems worthy of a celebration to me."

Patrick doesn't actually do a full-blown spit take, but a little bit of the champagne catches in his throat and kicks up into his nasal cavity. How could she *possibly* know about this? There was only one copy of that speech, and he assumed it would have died on the day he nearly died.

"How on Earth?" he asks.

"On the night of the shooting, Dr. Kim came to speak to me in the waiting room," Nora says. "I was so scared, Patrick—I thought he was going to tell me they had lost you. And I was convinced that it was all my fault. Because I was the one who was experimenting on you, and I pushed the experiment too far. I was Dr. Frankenstein, and you were the goodhearted monster the angry villagers chased to his death."

"Wait a minute," Patrick interrupts. "Is the monster in *Frankenstein* supposed to be *goodhearted*?"

"Isn't he?"

"Isn't the point that he really *is* a savage—that Dr. Frankenstein basically created this expression of his own grotesque inner-self?" And it's funny to both of them, though at this point in their lives they no longer bother to acknowledge it, that all these years later nothing has changed. They are still two bright, determined kids trying to bluff the world into thinking that they know a little more than they do.

"Besides, the comparison doesn't hold," Patrick adds. "Because I was a willing participant in the experimentation."

"Anyway," Nora says, "Dr. Kim told me told me that when they were cutting you out of your clothes they found a bunch of papers in your jacket pocket that he thought I might want. He pretended like he hadn't read them, but I'm pretty sure he did. He had this expression on his face that actually made me think he was disappointed in you."

Patrick shifts uncomfortably against the sofaback, twists the wrong way and causes a painful twinge in his still-tender stomach. He wishes he could find some way of insulating Nora from what he sees now was a pretty spectacular act of Patrick Francis Monaghan vanity—and from what she probably regards as an epic *fuck you* against her.

"I don't want you to think I'm anything but grateful for everything you've done."

"Oh, I'm not mad about it," she says. "I was a little taken aback, but seeing as you were near death at the time, I couldn't really be angry. I do have one question, though: Were you really going to go through with it?"

"I don't remember," he tells her. "I remember having made a decision. But I can't remember what I decided, whether it would have been my speech or Oscar's. It's the one thing leading up to the shooting that I can't seem to remember."

"You lay out a provocative argument," she says, and reaches down and opens her bag on the floor and pulls out the pages in question. They are folded in eighths, and the white of the now-brittle paper is painted with rust-colored streaks—the residue of Patrick's dried blood. "When the game is rigged, is it actually nobler to bow out rather than carrying on playing? By betraying the people who supported you, can you actually succeed in opening their eyes to inequality and inspire them to greater change?"

"Obviously you don't think so."

"Well, it's an academic debate. The speech was never delivered. In addition to rescuing you from a gay pornography scandal, Curtis Huber also stopped you from self-destructing. I'm thinking maybe we should cut that guy a bonus check from the campaign account to thank him for his efforts."

"Would you have ever forgiven me?" he asks.

"Of course I would have forgiven you," she comes right back. "But I'm not sure you would have forgiven yourself."

"I felt compromised, besieged—I don't know, I guess I was going a little crazy."

"I was turning you into someone you didn't want to be. I'm sorry for that."

"Don't apologize. You wanted to win. I'm the one who should be apologizing for not being the candidate who could bring you the victory you deserve."

"We can always run you again for Senate in 2018," she says, and playfully cocks an eyebrow.

Just then there is another knock on the door. Oscar announces himself and begs them to please tell him what they've heard. Nora asks him to give them just one more minute.

"We broke up today," Patrick says softly.

"According to your mother," Nora answers, "you need to find someone with whom you have more in common than just sex. She said that to me fifteen minutes after she first met Oscar."

Patrick laughs and tells her, "I think there's someone back in Staten Island she wants to set me up with."

Nora finishes her champagne, pours herself another, takes a long slug and tops off her flute. She says, "Do you ever regret it, Patrick—us carrying on as friends, when maybe at some point we should have gone our separate ways? Do you ever think that what they all say about us—that we have each other so that we don't have to have normal romantic relationships—might actually be true?"

Her voice is unsteady now; the alcohol has brought even more red into her already-rouged cheeks—Patrick realizes that this is the first time in months he has seen her tipsy. They really do need to get back to those long, lazy Friday nights, he thinks, when they would do nothing but talk and cook dinner and make their way through a couple of bottles of wine.

"Of course it's true," he exclaims. "But what does *that* matter? So *what* if we've messed each other up for life? Think about what we got in the exchange—just think about this incredible, twenty-two-years-long-and-counting adventure."

Nora looks away, toward the window on the far side of the room. Again there is a knock at the door, Oscar asking to be let in, but this time they both ignore him. When Nora turns back to Patrick, there are tears running down her cheeks.

"No, no, don't mess up your makeup."

"I don't know what I would have done if you hadn't pulled through, Patrick," she says. "I can't even fathom how boring my life—this whole world—would be without you in it."

"Lucky for us both," Patrick says, a rueful sweet smile on his face, "I didn't have to die for our sins."

7:43 p.m.

In the final hour of his life as a candidate for the United States Senate, bodies drift into and out of Patrick's suite, cell-phones buzz and ring, a steady murmur emanates from two televisions, one tuned to CNN in the sitting room, another to MSNBC in the bedroom. Polling stations on the East Coast have begun to close, and Senate races in Maryland, Rhode Island and New Hampshire have already been called for the favorites.

"We still might see a surprise out of Texas, where Patrick Monaghan has pulled very close to Republican businessman Andrew Cisneros in the last few days," says Donna Brazile on CNN—though Patrick suspects that she too has seen the exit polling data and is merely manufacturing a sense of drama for the cameras.

Oscar is sitting at the desk in the bedroom, hunched over his laptop, making final changes to Patrick's concession speech. If he's smarting over their breakup this afternoon, he doesn't let on—not when there is still work to be done. For her part, Nora is standing in a far corner, fielding phone calls from reporters, unwavering in her false conviction that their side has "a *very* good chance of pulling this out." Watching her, Patrick briefly feels pity—at this point, she isn't Napoleon at Waterloo, she's that rogue Japanese soldier who kept fighting World War II from an island in the Philippines until 1974. Until he realizes that she's just doing what she loves to do, hustling and cajoling, trying to sell the story of Patrick Francis Monaghan to anyone who's still buying.

Patrick's mother is here also, wearing a black Calvin Klein gown that Nora helped her pick out this afternoon and the diamond "re-engagement" ring that James Monaghan gave her on their thirty-ninth wedding anniversary, only a few months before he died. Patrick is filled with tremendous pride when his staffer Alison Bennett comes up to him and whispers, "Your mother is so beautiful. I can see where you get your good looks."

At eight o'clock, the suite begins to empty, after Nora instructs everyone to head downstairs and enjoy the party. The press secretaries and fundraisers and treasurers and assistants and interns—there were more than two hundred people working on this campaign by the end—all seem to evaporate like mirages in the desert: Who knows what you really saw, and who knows what was just your fantasy?

Now it is just Patrick and Nora and Patrick's mother.

A gay man defined in terms of the domineering women in his life—what a cliché! Patrick thinks.

But an instant later he has another thought: *Oh, whatever. Clichés can be vastly underrated.*

CNN calls the race at 8:07 p.m. "Breaking news out of Texas… the first openly gay man in history from a major party to run for the United States Senate… a former reality television star… shot and nearly killed just three weeks ago… Democrats knew it was a long shot, but were holding out hope…"

"I'm not going to let you watch the analysis," Nora says, coming up from behind him, the remote control in her hand.

"Wait, I want to hear what they have to say," Patrick protests.

"It will just be a bunch of insults. More people telling you what's wrong with you."

"No, leave it."

And before the argument can carry on, they hear Patrick's mother from the other room, where she is sitting by herself on the edge of the bed.

"A & E "—she says it like it's one word, *aehnee*—"is having a marathon of *Dallas Three Ways*. Put that on."

Patrick and Nora make their way into the bedroom and at the exact same instant ask: "What?"

Marilyn stands up and takes the remote out of Nora's hand and points it at the television and begins flipping through the channels.

"In honor of Election Day," she explains, "they're showing all twenty-two episodes of the show. I watched a few while you were still sleeping this morning, Patrick. You looked so handsome that first season."

"But not the second season?" Patrick asks.

Marilyn ignores this and carries on clicking. "There," she pronounces, arriving at A&E, where fractured images of the glittering Dallas skyline are flashing on the screen.

"There," Nora says.

"There," Patrick adds.

And then the three of them watch, as the techno-music score thrums on the soundtrack, as Gabriel Vasquez takes off across an extravagantly appointed Highland Park living room with a margarita glass in his hand, as Gabriel starts shouting at a Patrick Monaghan six years younger than he is now, as Patrick lamely tries to defend himself. And then Marilyn—who has never before seen this episode—barks out a laugh when she sees Gabriel throw his orange-hued cocktail into Patrick's face, and Patrick and Nora can't help but laugh too.

All things considered, it is not bad television.

9:05 p.m.

The suite is once again filled. There are hugs and pats on the back and assurances that he'll get 'em next time. A congratulatory call has just been made to Andrew Cisneros, along with an apology for allowing the campaign to get so negative. A class act to the end, Cisneros told Patrick, "This will sound crazy, but a part of me was rooting for you to win," and then he invited Patrick to lunch the next week to solicit his ideas on what he should focus on once he gets to Washington. Patrick's concession speech is scheduled for 9:30 p.m. and will likely be carried on both the broadcast and cable news networks—his last hurrah, at least for now, as the subject of national news. He is standing next to Nora, reading through the speech one last time, when Oscar suddenly appears beside them.

"Two messages that I figured I should run past you guys," he says.

"No press interviews until Friday," Nora says, "and then we'll talk to whoever's still interested in talking to us."

"Well, the first message is from your old friend Rebecca Lowenthal," Oscar carries on. "Calling from her new perch at *The New York Times Magazine*."

"Someone's moving up in the world," Nora says.

"This can't be anything good," Patrick murmurs.

"She wants to write a profile of you," Oscar explains. "'Patrick Monaghan's Next Act.' She says the editors are willing to make it a cover story."

"You know, Patrick…" Nora starts.

"No, absolutely not."

"… it's not the worst idea in the world… "

"Are you *insane?*"

"She's willing to be on the first plane down here tomorrow morning," Oscar adds.

"Who's the other message from?" Patrick asks, determined to change the topic.

"Well, there's this woman downstairs begging for five minutes with you."

"No, Oscar," Nora interjects. "He talks to one person, he'll end up having to talk to everybody."

"She says they knew each other as kids." And then, addressing Patrick, he asks: "Does the name Jessica DeStefano mean anything to you?"

9:15 p.m.

She knows that to explain it makes her sound ridiculous—like some kind of desperate housewife. She knows that they must all be looking at her—in this expensive dress that doesn't fit, with her tangled nest of hair that she keeps forgetting to get cut and colored—and wondering if she might be another of Patrick's lunatic stalkers.

But she can't stop now. She's got to keep trying.

She only needs a few minutes of his time.

She never would have said that she was unhappy all these years, only that there seemed to her so little opportunity as she was growing up to veer off the expected path.

She wasn't a dumb girl, but by no means was she a scholar—and so she did as her older sister had done and studied at Rutgers to be a paralegal. She wasn't unattractive, either, but she had also never lost her childhood pudge and could never seem to attract the attention of the best-looking boys. All through her twenties, as she served as bridesmaid at a dozen girlfriends' and cousins' weddings, she kept faith that her own turn would come, and that this nagging melancholy she suffered would eventually fade away.

Surely what everyone told her had to be true. There's someone out there for everyone.

She met Bob when she was thirty-one, just when that faith was starting to waver. The bachelor brother of one of her colleagues, he weighed at least a hundred pounds too many, and had black, bristly hair sprouting every which way from his shoulders, and he seemed a little too invested in his work as a junior partner in the audit department at Ernst and Young. But he knew what he wanted, which was a wife and a family and a house in Franklin Lakes, and Jessica felt that those were basically the same things she wanted—or at least that she would be a fool to turn such things down. They married on May 6th, 2006, and Jessica told everyone she spoke to that day that she had never been so happy in all her life.

She hated the idea that others might regard her as ungrateful. They did in fact move to Franklin Lakes, into a four-bedroom colonial with a built-in swimming pool and an enormous backyard shed that they converted into a guesthouse. Bob earned upwards of $600,000 a year, a salary that afforded them luxuries—new cars and trips to Europe and dinner once a month at Peter Lugar's—that she never could have even fathomed growing up. When he urged her to quit her job, because why should she have to commute ninety minutes each way into the city every day when he was making more than enough money for both of them, all of her girlfriends cooed and burbled with envy. She had found herself that rare specimen—"a real provider."

Who was Jessica to argue otherwise?

Yet all this time she never forgot about Patrick; and once the twins came along in 2009—Robert, after his father and grandfather; and Patrick, because she told Bob she'd always liked the name—the memory of that day suddenly loomed larger. Or, to put it another way: the lessons she had failed to absorb in her own childhood now seemed to her *essential*. How was she going to inspire her boys to lead lives that were untouched by compromise? How was she who had only the vaguest notion of the concept supposed to teach Bobby and Pat about *integrity*?

What happened next was a coincidence, or some sort of sign from God, or maybe both—how could she ever know?—but there was Jessica, stuck in the pediatrician's waiting room with the twins who were then just two months old. The instant she saw the photograph in the year-old issue of *Rolling Stone*, she knew that it was him. She read through the story without pause, and twenty minutes later, when the boys' names were finally called, the nurse had to ask if she was okay because she couldn't stop crying. She was crying for Patrick, and the struggles he had faced just to feel comfortable in his own skin; crying for herself, because she now felt her own past mistakes more acutely than ever.

And she was crying of course for her sons, whom she feared would never have an example like Patrick in their own lives to follow. The worst thing in the world, Jessica thought, would be instead for them to grow up to be just like their father, so stolid and ordinary; so wholly *uninspired*.

Was it just that she was bored and home alone all day and spending way too much time inside her own head? Was her sister Mary—the one person to whom she tried to explain the whole crazy story—speaking the truth when she said that it sounded like Jessica had a crush on some gay guy who probably had zero memory of her? She wasn't sure. All she knew was the urgency she felt in following the twists and turns of Patrick's adult life. She wasn't at all surprised when he went into politics—yes! *that's* what she wanted her sons to learn, how to be *leaders* like Patrick, and not merely crafty followers like their father. She wrote checks to his campaigns from an account Bob didn't know she kept, along with notes explaining her personal connection to the candidate. She hoped the result might be a phone call from him—and thought that *that* might be enough to quell this restlessness that increasingly roiled her insides—but all she got back were boilerplate thank you notes with a hand-stamped version of Patrick's signature.

When she told him of her plans, Bob wondered if she was depressed and asked if she might want to consider beginning a course of psychotropic medication. She considered it the ultimate declaration of her sanity that she ignored him and bought the plane ticket anyway. By now she understood that there was no other way to do this, except in person; and that for her own sake and the twins', *absolutely* this had to be done. Indeed, what a strange moment in her own life for Patrick to be making his historic Senate run. A few months earlier, she had noticed a series of five-hundred-dollar transfers out of the joint checking account that Bob didn't know she kept tabs on, and then she found an undeleted text message on his phone—evidence that his increasingly frequent business trips to Boston were being spent in the company of paid escorts. She wasn't yet ready to confront her husband, but she believed that traveling to Fort Worth for the rally was an important next step. She had to make amends with the first man in her life who had ever shown her *decency*, if she ever hoped to find such decency again.

The shooting was of course terrifying: the bloodcurdling screams of everyone around her; the sulfurous smell of gun smoke hanging in the hot air; the sight of her childhood friend now quite possibly dying in front of her. Yet once she returned home to New Jersey and learned that Patrick would survive, her resolve to meet and talk to him only strengthened.

Now more than ever Patrick needed someone to tell him that he was a hero.

Now more than ever Jessica needed to be the one who told him.

She had been planning to wait until *after* the election, when the chaos and security surrounding Patrick finally relaxed. But then the email arrived out of the blue, just six days before the party. *Please join us in cheering on Patrick Francis Monaghan to victory.* She later found out that it went out to everyone who had donated more than $2500 to the campaign, though in the moment she was convinced it really was divine providence.

She arrives at DFW airport at three o'clock on Tuesday afternoon. The traffic on 183 to downtown Fort Worth is beastly. By the time she checks into the Worthington and changes into her dress and takes the elevator back downstairs, the party has already commenced. For the next ninety minutes, she tries to penetrate assorted circles of conversation, hoping she might find someone who can help her get to Patrick. The room is packed with people, hundreds of them, all of whom probably want an audience with the candidate. But each time she worries this might be a fool's errand, she recalls that day so many years ago, and then she thinks of her twin boys and what she most hopes to teach them: that sometimes it takes courage you don't have to do what is right; that no one is born with such courage—you just have to recognize the moment that calls for it, and then summon it with all your might.

She talks to sixteen people. Just trying to explain it, she knows it must sound ridiculous. But *truly*, she's no desperate housewife. She just needs a minute of his time.

Eventually she finds a college kid, his blazer festooned with dozens of campaign buttons—she figures him to be some sort of intern. He tells her to wait in the hotel lobby, and then he returns a few minutes later with a handsome African-American man who introduces himself as Patrick's deputy campaign manager. This man listens to her story—he's the first person all night who doesn't look at her like she's nuts—and then says no promises, but he will see what he can do. He disappears for more than an hour, before finally finding her again at 9:15 p.m. By then, Patrick has been declared the loser of the Senate race and some of the other guests are already starting to skip out on the party.

"Oh, you're still here," he says, and her heart sinks. This was never going to be.

But then he adds: "Follow me. He's got two minutes for you."

9:27 p.m.

She is waiting for him in an alcove in the hotel's kitchen, adjacent to a long corridor through which white-tuxedo-jacketed waiters pass with trays of mini crab cakes into the buzzing ballroom. Nora raised an objection; said she just wants to get him out there and get the concession speech over with. Patrick insisted one last time that things be done his way. It's not every day that someone turns up claiming to have known you when you were a kid—surely he should at least say hello.

She is the picture of what he has come to term the American indistinguishable: frizzy brown hair streaked with gray; brackish brown eyes; a too-wide mouth that seems to drag down the rest of her face. She could be any one of the thousands of people whose hands he shook on the campaign trail.

"You don't remember me, do you?" she asks.

He sheepishly shakes his head. "I don't think so."

"It's funny that a person can have an impact on your life that you carry with you," she says, "but they don't remember you. The moment barely even registered for them."

Patrick looks into her crestfallen eyes. He hates the idea that he has let her down. He knows it's silly to react this way, but he can't shake the encroaching worry that he is screwing up yet another important moment in his life.

"Tell me your name."

"Jessica DeStefano," she says. "I moved away from Staten Island after the first grade. But I was hoping you might remember."

Patrick again shakes his head and says, "No."

"I was in the audience the day you were shot," she tells him. "A few seconds before it happened, you looked into my eyes."

And now Patrick starts to wonder if maybe this *was* a mistake to agree to see her; if this unhinged-seeming woman might have come here to do him harm.

"Well, I very much appreciate your support," he tells her, in the politician voice he uses when a constituent is carrying on too long and he needs to get away.

"You were my pint-size savior," Jessica DeStefano carries on. "It was the first week of kindergarten. We were seated at the wrong table in the lunchroom, and we were about to be put on the wrong bus. I was more afraid than I've ever been before or since."

Patrick freezes in place and narrows his gaze, trying to identify in the woman's face some vestiges of the sad, sallow face of five-year-old Anne Wade—her name was Anne Wade, he is certain of that. His brain gave him a clear picture of her, on the day of the shooting, it was like he had been transported back thirty-five years in a time machine and he could see everything so clearly. But now he can't discern any resemblance between that girl and this woman standing before him.

"That girl was Anne Wade," he pronounces, a note of defiance in his voice. Why is this stranger—this Jessica DeStefano—trying to fuck with his head?

"No, that was me."

"I don't remember you, I remember Anne Wade—"

"There was an Anne Wade in our class," Jessica says. "But honestly I think she was one of the kids who used to make fun of you."

Patrick opens his mouth, but no words come out. He is afraid that for all she knows and remembers, right down to the taunts he once suffered, this woman is still somehow lying; that Jessica DeStefano *isn't* the Anne Wade of his memory but an impostor; that she has arrived here to play one last trick on him and remind him that, no matter how far he progresses in life, he will always be faggoty little Peppermint Patty.

For a few anguished moments, he even wonders if when Curtis Huber shot him he did in fact succeed in killing him and everything that has happened since has only been a dream. Patrick has done his time in purgatory. A decision from on high has finally been proffered. An angel of death named Jessica DeStefano is now here to invite him into heaven—or perhaps escort him to hell.

It is not outside the realm of possibility.

"What do you want?" he asks.

"I wanted to find you and thank you," she says. "I know it sounds stupid, but it's something important that I had to do. I have twin boys—one of them we actually named Patrick—and when I look at them I think of you when you were their age. I think about how much I want them to grow up to be the kind of man you are."

"I don't understand..."

"When you were just five years old, somehow you knew what the right thing was to do and you did it. And so I thought if I could somehow see you and thank you for that... well, then maybe it would help me in my own life and in raising my boys.

"Life hasn't turned out the way I dreamed it would. But I'm not here trying to solve all my problems. I'm just trying to set this one thing right. All my life I've lived with such regret that I never said thank you that day; that I never stood up for you when the other kids made fun of you. That I never made you understand that you were special.

"I know I'm thirty-five years too late, but I wanted to tell you all of that now. I just wanted to let you know that what you did that day meant so much to me."

Patrick is dumbfounded; wide-eyed; suddenly breathless. This time when he looks into the sad, anxious face of Jessica DeStefano, he sees five-year-old Anne Wade staring back at him. Now he sees that she isn't a fraud or a liar. She was there with him that day.

The only thing is that she remembers it differently. She is under the impression that he acted as some kind of hero.

This is how it ends. With Patrick Francis Monaghan getting to find out how it all began.

Not the worst deal, he thinks.

And then he also thinks: *What a ludicrous carnival! How lucky I have been!*

He looks around him in hopes of finding a chair where he might rest, but there isn't one. He decides instead to lean his body against the wall. He is about to ask Jessica to carry on when into the kitchen comes Nora, pointing at her watch.

"Come on, Patrick," she says. "We need you out there."

"Give me another minute," he answers, and the urgency he feels must be palpable in the air, because without protest Nora takes a step back and stays quiet.

"I failed you that day," Patrick says, turning again to Jessica. "I abandoned you —"

"—no, no you didn't—"

"—I waited too long. I sat at the lunch table too scared to do anything, and when we did finally get the aide's attention, I pulled you along too hard, and your lunchbox crashed to the floor, and I could have helped you, but I didn't. I left you behind so that I could get on the bus."

"No, Patrick—"

"—this first major test of my life I completely failed."

"No, you remember it all wrong. I mean, you did seem kind of annoyed at being stuck having to be my keeper, and at some point you called me a stupid crybaby. It's funny—I remember you being such a *righteous* little boy."

"Patrick, please, we should go," Nora tries again, moving closer and taking his arm. He can tell she's worried that this strange woman is working him into a nervous frenzy, and that he will be in no state to take the stage and deliver a concession speech. But Patrick won't move. No way. Not now. This he must finally see through.

"What did I do?"

At the end of all this, he is fighting back tears.

Jessica DeStefano smiles and steps forward, opens her arms and takes Patrick into an embrace. Then she laughs—a gentle and breathy laugh that Patrick hears as his salvation, and that seems to lift him off the ground and carry him far away—and she whispers into his ear: "You did everything right that day. I'll never forget it. You stood up and went towards one of the aides, and when she yelled at you to sit down, you yelled right back. You told her, 'I'm *not* going to sit down.' And I did drop my lunchbox, but you stopped and you picked up all the pieces for me—I was too much of a basket case to do anything for myself at that point—and then when we got outside, you saw that the bus driver was about to pull away, and you shouted at him to stop. Even then you must have had a voice that people paid attention to, because the driver stopped, and we got on the bus, and we walked all the way to the back and sat down in the last seats.

"Thank you for that, Patrick Monaghan. Because you did *everything* right that day. And all the way home, you held my hand and wrapped your arm around my shoulder—even though the other kids around us were making funny faces and calling us names—and you told me not to cry, to take deep breaths, that it was going to be okay. I've never forgotten. I remember it so clearly, that you said to me: 'Don't worry. Next week, I'll make sure we're on the pink bus.'"

ACKNOWLEDGEMENTS

My deepest appreciation and thanks to the following: for providing a space where I could complete the first draft of this novel, the staff of City Library on Flinders Lane in Melbourne, Australia; for her nuanced reading of and insightful feedback on the earliest pages, Sarah Ellenberg; for her editorial guidance and tenacity on behalf of my work, Emma Parry; for his wise counsel and encouragement, Wayne Hoffman; for taking *The Pink Bus* on and giving it such vibrant life, Steve Berman; for his gorgeous evocation of Patrick Monaghan's universe on this book's cover, Matt Cresswell; and for her tireless support and boundless empathy, Julia Heaberlin. Finally, a special note of thanks to my husband, Neritan Xhaferi, who has seen me through the highs and lows of these few years with his characteristic patience, kindness and profound decency. *The Pink Bus* wouldn't exist without him.

ABOUT THE AUTHOR

Christopher Kelly is a novelist, editor and critic whose work has appeared in *Texas Monthly*, *The New York Times*, *Slate*, *Salon* and numerous other publications. His first novel, *A Push and a Shove* (2007), was published by Alyson Books and won the Lambda Literary Foundation Award for Best Debut Novel. A graduate of Dartmouth College, Kelly lives in the New York City area with his husband, Neritan Xhaferi. His writing can be found at **www.thepinkomnibus.com.**